THE
BOOK
BINDER'S
SECRET

A. D. Bell lives in Oxford, haunting the city's bookshops of a weekend, writing in their cafés, and walking the winding paths of her characters.

THE
BOOK
BINDER'S
SECRET

A.D. BELL

H Q

ONE PLACE. MANY STORIES

HQ
An imprint of HarperCollins*Publishers* Ltd
1 London Bridge Street
London SE1 9GF

www.harpercollins.co.uk

HarperCollins*Publishers*
Macken House, 39/40 Mayor Street Upper,
Dublin 1, D01 C9W8, Ireland

This edition 2025

1
First published in Great Britain by
HQ, an imprint of HarperCollins*Publishers* Ltd 2025

ISBN HB: 9780008755942
ISBN TPB: 9780008755935

This book is set in 10.7/15.5 pt. Sabon by Type-it AS, Norway

Printed and bound in the UK using 100% Renewable
Electricity by CPI Group (UK) Ltd

FSC
www.fsc.org
MIX
Paper
FSC™ C007454

For more information visit: www.harpercollins.co.uk/green

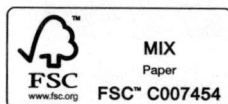

For those who love getting lost in a good book

1.

Oxford, 1901

The cold was fierce in the bindery. The late October chill so deep in the stones even the most willing fire could not coax them to warmth. My fingers were numb as I sat back, admiring the finished volume of poetry by Samuel Rogers. The buyer had wanted to turn the drab binding into a lavish gift for the bibliophile father of the girl he hoped to marry. I ran my finger over the raised bands of dark blue morocco along the spine, etched with gilt and inlaid with red flowers, a design inspired by an early work of Sarah Prideaux, a woman bookbinder I so admired.

'You should go home, Miss Delaney,' came Mr Caxton's voice from the other side of the workshop.

I had been apprenticed to the esteemed bookbinder Mr John Caxton of St Giles, Oxford, for the past three years. No relation to the great printer but a name he leaned on as a credential, nonetheless.

'I will when you do,' I said and saw his bright, round face in the lamplight. He was a small, thin, crooked-backed man who looked every bit of his sixty years.

We were two islands of yellow light in a dark expanse. The bindery workshop was not big but felt it at night. The walls lined with books in all stages of undress, endless drawers of cloths, vellum, leather, paper beyond measure of all grains and grades and hues, of marbled and painted endpapers, of gilt leaves, presses, blocks, and sewing frames. Tools so numerous it would take a lifetime to use them all. Tools so specific one may use a dozen on a spine alone. Drawers of awls, knives, scalpel blades, bone folders, rulers, and brass trindles. Trays of needles, curved and straight, shears and hammers. By the back door were sacks of dried glue ready to be mixed and laid with hog-hair brushes.

An Aladdin's cave of riches and chaos and it was my unenviable task to maintain order. To find places for the dozen new awls Mr Caxton would arrive with one morning, or the new order of goatskin he had failed to inform me was being delivered. But he was kind-faced, patient, and rather funny.

He appeared at my desk, his small, bespectacled eyes peering down at my work. He lifted the slim volume and turned it over, opened the covers to see how it lay.

'No doublures?' he asked, inspecting the inside of the covers where I'd glued marbled papers rather than matching morocco-grain cloth.

'They did not pay enough.'

He said nothing but lifted the book to his ear and flicked through the leaves as if to hear for mistakes.

'You have bound the book upside down, Miss Delaney,' he said and handed it back.

My jaw fell. I could not have. I grabbed the book, panic fluttering through me and whipped it open.

Then I heard him laugh. For a sixty-year-old man he laughed like a child.

I raised my head and locked my weary, aching eyes on him. 'You are a terrible teacher.'

'And you a mirthless student!' He continued his creasing as he ambled back to his desk.

'You win. I shall go home,' I said, unable to look any longer upon the Rogers.

I wrapped the book in a clean cloth and locked it in the cabinet behind my bench. I would send a note in the morning to the buyer to collect. Despite doing all the work, Mr Caxton's name would accompany the binding and the sizeable fee would go to him, less than a quarter then would come to me. It stung, when I saw the bills changing hands and saw so little of it cross my own palm, but it was the price I paid for learning. To be able to say I trained under John Caxton, who once bound books for the queen's personal library.

I wrapped myself in my cloak and put on my gloves. Warming my aching hands in the wool.

'Goodnight, Mr Caxton,' I said as I passed him.

'The binding is beautiful,' he said, eyes shining up at me. 'I shall be writing to Frank Karslake about you.'

Frank Karslake, the founder of the Guild of Women Binders. They had been established for three years now. I had written to them before with request to join but those letters had gone unanswered. With Mr Caxton's recommendation, it would open a door I'd thought closed. I felt a great surge of warmth. A dream, to be recognised.

'I shall tell him you are a hack of course, with little talent beyond sewing.'

'Only the truth.'

'I speak nothing else,' he said. 'Goodnight, Miss Delaney.'

I stepped out into the freezing air with a light step. What a joy it was to love your work. My father had loved his, perhaps more than he should, and now I mine. Though as apprentice, twenty-five and unmarried, I did not earn enough to keep me as comfortable as I wished nor to give me the freedom I craved. I still lived in my childhood room, above Delaney's Rare Books – my father's bookshop – on Victor Street, and when I was not binding books, I was cataloguing and selling them.

When I was a child, rare and fusty tomes had been the boundaries of my life, giving it shape and meaning. There were books in the winding rooms of my father's shop older than my child's mind could imagine, volumes that had seen kings rise and fall, buildings crumble and wars fade from memory. Books endure, my father would say. They endure, as we do not.

The walk between Mr Caxton's workshop and my home was short, a few turns only. I had little time for myself and, in truth, I wasn't sure what my life looked like when I was not ink-deep in book blocks and cover boards.

My world was small, bound between Cotswold stone walls, pressed thin as paper. I loved it, yet I chafed against it, and when an opportunity came to break open those walls, I seized it with both hands and little thought of consequence. For really, I thought in my naivety, what danger could lie within a book?

2.

Father banged around downstairs as I tried to stretch out the last few minutes of sleep. He had received a delivery of works from another bookseller who was going out of business. When this happened, the dealers of the city and nearby towns would clamour, sifting the shelves for a lost Donne or well-bound volume of Shakespeare, and Father was no different. He'd been there and back to St Aldates while I slept.

'A taste for gin and a weakness for horses does not sit well beside books,' Father said as I stepped down into the shop. 'Before the drink took him, Forstatter had a good eye. Can you see the value in this lot?'

A test, as always. My eyes still blurry from sleep, I knelt to the stacks he had set up. I knew his way. A fastidious old man, he could not help himself from sorting, thinking everyone would see the order he proposed as if it was the only natural way to arrange the world. Indeed, several years ago he had spent a weekend reorganising the shelves, not by name of author as is proper, but by date of publication. How was a lady looking for a volume of children's stories to know the day it was published, I'd asked, to which he replied, she must ask me, the bookseller, for that is my job. The shop had stayed like that for a month until Father grew weary of the constant questions and drop in sales and put it back to usual.

I looked over the books before me. In one pile, Father had grouped the common fare. The editions that would fetch a few pounds from one beginning their collection or from one who just wanted a good read. In another, he had grouped theological works of varying pedigree. I spotted a Milton, bound in red cloth, the cover etched with a depiction of his Hell. The binder had not worked well, for the tooling was not deep enough in places and had begun to flake. The frontispiece told me it was a modern printing and worth little. I checked Father's eye, a gleam in it as he thought he would catch me out.

I moved on to the final pile. These were the older, the rare, the keystones for all collectors. Shakespeare. Dryden. Keats. Shaw. And there it was. I pulled it from the stack, for he'd tried to conceal it to better test me, but a glance at the binding told me its truth.

'*Pilgrim's Progress*,' I said, running my hand over the smooth cover. 'Half sheep-skin binding, clean, no tears or discolouration.'

'A ten-a-penny book, don't you think? Any man with sixpence may find himself a copy.'

I opened it to the title page. 'This is a first edition. Published by Nathaniel Ponder in 1678.'

But he still meant to test me. 'How do you know it is a first edition?'

'It is only the first part of the story, the second was published in 1684 and both together in 1685. All editions thereafter contain all three parts.'

'Well done, Lilian,' he said, and took the book from me

with a tender hand. He had more affection for the books than for me and I had long ago given up trying to compete.

He held the book as one might a new baby and moved through the stacks to his office.

'Wait,' I said. 'You missed one.'

He turned, a frown above his eyes. 'I missed one?'

I handed him a book from the common pile. 'A rare and valuable thing indeed.'

He checked the spine and handed it right back. 'Your eye is failing. This is nothing but a standard collection by a middling poet.'

'*This* is the 1810 edition of Percy Bysshe Shelley's *Original Poetry by Victor and Cazire*. Written with his sister, Elizabeth, and published by John Stockdale. This edition was supressed. It included a poem by Matthew Gregory Lewis, used without his permission. Stockdale recalled it. It was republished years later in an edited edition but this –' I held up the slim, nondescript volume – 'is one of only a handful that entered circulation containing the Lewis poem. It is rarer than any book in Forstatter's collection, though I doubt he knew what he had.'

Father picked up the volume again and inspected it more closely. 'How did you come by that knowledge?'

As if I had to justify the provenance of any fact he didn't know. I could not say I had read it in Walton's *Notes on a Collection* because he believed Walton to be a fraud who inflated the value of works. So I told a lie to my father, not the first and far from the most egregious, but still if a lie was what it took for him to see the value in me, a lie I would tell.

'Mr Caxton told me. He bound an edition for a gentleman's

library two decades ago and the gentleman had been acquainted with Stockdale.'

My father gave a 'hmph' noise but did not dispute it, for if he believed anyone it was Mr Caxton. 'Stockdale was a pornographer. You know a copy of Harriette Wilson's memoir went for five hundred pounds last month. Said to be the one Stockdale sent to the Duke of Wellington to try to blackmail him.'

'I would have asked for eight hundred,' I said and my father looked at me, rather than the books, for the first time that day.

'I'm sure you would have got it, too.'

He took the Shelley and nestled it beside the Bunyan still in his arms. Two books, bound paper and skin, worth more than I would make in a year, maybe two to the right buyer, but those buyers were rare and those books could sit in Father's office for months, even years, before the one he deemed 'right' came along. As Father went about his morning routine, I had mine, which I undertook without instruction for one needs no instruction after years of the chore.

I catalogued the Forstatter collection in the ledger, alongside estimated values and shelved them where I could find space. I stopped sometimes to admire a finely bound volume or despair over a bad one. I stopped more to smell them, for there is nothing like the smell of books to awaken the soul. It's the earthy, sometimes sweet scent of the calf's leather, the fatty glue on paper and ink. Anyone who loves books knows that smell. Breathes it. That particular perfume that invades and stays. The aroma of imagination, of knowledge waiting.

Some of the cheaper but more popular items I stacked upon the table at the front of the shop where a passing customer could see them, but those of true value went behind glass or out of view entirely. Father would write to his chosen customers that he had acquired a *Pilgrim* or a finely bound Swift and they would flock to him. Should several customers want it, my father would take it to the auction house. But sales like these were too few and the cost of acquiring the books in the first place high. Bookselling was never something one did for the money.

Every collector begins with a love of books, a desire to possess knowledge, but all, over the course of their lives, begin to love the chase more. They crave the ownership of something precious, and the notoriety and admiration a good collection brings. I do not believe many read the books they acquired anymore but instead sat them upon a shelf and let them wait. A sad fate for a book meant to be known.

'I must go,' I said as I buttoned my cloak about my neck. 'I will stop by the market on the way home. The cupboards are bare. Are you eating?'

Father was in the office and I heard only an impatient murmur for me to stop making noise and be gone. A lonely man, forever heartbroken by the loss of my mother nearly fifteen years ago, who sought solace in books. She had been sick, though she kept the extent of her illness from me until the end. They both had. When she died, my father retreated into his work and I was alone most of the time. I had to learn those books, their histories and hidden values, if I wanted to speak my father's language. And I did, for then his love of books would turn fleetingly into a love of me. I endured the games and tests, told the lies I needed, for just those few moments he would look upon me as me, not as a shade of my mother or a nuisance in his home.

I did not call a goodbye that morning or wait for an answer. I stepped out of the door, let it close behind me, and doubted my father even knew I was gone.

I arrived at Mr Caxton's workshop not ten minutes later, for I was eager to be out of the cold. The fire was lit, the high windows free of shutters and the room flooded with thin winter sunlight. A haven, after the airless confines of my father's shop.

'You're late, Miss Delaney,' said Mr Caxton, not looking up from his work.

'I'm not and you know it. Father came into possession of some of Forstatter's stock. I had to help him.'

He looked up then. 'Did he get the Bunyan?' I nodded and the old man smiled. 'Good for him.'

'He also got the plagiarised Shelley from 1810, though he didn't know it. I told him you heard the tale of the suppressed volume from an acquaintance of Stockdale.'

He leaned back and fixed me with his sharp eye. 'You dragged me into a heinous lie, sullying my good name?'

'I did and I shall do so again one day, I'm sure.'

Mr Caxton laughed then fell quiet. I could feel him watching me as I unfastened my cape and hung it upon a hook near the fire.

'What bitter irony, though not altogether unamusing, that you must lie to be believed.'

'Indeed.'

'He will see your worth soon, I'd wager,' he said, and gave me the kind wink he often did.

Some would say Mr Caxton was inappropriate or ungentlemanly but I had known so-called gentleman and none were as gentle as Mr Caxton. He had in him the heart of a true booklover and saw in others not their sex or station, but their shared passions. I was born with a desire to turn something broken into something beautiful and Mr Caxton had seen that in me the moment I'd stepped into his workshop and gawked, wide-eyed and open-mouthed, at the riches on display. Beyond reading the books, for that was only half my interest, I learned to take them apart. Know their anatomies. Found what was under their binding, as if I'd find some deeper meaning to the words by studying their bones and piecing them back together.

'I have received a most interesting request,' Mr Caxton said, handing me a letter.

It was from Dr W. Ashburn, physician to dukes and earls, and well-renowned book collector. He had come into possession of some new volumes at auction, curios rather than outright valuable and there was one he wished bound as a gift.

'Dr Ashburn lives near Bath,' I said. 'Why would he not engage one of the binders there?'

'Read on.'

I did and saw the words I thought I never would. 'He requests me?'

Mr Caxton nodded. 'I should feel slighted. I have been wanting to get into Ashburn's library for a decade, but I shall not harbour any ill feeling.'

'How magnanimous of you, sir,' I said, smiling at him as much as at the contents of the letter.

'You star is rising, my dear. I hope you can hold on. You are to go to his estate today.'

I blinked. 'Today?'

'A man like Ashburn does not like to wait around. Take the

train. I shall inform your father. I have already sent a telegram back to say you will be attending.'

'You are not coming?' Sudden fear caught me. I had never been alone to visit a client.

'I am old and tired. You would drag me across the country in this weather? No, you are capable and earnest and have been on enough calls with me to know the dance.'

'But . . .' I had stood alongside Mr Caxton in those meetings, made notes and been all but invisible to the earls and reverends and barons whose collections we admired. I had been secretary, now I was to be a bookbinder in my own right and I was not at all sure I was as ready as I thought.

Mr Caxton took my hand. His skin was worn smooth and warm like fine vellum and his fingers permanently crooked from a lifetime sewing spines. His joyful demeanour was gone and his serious nature emerged, something I had seen only a handful of times in my apprenticeship.

'Doubt has no place here. You cannot be tentative when gluing leather to board, it must be a firm, confident motion, as must life.'

I nodded, though felt neither firm nor confident.

'You will miss the train,' he said and unhooked my cloak from the peg.

I collected up my notebook, pencil, a recent auction catalogue so I might be prepared should Dr Ashburn test my knowledge, and with one of Mr Caxton's satchels over my shoulder, I embarked for the station.

3.

The train to Bath was swift, taking only a few hours with one stop at Didcot where I changed trains onto the Western line. I took a hansom cab, drawn by a beautiful white mare, from the station to the home of Dr Ashburn. I had spent the train ride studying my notes from previous meetings with Mr Caxton, the questions he asked clients and information he gave. I spent the taxi ride making my own.

Tynesdale House, Dr Ashburn's estate, stood on the side of a gentle sloping hill some five miles outside of the city. We wound up the long driveaway; all the while views over the Avon Valley grew more spectacular the higher we climbed. Mist clung to the valley sides like floating smoke, turning the city below to a spectre, like the vague outline left when the ink had run out of a printing.

As we crested the top of the hill, the house came into view. A building of pale Bath stone in the Gothic Revival style. It was a magnificent example and, as I exited the taxi, I had to stand for a moment to simply admire it. Tynesdale was replete with crenellated towers, high arches, deadly pointed spires and pinnacles, a riot of expression beside the sedate, classical stylings so often favoured by the well-heeled.

The cab drove away and as I approached the entry – eyes still fixed on the glorious oriel windows – the great door opened. Standing at the threshold was a large man with a severe countenance that immediately set a chill in my bones. He wore a black suit, pin-sharp, and a white collar starched to a blade. I at once felt the shabbiness of my own dress, its dark red wool that hid the ink stains, my simple, comfortable blouse hidden beneath my cape that had a badly repaired tear at the shoulder, and then my jacket on which, if one looked closely, one would see loose threads at the hem. I imagined this butler looked at everything closely.

'Good day,' he said with a slow bow. 'Miss Lilian Delaney, I presume?'

'Yes, I am she.' I tried to sound more confident than I felt. 'There are some books, I believe, that Dr Ashburn wishes me to look at.'

'Of course.'

His voice was as cold as midwinter and I wondered how long he would see me shivering – for I hadn't had time to go home to change into warmer clothes – before deeming me worthy to enter. I wanted to straighten my back and raise my chin and say, *I am here at your master's request, let me in at once.* But a man like this, a butler in a house of this size and provenance, was so far above my lowly station that I would not have been shocked if he bid me use the back door.

He finally stepped aside and swung his arm inward. 'Please come in. Dr Ashburn awaits you in his library.'

The library where he housed the Ashburn Collection. I would tread where my master had not and see and touch books he never had. A thrill ran through me and I did a poor job of concealing it. I believe I caught the butler frowning.

The Ashburn Library, renowned in bibliophile circles as a hushed sanctuary of knowledge and science, was a pleasant room on the far side of the house which, I guessed, did not receive direct sunlight. Even the door was worth admiring. Elegant walnut with brass inlays with carved scroll detailing above. The butler opened the door and ushered me inside. The room was bright with arched windows framed with heavy green curtains. Two armchairs sat before a fire, a table between them. In the far corner was a piano that seemed more decoration than entertainment, and on the three walls, were the books. The doctor's collection had the reputation as the foremost collection of medical texts in the country, if not the world, and it was easy to see why.

I breathed in the smell of the place, the hint of age and leather alongside the smell of cedar wood burning in the hearth. Cedar was a favourite among the serious bookmen. A hardwood, it burned slow and gave off little smoke, which might stain or damage their works. There was a second door at the far end, barely visible between the shelves, which I imagined led to a study. As I stepped tentatively over the threshold and into the sanctum, this door opened and Dr Ashburn appeared.

A tall man, stout and wide in the shoulder, but he carried his weight well. Despite his age, well over fifty, he sported a fine head of light hair and was dressed in a dark grey suit.

'Miss Delaney,' he said and strode towards me, hand outstretched. 'A pleasure.'

'The pleasure is mine, sir. Thank you, for asking me here.'

I almost missed his hand, for I was barely looking at him, my eyes drawn always to the shelves and the thousands of volumes they contained.

'I can't quite believe it,' I said, almost to myself. 'This is the Ashburn Collection.'

'Some of it,' the doctor said, admiring the shelves beside me.

I looked at him then, towering more than a head above me. An imposing man, but affable, and should the stories about his work be true, gentle with his patients.

'Is it true, sir, if you don't mind me asking, that you have *Della Simmetria* here?'

He regarded me with a tipped head. 'You are well informed.' Then he stepped to a shelf a few rows to his right and, barely looking, slipped from its bed a slim volume.

'Albrecht Dürer, 1591,' he said. 'His masterwork, detailing the hidden symmetries and proportions of the human body.'

He opened the book to around two-thirds in and carefully unfolded a page so it lay double width across the book. My mouth fell open.

'To see this work, of this age, with the folds still intact is incredible,' I said. 'This is the Italian translation? But the binding is newer.'

'You have a keen eye, Miss Delaney. I had to have it rebound owing to water damage from the previous owner.'

'It is beautifully done. Simple and elegant.'

He put the Dürer back on the shelf. 'I have a fondness for the history of medicine as you may guess, and my library focuses on such, but lately I have found a liking for more modern fare. Which is why you are here. Please, if you wouldn't mind.'

He gestured to the study and walked ahead. I followed, as

slowly as was polite, scanning the spines for names I knew. I spotted a volume of Thomas Gibson's *Anatomy of Humane Bodies* from the late seventeenth century, bound in a stunning style I took to be Dutch, for it was a pale vellum spine laced to the boards. And on a shelf near to the study, an eighteenth-century German edition of Hippocrates' *Aphorisms*, and hundreds, thousands, more.

The study was a much smaller room lined with glass-fronted cabinets, behind which sat the true gems of his collection, including a very early *Treatise on Painting* by da Vinci. There was a smell, though, that did not fit and, in fact, was the horror of any collector. The smell of burning.

On a desk in the centre of the room sat several books. Dr Ashburn rounded the desk and picked up a volume, handing it to me.

'This is to be a gift for my wife. I had wanted an elegant binding for it; as you can see, the boards are plain, the cloth dull.'

'*A Manual of the Medical Botany of North America* – she is a lover of plants?' Still, the burning smell bothered my senses. I looked for the source and set my eyes upon a crate in the corner.

'And the Americas. I had heard from collectors that John Caxton had been putting out some fine, exquisite bindings, which never quite sat well with me, for I know Mr Caxton to be traditional in his style. Then I learned of his woman apprentice and the mystery was solved. I would like you to rebind this book in a manner you see fit, for a lady of my wife's standing. She enjoys modern fancies.'

A rush of excitement ran up my arms, as if radiating

from the book itself. I leafed through the pages. The text was neat, only printed a handful of years ago in New York and accompanied by coloured plates, fine illustrations of flora of all kinds. The dustjacket was gaudy, as were most to come from New York, and the quarter-bound cloth beneath an uninspiring shade of brown with a contrasting cream paper.

'It is a beautiful book. I hope I will do it justice for you.'

'I'm sure you will. I need it back in three weeks. Will that be a problem?'

Where was that smell coming from? What in that crate had burned and why was it here? 'Not at all.'

'You are distracted?'

I hadn't realised but I had not looked at Dr Ashburn for several minutes and he had been talking.

'My apologies,' I said and felt my cheeks redden. 'The crate, there. Is something burnt?'

His features took on a dark countenance. 'Yes. I bought the *Botany* along with a few others.' He went to the crate and with his large hand, took out a book, badly fire-damaged. 'But this was in the crate with the rest and now I must air the volumes. It's inconvenient at the least and sabotage at the worst.'

'May I?' I reached out my hand.

It was a small volume. The covers were blackened and the leather had been eaten away by fire. The page edges were singed but mostly unharmed, as if it had been pulled from the flames at the very last moment. There was no gilding on the edges, they were plain, trimmed. I could not tell if the binding was old or new but it was distinctive in its colour and style. I opened the cover, my hands already dusty with soot. The endpapers were dark red and felt thick to the touch. There were smoke stains across the paper and the title page was burned at the foot.

A Song for a Knave by Abel Bell, published in 1851, but the publisher name was blackened and unreadable. I'd never heard of the author and, without a publisher, had little clue to where it came from.

'Miss Delaney.'

I looked up and Dr Ashburn was staring down at me, a hint of impatience in his face.

'My apologies, sir. I hate to see a book so damaged.'

I moved to give it back but he put up his hand. 'That is a volume with no value, and in which I have no interest. Clearly nor does Grieves who sent it to me.' Another name I did not know. 'You may take it and do as you wish for, if left with me, it will be back in the fire.'

I flinched at the thought of a man carelessly committing page to flame but he was right. This book was worthless and yet, someone had cared enough to save it from burning. I realised I cared enough to do so again.

'I will gladly take it off your hands. And I will of course bind the *Botany* for Lady Ashburn.'

'Three weeks, Miss Delaney.'

'And not a day later.'

His affable nature returned, despite my apparent rudeness. He gave me a cloth for the burned book then rang a bell in the wall. I wrapped the book and wiped my hands on my cloak to rid them of the soot. We went back into the main library. The light had shifted and the room glowed as the light touched the golden inlays and gilt edging of the books.

'Do a good job and there will be more work for you as I add to my collection.'

I could not help but smile. 'Thank you for your faith in me.'

'Don't let me regret it.'

My smile tightened at this tone. This was an opportunity beyond all others. An ongoing commission from one such as Dr Ashburn could open every library door to me and cement my career as a bookbinder. No longer would I rent my corner from Mr Caxton, but I would run my own workshop, take my own apprentice, just as Sarah Prideaux did.

I put the cloth-wrapped book in my bag, alongside the *Botany*, just as the butler appeared at the library door. I was led out of the house. A fine carriage awaited outside with Dr Ashburn's family crest on the polished black door.

'The driver will take you to the train,' said the butler and he made no move to assist me.

A footman held open the carriage door and I climbed inside, pulling my satchel onto my lap.

The weight of the books was a comfort in my surroundings. I did not know such finery, nor how to act around servants for I never had any. I knew books only. As soon as I'd stepped into the library, I felt like I'd belonged, and the moment I stepped out, I was an imposter again. I clung to my satchel, to the books therein.

Despite Dr Ashburn's request, the *Botany* book held no interest to me, but the other, the burned volume from an unknown author, a name that seemed plucked from the air rather than given at birth, intrigued me greatly.

Who would burn a book and then save it? Who would slip it into the hands of a collector who cared nothing of it? From where did this book escape and why did someone go to such length to preserve it?

My fingers itched to explore it but the binding was fragile from the fire, and I did not want to risk the jolting of the carriage causing further harm.

But once on the train, I could not help myself.

4.

I bought a sandwich from a cart at the station before boarding the late afternoon train but forgot it entirely as soon as I pulled the burned book from my bag. I laid the cloth over the train table and gently set down the volume, *A Song for a Knave*. The train was not crowded but across the aisle I caught the eye of a lady in green whose nose wrinkled at the smell of burnt leather. I offered an apologetic expression and expected her to look away but she did not.

In the full light from the carriage, I saw details I had not in Dr Ashburn's study and in those details, further questions arose.

The fire had eaten through the top layer of leather and stained the rest with soot. At the spine, where it had escaped the worst, I could see the leather was dyed a deep, almost black, purple. There was no tooling on the spine beyond the title and author, no detailing to speak of value or collectability and yet, had this been a printing for everyday use, leather was an expensive choice when cloth was available.

I lifted the cover, wary that it might come off in my hands. It didn't, though by rights should have as the fire had bitten through the spine hinge. Something held this book together and I was not at all sure what.

The title page was sparse, giving little in the way of information about the book itself. It held the name of the book, its author, the date 1851, but the publisher was obscured. No woodcut colophon of the publisher, no opposing frontispiece, no illustration to mark this as a fine volume and no detailing of the content or editor. It was curiously sparse for a book bound in such a way.

I inspected inside the cover. The red endpapers were glued roughly, with uneven spots and lumps that made me itch to correct them. The fire had caught the top corner and melted the glue, allowing the paper to curl, its edge singed. With my nail, I prised it further and, beneath, caught a glimpse of a second paper.

'How curious,' came a voice. I looked up and saw the lady from across the aisle was now seated at my table. 'Will you save it?'

I was too shocked to speak, for I had been so absorbed I had not noticed her move.

'Can it be saved?' she asked.

'It can,' I said quickly to make up for my staring. 'It will, should I have the time.'

'I apologise for surprising you. I've never seen someone as intent on a book.'

I tried to be polite, but I did not wish to talk. 'That is all right.'

'You are a bookseller by trade?' she asked, her eyes bright and eager to chat.

'A bookbinder.'

She nodded. 'My husband is one also. It is a work that quite consumes the soul, is it not?'

I did not know how to answer that, for I'd never heard it put that way and saw immediately the truth in it.

'Books have that way about them,' I said only.

My mind raced for a way to end the conversation but I still had an hour left on the train and the carriages were busy enough that moving would not guarantee me a table on which to work.

'Indeed,' she said and, for a blissful moment, fell silent and I took the opportunity to study her.

She was well dressed, in a pale green skirt and matching jacket, heavy and warm for the weather. On her own table was a wide-brimmed hat with a plume of dried flowers in the ribbon. She was not rich, nor was she poor, but I wondered why she travelled in the middle of the train and not in one of the carriage compartments.

'Where are my manners,' she said, her eyes flitting between me and the book. 'I am Mrs Chand.'

My ears pricked. Chand. 'And your husband is a book-binder?'

She nodded, and her mouth turned in a smile.

'Mohan Chand?'

'His reputation precedes him, clearly.'

'His work is beautiful. I saw a copy of Johnson's *Dictionary* he'd bound for a client. The marbled calf leather and gilt morocco spine label were exquisitely done.'

She appeared impressed. 'You know your books, Mrs . . . ?'

'Delaney. Miss Lilian Delaney.'

'Delaney . . . not the Oxford bookseller?'

'Indeed.' I wasn't sure if I felt pride at my father's reputation or invaded somewhat by this stranger knowing of him.

She nodded, again, and her eyes fell to the table. 'Tell me about this book you're hoping to save, Miss Delaney.'

'I fear there is not much to tell. The fire took the name of the publisher. The author hides behind a pseudonym, I believe. I do think it has been rebound, though, as there is some binder's waste below the endpaper.'

I turned the book to show her the hint of a page beneath the ends. Her eyes widened as mine had.

'And somebody burnt it? On purpose?'

'I'm not sure. Somebody certainly saved it on purpose, but then it ended up in a delivery of books to a client without his knowledge.'

'A mystery indeed. Perhaps if you find the bookbinder, they can shed some light. It looks like a library edition, simple and uniform, but an odd colour choice.'

'That was my thinking but I can't see a mark.'

The train whistle blew and Mrs Chand started. 'This is my stop. I quite forgot the time. I travel so much around this country, I cannot keep track of the stops.' She stood and took her hat and bag from her seat, her eyes lingering on the book. 'My husband often hides his mark beneath the back endpaper. He says he cares little if the collectors see it but wants to be sure another binder will.'

Most stamp their mark plainly, either in the corner of the inside front cover or some even right on the cover itself, making their initials part of the tooling. Now my fingers itched to check every inch of the book for a mark, should one exist.

The train slowed and stopped.

'I hope your mystery proves fruitful, Miss Delaney.'

'Thank you, Mrs Chand. It was nice to meet you,' I said, then looked up but she was already gone along the aisle.

I turned eagerly back to the book. I had not the tools with me to undress it so could move no further in my search. Instead, I turned to the pages themselves. They were cleanly, if not perfectly printed. There were areas of pale type speaking to poor ink coverage and several typographical errors, misspelled words, and errant commas. It was not a book anyone took any care over and seemed rushed together. The text itself, as I read the first few pages and flicked through more, appeared to be a tale of an illicit love affair set among the cloistered halls of a convent. It was little better than a penny dreadful.

The damage was mostly on the front cover. The burned leather flaked off in my hand as I attempted to open it.

The train jolted and my hand jerked forward.

The cover ripped away from the binding.

'No, no, no,' I whispered, cradling the broken board.

As I tried to piece it back together to wrap up, a scrap of singed paper fell from the board. It was not unusual for binders to use paper to back the boards and paste the spine but it was generally used on older books, not those printed by the modern machines. I would have disregarded it entirely were it not for the few words written upon it.

I set the cover gently atop the book and picked up the scrap.

In a looping, cursive hand, someone had written, *I wish you had not killed him.*

5.

Once off the train in Oxford I hurried across the Hythe Bridge, turned left up Walton Street into Jericho towards home. It was cold and I had not paused to put on my gloves. My hands ached from the chill. The books were heavy in my bag, dragging on my shoulder.

The words on that slip of paper haunted me. I was sure they were written by a woman given the hand, though who she was writing to and who this person had killed was a mystery. The scrap had been part of a page of text – there were hints of other letters at the edges. Whether it had been burned before being bound into the book or burned within the book, was unclear.

It was early evening and I knew Mr Caxton would not expect me back today. I needed to go home to check on my father, to see he had eaten and remembered to keep the fire lit. I wanted to go to the workshop and delve into the burned book. But also, I wished to be the good daughter, to have a golden-eyed father look dotingly upon me, but my father was not that man. Yet, he did need me. And his need was greater than my desire. I slowed my pace as I came to the corner of Jericho Street, which would lead on to Victor Street and my home. I wished to bury myself in books and yet the real world called.

The lights were on in the bookshop windows, sending an orange glow into the street. Oxford at night had that glow about it. The golden tones from the new electric streetlamps illuminated the pale stone and gave the city its lustre. The lights were not yet on upstairs and I could not see my father through the windows. He would be in the office and would have forgotten to extinguish the lamps in the shop. He would be bent over a book or ledger, a pen in his mouth, a black smudge on his lip from the ink.

My face was numb from the cold. My nose, I imagined, had taken on an alarming red hue and as I went to open the door a fierce chill hit the back of my neck. Not the chill of cold but of someone watching.

Lamps stood at either end of the short street, throwing its centre into shadow. I watched, the hairs on the back of my neck still standing, but no shadow moved. Nothing stirred in the dark.

A light went on in a building opposite and cut a rectangle of light across the street, showing the dark spots for what they were and revealing nothing, and no one, hidden. I chided myself for my worry. I had felt a chill, out at night, in October, dressed poorly for the cold – nothing more.

I shook the remnants of the feeling away and let myself in to the bookshop.

'Closed!' came an impatient shout from the back of the shop.

I was too weary for his tone and I matched it with my own impatience. 'It's me, Father.'

He appeared in the door to the office. 'Where have you been?'

I moved past him to the stairs. 'At work. Where else?'

I did not want to explain the minutiae of my trip as I would have to. I wanted to be upstairs, in my room, with the book.

'A long day,' he said.

I nodded. 'I am tired. I'll go up now.'

With my foot on the step, he said, 'Wait, I have something for you.'

I tried not to let my frustration show. 'What is it?'

'Come, come.' He waved me after him as he shuffled back to the office.

The office was chaos as always. The desk heavy with papers and books, the shelves bursting with the same. A small window let in a little light through the day but it was grimy and he refused to let me clean it. He preferred the softer light, better for the books he said. A waist-high safe of green metal stood proudly below the window, purchased after a robbery some years back, and beyond the lock on the front door, the only concession to security in the shop.

Navigating the small room was a feat in itself. Piles of books formed labyrinthine pathways to the far side of the desk and the only clear spot was a chair he kept free for visiting collectors and his favoured customers.

I noted the crumbs and wax paper on the corner of the desk, which had not been there this morning, and was relieved at least that he'd eaten. Father, slightly stooped now and thinner than he'd ever been, weaved his way to the desk and bent to the lowest drawer. He brought out a locked wooden box and, taking the key from his pocket, unlocked it. The safe was for important books, far more valuable than coins and notes but this was the moneybox where he kept the sales of the day.

He took a thin fold of notes from it and handed them to me.

'What's this?' I asked.

'I sold the Shelley you found.'

For a moment, the burned book and its secrets were forgotten.

'That was fast; it was only this morning,' I said and counted the notes.

'Mrs Rowley is a Shelley collector, among other poets. I sent her a note and she came right away.'

I held twenty pounds in my hands. 'This is mine?'

He nodded. 'Mrs Rowley paid one hundred and fifty.'

I believed that volume to be worth closer to five hundred but I would not sour the moment. 'That is quite something. I can't accept this, though; it's too much.'

I attempted to give the money back but he pushed it to me. 'A portion of the fee for the finder. You may use it as you wish. A new dress perhaps.'

I did need a dress though it riled me that one, with all it entailed, would see me with pennies left. I wrapped the notes and held them tightly.

'Thank you, Father. This is wonderful.'

He nodded and set about returning the moneybox to the drawer. As he lifted it, he stumbled. The box crashed onto the desk.

He tripped on the leg of his chair. I dropped my satchel, dropped the money, and caught him before his head hit the wooden shelf.

'Father!' His face was twisted in pain and he clutched at

his chest. I lowered him down in his chair. 'Are you well? What is it?'

'It's nothing. It's nothing,' he kept saying. His face red and sweating, as if he'd run a mile in the hot sun.

I held on to his hand and realised, with a sinking in my chest, that this was the first time we had touched in years. I felt the weakness in his body as I caught him. I hadn't noticed how old he had become.

'What happened?' I asked as he regained himself.

'A turn is all. I twisted with the heavy box,' he said, scowling. 'Don't fret about me, girl.'

'I shall call for Dr Ingram.'

He grabbed my arm and fire set in his eyes. 'You'll do no such thing. I am fine. Get me some water if you want to be useful.'

I did not want to leave him but the danger appeared to have passed and he was as himself again, if a little breathless. I fetched water and he drank it with a shaking hand.

'I think I'll go to bed,' he said, as if admitting defeat.

'Father . . .'

'Not another word, Lilian. Clear up this mess, would you?' He stood, waving away my concerns, and without a backward glance disappeared from the office.

I listened for his steps on the stairs, a sound I'd heard a thousand times and yet this time it felt momentous. Like it would be the last time.

His steps were slower than usual and halted for a brief time about halfway up, but he did not fall nor call out for me. I waited until I heard his bedroom door close then set about tidying. I collected the notes from the floor, folded them and

31

tucked them into my satchel, then put away the moneybox and straightened the books on the desk. A letter caught my eye.

It was headed the London and County Bank and spoke of a credit note soon to be repaid. I took up the letter and saw the sum. A lump formed in my throat. The bookshop did not make that in a year. I set the letter back where I'd found it. My father would think me snooping. I put the notes from the Shelley back in the moneybox and kept only a few pounds.

I went upstairs with the debt weighing heavy upon me. At my desk, I took out the burned book and the *Botany*, which had of course been the whole point of my visit to Dr Ashburn. It was clearer to me now more than ever that I had to focus on my work, bring in enough money to pay my father's debt. Clients like Dr Ashburn were the way to do that, albeit slower than the bank would like judging by the urgency of their letter.

Under a flickering oil lamp, I studied the *Botany*. It was a beautiful, neat volume with a plain, average binding. The illustrations were bright and detailed and the type clear.

But I did not care.

As much as I tried to ignore it, the burned book called. Shouted. The smell of the charred leather caught my senses and would not let go. The scrap of paper speaking of death pulled me like gravity.

One quick look would not hurt. I set aside the *Botany* and took up *A Song for a Knave*. I slipped the scrap from where I'd kept it beneath the back cover. The front cover had detached completely but for a few strands of yellowed thread. I snipped them clean away, for I had a few tools at home should I need to work late into the evening as I often chose to.

I carefully pried the leather from the board. It flaked and

cracked, peeled like onion skin until the outside of the board was exposed. On the inside, I cut away the endpaper to reveal the board. But it was not the board. It was paper. A fine grade too, expensive, durable. This had held the book together when the fire took the spine.

Using a small blade, I teased the page from the board and found, to my astonishment, it was not one but two pages. Only the edges of the topmost had been glued and it came away easily, revealed beneath it a second piece, eaten away in places by the fire and pasted down fully against the board.

There was writing on the page, faint against the calfskin turned dark by the heat, but still legible and unmistakably a letter.

I felt a sharp chill run through me upon seeing it. Someone had gone to great lengths to hide it but, clearly, it was meant to be found.

With shaking hands, I turned up the lamp and began to read.

To my Knave,

Our story. Our love. I send it out to the world in the only way . . .
   Here we are hidden. Between me, God, and the binding.
   . . . will not look here. His man does not read nor see books for more than paper but we know different, don't we?
   My confinement now has meaning. As do these books . . . . . .
   . . . . . . will find their way to you . . . there is little chance. But it is my last hope.
   The money is mine. They cannot take it while I breathe and they dare . . . . . .

My Knave. How . . .

But I am glad he is gone. This story is the truth of . . . . . . It will set us both free.

There is not much time . . . you must . . . . . .

I, Your Queen,

The fire had taken words here and there but the meaning was clear. I took up the scrap and set it at the burned edge. *My knave. How I wish you had not killed him.* Yet the writer was glad of it.

I put the board down and rubbed my eyes. They itched from the light and a long day, from the faint, almost-gone words of this woman's letter which I could not stop staring at. A queen and a knave. A love ending in tragedy. And money in the centre of it, as it so often is.

I looked again at the binding. It was rudimentary, though not without skill, and clearly done in haste. I stifled a yawn, for it was close to midnight. My careful prising of the leather took far longer than I expected.

I checked the back cover. It was not as badly damaged. I took my knife to the endpaper and lifted it. On the overhanging leather beneath, a mark caught my eye.

FFG

Finally! A binder's sign, three initials inside a simple box blind-stamped into the leather. Hidden of course, as this book seemed to like.

I pulled aside the endpaper, expecting a second page, another letter, but there was nothing. The board was blank. I confess I was disappointed.

I picked up the front cover and read the letter again, copied it onto clean paper, read that over and over until my eyes hurt and lids drooped. I imagined this queen falling for her knave and forces around them conspiring against their union. She imprisoned by some unkind lord, and he fighting to reach her. Her only hope, her last hope, to hide a letter in a book that he may, by chance, find.

As I fell to sleep, my head on my desk, one word, and its final letter, floated up out of the darkness.

Books . . .

6.

Father seemed none the worse for wear for his turn the night before, though he did his best to avoid my questions and shooed me off to work the moment I stepped off the last stair. I said nothing of the debt, though I lingered a moment to watch him. His cantankerous manner infected the very bones of the bookshop, turning it from haven to dungeon. His worries weighed heavy and, knowing him, he would ignore them until the moment he no longer could and by then, all chance of help would be passed.

I stepped out of the shop and, for the first time, felt the moments I would see him walk in and out of our home, hear his banging and cursing, were numbered and counting down all too fast.

'You look like you slept in a hedge,' Mr Caxton said from his desk as I walked into the workshop.

I stifled a yawn. 'Thank you.' It was not my usual quick snipe and Mr Caxton noticed.

'What is it? Was Dr Ashburn unkind?'

I hung up my cloak and all but fell into the armchair opposite his desk. My neck hurt from sleeping on my desk and I still had the faintest impression of the woodgrain on my cheek. I kept my satchel, and the pieces of the *Knave* safely on my lap.

'No. He was fine. He gave me this.' I took out the *Botany* and handed it to him. 'He wants it rebound as a gift for his wife.'

Mr Caxton turned the volume over his in hands. A practised, almost unconscious, motion where he checked the spine, ran his hands over the boards feeling for warps or creases, eyed the page edge for tears or bad trimming, and finally opened it. He flicked through the pages, caring less for the content than its packaging. His small, round glasses flashed in the lamplight, for he refused to install electric fearing it would discolour the books and set the walls alight.

'Very nice,' he said. 'I suppose he gave you a month?'

'Three weeks.'

'The cheek.'

I took the book back and held it with little regard. And again, Mr Caxton noticed. For a man so consumed with the page, he had a remarkable eye for expression.

'Good Lord, Miss Delaney, your excitement is near bowling me over. Contain yourself, would you?'

'I am excited.' *But not about this*, I thought, and wondered if he could read my mind as he could so easily read my face.

'I do hope you put on a better show for Dr Ashburn.'

I rolled my eyes but not did quip in return. I stayed in the armchair for a spell as I willed my limbs to move and watched Mr Caxton work. I had not for a while, for beyond a little mentorship here and there, we largely worked apart. His hands moved effortlessly as he sewed the signatures of an early edition of Voltaire's *Candide*. He was truly a master at his work and

I'd forgotten how much I enjoyed simply seeing the process of a book being brought back to life. I pressed my hand to my satchel, felt the *Knave*, its pieces wrapped carefully in linen, every scrap of leather accounted for. Would he think me foolish for caring for a book past saving?

'You're staring,' he said, without missing a stitch.

'I'm enjoying your needlework. You'd make a fine seamstress.'

'I'm sure my apprentice would not be so bone idle as you.'

We settled into a silence born of years of familiarity. I had to tell him. I needed to. Wanted to. The secret burned in me like the leather on the book itself.

Mr Caxton sighed. 'You're staring and it's not at my sewing. Spit it out.'

'Dr Ashburn gave me something else.'

His eyebrow raised and he peered over his glasses at me. 'I hope whatever it is, it's decent.'

I pulled the wrapped book from my bag and set it on his desk. He set aside the Voltaire as I unwrapped it.

He wrinkled his nose at the smell of burned leather. The book, pieced loosely back together after my dissection, lay before him. He stared at it, then at me.

'It's dead. He wants you to resurrect it?'

'He was ready to throw it back in the fire.'

Mr Caxton lifted the burned book and winced when he saw the detached cover. 'Poor thing.'

'Someone saved it from the flames.'

'And not a moment too soon. The pages are in good shape.' He turned it over. '*A Song for a Knave*, not one I'm familiar with. The author too, Abel Bell.' He shook his head. 'Sounds like a romance novel, not one I'd expect in Dr Ashburn's collection.'

'Indeed.' I leaned forward, a conspirator's smile on my face. 'Dr Ashburn said this was in a recent delivery. He'd not bought it.'

The eyebrow raised again as he examined the book. 'Intriguing.'

'There is more,' I said and lifted the detached cover, turning it over to reveal the letter.

Mr Caxton settled his glasses and turned up the lamp.

'I took up the endpaper and found that beneath,' I said.

'Well, well,' he murmured, reading the fragmented letter.

'Isn't it interesting? It seems as if this letter was hidden with a purpose. A queen to her knave. Whoever they may be. Talk of a murder and confinement and money. Someone cared enough to save it, then it was carelessly tossed into a shipment of other books. And look, here.' I pointed to the line reading: *As do these books*. 'It says "books". There could be more out there with more of these letters.'

'A curiosity but this letter is binder's waste. Could be from anytime, anywhere. Could be a page from a novel or a play.'

I gave him a stern look. 'You know it is not.'

'I know very little, as you well know.'

He turned away from the letter to the rest of the book. He squinted at the corner of the back cover, near the top right edge of the board. 'What is that . . .' He pulled his magnifying glass close and held the corner beneath the lens.

'What do you see?'

'A mark.' He pushed the glass to me and indicated where to look. I saw it then, faded by exposure to the glue but unmistakable. Five tiny pinpricks arranged like the dots on a playing card. Yet they were not arranged as a five would be, but rather a six with the top left-most pip missing.

<pre>
      *
   * *
   * *
</pre>

'Have you seen a mark like that before, Mr Caxton?'

'I have not.'

'And here,' I said, peeling back the endpaper at the foot of the cover and showing him the binder's mark. 'Do you know any binders with the initials FFG?'

He tutted. 'I'm old and barely recall my own name most days. FFG could be the binder themselves or the bindery or even their guild.'

I slumped back into the armchair. No publisher, no idea of the binder, no notion of who the letter was for or from. Just an author neither of us knew and their low-brow novel.

Mr Caxton examined the rest of the book for a few more moments but quickly lost interest and returned to his Voltaire. Eventually, when he realised I was not moving, he set down his needle once again.

'You care about this?'

'I do.' More than I perhaps should have but with so much spiralling from my control, this felt like something I could grasp.

'Where did Ashburn get the book?'

'He said it was in a delivery from a bookseller named Grieves.'

Mr Caxton's brow furrowed. 'Grieves. Grieves. Grieves . . . it rings a bell but not a loud one. If this matters so much to you, I will ask around.'

A spark returned to me and I shot up from the chair. 'You will?'

'If it'll stop you sulking and get you back to work. I don't pay you to be sitting in that chair.'

'No, sir. You pay me to sit in *that* chair,' I said, pointing to my own desk.

I collected the pieces of the *Knave* and wrapped them back up in the linen. I put it in a low drawer on my desk, hoping out of sight meant I could keep it from my mind long enough to get some work done.

I began on the *Botany*. The binding was simple, quarter cloth over plain, paper-covered boards. The endpapers were a peacock marble but mass produced and lacking the lustre of handmade papers. I threw the dustjacket in the bin and took up my knife.

I tested the blade on my thumb and, finding it dull, sharpened it on a strip of thick leather. When it would slice a hair from my arm, I carefully cut the endpaper along the spine. Only enough pressure to slice one sheet, no deeper or it might damage the binding itself.

With a little force, I prised the board from the book block and exposed the spine. The backing was discoloured and made of cheap paper, which – despite the book only being printed a few years ago – was already cracking. With a little thrill of excitement I knew I would have to replace it. Breaking into the guts of the book, tearing away the factory remnants was my favourite part of the process. I would take something weak and dull and turn it into something strong and beautiful that would outlast its owner.

I was making myself a small part of the story of this book. For what is a book but a collection of stories? The story inside the pages, the story of its author, its journey from ink on a page, through a publisher, into the hands of its owners, its binders, its restorers, and readers. I was a small part of this book's story, and the stories of every book I'd worked on, and that gave me an invisible immortality. Books will outlast us all and I was content to be but a footnote in their lives.

With my paring knife, I peeled the paper from the spine and revealed the threads. I hadn't yet decided how to finish this book. It would take me a few days to find something suitable – Ashburn had said his wife liked modern fancies – then a few days more to sketch and refine the design, but there was plenty to do in the meantime. With the spine free, I cut a strip of mull and another of thicker paper for protection and prepared the glue.

While I boiled and stirred the glue, I watched Mr Caxton. He was still sewing the Voltaire, moving slower than he usually did. I suddenly felt a sharp stab of worry over him, as I had my father. The two men, two mentors in my life were frail, ageing too fast, and I was not at all prepared to live without them.

'Your glue is burning,' Mr Caxton said, without looking up.

The smell reached me then. The glue, simply water and a handful of rabbit pellets, had thickened and caught on the pan. 'Damn!'

He laughed as I scraped the ruined glue into the bin. 'Miss Delaney, mind your manners in front of a gentleman!'

'Why, is there one here?'

He stood then and came to see the mess I had made. 'Distraction leads to mistakes. What is it? A boy?'

I rolled my eyes as I wiped out the pan and started again. 'When would I have time to court?'

'One can always find time when one is young.'

'Not if you're a bookbinder.'

'Touché. You are not yourself, however. I understand if you don't wish to tell me; a young woman's life is her own these days. Is it that book? The letter?'

'Partly. My father took a strange turn last night. He collapsed, pain in his chest.'

Mr Caxton's smile fell away. 'I'm sorry to hear it. Has he seen a doctor?'

I gave him a look that gave him his answer.

'I will call on him this afternoon,' he said. 'Impress upon him the need to stay alive.'

'He will listen to you far more readily than he'll listen to me.'

I toyed with telling him about the debt. The large loan my father had taken out, though I couldn't think why we would need it, but could not bring myself to air any further secrets. My father would hate me for it.

'If there is any additional work I can do for you, I'd appreciate the extra pay,' I said.

'Ha! You do have a sweetheart.'

I scoffed. 'I just could use some extra is all.'

His bright eyes watched me a second longer and I thought he could tell I was lying or, at least, hiding a truth, but he knew better than to press.

'There is a three-volume set of Ueberweg's *History of*

Philosophy to be bound in black calf, in the style of the Wellington library.'

'I'll take it,' I said quickly. Three volumes would keep me busy while I worked on the *Botany*. 'Thank you.'

With that, we went back to our work. I made the glue without further incident and as it cooled enough to use, I examined the *Botany*. The pages would not need further trimming but the spine was a little flat and uneven due to the mechanical rollers. I took up my hammer and with judicious hits, rounded the spine to an even curve.

I put the book into a press, shaped the spine further into a profile resembling a mushroom. I sat with the book, naked and exposed, as I tried to imagine what the end result would look like, for I could do little more until I had an idea, a colour, a theme. But it did not come quickly. For some books, their final form was a simple thing, a uniform library binding, or it came about so quickly it was inevitable, yet others took a while to show their style. This one, I feared, would be the latter.

All I could think, staring at the book and knowing the multitude of steps and pieces to be assembled before it was complete, was how many places there were to hide something within its binding. The mull and backing of the spine, the endpapers, the cover, and board, whether wood or card. One could inscribe a sonnet on the underside of the calf's leather and it would be forever preserved, never read. One could carve a portrait in a wooden board and cover it in vellum so not even the faintest impression would show through to the cover. One could hide pages, letters, stories, confessions, behind the endpapers. One could even write a message on the spine itself. A book is a many-layered thing and we see but a fraction of its depth in the reading of it.

The doorbell rang with a sharp trill that snapped me from my thoughts.

Mr Caxton did not move, for it was my job as apprentice to answer callers. It was only the lunch boy delivering sandwiches as he did every day at one o'clock. The morning was gone to idle thoughts and burnt rabbit glue.

After eating, I turned my attention to the Ueberwegs and did as I had done to the *Botany*, stripped them of their covers, cleaned up the spines. I had bound books for the Wellington library before and they took little thought or creativity. It was nice to focus on a simple, mechanical task when the worries of the day, the intrigues of the book, threatened to overwhelm me.

So, I cut leather, pressed the books, prepared the endpapers, found we had little in the way of gold leaf in the stores and wrote to the supplier for more. I opened the post, swept away the slivers of paper from edge trimming, refilled the oil lamps, and did everything I could to keep myself busy.

As the day wore on and darkness fell against the windows, I felt Mr Caxton watching me. I was tidying the endpaper drawers, organising them into colours and types. Marbled, speckled, plain, patterned, painted.

'I've never known you to be so industrious,' he said.

'We need to keep a tidy shop.'

'Do we?' He sighed and I heard the movement that meant he had taken off his glasses and was rubbing his eyes. 'It's past seven. You should have left more than an hour ago.'

I looked at my watch and saw he was right. 'This needs doing.'

'Not today. You should go out, have some fun at your age. Don't you have any friends longing to see you?'

The question caught me by surprise. It was one of the only questions he'd ever asked about my life outside these walls. Truth was, I was ashamed by the answer. I had made books my life and left little room for anything else.

'I am too busy for that,' I said, knowing he would see through the lie and ask no further of the truth.

'You're as bad a liar as you are apprentice so I will do as any good master would and throw you out.'

I gave a small laugh. 'Throw me out?'

'Just for tonight – I'm not a monster. Leave now and take this to the post box on your way.' He handed me a letter addressed to someone I didn't know. 'It is an enquiry after your man Grieves. I'll help you, where I can, as long as this flight of fancy does not interfere with your work as it has done today.'

A tightness I'd held in my stomach all day loosened at his words, stern as they were.

I took the letter from him. 'Thank you, Mr Caxton.'

He did not look so happy as he usually did. He was a man of simple pleasures and interests and had all the time in the world for those who shared or respected them. But today, I had shown him impatience and frustration with the book entrusted to me by an important client. Mr Caxton noticed everything and I felt a terrible sadness for having let him down.

'I am sorry,' I said but he waved me away.

I took up my cloak, put the burned book in my satchel, and stepped out into the dry, cold October night.

7.

My breath misted before me as I walked down St Giles to the turning towards my home. When I got to the corner, I faltered and what Mr Caxton said returned to me. Did I have any friends . . .

I hadn't had friends for years but I did have someone I missed. Someone I thought of often when the day had been hard or interesting and I wanted to share it, when I walked by the canal or smelled the chestnut roasters at Christmas time. I thought of the letter, the love expressed in those few burned words, the queen calling to her knave as I had once called for him. I wondered if he would still want to see me as much as he once had. I decided, quickly, that I needed to find out.

I hitched my satchel more comfortably onto my shoulder and headed south on St Giles to where it met Broad Street. The city was busy, the lamps burning, casting golden pockets of light between the darkness. The colleges were lit from within, their dining halls bustling, students and scholars coming and going through the porters' lodges. I passed Balliol College and weaved my way through the well-dressed revellers outside the Sheldonian Theatre. Passing the great and imposing Clarendon Building, I turned down Catherine Street. I had always loved this part of Oxford where the old world met the new. This road had been Mousecatcher's Lane once, then Cat Street for a spell. How odd it was that a city could change its skin, its names, its buildings, as easily as a book could change its cover.

Before I reached the Bodleian Library, I turned down New College Lane and passed beneath the Bridge of Sighs. Immediately to the left, and easy to miss, was Hell's Passage, a narrow opening between two buildings, not even wide enough to stretch out an arm.

I followed the passage to its end where, nestled within the towering buildings of the colleges and the old city wall, was the Turf Tavern, once a haven for criminals and now a haunt of students and those who knew where to find it.

I heard the place before I saw it. The muffled talk and clinking glasses. Braziers warmed and lit the sheltered courtyard and, despite the cold, it was full as it often seemed to be. There was always a spirit of merriment about the Turf, as if every day here was Christmas Eve. I always expected a man in the corner to be selling cones of roast chestnuts, and the smell of mulled wine and hot cider seemed to permeate the very stones beneath my feet. Today, the crowd was joyful, students letting off steam in the way only students could.

I eased my way through them and into the tavern itself. A warren of crooked and uneven rooms, sawdust on the floor, where the landlord's head brushed the low beams and small groups of red-faced young men and women huddled against rough stone walls. It was a place out of time.

Standing behind the bar, pouring a pot of ale for a man who'd already had too many, was Harry. He was stooped beneath the beams, though that was more because of the height of the ceiling than the height of Harry. I'd known him since childhood, schoolyard days and running the streets of Oxford, languishing on Port Meadow in warm summer evenings. We'd been inseparable, best friends at first then, inevitably, more. Until we weren't.

The drunk man staggered away and I approached. Harry cleaned the bar, registering a new customer but not who I was.

'What can I get you, miss?'

'A pot of mild, please.'

Perhaps it was the sound of my voice or my order but he looked up. Saw me again for the first time in years.

'Lily?'

'Hello, Harry.'

There was the smile. Broad and bright. It lit the way. 'How long has it been?'

'Too long. How are you?' It was good and yet strange to see him again.

'Can't complain. You still selling books with your dad?'

'I'm a bookbinder now but I still help out at the shop now and then.'

He pulled down on tap three to pour my drink. 'Are you meeting friends here?'

'I hope so.' I smiled. Nerves sent my hand shaking. 'I wondered if you had a break coming up?'

His brow flickered as if confused but his smile didn't falter. 'I'm finishing soon, if you can wait?'

*

We walked together along the lamplit streets, coats drawn up to our chins. Old lovers on old streets, we fell into an easy rhythm, our feet and our shared memory taking us without our instruction. It is easy to speak when walking alongside someone. Not having to look at their face makes the words flow. And they did. We spoke of our lives since we last saw one another. Three and a half years, close to four. The enmity of our last few months forgotten.

I'd seen him once or twice from afar, at the end of a street or entering a shop as I had left but never to speak to.

'I've been here and there. Spent a little time working on the railways down at Didcot but it weren't for me,' he said.

'And now you're serving ale to the toffs,' I said.

He laughed. 'They're not so bad. Most of them don't even notice me.'

'They should.'

He glanced at me and I at him. I felt a blush rise and was glad of the darkness. Years had passed and yet our conversation flowed as if it had been just a few days.

'And you're a bookbinder.' It wasn't a question but nonetheless I heard uncertainty in his tone.

'Apprenticed to John Caxton, on St Giles.'

He nodded slowly, as if he knew the name. 'Huh. I didn't know girls could do that.'

'I'm a woman,' I said, arching my eyebrow in amusement. 'There are plenty of women bookbinders; there is even a guild I hope to join. I dare say the profession is beginning to modernise.'

'Too right. More should. Are you hearing the talk of women getting to vote? It'll be soon, mark my words.'

'I never took you for political. From what I remember, you'd pelt tomatoes at the speakers on Carfax corner.'

'Only because you'd stole the basket and they had to go somewhere.'

I had been an angry, motherless child, and when the confines of the bookshop and my father's grief pressed too close, the city and those within became my playground. I'd forgotten a lot of the mischief, but with Harry beside me, it was all coming back and, with it, a deep sense of disconnection from who I was now and who I used to be.

We walked in silence for a while and found ourselves at a familiar spot at the canal.

'Remember this?' I said as I ducked off the pavement and onto the towpath.

Trees lined the path and the water was high after an autumn of relentless rain. A few barges were tied up, their windows dark, engines cold.

'I remember you unmooring a half dozen boats down this stretch and me getting chased for it,' Harry said.

'I've never seen you run so fast.'

'You were a terror, you know. God, I'd have followed you right to Hell back then. Once you got an idea in your head, you'd never let it go. Dog with a bone, you were.'

I still was. I felt the weight of the book in my satchel. 'I've got a new bone now.'

'Lord, save our city!' he cried. 'What is it?'

'A mystery. Inside a book,' I said and he looked confused.

I told him of the burned book, the letter, the dotted symbol and how it came to be in my possession. Speaking it all aloud felt thrilling, like a story from a novel or a pulp pamphlet.

I realised this was why I'd sought him out, a friend to tell a story to, but now I was with him, the story didn't matter so much.

'You think it's real?' he asked and the question hit me like a fist.

'Of course it's real.'

'Sounds a bit mad if you ask me. Why would this lady put a letter under the cover of a book like that if she wanted it found? Who's going to go looking there? Could be a joke, couldn't it?'

Mr Caxton had said something similar and I'd ignored him in favour of my own excitement. Now with Harry saying the same, doubt crept in and, once there, I could not shake it. It could be a fake, a piece of binder's waste with little more to it than a forgotten scrap of paper on a bindery floor used for backing. I hoped, though, there was more to the story for then, I felt, there would be more to me.

'You've gone thoughtful,' Harry said, bending to look me in the eye. 'I'm sorry, Lily, I didn't mean to . . . you know.'

'It's all right,' I said it but didn't quite mean it.

We settled into a sad silence, which eventually he broke.

'What made you come out tonight?' His voice was softer, the boyish quality gone, replaced with the man's.

'Truthfully?' I looked at him. 'You did. I wanted to see a friend. Father said he'd heard from your mother at the market that you were at the Turf.'

'Well, Mother's gossip aside, I'm glad you did. It's good to see you, Lily. Can you believe so much time has passed and here we are, still the same two townies?'

'Not quite the same. You've grown into your ears finally.'

He barked out a laugh and stuck his hands either side of his head.

'You brush your hair now,' he snapped back and I saw in this man the fun, loving boy I'd known as a girl. 'Must be fighting off proposals.'

The blush returned, unbidden and unwanted. 'Several every day. And you, married with three strapping sons?'

'Four. And six dogs!' He grinned and shook his head. 'No, no time for all that. Just me and my mum. I'm all she's got since Dad run off.'

I nodded. I'd heard the gossip from my father. Harry's dad spent the family savings on the horses, lost it all, then ran off with a girl from the track.

'You've turned into a good man, despite my best efforts,' I said.

'And you a fine lady, despite the ink on your fingers. Who'd have thought it, hey?'

The smiles turned sad and we both knew the evening had come to an end. Talk of sweethearts, of blushes, flirting without meaning to; now there was nowhere left for us to go.

'I'd better get back to my father,' I said.

'My ma will be wondering after me too. I meant it when I said it was good to see you, Lily. I'll call on you next time.'

'I'd like that.'

We walked back to the street together and he turned right and I turned left. He looked back once and I remembered the event that parted us. One I'd tried to forget. He said he'd have followed me to Hell and he did. But I'd escaped and he hadn't.

I blinked away tears, blaming the cold night for stinging my eyes, and headed home.

8.

It was a slow week, which saw October give way to November, and I'd spent the time on the *Botany*. I'd finally deciding on a crushed green morocco leather with a hand-tooled golden celandine and fine line dentelles around the edges. I spent half a day sewing the head and tail bands in green and yellow thread and the rest of the week sketching a design and creating a template so it would be as second nature when I came to tool it onto the cover. Dr Ashburn had paid for unique, for modern, for special and I would deliver. Despite my early disinterest in the book, the love of my craft had returned and I was enjoying the work. I had just under two weeks left to deliver it and was confident that if nothing went wrong and I did not have to strip and recover it, I would complete it early.

After seeing Harry, and hearing his doubts about the burned book, my curiosity waned and the constant pull to check it, examine it, search out further secrets within the binding, eased to a dull ache in my chest.

That is, until Mr Caxton received a letter and the feeling returned tenfold.

'Here, Miss Delaney, your bookseller has been found,' he said, handing me the letter.

It was from a friend of his in London who knew of Edmund Grieves. Grieves, it turned out, was a bookseller of some small renown, with a reputation for finding volumes nobody else could.

'My dear friend says he also has a knack for getting collectors to sell, even if they don't particularly want to,' Mr Caxton added with a knowing tip of his head.

'An unsavoury character then. Why would Dr Ashburn have dealings with him?' I asked.

'I wouldn't dare speculate, but every collector I've known has a book they can't forget. A volume they would do anything to acquire. I believe you understand something of the obsession of a particular book.'

I heard admonishment in his tone. I focused on the letter and not the growing urge to rush to my drawer where I kept the *Knave*.

'Your friend, he says he hasn't found anything out about the author or publisher. You told him about the book?'

He frowned. 'I did.'

I felt small before him then. Questioning him like that was not my place, nor my person. He would have done it to help me, to find more information than the book could give and besides, there was no reason to keep it secret. Yet I found myself protective of it all over again, of not wanting to let others see, except those I trusted or wanted close. Mr Caxton. Harry. But I had not told my father and this new understanding of why saddened me in a way I didn't expect.

Mr Caxton, the man that he was, noticed my downturn. He patted my arm and the matter was forgotten. An apology now would only aggravate the situation so I smiled awkwardly and read further.

'Grieves has a shop in London, in Cecil Court,' I said, my voice rising with excitement. 'I could visit at the weekend.'

Mr Caxton shook his head. 'When you're meant to be working for your father.'

I opened my mouth to object but he was right. I spent Saturday in the bookshop and my father couldn't spare me. Sunday was out as I was sure Mr Grieves would be closed.

I lowered the letter and felt the desperate disappointment of a road closed to me. 'Of course.'

On my desk, the bound, glued, and pressed book block of the *Botany* was ready to be covered. A crucial step, not to be hurried. I still had two of the Ueberweg's *History of Philosophy* volumes to complete, both in various stages of undress. Much to do, and all more important than half a letter in a novel nobody cared for.

'Another time,' I said and handed the letter back. 'Perhaps the New Year will bring an opportunity.'

I went back to my desk, took up my paring knife and began to thin the green morocco at the edges so it would lie flat against the boards.

'Good Lord, woman!' cried Mr Caxton. 'I won't have you moping about the place making us all miserable. I have some books that need to go to a collector in Bloomsbury. They'll be ready on Wednesday. I was going to post them but you'll do just as well.'

I dropped the knife. 'Do you mean it?'

'Yes, yes. But cover that book first, will you, for decency's sake.'

*

I was on the twenty past eleven train on Wednesday morning – after spending the first hours of the day unpacking an order with my father and checking that the cover of the *Botany* adhered well in the standing press. The train brought me into Paddington Station at half past two. No matter how many times I'd visited, the awe of the place still caught me off guard. A great monument to steel and glass, Brunel's workaday masterpiece, used by thousands until, for them, the majesty had worn to the mundane. On a day like today, with the winter sun shining low through the vaulted glass, the concourse was filled with wide beams of light and the majesty was restored.

I carried a package of books under my arm, three volumes of John Fletcher's comedies for a collector who yearned to be a playwright. He took himself to be a resurrected Shakespeare but in fact was just a rich man with flattering friends. He had a townhouse on Tavistock Square in Bloomsbury and I took a carriage directly there. The books were heavy and I wished to be rid of them so my true purpose in the city could begin.

After delivering the books, I made my way to Cecil Court.

It was a pleasant enough walk on a dry day and, impatience carrying me, I arrived at the St Martin's Lane entry before the clock struck half past three.

Cecil Court, a busy thoroughfare connecting St Martin's with the theatres, offices, and eateries of Leicester Square, saw endless footfalls and chatter. It was a place steeped in the arts, a bookseller's row, where Mozart once lived and *The Dome* was published and the first of the moving picture makers had taken up. One can't reach out an arm without hitting an esoteric bookshop or aspiring poet or publisher. The buildings were new, only a few years old, and the former slum was now a well-to-do area of the city, with sharp heels clicking on the stones and the air full of the scent of ageing paper.

Mr Grieves had his premises at the far end, number twenty-five, beside the new shop set up by John Watkins, a long-term friend and client of Mr Caxton.

Already, the winter sun was lowering itself behind the tallest buildings, casting the narrow court in deep shade.

On the corner, a flash of light caught my eye. A man in a bowler hat leaned against a dark doorway. The flash was him striking a match for a pipe. He watched me pass, a cloud of smoke erupting from his mouth. His eyes didn't leave me and I felt a chill that had little to do with the weather. I hurried on, thankful Cecil Court was not a long passage, and came to Grieves's shop. The light from within cast out into the court, briefly catching browsers and those rushing to business elsewhere.

I stepped inside and immediately felt at home. Despite Grieves's reputation, his shop was impressive. A long gallery with tightly packed shelves either side, opening to a wider room off to the left. That room held a counter and till, more shelves and stacks of books piled on the floor and any available space.

I ran my eye over some of the spines, to give myself time to build up my courage enough to speak with him. I could hear someone in the other room, gentle sighs and shuffles, the scratch of a pen on paper.

I spotted volumes I knew well, the common titles for those looking for a book to read: Dickens, Doyle, Twain, Wells. And deeper along the shelves, the more obscure titles, Findlater's *The Green Graves of Balgowrie* and two novels by Amy Levy who had died so young. I saw religious texts sit alongside salacious novels and there appeared little in the way of organisation. I imagined, if Grieves was anything like my father, he alone knew the location of every book in his shop.

I pulled a book from the shelf, less for the book itself and more for the binding. Quarter bound in red calfskin with blind tooling. Expertly done. I checked for a binder's mark and found the back endpaper unglued. I peered beneath and spotted MC with a dot in the C: Mohan Chand.

'Looking for something?'

I jumped, dropped the book. The sound it made as it hit the floor was like a musket shot in a silent room.

Standing in the entry to the other room was a slim man about my height with a moustache and spectacles. He was in a shirt and buttoned waistcoat, sleeves rolled up revealing taut, muscular forearms that did not suit his age, which must have been close to fifty. Dark hair shot through with grey, moustache untidy at the edges.

'Uh . . .' I began as he fixed me with a sharp, unwelcoming stare. I rushed to pick up the book, checked it was undamaged and slid it back on the shelf. 'Are you Mr Grieves?'

'I am. And you are?'

I stepped forward, hand outstretched. 'Lilian Delaney. I'm a bookbinder, apprentice to John Caxton.'

He took my hand but in a wary, weak grasp. 'I've seen his work. Very fine. What can I do for you?'

I could tell he did not want me to be there but I persevered. 'This will sound strange but I've come into possession of a book I believe once was yours. It's called *A Song for a Knave* by Abel Bell and it was terribly burned.'

His demeanour changed then. He crossed his arms over

his chest and the opening I'd created with Mr Caxton's name was rapidly closing.

'I don't know what you're talking about.'

'I think you do. It was in the collection of Dr Ashburn and he passed it to me. He said it was in a delivery by mistake.'

'And you've come to return it?'

'Not exactly. I . . . well, I wish to know more about it. The publisher, for example. Were there other books by the author? I believe there is more to its story, you see.'

He glanced out the windows as if fearful of being watched. 'You'd better come through.'

Grieves led me through the other room, through a door behind the counter and into an office. A pleasant enough room, heavy with papers and ledgers but a small, high window let in enough light for it not to be gloomy.

'Charlie!' he shouted and almost immediately a young man about my age, maybe a little younger, appeared, somewhat out of breath.

'Sir?'

'Fetch some tea, will you. And lock the front door.'

He nodded. His attention lingered on me and he gave a smile before hurrying away. I confess, I was a little uncomfortable with the idea of being locked in but the mystery of it compelled me to put those worries aside. I had to know and I suspected Grieves knew far more about the burned book than he would be happy to tell me.

'Do you have the book with you?' he asked.

I nodded and moved to take it from my satchel.

'Don't,' he said sharply. 'I don't wish to lay eyes on it again.'

I closed my bag. 'Why not?'

He flattened his moustache with his thumb and index finger, a nervous habit more than a necessary act. Grieves was not what I expected. He was rakish and had an air of danger about him I'd never known in bookmen. They were all gentle, solitary creatures, focused on learned pursuits and displays of knowledge but Grieves was not.

'It's burned. Worthless,' he said, his eyes darting away from me to the table.

'But it's not worthless,' I said carefully. 'I found something.'

His eyes shot up. 'I don't want to know. Those books are cursed.'

'Books? I knew there were more! Do you have them?'

His moustache twitched and again he smoothed it with thumb and forefinger. There was a knock at the door and the man, Charlie, came in with a tea tray.

'Please, do you at least know the publisher? Why would you have put the burned book in with the Ashburn delivery? He didn't order it.'

Charlie looked from his boss to me and back, then set down the tray. 'Anything else, sir?'

Grieves waved him away with a scornful look. 'Miss Delaney, was it?' I nodded, watching Charlie as he left the room. He'd left the door ajar and I wondered if he stood the other side to listen.

'I can't help you, Miss Delaney. You're right, there was another book by Abel Bell, both in the same dark purple leather. The other was sold and I cannot divulge the names of my customers.'

At once a deep disappointment and a rising excitement. Another book existed and there would be a way to find it.

'Could you tell me the publisher? The name of the book?'

His jaw flexed in annoyance. He took up a pair of reading glasses and opened the ledger before him. He flicked back a few pages and ran his finger down a long, handwritten list of sales. I saw from other entries he catalogued the title, author, publisher, and the buyer, as well as the date and price. Meticulous and neat, not what I expected from an office so messy.

Outside the door, a floorboard creaked and my suspicions about the tea boy were confirmed. I tried not to smile. I would have done the same if my father were meeting a young woman alone in his office.

'I'm afraid I didn't record the details.' He flipped the ledger closed. 'How forgetful of me. I can't help you any further.'

Not can't, but won't. I refused to let my frustration show. 'You had two of these books, is that right?'

'I did.'

'Do you know if there are more?'

'I don't and I don't care. Listen, Miss Delaney, these books have brought nothing but misery upon me. I don't want them here, I don't want to talk about them and should one cross my path again, I'll destroy it.'

His anger both concerned and intrigued me. What power these two books held over him. I doubted he'd found the letter as it was still properly glued when I freed it. But there must have been something else to it for him to become so riled up.

'I can see I've taken enough of your time,' I said, standing and lifting my satchel onto my shoulder. The tea lay untouched between us and, as I stood, I heard soft footsteps retreating from the door.

'You'd do better to forget you ever saw that book, Miss Delaney,' Grieves said, standing too.

'I don't believe I can do that.'

'I mean it,' he said, leaning close, his eyes wide, almost manic. 'The books are dangerous.'

I let out a nervous laugh. 'How could a book be dangerous?'

He sneered as if my question was absurd. 'You should leave. Burn the book you have. Forget you ever saw it.'

He said it with such force, such fear in his tone, that my laugh died, and my smile dropped.

I opened the door and air rushed into the room. I almost fell out into the main bookshop where the young man, Charlie, was shelving books. He looked up from the spine of a volume in his hand when he heard me come in.

'Miss, you all right there?'

'I'm fine,' I said, straightening my jacket and holding on to the strap of my satchel as if it would balance me.

Mr Grieves came out behind me. 'Miss Delaney is leaving. Show her out.'

Then he was gone and the office door slammed. Charlie gave an apologetic smile and set the book down.

'Don't mind him. Since a friend of his died, he's not . . . Ah there's me talking out of turn again. This way.'

He ushered me into the long gallery and to the door. Taking a key from his pocket, he unlocked it, opened it and I pushed my way outside.

I wasn't in the shop for long but the day had grown dark and the lamps were not yet lit. Cecil Court was only lit by a few windows and it had the feeling of being the middle of the night, not the middle of the afternoon. The cold hit me too and my bones felt like they would shake apart.

I hitched my satchel, felt the weight of the *Knave* within and it wasn't the comfort it was before. Grieves's words repeated on me like a bad oyster. Such fear, such warnings. Burn the book. Forget I ever saw it. But I was no closer to understanding why.

I tried to put Grieves's warnings from my mind as I walked through Cecil Court towards St Martin's. I came to a darker stretch, where the shop windows were dim and the awnings cast even deeper shadows.

I did not hear the man until he was upon me.

He barged into me, grabbing my satchel and yanked it from my shoulder. The wind went out of me and I instinctively held the strap, pulled it back.

The man was tall, well-built and wore a bowler. I told myself to remember the details for the police but my mind raced. I focused on all the wrong things. Tweed jacket. Brass buttons. Scuffed shoes. Smell of pipe tobacco.

He huffed and growled like a dog in our tug-o-war. He wrenched the satchel and my shoulders screamed, felt like they would tear from their sockets but I held on.

I shouted for help. Screamed it. A few doors opened along the court. People stopped. Another man walked towards us.

'Hey!' he called out.

My assailant looked here and there, his panic rising, pulling on my bag but I wasn't letting go.

Running feet along the court. He had to let go. He had to. Else he'd be caught.

He raised his head and beneath his hat I saw his eyes. Cold.

Empty. A wolf's eyes. He bared his teeth and one glinted silver in the shop lights.

Then the satchel strap went slack and for a moment. I thought he'd let go but he was rushing towards me. He cracked his elbow into the side of my head and drove his fist into my stomach.

The world spun. I hit the ground and my satchel was gone. Out of my hands. The burned book stolen. The man ran, barging people aside.

'No!' I tried to get up but well-meaning people kept me down.

'It's just a bag,' they said. 'Better that than your life,' they said.

'Miss Delaney!' came a shout from behind and the people moved away. Charlie lifted me up.

'He got my satchel. My book!' I could barely catch my breath and pointed to the man who had reached the end of Cecil Court.

Charlie took off sprinting. Both men disappeared onto St Martin's Lane.

I limped up, someone guided me to a chair outside a shop and I didn't stop them. I felt empty without that book. As if all possible futures were ripped from me in one senseless act.

A kindly woman took a handkerchief to my temple.

'Got a cut there, love,' she said and showed me the dark stains of my blood.

My head throbbed, my vision swirled, turned to spots and sparks, and suddenly Charlie was back. Panting. Hair mussed. Collar open and torn.

But he had my bag.

I cried out and threw myself at it, at him, at the overwhelming tide of relief crashing into me. I pushed off him and immediately opened my bag. There, safe within, was the linen-wrapped book. My fear melted away and, in its place, came pain. A bone-deep ache in my head, as if someone were taking a hammer to my skull from within. And my stomach. I dreaded to think what would await me when I finally got home and examined myself. I could feel the thickening of the bruise, the muscles hanging on by a thread. I tried to stand but pain lanced through my gut and I almost fell.

Charlie caught me and eased me to my feet. I wrapped my arm around my satchel and held it against my chest.

The side of my head itched and stung. I pressed my hand there and it came away sticky with blood. Charlie gave me his handkerchief and I held it there.

'I think you need something stronger than tea,' Charlie said.

'Whisky. I need whisky.'

9.

The whisky was warm and as I sipped it, I felt a spark of life returning to me. Charlie and I sat in the Salisbury Pub on St Martin's Lane. It was a relatively new place, Charlie said, opened only two years before. It was lush inside, with red leather banquettes, golden columns in a Roman style and grand chandeliers a little too big for their situation. Behind the bar were smart young men in bow ties and white aprons rushing before bright mirrors covered in gold scrolling. The clientele, at this time of night, were largely clerks and suited folks, along with young courting couples and, in the next bar, all women enjoying their own company.

The pub wasn't too loud or rowdy, the drinkers calm, and I imagined the owner paid a policeman to keep it so.

Charlie sat beside me, hands on the table, glancing at me every now and then, wincing at the cut on my head and muttering something about getting there sooner. He had fixed his collar and his hair but still, what a pair we made.

I shook a little, as the shock wore off. I'd never been robbed before, though I had been in a few schoolyard brawls with other girls. A grown man with ill intent was entirely different. I tried to reason out why the man in the bowler hat would think I had anything worth stealing. I did not dress richly, nor wear jewellery. My satchel was old, worn, covered in scuffs. I supposed I was an opportunity to him; a woman alone attracts the wrong kind of attention in a city like this. Yet I could not shake the idea that there was more to it – the way the man looked at me, the glint of steel in his eye. It made me shiver.

'What an end to an otherwise dull afternoon,' Charlie said, breaking the long silence between us.

I put aside the image of those eyes and took a drink. 'Thank you, for getting my bag back.'

He shrugged as if it was nothing. 'Least I could do. That bloke had a fist on him. He was fiddling with the buckles when I tackled him. He clocked me one then ran off. I reckon after the tussle with you, he didn't fancy another.'

'It was very brave of you.'

'Must be a special book you have in there to risk being hurt over.'

'It is.' I'm not sure why, but I found myself telling him all about it. The whole story, from its origins in Dr Ashburn's collection, to the letter pasted on the cover board, all leading me here. He sat back with a whistle as I finished and knocked back his own drink.

'What did Grieves tell you about the other books?' he asked.

I raised an eyebrow at him, though it hurt to do so. 'You tell me. I know you were listening at the door.'

'You got me, guv,' he said with a laugh. 'We don't get many visitors in the shop, especially ones so beautiful.'

Despite my best efforts, I could not help but be flattered. He was handsome, in a roguish, dishevelled way, with kind brown eyes and a glow of life and fun about him. He had dark blond hair in an easy wave and I found myself daydreaming of running my hand through it.

'I shouldn't be telling you this,' he said, leaning closer. 'But old man Grieves was lying to you. Said he had two of those Abel Bell books, right?' He shook his head. 'He had three.'

All thoughts of hair and flattery vanished. '*Three?*'

'Someone paid him to find them but something went wrong with their arrangement and Grieves stopped. Couldn't sell them because who'd buy them? They are worthless by any account, but he didn't want the buyer getting them. He sent them off to his clients. One to your Dr Ashburn, another somewhere else and the last one is still in the shop, all packed up and ready to go. I can get it for you.'

The urge to grab him and shout 'yes, now!' was overwhelming. I fought against it and kept my hands to myself. 'For what price?'

He grinned. 'Dinner and a show?'

He was the rogue in more than looks, it seemed. The thought of spending an evening in this man's company didn't fill me with dread or revulsion, as these things often do, but rather a growing sense of excitement.

'I don't live in London.'

'Oxford, right? That's where John Caxton has his bindery.'

'You were paying attention.'

'I always do, Miss Delaney.'

'You may as well call me Lilian, if we are to go to dinner.'

His smile broadened. 'Will you come back on Friday? I'll have the book.'

'Won't Mr Grieves miss it?'

'He hates the sight of them. This one is in a box ready to go to a collector in Edinburgh who isn't expecting it. Nobody will be looking for it.'

Except, I thought with a sudden drop in my stomach, the person who paid Grieves to find them in the first place, who-ever that was. I wished away the dark cloud and focused on the young, handsome man before me.

Then I realised the time.

'I must go!' I stood up quickly, satchel always in my hand, and the blood rushed to my head. I swayed, caught myself on the table, then Charlie caught my arm.

'Careful there,' he said, holding me closer than perhaps he needed to.

I politely pulled away. 'I must go. I'll miss my train.'

Charlie helped me from the pub and hailed me a carriage. 'Paddington Station,' he said to the driver, then to me: 'Friday? I'll meet you here, say, six o'clock?'

Despite my panic at missing my train I could not help but smile. First at the idea of his company but then, too, at the notion he may know more about the books. 'Yes. Six o'clock.'

His hand lingered in mine as he helped me into the carriage. A hand that had saved my satchel, rough and strong, not like the hands of bookmen I'd met before. I wondered about him, this stranger who had done me a good deed but who I knew nothing about. He could be anyone. But despite that, I found myself looking forward to our next meeting before I'd even left this one.

The carriage driver cracked the whip and Charlie closed the carriage door as we pulled away, raising a hand to wave. I sat back on the seat and blew out my reddened cheeks. My smile returned and didn't leave me until I boarded the last train to Oxford. Then, the smile died and, in its place, panic.

Because on the train, I took the burned book from my satchel and discovered the loose board with the letter was gone.

10.

I checked every inch of my bag. Replayed every moment of my attack and Charlie's rescue and our time in the pub. The only time the bag was out of my sight was the few minutes between the man taking it and Charlie returning it. Had it been a few minutes or longer? My memory was a mess of sensations and everything felt at once too clear and sharp and yet not. I searched again for the letter. Could it have fallen out? Had my buckles come loose while I tried to save it? The thief unclasping them as he ran? But I had undone the buckles to check the book. Hadn't I? My head ached, the pain blooming behind my eye like a swelling mushroom. My memories of the day were not solid things, but cloud-like, drifting into new shapes with the slightest thought.

Had I really seen the linen still wrapped around the book? I had. That I was sure of. And yet as soon as the certainty hit me it left me again.

The only possible solution dawned on me. The thief must have taken the letter. That meant he had known what he was looking for, known I had it, and waited for me. Charlie said someone paid Mr Grieves to find the books until the arrangement soured. But how could anyone possibly have known I had the book? The questions swirled and swarmed like a mass of starlings, as soon as the shape of an answer came, the pattern twisted and new questions emerged.

The books are dangerous, Mr Grieves had said and I was beginning to understand what he meant.

I felt suddenly exposed in the busy train carriage. Suddenly saw a dozen men in bowlers, their wolfish eyes staring at me. Women looked at me with sideways glances and every person knew what I carried and wanted to take it from me. I wrapped my arms around my satchel and tried to make myself smaller and smaller, as if I would disappear into the upholstery if I pressed against it hard enough.

The man in the bowler had been in Cecil Court when I arrived. I tried to believe it was a robbery, an opportunistic criminal saw a woman alone and tried his luck. I had to believe it because the alternative was too big, too terrifying.

The train pulled into Oxford and I all but ran off and out of the station. I kept my head down, my satchel clutched to my chest, as I hurried through the streets of my city.

Oxford was a stranger that night. Every shadow held a fiend, and I could not move fast enough to get to my front door. When I finally reached Victor Street and could see the light from my father's shop window spilling into the street, the knot in my stomach, if not the ache in my head, began to ease.

I was a few feet from my door when, from the shadowed centre of the street, where the lamps did not reach, a man stepped.

I screamed and the man rushed towards me, his hands out as if to grab me.

I ran and at my door, his voice cut through the dark.

'Lily!'

I turned and saw him in the light. *'Harry?'* The air left me and I almost collapsed against him. 'What are you doing here?'

'Waiting for you. I said I'd call on you next time,' he said, smiling though he seemed a little shaken by my scream. But there was that easy charm I fell for once. It was so good to see him, better than I ever expected and it took all the strength I had left not to throw myself into his arms.

He stepped onto the pavement beside me. He quickly saw the crusted blood at my hairline and his hands went to my face. 'What happened?'

I flinched away, an instinct only, but he dropped his hands at once.

'I wish I knew how to answer,' I said.

'Did you fall? Did something hit you? Someone?'

I met his eyes at the last.

'Christ,' he said and I could almost see the armour settling over his knightly shoulders. 'It looks bad. Who did it? Was it the Barrows? I'll pay them a visit. I swear I will.'

I shook my head and my brain bounced around inside my head. 'No,' I said, forcing down a surge of sickness. 'It wasn't in Oxford. I've been away today.'

His anger appeared to fade with no one close enough to fight. He took my elbow and I let him. 'Let me take you to the doctor at least.'

'No, no, it's not as bad as all that. I just need to rest. A good night's sleep heals all ills, so they say.'

'They're usually right,' he said. This was clearly not the way he hoped this evening would end. His voice softened. 'Are you all right, Lily?'

74

I took his hand. 'I am. I will be. Can we meet tomorrow for lunch? I'll explain, I promise.'

He nodded. 'I'll come by at noon.'

I held his hand longer than needed, than a young unmarried woman should, but he was warm and real and I had never been one for propriety.

'Lily . . .' he began, his voice barely above a whisper. I had an idea what he might say but I hadn't the life left in me to hear it.

'Goodnight, Harry,' I said gently and let go of his hand.

I could see the sadness in him; I felt it too. I brought my hand to his cheek and he pressed his face into my palm. I felt the familiar ache in my chest when I was around him. The ache focused to a sharp pain and memories I'd buried began to surface.

I stepped away and a rush of cold air came between us. 'I'll see you tomorrow.'

He nodded and, as I knew he would, watched until I was inside.

I leaned back against the closed door and tried to order my thoughts. But my head throbbed and my chest hurt and all I wanted was to collapse onto my bed and dream it all away.

But from the back office came a strange sound. A low rumble that was not at home here among the books. The man in the bowler had found me. Was searching my home for more books or waiting for me. I took an umbrella from the stand by the door because there was nothing else. I inched towards the back room, the noise coming at odd intervals but forming a rhythm.

The office door was ajar and I pushed it open, expecting to see those wolfish eyes, that glint of silver.

But no demon jumped out at me. There was only my father, asleep at the desk. The rumbling noise had been his snores.

I lowered the umbrella and a deep weariness came over me. 'Father, wake up.'

But he did not stir and I soon saw why. An empty bottle of whisky lay at his feet. He did not drink beyond the occasional porter with a friend or client but tonight had decided to drink himself into a stupor. He lay face down on the desk, a pile of letters for a pillow. I could not see their content but they were headed the London and County Bank. My heart broke for him, for us, for what it might mean.

I could – should – wake him up, take him upstairs to bed, but then he'd know I'd seen him like this, saw the letters and knew of his debt. He would be ashamed and retreat further into himself. Or I could leave him here, sick as he was, until it got cold enough for him to wake and take himself to bed. Pretend like none of this was happening. Smile while the house came down around us.

'What do I do?' I whispered but there came no answer.

11.

The cold had deepened and, as the morning wore on and I worked on the *Botany*, snow began to cloud the upper windows of the workshop.

Instead of my usual practical chignon, I wore my hair looser, with a fringe to hide the cut on the side of my head and Mr Caxton did little more than raise an eyebrow and ask again if I had a sweetheart. Several, I'd said, and he laughed but for the first time, I was not joking. Both Harry and Charlie occupied my thoughts as I measured and cut the endpapers. I'd chosen a pale blue and yellow marble, which looked like abstract cornflowers and thicket. As I folded the first endpaper and flattened the crease with my bone folder, I thought of Charlie, his easy smile and open flattery, the heat as he'd taken my hand and held it, of how far away Friday felt though it was only tomorrow.

As I measured the second paper and brought it to the blade I thought of Harry and all he was and had been and should have been to me. They were twin devils dancing in my mind and behind them both, the burned book, the mystery in its pages and the thought that there were other books by this author, bound in the same way, and someone wanted them. Wanted them so much they thought little of resorting to violence.

Sudden pain shot through my finger. Blood spotted the blue marbled paper and I stared for a moment before I realised I'd sliced the tip of my little finger clean away.

Mr Caxton was at my side before I could call for him. He squeezed his small hand around my finger and, with nothing else to hand, grabbed a strip of mull cloth and wrapped it around the wound.

'Don't worry, my dear,' he said. 'No bookbinder worth their needle has all their fingertips.'

'I don't know what happened.' My voice seemed barely my own.

Mr Caxton led me to my chair, his hand still tight around my finger to staunch the bleeding.

'Here,' he said, 'hold on to this while I fetch a bandage.'

I did as he said. The mull was soaked red and I saw again the woman's handkerchief in Cecil Court, felt again the sticky blood on my face. My finger pulsed and each beat of my heart brought another wave of sickness. Mr Caxton returned with a bottle of brandy and a small bag.

'I hope that's for me.' I nodded to the bottle.

'Fortification, my dear. I can't abide the sight of blood.' He took a swig and looked for a moment like a dock worker or labourer at the end of a long day. 'Come on then, let's have a look.'

He gently peeled away the cloth from my finger and, now I had a free hand, I grabbed the brandy for myself. He set about cleaning the wound and I found myself suddenly curious about his fatherly manner.

'Do you have children, Mr Caxton?' I asked.

'Never cared for them – too sticky.'

'What about a wife? Were you ever married?'

He paused in his work for a fraction of a moment. 'No, dear. I love my books; there is little room for anything else.'

'Are books enough?'

To that, he gave no answer, just one of those smiles of his which could mean anything or nothing. I thought of my father, so consumed by books he would be buried by them and I knew, despite my love for them too, that I didn't want to end up that way.

I winced as he wrapped the bandage.

'All done,' he said and patted my hand. Then he turned grave. 'Did you find your Mr Grieves?'

My hand instinctively went to my head, ensured my hair was still covering the wound. 'I did. He was helpful.'

'Good. I trust that's the end of the matter. You only have a week left on Dr Ashburn's order and you've bled all over the endpapers. No more distractions.'

'Yes, sir.' I felt wretched for failing him. And felt even worse for what I would have to do next. 'But I do need to go back to London. Tomorrow.'

I had never seen Mr Caxton angry. I don't believe he had it in him, but the set he had in his features then was the closest I'd come. 'Oh?'

'Mr Grieves has a commission. He's acquired a damaged edition of a Rabelais and wants it rebound for a client. I offered my services and need to go back tomorrow to collect it.'

Mr Caxton watched me for a moment, his eyes intent on mine, looking for the lie. 'Which Rabelais?'

He expected me to say *Gargantua* but that would be too obvious. '*The Third Book*. Grieves's collector likes books with controversy attached.'

'And why would he ask you?'

I acted affronted for a moment then shrugged. 'I told him I'd do it cheaply. I reasoned it would be worth it to secure a new client.'

Mr Caxton softened enough for me to know my lie had worked and I felt all the worse for it.

'Very well. But you must not be late on the *Botany* book. A client like Dr Ashburn is more valuable than a West End bookseller.'

I nodded and went back to my work. I thought it best to give a show of my dedication. I cleaned up after my accident, threw away the bloodied endpaper and cut new ones. I glued the edges and tipped them onto the book block, back and front, then it went back into the press. While the glue dried, I worked on the second Ueberweg.

As the clock struck the hour, a knock came at the door. I set down my paring knife and opened the door to Harry. Handsome, expectant Harry. And my heart sank. I'd forgotten our lunch.

'Ready?' he asked.

I would have to explain to him what was going on. The attack, the reason for it, and he'd tell me to stop, to forget the books and then we would argue and I hated to argue with him. He'd see me differently, as a fragile thing in need of protection. He would probably wish to come with me tomorrow and I couldn't have that.

'I can't . . .' I said and his face fell. 'I'm sorry, because

I missed so much of the day yesterday, I have so much to catch up on.'

He nodded and gave a tight smile. 'How about tomorrow?'

'I'm sorry,' I said, wincing. 'I need to go back to London.'

He shook his head. 'I see.' He turned to go but spun back to me. 'You know when you showed up at the Turf I thought you'd finally come to say sorry but I suppose I was wrong.'

Long-buried indignation flared within me. 'What do I have to say sorry for?'

'You don't remember? Christ, Lily. I can't believe I thought you'd changed.'

'I have changed.'

'I was ready to marry you.'

Tears welled in my eyes but I fought against them. 'You should go.'

He rubbed his face, his cheeks red with anger or sorrow or both. He left without saying anything else, afraid perhaps of saying something he could not unsay. I took a moment to compose myself, to release the tension from my voice, clear my eyes of unfallen tears, then I stepped back into the workshop.

Mr Caxton, who I knew had heard it all, for there was barely a vestibule between the front door and the workshop, looked at me with a strange expression I had seen once or twice upon my father's face. The particular sadness of a parent towards their hurting child.

'Books are a poor substitute for love, my dear,' he said with a kind tone.

'Books don't break your heart.'

He shook his head and went back to his work. 'Of course they do.'

I wiped my eyes and slumped down into my chair. I ripped the cover from the third Ueberweg and we spoke little for the rest of the day.

Friday came and I took the afternoon train to Paddington. I left the burned book at home and in its place in my bag I took a paring knife. I did not see my father that morning and barely spoke with Mr Caxton. We were both sore and I would have to work hard to make it up to him but I couldn't think about that yet. The book was more important to me. My world was collapsing around me but this one thing, this one mystery, this I could control. If I could just figure it out, find the queen, her knave, hear their story, I would be free of it, and my life – my small, confined life – would have meant something.

12.

I was late to the Salisbury but not by much and, as I approached, I saw Charlie's tall, rangy figure loitering by the door. He had his hands deep in his pockets, a bag over one shoulder, and a scarf wrapped around his neck to stave off the chill. I watched him for a moment as he checked his pocket watch and no doubt wondered if I would show up. He was handsome, in a windswept, dishevelled way. In a way Harry wasn't. The sour thoughts came and I did little to stop them. Our argument played again in my mind and I found myself walking faster towards this other man. This person who knew nothing of me and who I used to be.

Charlie spotted me and a wide smile spread across his face. 'Lilian,' he called, waving.

I crossed the road to him and let myself relax into his presence.

'I thought you weren't coming for a bit there,' he said. 'How's the head?'

'Still attached,' I said and my eyes went to the leather shoulder bag. 'Is that what I think it is?'

'Right down to business. I like that in a woman.' He grinned and offered me his elbow.

'You're a bit of a rake, aren't you, Mr . . . ?' I said as I slid my arm through his.

'Cutter. Charlie Cutter, Hastings born and London bred.'

We found a table in a small restaurant famous for its roast meats and fruit pies. The place was cosy and full but Charlie said he knew someone and we were shown quickly to a quiet table in a snug corner.

'Figured you'd prefer a bit of privacy while we conduct our business,' he said, and there was that grin I couldn't help but return.

He cast around in a theatrical way to make sure no one was looking and brought up the leather bag he carried and set it on his lap. From within, he brought out the book and handed it to me. It was as if the *Knave* was before me, complete and undamaged. The leather was clean and dark purple, almost black. On the spine was the barest decoration, just the title and author in silver foil. *He Sings His Devotion* by Abel Bell. Two books, two titles suggesting love and romance. I opened it to the title page. Simple, pristine. The publisher, Montague and Cliff, based in Manchester, and the year 1850. Excitement buzzed inside me. I flipped to the front endpaper and ran my hand over it. Over the place the letter had been in the *Knave*. I felt a small ridge right before the endpaper met the leather. A ridge that should not be there. Something was underneath.

'Is it everything you hoped?' Charlie asked and I remembered where I was.

'I believe so.'

'Then this calls for a celebration! Gin slings and roast beef.'

Charlie got up and went to the bar to order while I ran my hands over every inch of the book, felt every join and crease.

I was about to take the paring knife from my bag and begin slicing into its secrets when Charlie returned with two drinks and raised his in a toast. His charm was infectious and it was with only a little reluctance that I put the *Devotion* in my satchel and picked up my glass.

'To books and those who love them,' he said and I clinked my glass on his.

As the gin warmed my insides, I felt them loosen. 'How long have you been with Mr Grieves?'

He rocked his head side to side as if weighing up the time. 'A year, give or take.'

'Is he good to you?'

He laughed. 'Old Edmund isn't good to anyone. Not anymore.'

'Is this what you wouldn't tell me last time?'

'You'll have to buy me another drink before I sing about that.'

I smiled. 'It's a good job I don't have anywhere else to be.'

He cocked an eyebrow. 'Miss Delaney, I don't know what you're suggesting.'

'A business arrangement of course.' I rested my elbows on the table. 'You have information I want, and if it takes a few more gins to get it, that's a good investment for me.'

He fixed me with that grin, that roguish eye, and called for the barman to bring two more.

'Ask your questions and I'll see if I've drunk enough to answer them.'

I sat back, sipping my gin. 'When did Mr Grieves start collecting these books?'

'He already had the burned one when I came to work for him. The other two came quite soon after.'

'When did the arrangement turn bad?'

'About six months ago. He couldn't find any more of them and the buyer didn't take kindly to that, let me tell you. Threats and all sorts.'

I could well imagine it. Maybe the man in the bowler was working for the same person. Still looking for the books, taking them by any means.

'Who was the buyer?'

The drinks arrived and Charlie drank half of his in one mouthful. 'That I don't know. It was all done by letter. Don't think the chap ever came into the shop. But Edmund said the buyer paid a king's ransom for those books and more besides.'

I sat with the information, tapping my finger on the edge of my glass.

'I don't understand,' I said. 'These books are pulp romances and adventures, not even that well written by most standards. They have no collection value and the binding is plain. So why would someone want to pay so much for them?'

Charlie shrugged and I realised his second glass was empty. I finished my first to catch up.

'I wish I knew,' he said. 'Maybe that letter you found in the burned one has something to do with it.'

It had to. Someone was after what these books held, not the books themselves. I wondered over telling Charlie the letter was stolen but I was more taken with his master's story.

'Mr Grieves didn't give the buyer the three books, so why make a record of their destinations in his ledger?'

'He refused to give over the books, said the buyer didn't deserve them, whatever that meant, and he wouldn't be party to it anymore. As for the records, he's a strange soul, has trouble when something isn't just right, so, for him, not record-ing where these books went . . . he couldn't *not* do it, you understand? I don't think he cared that the buyer could find where the books went, though he'd made it hard for them.'

I knew obsessive men. Obsessive in act and detail. My father was the first. His obsession was his shop, his books, his shelves and their arrangement. I supposed Mr Grieves was the latter. Fastidious with record-keeping and knowing his trade. When I'd first walked into his shop I'd got the sense he knew every book on the shelves.

'What happened to Mr Grieves to make him stop collect-ing?' I asked. 'Have you had enough to answer that one yet?'

'Someone he cared for died. In a bad way.'

My eyes widened. 'Died? Or was killed? Did the buyer do it?'

He sighed. 'I don't know. He won't talk about it. Look, is this all you came back for?'

'What do you mean?'

'If all I'm good for is gossip about something that happened months ago, then I've told you all I know,' he said, his eyes downcast, his tone flat, and sat back, away from me. 'You got the book so you can go home now. I won't hold you to dinner.'

I grabbed his hand before he could stand up and leave. 'I'm sorry. I get . . . absorbed in this stuff. A dog with a bone, someone said about me once. You're right, I wanted to come back here for the book but I wanted to see you too.'

His gaze met mine. 'You did?'

'Don't let it go to your head. You're a nice man is all and you helped me.'

He leaned close to me. 'Just nice?'

I pushed his face away. 'Get another drink.'

87

'Landlord!' he shouted.

Our meals arrived and we ate and drank and laughed more. I had not laughed so much in years. The cares of my life fell away, didn't exist with him. We talked of things that didn't matter. He asked after the bandage on my finger and I told him the story, though not that I was thinking of him while I did it. I asked after his life before books and he spoke of summers by the sea in Hastings where his grandparents still lived though he didn't visit as much as he wanted. I spoke of summers by the river, my wild younger days of stolen cider and canal-side pranks. I was not what he expected, he said, and he was everything I expected.

I didn't notice the hour, the last train long gone, until we emerged from the restaurant into a frigid night. I didn't care. I'd get the first train in the morning and be back to work in the bookshop before ten.

Charlie made a show of gallantry. 'Let me walk you to the station.'

I rolled my eyes. 'You know very well there are no trains.'

I was drunk, as was he, but joyfully so. My face hurt from laughing and my hands were warm in his as we swayed through the revelry of the West End. Theatres were letting out and music and revelry spilled from pubs calling for their trade. Everything seemed to sparkle in the lamplight and nobody seemed to notice us, not that I cared. I was past caring about the looks and judgement of others. A lady should do this; a lady should do that. Propriety was for those who had status to lose and I had precious little of anything left to lose.

'What will you do, Miss Delaney?' Charlie said, grinning. That grin! That face!

'Suppose I'll have to find somewhere to sleep.'

A group of drunken men passed us and we were forced into a doorway. I don't recall how we began kissing but we did and did not stop for what felt like hours. His kiss was firm but not rough and his hands did not roam as they might.

'I've wanted to do that all evening,' he murmured. He tasted of gin and beer and I was drunk on him. Every thought and worry fled me and it was only here, now, and what would follow that mattered.

'Do you live far?'

He shook his head. 'You'll cause a scandal.'

'I don't care.' I reached up and pulled his face to mine again.

Charlie had a room above the bookshop and we were there in minutes. I knew I shouldn't have, but I had learned years ago to live for myself, that my body is my own to do with as I wished. Feeling this way with a man I barely knew was better than feeling the pain and nothingness I had endured for so long after my life with Harry had come to such an abrupt end.

Charlie's kiss turned fierce and mine matched it, forced away the memories of Harry's, of what happened between us. My hands ran over him, into his hair, down his back, to his belt. His circled my waist and drew me close and then we were undressing. I cursed the number of buttons on my dress, the knots in the corset laces, the catching hooks. Finally free of them, I stepped out of my pile of skirts and into his arms. The chill bit my bare skin but he was fire atop and within me and this, just this, this moment and I'd live in it for as long as I could.

13.

I woke with a start to full, blazing sunlight through the window and knew I'd missed the early train and probably the one after. I scrambled out of bed and woke Charlie.

'What's the rush?'

'I need to get back to the bookshop. I'm late for work.' I dressed fast – corset, petticoats, shirtwaist – while Charlie lit up a cigarette and watched me from the bed, one arm hooked behind his head. 'I'd like to see you again.'

I smiled as I fastened my skirt. 'You would?'

'If I'm still of any use to you, of course.'

Dressed now but for my jacket, I turned to the glass on the wall above the dresser and tried to tame my hair. 'I don't suppose you have a brush.'

He opened a drawer in the nightstand and handed me a comb. I made myself into a more respectable mess but time was slipping away and it would have to do.

'When will you be back in London?' he asked.

'I don't know.'

He sat up, swung his legs over the edge of the bed. 'Will you call on me?'

'I'll try.'

I checked the book was in my satchel and slipped on my shoes. I leaned over to kiss him and he tried to pull me back into bed. Part of me wanted to let him.

Downstairs was quiet, Mr Grieves not yet arrived. Charlie had put on his shirt and trousers and followed me to unlock the door. The clock on the wall said half past ten and my heart sank further. I would be back so late and I had no idea what my father would say.

I left Charlie with a kiss and a promise to see him again, one day. I took a carriage to Paddington Station and boarded the Oxford train as the whistles were blown. The train took three hours. I had intended to examine the *Devotion* volume but the exertions of the previous night got the better of me and I slept the whole way only to be woken by the conductor when we were already in Oxford.

Off the train, I hurried home though the morning was gone and afternoon in full swing. I arrived at the bookshop close to half past two and walked into a crowd, though not of customers. My father, with Mr Caxton trying to keep him calm, Mrs Hawes from next door and a local constable, Officer Bolton, one known to my father for all the wrong reasons. He was so much older now, with white whiskers, and had arrested me once for disorderly conduct. Harry and I, in our wild youth, had pelted the Christchurch porter with eggs.

'Lilian!' my father cried. 'Where in God's name have you been?'

I met Mr Caxton's eye and saw the worry in his.

'In London,' I said. 'I missed the last train yesterday evening.'

Mrs Hawes looked overjoyed at the state of me. The gossip

of Victor Street, she was a rich, old woman with little to occupy her. I suspected, by the look of my hair, my crumpled dress, and the blush I still felt in my cheeks, she knew exactly what happened. A woman often does.

'In London! An unmarried woman alone, heavens!' she crowed.

'Miss Delaney,' Bolton began in that drone of his. 'Glad to see you safe and sound. I hope you stayed out of trouble.'

'Of course,' I said, my voice clipped and tense under their judgement. I found my father and went to him, took his hand. He was a shadow of himself and the concern was writ deep in his face. I had to admit, it lifted my heart to see it, to see he still cared. 'I'm sorry. I took a room and was so exhausted I slept through and woke only to catch the eleven o'clock. I am perfectly fine.'

My father's eyes widened. 'Except for that, where'd you get that?'

He pointed to my head. To the still-healing cut at my hairline that I'd failed to conceal. I cursed myself for missing it. Mrs Hawes made a show of sympathy and I dared not look at Mr Caxton, who had been suspiciously quiet.

'Oh. It's nothing,' I said. 'I tripped and hit my head is all.'

I hoped I was convincing. I didn't feel it.

Bolton turned to my father. 'Well, now that's cleared up. I don't believe I'm needed here any longer.'

My father shook the man's hand. 'Thank you, Bill.'

Bolton passed me and stopped. 'Miss Delaney, I suggest next time you intend on spending a night in London, you tell your father first.'

'Yes, sir,' I muttered though felt no deference to the man.

I remembered how he'd behaved when he arrested me. How I'd fought back at the roughness of his grip on my wrists and how he'd laughed at me, just a girl of fourteen.

He left, finally, and a little air came back into the room.

'Oh, Lilian dear,' came Mrs Hawes, tutting at me. 'You gave your father such a fright.'

'I am sorry,' I said again. 'Thank you for being here to help, Mrs Hawes.'

'Tea? Shall I brew a pot?'

Mr Caxton stepped forward. 'I think we should get out their hair, Mrs Hawes. The Delaneys have a shop to run. Come on now.'

He eased her away, despite some high-pitched protests, and when he came to me, he did not look at me. 'See you on Monday, Miss Delaney.'

'Yes, Mr Caxton,' I said and felt my heart break at his tone. The dullness of it. The disappointment.

When they were gone and my father and I alone, I went to him. 'I am sorry, Father. I didn't mean to worry you.'

His hands shook and he balled them into fists so I would not notice. 'You're an adult now, I accept that, but you were late for work. I needed you here to open the shop while I went to the auction this morning.'

I felt as if a cannonball had hit me in the chest. 'You weren't really worried about me, were you?'

'I had business to attend. I missed it because you were off galivanting God knows where.'

Anger rose in me and I had a mind to release it. Say all the things I'd never had the gall to say before. But I saw him trembling. Smelled the alcohol on his skin and breath. He was already broken. I could do nothing worse to him than he had already done to himself.

'You're right,' I said, letting the anger deflate. 'I'll get to work.'

I went upstairs to change without waiting for another word. I put my satchel on the desk and it fell open, revealing the spine of the *Devotion* book. I stared at it for a moment and felt a sudden surge of rage towards it. I wished I'd never seen that burned book, found that letter. It had caused nothing but grief and pain. I relived the attack in Cecil Court, touched the cut on my head and saw again Mr Caxton's expression, heard his tone when he'd spoken to me. I could not bear it. I took the book from my bag and put it in a drawer. Out of my sight.

I changed and quickly washed my face then went downstairs. My father was in his office with the door closed and I set about my duties with diligence born of guilt. I tidied, swept, took deliveries, helped customers though there were precious few of them, and when five o'clock came, closed the shop.

I made dinner for us both and when I knocked at his office, he told me to leave it outside. I ate alone and miserable in my room, trying to find in myself the will to make it through the rest of the evening. My thoughts drifted to Charlie. I wondered what he was doing, if he was out in the West End, charming another girl. A needle-jab of jealousy hit me and I replayed our night together as I gazed out of my window at the darkness of Victor Street. I felt his hands again, his hair, the smell of him. The surprising, gentle way he had. Remembered the laughter and falling asleep beside him. I wasn't sure what it meant. What it could become, if anything. It wasn't love, not yet anyway, but sharing a bed with someone always meant something, whether I wanted it to or not.

I glanced at the drawer, which held the two books. The burned *Knave* and the pristine *He Sings His Devotion*. I'd felt something below the endpapers. Perhaps just binder's waste. What were the chances this book also held a letter?

Before I could talk myself out of it, I was off my bed and to my desk, the *Devotion* freed from the drawer. I sat with it for a minute, studying the binding, trying to understand the binder: FFG. But the binding was so simple, so plain, the materials common and unimaginative, that I could discern nothing about them. Perhaps an apprentice learning their trade as I was, unable to sign their work freely so chose to hide their name beneath the fold. I should have done the same on my books.

I opened the front cover and ran my fingertips over the red ends. I only noticed then, on this undamaged book, how incongruous the colour choices were. Blood-red endpapers and dark purple leather. Without the soot and charring to disguise it, it clashed terribly.

I took my paring knife from where it still rested in my satchel, and paused, blade to paper. With the burned book, my entry had been simple, the glue brittle and easy to pry but this would be a different matter. Whatever was beneath went right up to the edge of the leather and I risked cutting it. I agonised, knife poised and trembling, but not for long. The need to know far outweighed the risk and I eased the blade along the edge of the endpaper.

The glue, like on the *Knave*, had been unevenly applied and some spots came away as if nothing held them, but others, it was like sawing through an oak branch. It was painstaking and slow and my eyes hurt by the time two edges were free.

But the reward for my labours was great and unexpected. My heart tightened and I dared not breathe. I had hoped for a letter, a missive between doomed lovers. But hidden in the binding were pages, covered in small, unbearably neat copperplate handwriting. They were not glued to the board and with shaking hands, I lifted them free. The pages were of bible paper, so thin and delicate to be almost see-through. I spread them, five in total, written on one side only, for the paper would surely rip if it were used on both sides. In the lower corners, the pages were numbered in Roman script.

IV . . . V . . . VI . . . VII . . . VIII

The first page of the set was the fourth by numbering. There were more pages elsewhere. A thrill went through me. I set the pages aside, too excited to read them with any attention, and went to the back cover, pried up those endpapers. After another eye-watering hour, I had the edges free but the board was blank. I sat back, deflated, but there had been more to the *Knave* than the letter and I was sure this book held further secrets.

I quickly found the binder's mark, FFG, where it had been on the *Knave* and then recalled the subtle, almost invisible mark Mr Caxton had found in the top corner of the inside cover. I turned up the lamp and brought it close. Without a magnifying lens, it was hard to see but if I angled the book in just the right way, the light caught on the mark.

Five dots, arranged as the sixth playing card. But it was not the same. A different pip was missing.

* *

  *

* *

On the *Knave*, it had been the first, and this was the third. I sat back. The third book. Of six? Mr Grieves had found three and stopped looking after a friend's death. A mysterious death? He had wanted to get rid of them. Perhaps he'd tried to burn them, or at least the first one, but for one who loves them it is as easy to destroy a book as it is to destroy one's soul. Maybe it had been Grieves who consigned the *Knave* to the flame but saved it at the last moment.

No. I remembered. He had said it was burned when it came to him.

But the question that would not leave me was why. What was so important about these books?

I looked down at the pages, the hidden story within the story. The handwriting was the same hand as the letter, albeit neater. Mr Caxton always said half the book's past is in its smell: the colognes and hair oils from past owners, the lingering of vinegar from a glaire not fully cleaned, the type of wood burned in the bindery for warmth.

I lifted the pages to my face, breathed them in, and past the ink, the paper, the leather, and board was the barest hint of a perfume. A sweet scent of orange blossom held in the fibres for decades, preserved in the binding, travelling through time to find me. It was with that smell, the idea of the woman who wore that perfume, who wrote the letter to her lost love, that I took up the pages to read.

governesses, each more dour and dull than the last. Most allowed me only to learn needlepoint and piano but one, the last, allowed me the books my father deemed inappropriate for women. Politics. Law. Economics. I learned the history of men's failing and hubris. The Revolutionary War with France. The South Sea Bubble. Lord North's many and varied faults. I read enough of the law texts my father kept in his library to understand the rights of man and woman and how disparate they were. I devoured knowledge and then my governess gave me novels. Stories of women, stronger than their circumstance, rising high above their class or manipulating it to suit them. I lived in books for my adolescent years, for – except important dinners where I was to be shown off as dutiful and quiet daughter – I was kept largely out of sight. It was only when I turned eighteen that my father began to notice that I had become beautiful and accomplished in all the skills a woman should possess, that I was now of value to him.

My father was a man who had gained his title with money and influence and believed himself greater than any man who had to rely on the uncertainties of birth. He was the grandson of a miner and had risen by his own tenacity and savagery to the ranks of Lord, with a seat in the House. He was patron to several MPs and therefore held considerable control over Parliament. He was, with few exceptions, one of the most powerful men in the country and had a reputation for bending the law to his will and using his vast fortune to bribe away any hint of scandal. I was little more than a tool for him to gain even more power, should I marry the right man. It was what I was bred for, after all, and with my mother dead so long, he had forgotten what it meant to love something, for I believe he did love her, in his way.

At eighteen, during the '51 season, I was launched into society. A whirlwind of debutante balls and parties across London's richest families. My beauty shone against other girls, daughters of earls and dukes, and I was quickly inundated with requests for visits from men far older than I. My father refused all but the most promising, though I was sure he had a candidate in mind.

'Act well, daughter,' he would say. 'Make them believe you are more interesting than you are.'

I bobbed. 'Yes, Father.'

I was to speak the right way, to nod and smile along to whatever the gentleman said, to defer to him, to laugh when he made a joke, but not too loudly. I was not to give my opinion for that was up to my future husband to grant me. I could not show an ounce of intelligence beyond the scope of what was deemed attractive for a young woman to possess. I had to be clever, but not inquisitive, yet I had to show interest in a man's endeavours though I was not to understand them. It was exhausting and by the end of a walk or tea with one of those men, I felt dull and useless.

I had grown angry at my confinement, of mind and body, and chafed against the limitations my father put upon me. One evening, I had had enough. I wanted fun and to be free of my name and my obligations and for that, I needed to lie. I went to my father but he was ensconced in the drawing room with men of business, talking over a deal, the details of which I did not hear.

'Father?' I asked at the door, keeping my eyes to the floor lest any of the gentlemen believe me impertinent.

'Not now.'

'But, Father, I have been invited to a ball. I wish to attend.'

'I said, not now.' He had his back to me and his voice had quickly turned to a growl.

'I hear the Duke of Arundel's son will be in attendance.'

He lifted his head a little but did not turn. 'You hear or you know, girl?'

My knees weakened but I held firm. 'I know.'

'Go then, and stop bothering me.'

I went quickly from the room so he would have no time to change his mind and, with my maid Daisy in tow – a comely girl who did not yet know my father's temper and was more afraid of me – we took the carriage to the home of a lord and lady I knew to be having a ball, for I had truly been invited. The carriage rode away to park somewhere nearby but Daisy and I did not go inside. Instead, I dragged her, complaining and fearful, to the West End. I wanted to see life and music and, under a cloak like a woman in one of those salacious novels, I went to the theatre.

I don't remember the play, if it even was a play, but I remember the rest. It was this night that my life would change and I would be set upon the path that would lead to my destruction. Yet I would not change a moment of it.

I sat near the back and watched the show. The audience exploded with laughter at the ribald humour, and the actors were wonderfully bright and bold and free.

I noticed you watching me some way into the second act. I pointed to the stage, as if to tell you to pay attention there. You smiled and dutifully turned your head. Though I soon caught you staring again. In the smoky, noisy theatre, you were a beacon. You had no beard or moustache and looked so wonderfully young compared to the men I had spent the season wooing. You were blond, hair the colour of limelight, and had blue eyes so bright

I could see them across the room. And you held in your hand a book, of all things.

My maid caught me staring, saw the smile in the corner of my mouth and tapped my arm.

'Miss, that's not proper.' Her voice was a mouse's whisper and I ignored it.

The seat beside me was empty and you took your chance. Such impertinence for a man to sit beside a woman without invitation, but you never did wait for an invitation.

'Are you enjoying the show?' you asked, raising your voice to be heard above the orchestra.

'I was,' I replied, 'until a strange man took it upon himself to bother me.'

'The devil,' you said, 'shall I chase him off for you?'

Your voice spoke to breeding but not too much. An accent from somewhere rural beaten out of you by Oxford or Cambridge.

'I wish you would.'

My maid bristled beside me, muttering something about scandal and my father. The fear of what my father might do should he discover I was here, speaking with a young man unvetted by him, haunted my thoughts and made me all the more keen to enjoy every moment.

I nodded to the book in your hands. 'Is the show not engaging enough for you?'

'I do not go anywhere without a book.' You lifted it and showed me the cover, an author I did not yet know but would soon adore. The name shone out: Abel Bell. 'My favourite writer. I've read everything he's written at least twice. Tales of adventure and romance.' You smiled at me at that last word and I knew I was blushing.

'It does not look like a romance from the simple cover.'

'A book may hold many secrets, my lady, if you know where to look.'

The play ended and you rose, offering me your hand. In the crowd of theatregoers getting up to leave, we were invisible to all but my maid who continued her hand wringing.

'Might I introduce myself? I am William Heathfield.'

I nodded as I was trained to and in return, gave you my name. I had not heard of your family beyond a dim recollection I could not place, but your eyebrows rose when you heard mine. I should have given another, or just my first, but I forgot myself. Giddy to be out, escaped for a night, in the company of a handsome man for the first time all season.

'May I call on you?' you asked.

'I don't think that's wise.'

'Then might I arrange to see you somewhere else? I could chase away a few more devils for you.'

'You are persistent for a stranger without a title.'

You only smiled at my dismissals. You knew I didn't mean them. Even at first meeting, you knew me better than my father ever had.

My maid tugged on my sleeve. 'Miss, we must be away.'

You took a step back, half-bowing, your hands clasped before you. 'I shall see you anon, then, fair Juliet.'

I stepped past you. 'Does that make you Romeo?'

'Should the lady wish it.'

I was shocked by you. I had never been spoken to so informally, so tenderly. Every meeting with a man had been transactional. An interview. But you were so different.

'I believe you are a knave, sir, and there was no bigger knave than Romeo.'

You laughed and I had never made a man laugh before that wasn't a polite titter at some useless small talk.

'If I may not call on you, then perhaps we will see each other again.'

'Miss!' The maid pulled on me.

'I doubt that. I am very busy. This Saturday for example, I am to attend the regatta at Henley.'

You shook your heard in mock disbelief. 'Would you believe it that I am to attend the very same?'

'I must insist we go, miss!' Daisy said.

'Perhaps I will see you there,' you said and then to Daisy: 'My apologies for keeping your ladyship. May I walk you to the door?'

I realised we were the last in the theatre. That the young boys with brooms were already sweeping away the debris of the evening. I took your outstretched arm.

At the theatre door, you donned a hat I noticed was scuffed in places and your coat had a tear at the hem. A gentleman certainly, but perhaps not a wealthy one. You saw me looking and did not make an excuse as I expected. But your smile faltered, as if in embarrassment.

'Thank you, for saving me from that awful gentleman who sat beside me,' I said, bringing us back to happier things.

Your smile returned. 'My pleasure.'

You watched us leave. I felt your eyes on me, the heat of your attention. Then reality returned, Daisy's urgings and how we would get home. I called for a carriage, my father's driver all but forgotten at the townhouse ball. He would be sitting there long after we were home and would have a tale to tell my father. That was a problem for the morning. For that night I wanted to revel in my daring, at this man I had met and felt wooed by. You, my knave, in a few brief minutes, you had stolen my heart and would keep it.

Do you remember it as I do? The easy way we spoke together and *the feeling that came with it? How I wished I could bottle that feeling and keep it always. It would be solace now, after what happened. I can still smell the blood on you, still feel your hands shake in mine.*

That doesn't matter. I live now in the past, but I will choose to live in a happier memory.

The sun-filled days of our stolen season. How we laughed! At last Saturday came and

And!

There the page cut off.

I flipped the pages over and back to check I had not missed anything but that was all there was. I sat back in my chair and tried to understand what I had read and why it had been hidden. At the foot of each page were three sets of initials: W.A., H.P. and I.C. Each page had been initialled as if it were a contract or legal document, but who those initials belonged to was another question to add to the ever-growing list. But I had a name. One name. William Heathfield who was perhaps twenty in 1851. He could still be alive.

This was part of a larger document; that was clear now. The letter had been its introduction, a note for the intended reader but what of the rest? And to what purpose? Why have this witnessed, initialled, only to split it up and hide it within obscure books? I sat back, a thousand questions forming and dissolving in my mind. A few thoughts gained clarity amid the confusion.

These pages were important enough for someone to attack me to steal the *Knave*. Whatever this story became, it was important enough for someone to pay Mr Grieves to track down the books, assuming the collector knew these pages existed and was not just a collector of Bells. Regardless, it was important enough to hide within the bindings of these books for decades in the hope the right person would find it. I would hide them again, but somewhere else. I glued the endpaper back into the book and kept the pages separate. If anyone looked, the *He Sings His Devotion* was a complete and unmarred edition. I set it on my shelf and took up the pages again.

I read them over and saw in this motherless girl, whoever she was, a mirror of myself. An uncaring father, a wish for more for her life, and a rebellious streak shot through the heart of her. I knew I needed to know who she was, what became of her, for perhaps if I found her path, her fate, I would discover my own.

14.

Where to begin. I had several avenues open to me and two lines of intrigue. The books themselves were the first. Grieves had found one more. I didn't know where he had sent it but I knew someone who could find out. I also had the publisher now and could seek out the author but they were in Manchester. Going to Charlie would require a trip to London and I doubted Mr Caxton would be willing to let me go during the week. It would have to be next Sunday. The bookshop would be closed and Father would be about his own business, for we rarely spent a Sunday together. Church was a distant memory, lost after my mother's death, and taking a meal together was inconstant enough to make it a rare exception to our routine. I only had to ensure I did not miss the last train home; though, with a blush rising in my cheeks, I did not regret the evening I spent when last that happened.

The next line of course was the content of the pages themselves and the name. William Heathfield. A gentleman, it had said, who attended at least one major event of the '51 season, no doubt more, and attracted the attention of the daughter of a lord. Surely that would have garnered attention from the gossipmongers of the day. There would be periodicals from the time in the Bodleian, if I could only get in.

The danger of the man in the bowler hat and the mysterious collector searching alongside me did not trouble me, though perhaps it should have. All my life I had been able to focus on a single thing – an activity, a person, a passion – to the detriment of others. Harry called me a dog with a bone. The house could be burning down around me and I would not look up from my task until it was complete. That trait of mine made me a good bookbinder but not such a good friend. Now that focus rested on these books, this girl whose story was hidden within them. Nothing else mattered.

I wish I had been able to look up. To notice the life I'd strived for slipping away.

*

Mr Caxton did not greet me in his usual fashion. No cheerful jibe at my lateness or comment on my weekend. He was intent at his work on a two-volume set of Burke's *Peerage*.

As I passed his desk, I set down a paper bag without a word, and took to my own desk and my own pile of unfinished bindings. It was a few minutes later, when the smell of the still-warm almond pastry got the best of him that he finally spoke.

'Bribes will not work on me, Miss Delaney.'

The lightness of his tone sent a cool wave of relief through me and I hadn't realised how tense and dark my mood had become.

'I wouldn't dream of it. I stole that.'

A little laugh and the rustle of the paper being ripped. Silence as he ate and I prepared the stencil to begin tooling the design on the cover of the *Botany*. It was more intricate than I had attempted before, with different depths and grades of linework needed. I would have to take another day to practise as I only had until the end of the week to complete it and I couldn't afford to make a mistake. I had wasted a lot of time I could have spent better on this book but there was little I could do about that now. I tried not to live in the past, to dwell on old mistakes and tussle with my regrets. If I did, I would never get out of bed of a morning. My profession was to take something old and make it new again, to take something broken and reform it. It didn't matter what came before with these books, only what was to come. I lived my life as a book rebound after every tear.

As I traced the design and thought which tools to use, a shadow came over my desk.

'Where is the third book?'

My heart clenched and I heard in the voice the man in the bowler hat growling in the darkness. Saw again those wolf-like eyes, the threat they held.

'Lilian?'

I looked up and Mr Caxton stood over me. It was as if the light came back into the room in one great flash. 'Sorry, what did you say?'

Mr Caxton frowned. '*The Third Book*. Rabelais. You were to collect it from that Grieves fellow.'

My lie came flooding back to me. I'd entirely forgotten.

'Yes,' I said, stalling to grasp for a new story, 'as it turned out, the volume was so badly damaged, it proved not worth it. I believe he was trying to test me or swindle me. He did not seem the decent type.'

'A shame. And so devastated were you that you took a drink at a nearby tavern and missed the last train?'

To that, I could not answer for fear he would see my actions in my expression, hear them in my lies.

'I was young once too,' he said in a wistful manner, a tone he always had when talking of his past. 'I know what it feels like to want to explore beyond the realms of what is good for us.'

'I don't know what you mean, sir.' But I did, of course I did.

'I once ran away to London for three days and three nights in the company of a friend. We drank until our bellies were sore and danced with the young and beautiful Dionysians of Soho. My mother was furious as I was only sixteen and was meant to be working on her market stall.'

'I cannot quite imagine you drunk and dancing.'

He smiled and his eyes sparkled as if living it all again. 'I was not always the dignified and well-mannered gentleman you see before you. I understand the desire to live without consequence or thinking but, Miss Delaney, actions do have consequences.'

'I understand,' I said. As much as I respected and admired Mr Caxton, this fatherly advice was beginning to grate.

'If you are to take over my bindery one day, I must trust you.'

My eyes shot to his. 'Take over?'

'Yes, yes, don't get too excited. I'm not dead yet.'

I saw immediately the errors I'd made. The weight of them. Putting someone else's past ahead of my future. I'd almost sabotaged myself and maybe I had meant to, for life was becoming too big and I was not ready to live it without a father.

'But . . . you would give all this to me?'

'I have no children. Who else am I going to give it to? But you must show me you care. You could have finished the *Botany* for Dr Ashburn a week ago. Without so many distractions, you could have been working on the repair of that sixteenth-century Herodotus that's been languishing for a month. You could have opened the damned post and seen the letter from Frank Karslake that's been waiting for days.'

The stack of letters on my desk had grown and I reached for it, shuffled through them until I found the one addressed to me. I held it in my hands as if I was holding a dove, precious and fragile and liable to fly away at any moment.

I set it down on my desk and met Mr Caxton's eyes. 'I must tell you what's happened.'

A frown flickered over his brow and he pulled over a chair. 'That sounds serious, my dear.'

'It is, I fear. But so is what you're offering me.'

He held up a finger for me to wait and shuffled back to his desk, returning with half the pastry and his cup of tea. He set the tea down and took a large bite from the pastry, showering his waistcoat with golden flakes.

'Go ahead,' he said, mouth full.

I smiled at this man who was unlike any other I had known. But it faded knowing what I was to tell him. I pushed my hair aside to reveal the still-healing cut upon my forehead.

'I was attacked in London last week. A man tried to rob me.'

He stopped chewing. 'Good Lord. I should never have sent you.'

I shook my head. 'I've been to London a dozen times and never had so much as a bad word directed at me. But this, this happened because of the burned book. You saw the letter, well, it appears there is far more to the story.'

I told him everything of my two trips to London, leaving out only my tryst with Charlie. I told him of Grieves and the collector who was after these books, the theft of the letter, showed him what I found in the *Devotion* volume, the tale of the young lady and the lowly gentleman hidden in the binding, how someone was willing to go to great lengths to secure them, how there appeared to be six volumes, each perhaps with a different portion of the full story. He listened, as he always did, and as we talked, his tea grew cold and his last bite of pastry went uneaten.

When I was finally finished, he was silent for a spell. Then he reached forward and popped the last piece of pastry in his mouth.

'I confess, I had thought that letter mere binder's waste, but it appears not,' he said.

'I told you because I am letting it go. Putting it behind me and looking to the future.' I picked up the letter from Karslake. 'Focusing on this, and this.' I nodded to the workshop. 'I don't want secrets and I don't want you thinking badly of me for following a trail of breadcrumbs to a foolish end.'

'You're going to stop searching for these books?'

I nodded, for I was resolute. It had cost me too much already and now, with Mr Caxton's offer, with the potential lying unopened before me, with my father's debt hanging like a spectre in the back of my mind, I had too much to lose.

'You will simply let go of the mystery of this girl and her lover?'

I nodded again. *'That way madness lies.'*

Mr Caxton let out a small laugh. 'We each have a madness in us, my dear. Only the lucky ones may make a career of it.'

I smiled. 'Do you think less of me?'

He stood up, shaking his head. 'If you only knew what tempted me away from my trade as a young man, you would be calling me a hypocrite of the highest order. I have learned from my follies and I hope I can impart some wisdom so you would avoid making the same mistakes, though it appears I don't need to as you've already turned the right corner. You are supremely talented, Miss Delaney. Focus on that.'

'I will.'

'No more talk of burned books and hidden love stories?'

'None.' A heavy sadness fell over me that I would not get to follow the path to its end but that also came with relief. No more lies, no more hiding, and no more fear over the man in the bowler hat.

With nothing more to distract me, over the next few days I completed the *Botany*. I'd bound the small volume in green morocco with a symmetrical gold celandine pattern. The gold shone in the lamplight as if it had its own sun behind it and the green was the deep, verdant green of a summer forest. It was the best work I'd ever produced and Mr Caxton was so pleased, he had it photographed. I packaged it up and sent it back to Dr Ashburn three days early.

Meanwhile, the letter from Frank Karslake, head of the Guild of Women Binders, was an invitation to visit his bindery in Hampstead and asking for samples of my work. At Mr

Caxton's urging, I wrote back to him, accepting his invitation and enclosing the photograph of the *Botany*.

Days passed and as winter bit harder upon the city, I focused on my craft. I was happy. Or, if not happy exactly, then content. Or perhaps, resigned. The books still nagged at me, at my edges. When I stopped for a moment the lover's story crept back into my thoughts. I kept busy. Stayed in the workshop until past nine each night, worked longer in the bookshop at weekends and watched my father retreat further into himself and the bottle. I saw nothing of Harry but I thought of him and wondered if there was still an ember between us to be rekindled. Mr Caxton looked upon me dotingly again and our easy manner returned. I only hoped it would last.

15.

It was with great excitement that I stepped out of the cab on Pond Street in Hampstead and saw before me the workshop of the Guild of Women Binders. The building was on a corner and commanded its presence on the street. Its lower walls were all windows half covered in white paper or paint to keep out the glare and the door had little to announce itself but a brass plaque on the wall beside. I rang the bell and waited, almost shaking with the anticipation of finally being inside the guild.

The door was flung open by a man in an expensive suit with a purple silk handkerchief tucked in his pocket. His hair was thinning and receding but strangely voluminous at the top and sides, giving him a peaked, tricorn shape, which was not as comical as it could have been. On his face, round spectacles and a wide smile.

'Miss Delaney,' he said and held out his hand. 'I am Frank Karslake. A pleasure to meet you. Welcome! Come in, please.'

I shook his hand and allowed him to lead me inside the workshop.

He made small talk, asked after my journey and my health, that of Mr Caxton also, and spoke of how excited he was to receive Mr Caxton's letter. All while I took in the sights before me.

Half a dozen women at their work across long, wide tables. All the tools and apparatus of my workshop multiplied tenfold. Each woman was bent over a book, their hair done up in neat buns, same as mine. They tooled the covers, specks of discarded gold leaf floating to the floor like snow. A row of bookcases, full to bursting with completed books, stood against the far wall and their overspill lay on the floor in piles. It was a factory line of bindings. They could not all be to order, else there would be no customers left for the rest of us, and I wondered how Mr Karslake managed to sell them all.

'This is the finishing room,' Mr Karslake announced, 'where the books are tooled and through here,' he said, ushering me on into a larger, brighter space, equally full of women and a few men, 'is the forwarding room.'

The women sat at benches, strewn with tools and scraps. The surface spread with large pieces of morocco and calfskin and atop them, naked boards and book blocks ready to be covered. The women worked methodically, pots of glue before them, pasting the leather, securing the boards, bone folders moving so fast it was like a dance. At the end of the room was a standing press where dozens of books were being pressed. It was a huge piece of equipment, standing as tall as I. A woman stood at the bar, turning and repositioning until the books were adequately pressed.

'I see you admiring our press,' said Mr Karslake. 'Made by W.O. Hickok. I had it shipped from Pennsylvania at quite the cost. But we can press a hundred titles at a time.'

'It is a beautiful piece.'

The woman at the bar caught my eye and I smiled but she did not. She wore a dark grey working smock and seemed weary. In fact, all the women in this room seemed sunken about the eyes. Their motions expert and practised by routine, not passion. It gave me an uneasy feeling.

We moved on then to another set of rooms. 'This is the studio, where the learners come to take their instruction.'

This room held twenty women, all sat along two long benches, one in front of the other like a schoolhouse. They had a set of finishing tools before them and were learning their use. The instructor was a young woman with a patient tone, though she was quick as she rattled off the names of the tools and the women scribbled furiously in their notebooks to keep up.

'Constance,' Mr Karslake said and I recognised the name of his daughter. 'This is Miss Delaney, a bookbinder with John Caxton in Oxford. You remember the photograph I showed you? Miss Delaney, this is Constance, my eldest. She runs the workshop.'

The woman at the front, who could not have been much older than twenty, nodded curtly. 'I did. Beautiful work, Miss Delaney.'

'Thank you, Miss Karslake. And thank you for inviting me.'

The scholars had paused their notetaking to listen.

Constance shared a look with her father, who beamed. 'We are in need of an instructor for finishing. Savoldelli has gone back to Hampstead.' She directed this at her father, more than me. His expression grew dark for a moment. I guessed she meant the Hampstead Bindery, which was Mr Karslake's 'traditional' bindery, rather than this experiment.

'Indeed. And your work is first rate, Miss Delaney,' he said.

I blushed at the compliment, for I'd still not learned how to accept them. 'Mr Caxton is an excellent teacher.'

'This way,' Mr Karslake said, ushering me into a smaller room that appeared to be a drawing room or office. He had tea ready and bid me to sit in one of the armchairs by the hearth. I took him to be quite the salesman, for he'd made me feel important from the moment I walked into the bindery.

'So,' he began, relaxing into his chair, 'what do you think of our operation?'

I kept the smile on my face, so as not appear rude, but I had a mixture of feelings within me. 'It is wonderful to see so many women at this trade.'

'And it is growing every day! We accept women with talent for art, for what is bookbinding but everyday artistry. They are trained for a full year, first in the classroom as you saw, then they move to forwarding, four or five months there and they are ready for finishing. Once they have completed their year they may do as they wish: set up on their own or continue working here.'

As he spoke, and he continued to at length, I noticed another stack of books, all with goatskin bindings nearby. The topmost was a gold-tooled volume entitled *Aventures de Huon de Bordeaux*, with a thick floral border and extravagant font, all gilded in *pointillé*, rather than a flat piece of gold. My hand ached just looking at it and imagining the work. It was an unbalanced design, in my view, for it seemed to use every border pattern and technique, yet the title was all aligned to the left and that gave it an uneven look.

'I see you admiring the *Huon*,' Mr Karslake said and reached past me to pick it off the top of the stack. 'Isn't it exquisite? Constance finished it, from one of Savoldelli's designs.'

That struck me. 'Do the women not design themselves?'

'Not as a matter of course. That is left to the most experienced, though Constance and the de Rhiems girls are beginning to create their own. But that brings us neatly to you.'

'It does?'

'Your work is beautiful and it longs to be seen and recognised. I wish to act as your agent, to sell your own bindings. I would take a small fee and you would be one of our premium binders.'

'That is very kind, Mr Karslake,' I said, for it was, truly, yet I was troubled. 'May I?' I asked, holding out my hand for the book. I wanted to see it up close. He handed it to me and right away I could tell this binding was not of the quality I was used to.

I turned the book over in my hands, opened the covers and let it hang. I felt the looseness of the board, the free hinge that should be stiff. The endpapers too were tipped in but only by the barest smear of glue and I knew that in a year or less, they would come free. Up close, the gold tooling, while fine enough, was missing in places, as if the glaire had not been evenly applied or had not been properly mixed.

'Constance also mentioned my other motive for asking you here. We have a space for a teacher and I would like you to consider it. You'd have to move to London, of course, but there would be a wage and you'd be given space to work on your own bindings, which I would sell. Artistic bindings by women are all the rage and we cannot make them fast enough.'

The piles of books and straining bookcases told another

story. I put the *Huon* back on its pile. 'Mr Karslake, I cannot tell you how flattered I am by your offer. Your guild is a remarkable place for women to learn the trade.'

'I am proud to have given so many artistic women a vocation and a way to earn their own money. We are now able to print and publish and can take orders for any such paper work from our customers. A full service with Karslake! I would list your work in all our catalogues and I'll show them at exhibitions all over the country.' I sensed a note of desperation in his voice and I tried to keep my polite expression as he continued. 'I have contacts with the great booksellers in New York. Your work would be seen by the world, Miss Delaney, as it deserves to be.'

I could see how this would work on others. This flattery and bombast, but I saw behind it. Saw under the cover, under the binding of this place. Women used as cheap labour, under the guise of progress. It reminded me of my days at the university press, being just one of many along an assembly line, not paid or valued as much as the men next door. I didn't think Karslake a terrible man, just one with little knowledge of the trade and an ambition that outstretched his talent as a businessman.

'You have given me much to think about,' I said, standing. 'I'm afraid I must bid you good day else I'll miss my train. This has been illuminating, Mr Karslake, and I'm grateful for your faith in me. May I think about your offer and let you know my decision soon?'

He stood to join me. 'Of course, Miss Delaney, though don't dally. I am interviewing others and need the position filled quickly. Should you not wish to teach, I would still be happy to act as your agent.'

He walked me to the door, past the factory lines of women

about their work. It gave me a sense of despair seeing them but most looked happy enough, unknowing they were sitting atop a crumbling foundation. At the door, I shook his hand and promised to be in touch.

I stepped out onto Pond Street with a strange feeling in my chest. I'd spent the last three years of my life dreaming of joining the Guild of Women Binders, thinking it a club of talented and spirited women who all shared a love of their trade. I imagined evenings spent discussing the latest techniques, or new tools, or laughing over mistakes we'd made in our early years. But I found a factory, a place of low-quality work, where each book had a different hand at each stage. It saddened me, to have a dream dashed, and my gratitude to Mr Caxton and his teaching grew. It cemented in me even more the desire to do well by him, to make him proud to call me partner rather than apprentice.

I had no time to dally, for I wanted to get the afternoon train home to Oxford. Though I did spare a thought for Charlie and wondered if he ever spared a thought for me. My decision to spend the night with him had been reckless, stupid even, but Lord, it had been *fun*. It had made me feel more awake to the world than I had in years. Part of me wanted to seek him out, to feel that bright vibrancy again, to see if there was more to our tryst than me trying to forget Harry, but I couldn't. I was beginning a new stage of my life, a calmer, more certain one. I wasn't sure yet if I was happy about it, but I resolved to at least try to be.

16.

My train was held outside High Wycombe for a time as the wind had blown a tree branch onto the line. I had brought with me a small volume of poetry to read on the train, but my mind was drifting and I couldn't concentrate on the words.

Over these last few weeks, the story of the young lovers had barely left me, however much I tried to forget it. The abrupt ending of the pages, where they had arranged to meet one another, lingered inside me. Had they met? Had it been as romantic and dangerous as the rest of those pages suggested?

I shifted in my seat and forced myself to stop. I had put it behind me. I would only know what I already knew and that would have to be enough. If, by some miracle, I came across another of these books by chance, then I would put it aside. That was my decision. My promise to Mr Caxton. As much as it pained me to do so, it was necessary, so I took up the book of poetry and read until my eyes ached.

It was past eight and ink-dark by the time we finally pulled into Oxford. Despite a stiff back from sitting so long on the train, I was in good spirits. I realised I had changed, somewhat, from the girl I had once been. The feral Lily who had unmoored boats and stolen food, then the obsessive, studious Lilian who had learned the binding trade to hide from her past, and in between somewhere, still prowling at my edges was the reckless me who had become fixated with a burned book, taken to the bed of a handsome stranger, and been attacked on the street. Now, perhaps, it was time for settled Lilian. Calm Lilian.

Whoever I turned out to be next, one aspect of my past behaviour nagged at me and I resolved to fix it before returning to my life.

*

'What are you doing here?'

I'd stood across from the alley to the Turf Tavern and waited for him. Harry saw me as he emerged and stopped, his manner changed in an instant.

'I wanted to say sorry,' I said.

'Go on then.'

We spoke across the narrow, cobbled New College Lane but it may as well have been an ocean between us. I had turned him away and it was up to me to bridge the gap. I stepped across the road to stand beside him. He was angry with me. Harry had been angry with me for a long time and I did not blame him.

'I'm sorry for the lunch,' I said.

'You think I'm upset we didn't go to lunch?'

'You're not?'

'I'm not a child, Lily.' He shook his head. 'You don't understand, never have. Just leave me be, will you?'

He walked away and I couldn't bear it. I rushed to him, grabbed his hand. 'Wait.'

This was the first time we'd touched in years and a wave of

feeling crashed over me. The warmth of his skin, the strength in his hands, the callouses and scars. I knew his hand like I knew my own. I held it in both of mine, ran my fingers over the lines. I brought his hand to my face and pressed it against my cheek. His pulse quickened and he moved closer. I hadn't known until then how much I missed his touch.

Then he took it away.

'Lily, this . . . what are you doing?'

'I'm sorry, Harry,' I said.

He sighed through his nose, pursed his lips. 'I'll never understand you.'

'I don't understand myself. But . . .' I said and reached for him again. He didn't move away, let me lace my fingers in his. 'I'm really hungry. Shall we have dinner?'

He shook his head. 'Damn you, Delaney.'

Not twenty minutes later, we were at a table in The Chequers. Another ancient pub down a lane, as was favoured in Oxford. This one was all dark wood and carvings of exotic animals, harking back to the building's past as a menagerie. It was lively but not busy nor loud and we were able to hear our own thoughts, though that would not last as the night wore on. I sipped a ginger beer while Harry had a porter and we sat in a not unpleasant quiet, waiting for our food.

'How is your head?' he asked, finally breaking the stalemate.

'Healed on the outside. The inside is still a mess.'

'What really happened?'

'If I tell you, you will scold me and I've had enough of that from my father.'

He leaned closer, a firm look in his eye. 'I won't. I swear it.'

I held his gaze for a moment, then more, and didn't ever

want to leave it. I wondered then if one can go back to a child-hood love. Should a first love stay a first, or become the last? I was not sure yet if I would be trying to recapture something that was lost or rekindle a fire that should never have been put out.

'I was attacked by a man. Robbed. He tried to steal my bag but I held on. He hit me. That's the truth of it.' But not the whole truth. That was buried now. Dead and growing cold.

Harry's face was a mask of shock. 'Jesus. Lily.' I expected him to tell me how stupid I was going to London alone in the first place, how I'd clearly been loose with my belongings, but he didn't. His shock melted away into kind concern and he took my hand. 'Did he get anything?'

I shook my head. 'A burned book cover is all. I think he grabbed anything he could.'

I almost told him of Charlie running after the man, retriev-ing my satchel, but that was a door best left closed.

Harry's shoulders relaxed. 'Good. Did you tell the police?'

'Yes,' I lied because I didn't want a lecture. 'They said there was little they could do.'

He rolled his eyes. 'What use are they?'

'Let's talk about something else. Mr Caxton says I will take over the bindery from him.'

Harry's eyebrows shot up and his face broke into a wide smile. 'That's incredible, Lily. I'm pleased for you.'

'Are you?'

He turned sombre a moment, matching my own feeling. 'Of course. You deserve it.'

We were dancing around each other, talking of the everyday when we should be speaking from the heart. I was sick of the dance, the tiptoe steps, dodging and weaving away from each other. I missed him; that was the truth of it. Despite what had happened between us years ago, my life had been colourless without him. I had a new resolve. A new direction for my life and I wanted him in it.

'Harry,' I said, finding the words and the courage to speak them. 'I—'

'Sorry for the wait,' came a loud voice, and a plate of steaming lamb cutlets was placed before me. Another plate, stacked with slabs of roast beef and potatoes, was set before Harry.

'No bother, sir,' Harry said to the man towering over us. He wore a dirty apron and his face was red from the kitchens, but he smiled and bid us enjoy our meal.

Harry picked up his knife and fork and tore into his beef. 'I've been on my feet since morning. This is the first meal beyond a mouthful of bread I've had all day.' He took the first bite and another before realising I had not started mine.

'Sorry, Lily, what were you saying?'

As if snapped from a dream, I took up my knife. The flush of courage I had felt was gone. 'Nothing that can't wait.'

We ate, drank, and joked about the old days and the new. My heart could wait, for I had a trembling thought that he would not wish the same from me as I would from him.

We stayed past our meal and drank a few more pots before finally, a mite drunkenly, he offered to walk me home.

The November evening didn't feel cold that night, despite frost on the stones and ice forming on the puddles at the side of the road. The warm glow of the lamps turned the ice to gold. The streets were quiet, empty and we laughed as we walked along them, finally turning into Victor Street.

At my door, we stopped, our hands entwined. Harry lifted my arms in a playful way, pulled them behind his back so I stumbled against him. He let my hands go and I held them against his back. His arms wrapped around me and I looked up at him, he down to me.

'What are we doing?' he whispered.

'What do you want to do?'

He dipped his head, then stopped, as if still unsure of my intent. 'We're in the middle of the street.'

'There is nobody here but us.' I reached up, put my hand on his cheek and pulled his lips to mine. He tasted of home. Of fire. Of love I once had and lost and now may have again. And was all the sweeter for it.

But he pulled away. 'I don't want this to happen when we're drunk.'

'I'm not that drunk,' I said.

'Lily, if we're to make a go of this, I want to do it right.'

Disappointed at the heat cooling between us, I nodded. I needed to do a lot of things right from now on. There was no rush, after all. 'What is the right way?'

'Well,' he said, looking around for the answer. 'I'd like to court you, properly.'

I laughed. 'All right. Go ahead.'

He looked surprised and fumbled for his words. 'I will. I'll speak to your father tomorrow.'

'He's not my keeper.'

'I know. No man ever would be. But it's the gentlemanly thing to do and I want to be a gentleman for you.'

I felt an ache in my chest at his sincerity. He'd held on to our love, though it had lain in tatters for so long. I reached up to him again and kissed him again because I couldn't not in that moment. He responded, his arms tightening around my waist.

I let him go and he remembered himself, though I could tell this time it wasn't with as much conviction and, had I pressed, I was sure he would accompany me upstairs. But I would not press. I would let the courting stretch out for as long as we needed to find each other again.

'Goodnight then, Harry.'

'Goodnight, Lily.'

I unlocked the door to the bookshop and stepped inside. Harry watched, smiling, biting his lip like a smitten schoolboy, until I was inside. I closed the door and leaned back against it, willing my heart to calm and the red blush to leave my cheeks in case my father was still up.

I set my coat and bag down and checked the office. A lamp burned low but I didn't hear snoring or the scratch of his pen. He must have left it on when he went to bed. I went inside, still dizzy with the evening.

My father was not there but a man sat in his chair.

I froze. Head to toe, ice prickled my skin. The man wore a brown bowler hat and twirled a short blade in his hands. His wolf eyes bored into mine and he grinned.

'Hello, Miss Delaney,' he said, his voice as cold as his eyes. The grin fell away and he gripped the knife, pointed it at my chest. 'Where are the books?'

17.

'What books?' I asked, voice trembling, hand gripping the door handle.

'Don't play that game, miss. Tell me where they are and we can go about our evenings.' His accent surprised me. None of the city or country twangs but an educated, almost gentlemanly lilt that hid any idea of his provenance.

'Who are you? Who do you work for?' The same someone who had engaged Grieves, perhaps?

He ignored my questions, stood up, and stepped slowly around my father's desk. 'Those books don't belong to you.'

'I don't know what you're talking about.'

He kept walking, getting closer. I backed away. His arm reached over me and pushed the door closed. I held my nerve as best I could, but now I was trapped in the dim, airless office.

'Lie again,' he said and raised the blade.

'What's so important about these books?'

He raised his shoulder in a shrug, the knife loose and casual in his fingers. 'Let's call it sentimental value. Give me the books, Miss Delaney, and you'll never see me again.'

This close I saw the intricacies of his features. Studied them while I tried to think of a way forward. He looked to be in his thirties. Pale skin, small thin scar across his right temple, dusting of shallow pockmarks across his cheeks, smell of mint on his breath. His hat hid all his hair but his eyebrows were dark yellow, almost gold, and I suspected his hair was blond. He would be handsome if he were not so coiled for violence.

'I don't have them,' I lied and his lip twitched. I couldn't give him the books. That thought shouted loud and clear in my head. *You can't have them. I won't let them go.*

'Where are they?'

'I sold them. At a market. Penny each. I don't know who bought them.'

He narrowed his eyes at me and leaned closer, until our faces were an inch from touching. His eyes were empty and I knew he would have no qualms in using that knife. 'You're a terrible liar, Miss Delaney.'

'Please . . .' Fear took me then and my defence crumbled. 'I don't have them.'

'Last chance. Get the books. Quietly. Your father would not be happy to be woken. He must sleep poorly these days, with the weight of thousands in debt on his mind.'

Mention of my father turned my blood to ice. I saw then the letters from the bank spread over the desk. He moved away so I could open the door. I thought about running, sprinting down the corridor and out into the night, shouting for Harry or a nearby constable. But it would only take this man a few moments to go upstairs and use that blade on my father.

I climbed the stairs. The *Devotion* sat on my shelf and the *Knave* was wrapped in a cloth on my desk. I pulled them close and ran my hand over the cover of the *Devotion*. I checked the binding, it was sound and well glued. Nobody would know it had been opened. The pages I'd found within were hidden in a drawer, but I hoped he wouldn't know to miss them.

I crept downstairs, terrified of waking my father. The bookshop seemed full of shadows. The warm book-lined walls were cold and distant. The books were heavy in my arms. I hated to part with them, though I knew their secrets were safe, for now. The man's shadow filled the glass of the office door. I edged closer, my heart beating so loud I was afraid it would wake my father.

I stepped back into the office, the room suddenly so small with this stranger looming over it. Taking ownership of it.

I handed over the two volumes. He unwrapped the *Knave*, checked it, and rewrapped it. He opened the cover of the *Devotion* and for a moment my heart stopped. *He knows. He'll discover the pages missing.* But he only flipped it closed and held both in one large hand.

'Where are the rest?'

The question struck me. 'I don't have any others.'

'A moment ago, you didn't have these. Where are they?'

'I don't have any; I swear it.' I backed against the bookshelf.

He set the books on Father's desk and pulled his knife from his pocket. 'You're lying again.'

He came at me, pressed the point of the knife beneath my chin. Cold metal bit into my skin.

'Give them to me.'

My voice came out in a weak whisper. 'I don't have any. I don't know where they are.'

'Then you'd better find them.' He pressed the knife harder. I felt it draw blood and I gasped. 'Or next time I come back, this won't be such a polite conversation.'

He held me there. Shelves digging into my back, blade pressing upwards, lifting my chin until my neck strained. He was so close I could taste his breath and I wanted to gag.

Then he let go. Air rushed back and my knees weakened. I caught myself on the shelf else I would have fainted.

The man picked up the books and tipped his hat. 'Until next time.'

I waited until he was gone. Until the front door closed. Then I rushed to it, locked it, pulled the chain across and the blind down.

I put my back to the door, my heart near galloping out of me. I put my hand on my chest, closed my eyes and forced myself to take deep breaths. The shop seemed to breathe with me and the walls tightened around me. The books had regained their warmth, the shelves their strength. The terror released me and my body was my own again. I gathered myself, touched under my chin. A spot of blood smeared on my finger, and a few more had dropped onto my shirtwaist.

'Just blood,' I said aloud, as if filling the shop with my voice would make it mine again.

I checked the door was locked, even though it had only been a moment. I put out the lamps in Father's office, which still stank of the man and I feared always would, then went upstairs. I looked in on my father, who slept soundly, unaware of the stranger in his home, the threats he had made.

I closed and locked the door to my bedroom. Checked the latch was on the window and it could not be opened. I peered out, onto Victor Street, expected to see the man in the bowler staring up at me, but the street was empty. Ice rimmed the window but I didn't dare light a fire. All the fight and fear left me at once and my hands began to shake.

From beneath several papers and books in my drawer, I took out the pages from the *Devotion*. Still safe. Still mine. I folded them neatly and slid them under my pillow, kept my hand on them. I closed my eyes but the moment I did, the man's face rushed into my mind and they sprung open. Sleep would not come to me that night and it felt as if it would never come again.

I had to find the books, give them to this man, whoever he worked for. I had no idea where another one was but I knew who to ask. I had to go to London, to Charlie, and ask him for a favour. But it would be the better part of a week before I could go and I couldn't wait that long.

18.

I was up as soon as the sun crested the spires and turned the black sky grey. My body ached and the spot under my chin when the man held his knife was bruised and stinging. I took the pages, put them inside a small book of poetry and put that in my satchel. The paring knife I'd taken on my last trip to the city was still in there, so I took the short blade and put it in my coat pocket.

I was away before my father woke and at the workshop before Mr Caxton. I left him a note that I was sick and please not to call on me as I did not want to make him sick as he is old and infirm enough. Oxford was still sleeping as I walked her streets towards Harry's house just off the Botley Road. I knocked until he answered, pulling on a shirt, eyes bleary from sleep.

'Lily? What are you doing here?'

'I need you to keep this safe for me,' I said and handed him the book holding the folded pages.

He took it, blinking. 'What . . . what's going on?'

'I can't tell you everything right now. There's no time. But you remember the book I told you about, with the love letter inside it?' He nodded. 'There is more to the story and others who want it. There are papers in that book.'

The sleep cleared from his eyes. 'You're scaring me. Tell me what's going on. I can help.'

'Not now. But soon, I promise. I need you to trust me and hide that book.'

'Lily, come on,' he said, taking my arm.

'Please, Harry. Just trust me.'

He saw the hardness in my eyes and the jitter running through me. I needed to go, get to London, find where the next book was; that was all I could think of.

'I'll hide it,' he said and the relief made me smile.

'Thank you.' I stood on tiptoes and kissed his cheek. He smelled of warm cotton and I wished I could wrap my arms around him and stay, bury myself in him and forget.

But I backed away, leaving him on his doorstep, half-dressed and confused.

I marched to the station, bought my ticket, and waited. A few others, bundled against the cold and early hour stood at intervals along the platform. As soon as the train pulled in, I boarded. It was empty. The guard strolled along the station, spinning his whistle with one hand and rubbing his eyes with the other. I found a seat near the carriage door and tucked myself against the wall. I could see anyone who came into the carriage and through the station.

We waited a while; it felt like forever. I shifted in my seat and craned my neck to look down the far side of the platform. I saw a man in a bowler hat step from the station. I shrank against the wall but when I looked again, I saw it was not the same man. He checked his pocket watch against the station clock then boarded a carriage away from me.

The train pulled away and I sank back into the chair,

breathing deeply for the first time since last night. I hadn't seen the bowler-hat man board and, for now at least, nobody else could get on this train. I was safe. The pages were safe.

A night of little and fraught sleep caught up with me and my eyes closed, rocked by the swaying train.

I burst awake to a shrill whistle as the train pulled into Paddington Station.

The carriage was almost full and beside me sat a woman with pink cheeks. She jumped as I woke, almost knocking some knitting to the floor.

'Lord!' she said, scrambling to catch the falling yarn.

'We've arrived?'

The woman smiled and her cheeks turned to bright, round cherries. 'Yes, dear. You were a tired one. Making all kinds of funny noises in your sleep. Just like my boys did when they were young.'

The heat of embarrassment rose inside me. 'I'm sorry.'

She waved her hand. 'No, no. It was quite entertaining. You were talking about books, of all things.' She gave a titter and packed away her knitting in a large bag.

I righted myself and smoothed my hair.

'I hope you don't mind me taking a seat by you,' she went on, looking at me with a motherly air. 'Pickpockets do love a sleeper.'

I checked my pockets and all, including the paring knife, were as they should be. 'Thank you – that's very kind of you.'

She stood up to gather her things. 'I tell my boys kindness is the only legacy anyone can leave. Goodbye, dear. I hope you find that book you're after.'

I watched as she trundled down the aisle and out of the carriage.

It was another moment before the fog cleared enough from my brain that I could follow.

The clock struck ten as I left Paddington. Chimes rang out from the station and the church towers beyond. Mr Caxton would have found my note. I wondered briefly if he was angry with me, or worried. I pictured him small and alone in the workshop and my heart flooded with guilt.

I took an omnibus from Paddington into the city and made my way to Cecil Court. In the daylight, it was a different place. The narrow street was bustling with trade. The bookshops set their wares outside for browsers and many were looking over the offerings. I could not help myself from looking in one such box outside Watkins', full of cheap volumes of esoteric and pulp literature.

It was in this casual browsing that a name popped out at me. Abel Bell. My chest tightened. It could not be so easy, and it only took a moment to see that it was not. The binding and the size were different. I picked it up. *The Death of Love* said the gilding on the spine. A small, slim volume in red cloth binding, faded and foxed at the corners. The publisher was listed as the same as the other books: Montague and Cliff of Manchester. This one was published in 1889 and was a first edition. Twelve years ago. The author could still be alive and may know who had bought and rebound six of their books. I checked the back, for the dots, but there were none and I could feel nothing under the endpapers. They were factory smooth. I put the book back.

Then I came to Grieves' Bookshop. I lingered outside, hidden at the edge of the shop, and peered in through the window. I didn't want to go in, see Grieves again and give him an opportunity to refuse me. I needed Charlie. I watched for a while. Grieves helped a customer and had a sour look about him the whole time. He called over his shoulder and, a moment later, Charlie appeared.

He had that ease about him, wide smile to the customer as he handed him a fat volume. The customer checked it and nodded, then shook Grieves's hand. They went about the sale, money changed hands and Charlie saw the man to the door, where I waited.

The man left and Charlie saw me immediately. That grin tugged at the corner of his mouth. He was as handsome as I remembered. Though it had only been a few weeks, it felt like half a lifetime had passed.

Charlie raised his finger, as if telling me to wait a minute, then went back inside. He said something to Grieves. I imagined he was asking for a break or telling him he was going for lunch. Grieves didn't object, just waved him away as one might a bothering fly. Charlie ducked into the back, emerged again with a coat and scarf, and came outside.

We walked a few steps, out of sight of Grieves, before speaking.

'Well, well,' he said, with a constant smile I tried to, but could not fully, return. 'This is a surprise. It's good to see you.'

'It's good to see you too,' I said and meant it. He was easy to be with and being close to him, I remembered again our night together. Remembered the feel of him, the heat, and then immediately, guilt struck me and I saw again Harry, standing before me. I didn't regret my time with Charlie, but it wasn't so simple anymore. That's not to say I wasn't tempted.

We walked to the far end of Cecil Court and stopped.

'Penny for them,' he said and I realised I hadn't spoken in a while.

'I need your help. I hate to ask but I can't ask anyone else.'

His face grew solemn. 'This about the books?'

I nodded.

'And here was me thinking you'd come back to see me,' he joked but I could see hurt in him, hear it in the edges of his voice.

I reached for his hand. 'I did. I wanted to come back sooner to see you but I couldn't and then . . .'

A group of passers-by forced us into a doorway.

'Then?'

'You remember the man who attacked me?' I said and he nodded. 'He found me again. Came to my home and threatened me. I need to find those books else . . . I don't know what he'll do.'

'Christ,' Charlie said and looked at me as if through a new lens. I knew I was pale, my eyes dark, and some deep part of me still trembled. He wrapped his arms around me, pulled me into him. I resisted at first, didn't have time for it, but a moment in his embrace, my head against his shoulder, and a piece of me began to relax. I held him back and breathed him in. This man who I barely knew but had shared something so intimate with. I had taken him for a rogue of sorts, a fast man with fast morals, much the same as myself, but he was more. He smelled of books and tobacco and cedar wood.

'What do you need me to do?' he asked and I felt his breath in my hair.

I could have wept. Help, at last, with no judgement. 'You said when we met that Mr Grieves had found three books. I have two. I need to know where the third went.'

He was quiet for a moment. 'That won't be easy. He won't talk about them and he put them in deliveries. I don't know if he made records.'

'Please? Will you try? I don't know what else to do.'

He kissed my hair and a shiver ran through me. 'I'll try.'

We parted and a wealthy-looking couple walking past gasped at our brazen familiarity. I didn't care. My thoughts were all on the book and on this kind man who would help me find it.

'It'll take me a while. Grieves goes out for lunch at noon. He's gone for at least an hour. I won't be able to get in the office until then. I'll meet you at the Madeira, the coffee house on St Martin's Lane.'

I nodded. 'I'll be there.' He moved away but I held him. 'Thank you.'

His smile returned. 'Don't thank me yet.' Then he was away but he cast a look behind him and winked.

I had a few hours to spend but the thought of sitting still, waiting in a tearoom, made my heart shrink and skin itch. I had to do something. I could not seek out the publisher of the Bell books, for they were in Manchester, but I could search out William Heathfield and his entanglement with the daughter of a lord.

The offices of the popular newspaper *The London Looker-On* were nearby, just off Covent Garden. I was striding towards it before the thought was finished in my mind. The paper was a favourite with Mr Caxton who had it delivered weekly. He said he liked to live vicariously through the gilded youths of the city and keep up with the latest fashions for gentlemen such as he. I was not quite sure what he meant as

I never saw him out of his usual tweeds but I didn't question it. More than once I had read society gossip in those pages on an idle lunchtime. Their archive would be vast, I was sure.

Cecil Court and Covent Garden were neighbours and the walk was short. The offices of *The London Looker-On* were in a handsome, whitewashed building on Bedford Street, with arched windows looking into a neat entry and reception. The paper had been around for about eighty years and instead of remaining steadfast to its origins, it had shifted and adapted to the world it was in and the readers it attracted so was one of the few that had survived.

I was at the door before I even knew what I was going to say.

A woman not much older than myself looked up from her typing as I entered. She had delicate spectacles perched on her nose and her hair done up in a stylish pompadour. She smiled neatly when she saw me. The office itself was sparse, with a tall, regal-looking plant in the corner and a few chairs for waiting guests.

'Good morning. May I help you?'

'Hello,' I said and my mind emptied. I had no clue what to say to convince this woman or her boss to let me into their archive.

A slight frown as I approached her desk. 'Are you lost? Do you need directions?'

'No. Thank you. I am . . . I uh . . .' I couldn't grasp a lie fast enough so I resorted to the truth. 'I am hoping to gain access to your archive.'

Her eyebrows rose, but not too much as to alter her poise. 'Our archive? It is not open to visitors unless by appointment, in writing, in advance.'

I was afraid of that. I looked at this woman, her desk, for anything that could help me, but both were neat and clean.

'I understand,' I said. 'But you see, I am a bookbinder by trade.' At this she appeared to relax as if I was now not some chancer off the street. 'And I came across a story so incredible as to beggar belief. A tale of love and tragedy between two young members of society in the Fifties. I have been unable to get this from my mind and I was hoping to use your archive to discover the truth of it.'

Her eyes widened with intrigue. 'Who were they?'

'The daughter of a rich and powerful lord and a penniless young gentleman. They fell in love and the story I have ends abruptly as they were to meet in Henley for the regatta. I am beside myself wanting to know what happened.'

'I am not supposed to . . .'

I leaned closer. 'There is a murder in their tale and I don't know of who but it seems this young gentleman was the culprit and I must know.'

Her mouth opened at mention of murder. 'Do you think he killed her father?'

'I don't know. It might even have been a duel.'

She gasped. The romance of a duel! A man fighting for their honour or the honour of their lady. It was the stuff of novels.

The woman looked to the door into the main offices as if to check nobody was coming, then stood. 'I can give you a couple of hours but you must leave by one o'clock. That is when the editor-in-chief arrives. The archive isn't tidy, I'm afraid.'

I wanted to hug her. 'Thank you. Truly.' I could not keep the smile from my face, much as I tried to maintain a professional guise.

She led me into the main office. The clatter of typewriters assailed me and I couldn't understand how anyone could work in such a din. The office was full of people. Young men barely out of short trousers sat at telegraph receivers, women typists working full speed, and in a windowed office at the far end, the editors and writers surrounded a table covered in papers. The boys rushed back and forth from telegraph to office, passing on the latest society gossip; the editors barked their orders and boys hurried from them to the typists, who would turn the scrawl into a story. It didn't pause or slow or stop. It was enough to take my breath from me as I imagined myself in this rapid, hungry life.

Nobody noticed the secretary and me as we skirted the edge of the room, past the editor's office, and into a corridor. There were doors off all sides, a small kitchen, a water closet, a room for photography, another of artists drawing the cartoons, and finally at the end, the door to the archive.

The woman opened the door, for it was not locked, and together we descended a set of stairs. At the bottom, she lit a lamp and held it high.

The lamp cast a soft yellow glow but did not reach far. The room was utterly dark beyond its halo.

'The Fifties, you said?' she asked.

'Fifty-one.'

She led me deeper into the room and the scale of it quickly became apparent. Either side of me were tall shelves full of boxes. Further boxes, some topped with stacks of loose newspapers, crowded the floor. It was blissfully quiet, cool as stone, and smelled of old paper. I felt right at home.

At the end of the row, a lamp hung on the wall and she lit

it, offering much-needed light. She turned to the left and we passed by rows and rows of shelves until she slowed, checked the labelling on the nearest box and turned to me. She handed me the matches.

'There are lamps at the ends of most rows. I'll knock at a quarter to one and you must leave.'

'I understand. Thank you for your help.'

She finally let herself smile. 'If you find them, will you let me know?'

'Oh yes.'

'How thrilling,' she said with a longing sigh and handed me the lamp. 'Good luck.'

I watched her for a few moments as she disappeared into the dark. Her clipped footsteps on the stone floor receded and, not long later, I heard her ascending the stairs. I lit the lamp at either end of the row and found myself in a pleasant cocoon of warm light. Then I turned to my task, for I only had a few hours and hundreds of papers to search.

I checked the labelling. Each box was labelled with a range of months and a year. So organised, this would be simple. I scanned them until I found April – June 1851. The regatta always took place at the end of June. Living in Oxford, one could not escape the furore in the days before and the celebrations, or commiserations, in the days after.

I pulled the box from the shelf and set it on the floor, the lamp close. Inside was a stack of about twelve folded newspapers. The masthead was bright and clear, shouting *The London Looker-On* in an overwrought blackletter type with a beautiful illustration of the city below. I checked the dates, flipping through them until I found a likely candidate: Saturday

June 21st 1851. The regatta was usually in the middle of the week and would have been reported at the weekend.

Flicking through, I found it quickly. I smiled. I would not need the hours.

Henley Royal Regatta, a Royal Showing as Oxford takes the Grand. The article reported on the races, the Oxford and Cambridge colleges competing, their colours, race times and results. It was reportage, not gossip, so I leafed through the paper to the society pages.

But they were not there. In their place, a neat tear along the length of the paper. The pages had been removed.

I sat back on my heels. Checked again, through all the paper, but it was no different.

I opened the paper from the week before and the gossip was present. It spoke of the singers and musicians playing in the capital, the artists showing new work, the balls and parties so far in the season, of an unnamed and married earl dancing with the daughter of an American politician. Of an altercation between two gentlemen over a spilled drink. Light fare. Nothing scandalous. I checked the week after Henley and the pages were present, speaking of largely the same.

It was only that week, those pages, that were removed. But why do such a thing and who could, in the archive copy in the newspaper's own basement? To remove mention of someone no doubt, but could that someone be William Heathfield?

I didn't realise how fast my heart was beating. Suddenly the dark room seemed darker still and every creak and clang from above was a footstep behind me.

'Focus, Lilian,' I told myself aloud. My voice filled the space and it didn't seem so vast. 'There has to be more.'

I set to my task, reading the gossip pages of every newspaper of the season. Balls, ceremonies, theatre showings, weddings, engagements, the regatta, the races. In a late July issue, it spoke of a grand ball, the event of the season, to take place the following week. But the following week, the pages were once again removed.

Another, in September, also removed.

This could not be coincidence or accident. These pages, which may have spoken about an event or person, had been deliberately expunged from all records. Neatly cut with a sharp blade. But surely a young gentleman, albeit of low means, and an inappropriate match for a lady, could not have caused such a thing. What could he have done? The lines of the letter returned to me. *I wish you had not killed him. But I am glad he is gone.*

Who could he have killed that would lead someone to try to remove him from history?

Time seemed to stretch here in the dim light and I wasn't sure at all how much I had left. I became desperate. I found the box for the season before and whipped through the pages for any mention of him, hoping whoever had done this had not cared to look before his dalliance with the lady.

Paper after paper held nothing. No mention of him or his family. The following year, '52, another two sets of pages were removed from March and May. Panic took me. I raced through the papers, fingers growing black with ink, piles of newsprint scattered around me, a disarray that would take hours to tidy.

A hand grabbed my shoulder.

I jumped, screamed, my heart burst out of me. It was him.

The man. The bowler. He'd found me again and there, a silver glint of the candlelight. A blade.

'Miss!'

The startled secretary stared, wide-eyed and as terrified as me.

My breath returned. 'I'm sorr—'

'I knocked twice. You must leave now; it's nearly one,' she said.

'Oh,' I said as the room changed from a shadowed dungeon to an ordinary basement. The person before me was no demon conjured by my memory but an annoyed woman who had gone out of her way to help me.

My heart slowed and I nodded. 'I'm so sorry. I didn't know the time. I didn't hear a knock; I swear it.'

She held out her hand to help me up and as I stood, a blanket of newspapers sloughed off me and spread across the floor.

'Look at this!' she cried. 'You've made such a mess. I hope you at least found something worthwhile.'

'I . . . found nothing,' I said and her face darkened. 'Except that pages had been cut out.'

She was already pulling me away but, at that, she stopped. 'Cut out?'

I picked up one of the papers and showed her. She ran a finger along the tear.

'Do you know who could have done this?' I asked. 'Or when?'

She shook her head slowly. 'These are fifty years old. I don't know how this could have happened. I could ask . . .'

I raised my eyes to her. 'You would do that?'

'This is the most exciting day I've had in years. Leave me

your name and where to find you and I'll see what I can discover.'

I couldn't believe my luck. I grabbed a scrap of paper from my bag and wrote my name and the address of the bindery. I also wrote down another name.

'This is who I am looking for.'

'William Heathfield?' she said, frowning. 'I've not heard of any Heathfields.'

'I believe that was the intent of whoever removed these pages.'

'How thrilling,' she breathed and held on to the name a moment longer.

Then she remembered herself. 'I must get back to my desk. The editor-in-chief will be here any moment and if he finds me gone . . .'

I followed her quick steps through the stacks. As I neared the stairs, the noise of the offices above began to penetrate the stillness and, as we climbed, the distant din became a roar. I emerged, blinking and startled, from the cave below into pandemonium. The young boys raced here and there, arms full of papers, pencils tucked behind ears, and the typists provided a steady thrum of click-clacking keys.

The woman, I still did not know her name, ushered me through the chaos and back out into the foyer. Nobody seemed to notice. She took her seat as the front door opened and in marched a formidable man in his seventies, with a moustache akin to a handle brush and an impeccably tailored suit.

'Good morning, Mr Darrington,' she said with a bright smile. Her cheeks were flushed red by our escapade but he did not seem to notice, nor care.

He did not stop, just fixed me with a glare so piercing I wanted to shrink, and to the woman, offered the same and not a word of greeting.

As soon as he was through the office door, the whole place hushed. The typists slowed but never stopped and I could no longer hear the heavy footfalls of running men, nor the barked shouts of the editors.

The woman's shoulders slumped and she let out a long sigh.

'Thank you for your help,' I said. 'I'm so rude, I didn't ask, but what is your name? If you should write to me, I should know it.'

'Evelyn,' she said. 'I will see what I can find but now you really must go.'

I stepped out of the office into a thick winter drizzle. With my coat pulled around my ears and my head pounding with questions, I made my way to the Madeira Café and hoped Charlie's search had been more fruitful.

19.

'Where have you been?' he said as I bustled into the café, cheeks puffing red.

It was nearly half past one when I finally arrived. 'Would you believe me if I said I was reading?'

'Must have been quite the novel.'

We sat together at a table by the wall. The place was bright, even on a gloomy day, with lamps burning every few feet and mirrors on the walls bouncing the light to every corner. The floors were polished walnut-coloured wood in a parquet pattern and the tables were all wood painted white. The effect was not of a cosy den in the West End but of how I imagined a Paris eatery. A coffee waited for me at the table. It had grown cold but I drank it in three mouthfuls, savouring the bitter burn as it hit the back of my throat.

Charlie watched me. 'What were you reading?'

'I found my way into the archive of the *Looker-On.*'

He raised his eyebrows. 'How did you manage that?'

'I am very charming.'

He laughed and I tried to smile, though after the last few days it did not reach the edges.

'You remember the letter in the burned book?' I asked. He

nodded. 'The other book you gave me also had pages hidden within. They spoke of a man and I went to the newspaper to see if I could find mention of him in the society pages from fifty years ago.'

'And did you?'

'No,' I said and his face fell. 'But only because someone had removed several pages from the newspapers of that and the following year. They'd cut them right out.'

'In the archive copies?'

I nodded. 'Not every page but I think it is because of him. This man. I think someone was trying to remove all memory of him.'

Charlie leaned back, tongue working on the inside of his mouth like he was picking at a stuck seed. 'Why would anyone do that?'

'I don't know. But whatever this man did, it must have been terrible.'

On the walk to the café I had tried to imagine what William Heathfield could have done to provoke such a reaction. He had killed someone, but did that warrant his name being excised from history? Who, exactly, had he killed?

'Did you find the name?' I asked, suddenly remembering the reason I was here.

'Grieves is a stickler. He keeps a record of every book passing in and out of his shop. But this one wasn't in the usual ledger. It was in a small book he had hidden but I found it.' Charlie leaned close. 'The other book is with a man named Mohan Chand.'

The name lit up my memory. 'Are you certain?'

'You've heard of him?'

'He is a bookbinder,' I said and my thoughts ran away with themselves. Mohan Chand. It seemed our orbits were linked: first meeting his wife on the train, then the chance look at the finely bound volume, then his name in Grieves's book.

'I have an address,' Charlie said with a smile. 'Fancy a walk?'

*

We stood outside a fine red-brick building on Rochester Row in Westminster. It was a good sight taller than its neighbours, standing out further in an already impressive street. Chand's Bookbinders stretched across two wide windows; the frontage painted a deep, attractive green. The colour of late summer oak leaves and the richest velvets. Either side were a gentleman's tailor and a milliner. A man may buy his suits and have his favourite volume bound for his library on the same trip. The mid-afternoon trade was brisk, and we watched several people come and go. I had not known a bindery so busy, for Mr Caxton's never took walk-in trade; visits were only by appointment, and were usually publishers placing an order. He always visited out and worked by correspondence. I was suddenly nervous.

Charlie squeezed my hand. 'What's the worst that could happen in there?'

'I could embarrass myself in front of a master bookbinder.'

He shrugged. 'You wouldn't be the first. Come on, else Grieves will have me skinned.'

I let him lead me across the street and into the shop. Upon entering, a great wave of comfort overcame me. It was everything I knew yet on a grander scale.

The whole shop was clean, shiny, almost looked brand new, and I realised how small Mr Caxton's workshop was, how dusty, how drab. This was a palace of bookbinders.

Upon first glance, the bindery was split into two sections. The shopfront, lined with glass cases filled with the most exquisite designs, and beyond it, shelving for the more everyday fare. An older man in a fine suit stood behind a redwood counter, speaking with a customer. The counter was so rich in its colour, gleaming with a mirror-shine. It seemed to glow all by itself.

Beside me, running along the wall towards the back of the shop, were glass cabinets full of treasure bindings. Jewel-encrusted books, silver and gold metal tacked onto wooden boards, polished and rounded gemstones fixed in lavish designs, leather inlays, and gilt tooling the extent to which I had never seen before. Some of the books were large and featured painted linens and carved ivory; others were small and simple, prayer books covered in bright gold with depictions of saints beaten into the metal.

One volume in particular stood out. It was by itself in the middle of a cabinet with nothing to crowd it. It shone, such was the gold on its cover. A frame of grapevines danced around the edges, linking large corner leaves I couldn't name, and in the centre, a curved, pointed archway put me in mind of pictures I'd seen of Indian palaces. The arch contained three peacocks, their feathers resplendent with red jewels. There must have been a thousand stones on that book. I could not take my eyes from it.

'*The Great Omar*,' came a voice beside me. I spun around to see the man from the counter standing beside me, a soft smile under a black, bushy moustache. Up close, I saw his moustache and his oiled hair were shot through with grey and his skin was brown as calf's leather. He was shorter than I expected and behind him, tucked beneath the counter, I spied a step.

'I've never seen anything like it,' I said and he admired it with me for a moment.

'Might I help you and your friend with something?' he asked.

I glanced behind me and found Charlie examining the cabinets on the other side of the room.

'Are you in need of our services?' he continued. 'Or perhaps in the market for a special edition as a gift?'

His eyes darted to Charlie. Neither of us were dressed for browsing in Westminster and I didn't blame this man for his obvious suspicion. Charlie affected an air about him, kept his chin high and a discerning look across his brow. I couldn't help but smile.

'Actually,' I said, bringing his attention back to me. 'I am looking for Mr Chand. I am a fellow bookbinder and I'm looking for a particular volume.'

The man's face brightened. 'I am Mohan Chand. A pleasure to meet a fellow binder.' He clasped my hand in both of his. 'Tell me about this book you seek.'

'There is a particular writer of romances and derring-do that my father loved when he was a young man. He is ailing now and I wish to find some books for him to enjoy in his last few years.' The lie, although partly true, stung deeper than I imagined and I found myself tearing. Charlie was at my side in a moment, his hand on my elbow.

'Are you all right?' he asked and I nodded.

Mr Chand pressed his fingers to his lips. 'May I get you a glass of water?'

'No. Thank you. Only, these books are so important to me, you see. My father is a bookseller and through his contacts, I came to discover that you may possess one of these books.'

He raised his eyebrows. 'What is the title?'

'I don't really know. I only know the author: Abel Bell.'

'My wife is also an admirer of his work, though I can't think why. I suppose the romances please her,' he said with nothing but affection.

I remembered her from the train, her kindness and curiosity. 'Is she here? I believe I met her once.'

'She has been travelling these last few weeks. She attends auctions and estate sales up and down the country you see, looking for rarities for the shop. She's been in Edinburgh, would you believe, for about a week. If you'd come in a few days, she would be here.'

'A shame,' I said. 'Abel Bell's earlier work, from around the Fifties is what my father is keen on.'

Mr Chand frowned, tapped a finger on his chin. 'We had a Bell just come in, a rare one I believe. I have yet to send word to my wife to see if it is one she wants, but I suppose letting you have a look won't hurt.'

He disappeared through a curtain at the back of the room. Charlie looked at the treasure books and gave a low whistle.

'One of these would set a man up for life. Look at those stones.'

'Don't you dare,' I said and caught his eye.

I wandered to the other side of the room. Through an archway was the workshop where large tables were covered in

154

skins and cloths and scraps of endpaper. Two men worked in there, one at a frame, sewing the signatures in a methodical, practised way. Watching him was hypnotic, the easy movement born of years of practice. The other was sitting at the opposite end, his head bent, tooling the spine of a burgundy morocco cover. He was quick and seemed to barely touch the leather, but I could see the muscles in his arms tense as he pressed the tool in a curve across the spine. I could hear, elsewhere, the sound of beating hammers on pressed paper and I guessed there was another room, or several, where the less glamourous stages of bookbinding were hidden away.

Mr Chand returned, book in hand. He set it upon the counter in a practised, salesman's motion. There it was, the simple purple binding that looked so out of place in this room, with this man, to be almost uncomfortable.

'May I?' I asked and, with his nod, picked it up.

I ran my hand over the leather. This one was in relatively good condition, though there were watermarks on the cover and more foxing to the page edges than on the *Devotion*. Charlie hovered at my shoulder.

I opened it to the title page, making more of a show when all I wanted was to check the endpapers. I flipped through the book, to the inside back cover and, now knowing exactly where to look, I quickly found the dots. My heart quickened.

'*Orpheus in the Tower*,' I read aloud. 'I do not have this one. What luck. How much?'

He took the book from me and appeared to almost weigh it in his hands. 'Unfortunately, I cannot sell it.'

It was as if I'd been dropped in a bath of ice water. 'You cannot . . . Why?'

'As sensitive as I am to your father's plight and your own, as I said my wife does love this author and asked me to keep his work for her should I come across it. I have never found mention of this volume anywhere in the publisher's listings of his work, so it is one I must keep until she has seen it.'

'Please, sir, I will pay good money for it. My father has so little time remaining and I don't believe he has read this. The thrill it will give him, I cannot express. I will even send it back to you upon his passing so your wife will have it eventually anyway.'

Mr Chand seemed genuinely torn. His gaze went from me to the book, to Charlie, to my wretched expression. He bit down on his lip. With a sigh, he finally said, 'I am sorry. Truly I am. But I cannot sell. I will search for another volume for you though and, should I find one, I'll give it to you for a very good price.'

My hopes crashed down around me. It was so close yet so far from my reach. 'I understand,' I said through a tight jaw, though I didn't, couldn't.

'Say, your dad might like a Dickens,' Charlie said, his voice suddenly large and loud beside me. I looked up at him and there was the wink. 'I spotted a nice little *Barnaby Rudge* over there. Would you show me, sir?'

Mr Chand, glad – I was sure – to be away from me, set the book on the counter and followed Charlie to the far end of the shop, where the more common books were kept.

I stared at the volume before me and felt unease grow within. How was I to find another to give to the man in the bowler? What would he do if I had nothing for him when he returned?

I looked at Mr Chand. He was bent down, reaching for a book on a lower shelf. Charlie glared at me, nodded to one side. To the book. To the book right before me.

'I was sure I saw it down there,' he said, still staring at me as Mr Chand pulled another book.

Charlie grew more frantic in his signalling. He mouthed two words. *Take it*.

'Do you have any adventure books an older gentleman might like?'

'I'm not a penny bookshop. These are fine bindings, sir,' Mr Chand said, growing impatient.

I had moments.

I picked up the book as if admiring it, slipped it into my satchel and in three steps was out the door, into the street.

I walked briskly, my heart thundering in my chest, and a moment later, the calls of 'Hey! Miss! Stop!' echoed behind me.

I broke into a run. My heels rang out on the pavement like pistol shot. People stopped to watch. I had to dodge their gasps and 'oh my's'. Footsteps hammered behind me. Heavy pounding on the stone.

I couldn't look. Couldn't bear to see Mr Chand and his men chasing, couldn't see the anger in them. Couldn't think on what might happen if they caught me. Police. Gaol. I ran harder, turned corner after corner, found myself in a quiet, narrow street full of the stink of the river.

'Wait!' came a shout but it wasn't Chand.

I slowed and there was Charlie, panting, red-faced. 'You've got some legs on you, Miss Delaney.'

The moment I stopped running, the weight of my act crashed upon me. I breathed hard and it wasn't from the sprint.

'What have I done?' I dug my hands into my hair. 'I can't believe I did that.'

Charlie took my arms, turned me to him. 'You didn't give

him your name. He doesn't know you from Eve. You need that book more than he does. His wife can find another romance to swoon over. There are plenty.'

He spoke in such an assured tone that I was put somewhat at ease. 'Yes. Yes, you're right.'

'I don't imagine he'll call the coppers for a worthless book but best we get out of here.'

He held my hand and I followed, in something of a daze, as we emerged onto the Vauxhall Bridge Road. Charlie hailed a cab and, in a few moments, we were on our way back to the West End. I watched the city rush by, my satchel on my lap, my hands on the shape of the book within.

'I used to do things like this all the time,' I said, with no pride. 'I thought I had left it behind me.'

'Our pasts have a curious way of popping back up when we need them.'

I thought of Harry then, while in a carriage beside a man with whom I'd shared a bed, and wondered if he was still the future I wished, or if, after all this, he would fade again into the vast country of my past mistakes.

'Why are you helping me?' I asked.

Charlie looked from the window to me, almost surprised by the question. His eyes were kind, behind the West End cheek, and when he smiled, it felt as if the smile was only for me. Did Harry smile like that? For a moment, I couldn't recall and a seed of guilt grew to a blossom within me.

He shrugged. 'I'm a knight, aren't I? A Prince Charming, always ready to help a lady in need.'

'You helped me commit a crime. You put yourself at risk for a person you barely know.'

His grin faltered and I believe for a moment I saw the real man behind the bravado. 'Well, suppose I like you. Simple as that. I know I'm not much, don't have anything to offer you, but I'm not all bad.'

Talk of offers made me want to shrink. 'I have nothing to offer you,' I said quietly, and I'm not sure he heard.

My heart beat with confusion. Every pulse was a different name. Harry. Charlie. Harry. Charlie. Both as loud and persistent as each other. Charlie put his arm around my shoulders and I let myself sink into him. The jolting carriage rocked us together, my head on his chest, my fingers interlacing his. The heat returned as I recalled those hands upon me that night, but with it came a melancholy and I wasn't sure where my true feelings lay.

I did not have time to dwell on it, for the cab stopped and we stepped out onto Charing Cross Road, at the mouth of Cecil Court.

Charlie pulled me towards the bookshop. 'Come on. I'll sneak you upstairs.'

But I did not move. 'I can't.'

'Grieves won't see; he's always in his office.'

'It's not that. I've put you in danger. The man who attacked me could find you too. I would never forgive myself if something happened.'

But that wasn't it either. I was worried, of course, that the man would find Charlie but really, it was that confusion. That guilt. If I went upstairs with him, I didn't know what might happen and I wouldn't risk that. I couldn't do that to Harry. Or Charlie. Neither of them deserved half my affection. But I wasn't yet sure I could give either my whole.

'I'm not afraid of him,' Charlie said, attempting a smile, but I pulled my hand free.

'I'm sorry, Charlie. I have to go.'

I turned and walked away.

'Lilian!' he called but I did not turn and he did not chase me.

20.

The next train to Oxford did not leave for several hours and I could not think to sitting still. I walked until my feet ached and my shoes pinched my heels. I found my way back to Paddington with still time to spare and took a table in a tea-room just outside. It was full of travellers, with luggage by their sides, counting down the minutes until their train was due. The place was cramped but at the back, a small table by the kitchen door was empty.

I ordered a pot of tea and it was brought promptly, with little in the way of service. This was a café with faceless patrons coming and going in a swift procession and I was thankful for it. Less chance I would be remembered.

I took the book from my bag. *Orpheus in the Tower.* Mr Chand had said he could not find this book in the publisher's listing of Bell's titles. I wondered if the same were true for the other two books I had found. I felt a terrible surge of fear and guilt come over me at thought of Mr Chand, of what he might think of me. I wished to build a reputation as a binder of fine volumes, for those volumes to be sold at auction for hundreds of pounds, for collectors to say, 'This is a Delaney binding,' and for them to seek me out as Dr Ashburn had. But I felt that future slip further from me with every day I was embroiled in this mess. Now I had burned a bridge not yet built with Mr Chand. He did not know my name but he knew my face and should he discover me, one word from him speaking of my theft and deceit could undo years of good standing.

My life, once safely kept within the pale-yellow stone of Oxford, was now precarious. A tightrope walk above a pit of spikes. I wished, for a moment, I had never seen that burned book; but now, with another volume before me, I could not help myself from delving deeper.

Orpheus in the Tower was the same on the outside as the *Devotion*. The binding identical, the tooling minimal, the spine neat. It was uninspiring and, though it used fine materials, was not made with care.

Inside, the title page was simple. The title, author and publisher, as the others. I brushed over it quickly in favour of the pages I knew lay within. I checked the clock on the wall – still nearly an hour to wait for the train. I turned to the back cover, found the dots.

* *

* *

*

The fifth book. The *Devotion* had been the third, and the *Knave* the first. Casting a glance around to check no one was looking my way, I took the paring knife from my satchel. I held it, half-concealed in my hand and began to peel away the endpaper at the front. Perhaps it was the water damage or the uneven glue on these books but it took the better part of the hour to free it without tearing. Soon I had two sides open and could see within several white pages.

The same thin, fragile paper, the same dense but neat copperplate hand. A thrill went through me. Each page again was initialled at the foot with W.A, H.P. and I.C, each in a distinctive style. Numbered too, beginning with XV.

As I began to read, the bustle of the café fell away.

21.

returning to our lives for a time. It was a small price to pay to be with you. We had a few months before my marriage to that toad Lord Beauchamp and much to do. We needed money to disappear and I, with reluctant help from Daisy, sold much of my own jewellery and dresses from previous seasons.

I still have our letters, though they are hidden as is every part of us. Father returned from France and life at home regained its familiar rhythms, though I burned inside with our secret. He talked of the marriage plans to Beauchamp and how auspicious our union would be for him and his business. He expected me to be as excited as he was, but I was half full of despair should our plan not work and half full of love for you, daydreaming our escape.

I invented a ruse to be able to see you. A friend who did not exist. My letters to you were addressed to Miss Lelah Whitfield to avoid raising Father's suspicions. I told him she was a girl I'd known at finishing school, just returned from Europe, and she wanted an escort for the remainder of the season. He did not raise an eyebrow; it seemed all notion of you was absent from his mind.

Of course you figured it out. Lelah Whitfield was Will Heathfield. We wrote in codes to one another, talked of love hidden beneath anagrams and wordplay. The housekeeper could make neither head nor tail of our notes and soon stopped bothering to read them. You sent me books, most by Abel Bell. Ones you'd favoured as a child and retained into adulthood. As I read them, I imagined us in those adventures, setting out into the great unknown, together.

And so began the whirlwind. With a female chaperone in the form of 'Lelah', I was allowed to attend the theatre, to go to parties and balls, allowed a degree of freedom because Father thought I was meeting a friend and, now I was engaged, no man would bother me. It was all lies. Every meeting was somewhere other than written, all code only you and I could decipher. Every stolen kiss all the sweeter for the deception.

Father thought me unimaginative, naïve, and perhaps a little stupid, so did not think to question my sudden social engagements. He never thought I had any power to defy him.

Daisy continued to sell my jewellery, small pieces here and there, enough not to arouse suspicion. Once I asked Father for the money to buy a new dress and necklace to better show off to society and he waved me away with a handful of notes. I soon had quite the saving. We would have enough to go in a few weeks. You were already checking sailing times from Liverpool to New York.

I had thought myself so clever.

I was due to meet you that evening, to take dinner at a small, discreet café and take stock of our situation. I dressed demurely, for to Father's eye, I would be meeting Miss Lelah for a quiet evening of bridge and gossip. I went to his study to say goodbye, as I had taken to doing when leaving the house. I knocked and was granted entry but everything was wrong.

The lamps were dark and only the fire in the grate cast any light across the room.

'Father?'

He sat in his armchair beside the fire, his features gilded by the flame, swirling a glass of brandy.

'Come in, daughter. Close the door.'

I did as he asked but he did not rise nor look at me. As my eyes adjusted to the low light I saw you. Lying prone on the floor before his desk. You were not moving.

I rushed to you, turned your body over and saw the blood. Your face was swollen, a mess of bruises and cuts, blood matted your beautiful hair.

I felt beneath your nose, found your breath, then pressed my head to your chest and heard your heart. Still strong. Still with me. I heard the creak of Father's chair as he stood and I rounded on him, clutching you to my chest. Rage filled me. 'What have you done?'

Father towered above us, his features dark, still swirling the brandy glass. I remember his voice so clearly, the danger in his tone. 'I said you were not to see this boy again and you defied me. Do you think I would allow you to soil yourself with him?'

'How did you . . . ?'

He went to the wall and rang the bell. I stroked your hair. You were so still as if sleeping, but your injuries were vast and I dreaded to think of the bruises or broken bones that lay beneath your clothes.

The side door opened and Daisy entered, with Uncle Silas behind. Seeing him, I knew how serious my father was. Silas was openly cruel, like his son, where my father hid his behind well-tailored manners. Daisy's face was red with tears and Silas held her roughly by the arm.

'Daisy here was caught selling a necklace I bought you last year,' Father said. 'At first I thought her a common thief and intended to turn her over to the police but what a story she told.'

Daisy would not look at me. I thought this day would come; I only hoped it would have been a few weeks later.

You stirred in my arms and I stroked the portion of your face that was still yours. My heart hardened and my tears dried.

'What do you want of me?' I asked.

Silas sneered and the Yorkshire tone he'd tried so hard to conceal in society came out. 'To do as you're damn well told and not open your legs for any pretty boy in tails.'

I winced at his words. 'How dare you, Uncle. You know nothing of us.'

Father's hand cracked across my cheek. It was not the first time, nor would it be the last. 'Impudent sow. Show your uncle some respect. You are chattel, girl. You have been bought. You will marry whom I tell you to. Do you understand?'

'I'd sooner die than marry that man.'

He smiled. Can you believe it? But there was no humour in him. He knelt down so he was face to face with me. 'You will not die, daughter. But **he** will.'

My blood turned to ice and everything in me froze. 'No . . . you cannot.'

'If you see this boy again, I will kill him. If you write to him again, I will kill him. If you do not marry Lord Beauchamp as and when I choose, I will kill him. Do I make myself plain?'

I held you to me perhaps for the last time. 'Father, please . . .'

Father grabbed my arm and pulled me up. Your head slid from my lap to the floor and you stirred again, tried to roll over.

Silas took you under the arms and you let out a pained groan. You were alive and the world was brighter for it. I could not let them kill you.

'I'll do as you say,' I said. 'But please, Father, let him live. If he dies, I will throw myself into the Thames and you will have no daughter to sell.'

'Very well.' He nodded to Silas and you were dragged away. Daisy followed and my father and I were alone.

My rage boiled. 'When you die, when all you have made comes to me, I will dance on your grave.'

'When I die, nothing will go to you.'

His tone chilled me. 'What?'

Father went to his desk and found a paper. 'Your judgement is not to be trusted and your virtue uncertain. I cannot allow my fortune to go to you, daughter.'

I had spent my life tolerating my father and his cruelties in the knowledge his fortune would one day come to me. 'Then where? To Silas?'

'A legitimate male heir. A child born in wedlock. You will bear a son to Lord Beauchamp, and he shall inherit. He alone.'

The thought crippled me. 'And if I bear daughters?'

'Then you try again and again, as many times as it takes. You will bear his children until it kills you for all I care.'

'And if I fail? You would sooner see your money in the hands of bankers and strangers than your own daughter?'

'The moment you defied me, you ceased to be my daughter.'

I could say no more. I went back to my room in a daze and when the door was closed behind me, I collapsed. My dress was stained with your blood. I remember how vivid it was, how it was all I could see. Your life draining out of you, all because of me. My own life now a shadow of what it was, hope and love snuffed out in one evening. Father had found you, hurt you so badly I wondered if you would even recover, and at once taken away our future. I am sorry, my love. I am sorry for that and what came after.

Those days were dark and I was not allowed to leave my room. I grew ill and pale and would not sleep. Daisy brought me food and tried to explain her betrayal but I would not hear it. I screamed at her to leave me. In the weeks that followed, I fell into a sickness I could not pull myself from. By way of a sorry I supposed, Daisy brought me a note from you. You were alive. Healed. The thought lifted my heart but then broke it afresh as I knew I could not see you again. I did not write back. I needed you to forget me.

When my sickness did not get better, the doctor was called. I needed to be fit to marry, Father said. He cared not for my welfare, only for my selling price.

Dr A, who I had known from childhood and who bears witness to this document, had always been kind and was the only man I had known, except you, to treat me with respect.

He asked me some questions about my symptoms. Weakness, tiredness, vomiting, an aversion to certain foods and odd pains in my stomach. He examined me and when he was finished, he sat on my bedside and took my hand.

'Dear girl, it appears you are with child.'

I cannot describe how I felt in that moment. The shock. The sorrow of you not being beside me to hear it too. The fear of what my father would do. My hand went to my stomach and I felt you there. The doctor stayed for a time. He didn't ask me questions of how I came to be so, but told me what I might expect of the next several months. He gave me some ginger tea for the nausea and left me. I cried for what felt like hours.

My father, who of course had been told, would not speak to me. He called our child a bastard; he called me so much worse. He would not allow visitors and checked every letter I received.

I was desperate to see you. To tell you of our child growing within me. I asked Daisy to deliver a note to you. If she was keen to made amends she would take it, I said. She did, though I believe she must have read it on the way, for when she returned, her demeanour was that of a mother hen. She fed me and looked after me in a way she had not before, and she brought with her a note from you.

Your joy at the news did little to temper my sorrow but, for a moment, it was a comfort to imagine our life together, with our child and my father's money. We passed notes to one another and my sadness began to lift, though I was always conscious of the danger I was putting you in.

The announcement of my impending marriage to Lord Beauchamp was made and the excuse Father gave of my absence from society was that I was in Paris, taking the tour and being fitted for my wedding dress.

The weeks went on, and my belly began to swell slightly, though if I was anything like my mother, I would not be obvious until far closer to the arrival. Your notes and our daydreams kept me going.

But nothing can be kept a secret in this world for long and rumours began to fly about me. Inevitably, the rumours reached the ears of Lord Beauchamp. He demanded his doctor examine me and confirm or deny my virtue. Father could not allow it.

Father came into my room in a terrible rage. He was red-faced, stank of alcohol and his fists were clenched so hard his knuckles turned white.

'You have ruined me, little whore,' he said. Such hate in him I'd never heard before. 'Beauchamp heard of your shame and wishes you examined by his physician. If I let him, he will know his future wife is a harlot. If I don't, he will suspect the truth anyway. But if you were no longer carrying that bastard, then all my problems would be solved.'

I pressed myself back against the pillows, drew up my knees.
He came to my bedside, trembling with rage, his eyes dark as
a devil's. He reached for me

No! It mustn't end there. I set down the pages, my heart beating wildly in my chest. The noise of the café had faded, half the tables now empty. I glanced at the clock and saw my train was due to leave in minutes and there would not be another for hours.

I scooped up the book, pages and my paring knife, left a few coins on the table for the tea and ran into the station. I boarded a moment before the whistle as the head of steam covered the platform.

I found a seat, cramped between a lady and her small dog, and an oversized gentleman, and lived again those moments in the pages.

Who was this woman who had endured so much? Who was this cruel father who would hurt an unborn child for the sake of his business? Another two names had come to light: Silas and Lord Beauchamp. I had heard of the Beauchamp line and resolved to find out if His Lordship married in 1851.

The scandal of an unmarried pregnancy would have been the talk of society at the time. Was this William Heathfield's crime? The reason someone, I supposed the girl's father, had him erased from the pages of the *Looker-On*?

And whoever was now looking for this confession could not be acting on her behalf. I sensed a need to protect this girl, whose name and life beyond these hidden pages was a mystery to me. When my seating companions had departed, at Aylesbury and Thame, I lifted my satchel onto my lap and cut a neat slit in the lining. I slid the pages inside. The book, I could do little about until I returned home.

The train eased into Oxford and the last few passengers departed. I walked home in the dark evening, barely aware of my surroundings, thinking only of what became of William and his love, and how I might find the other books, and learn more of this story.

The chill was deep and unforgiving and my navy-blue cape, the warmest I had, did little to stave off the chill. I hurried on, through the quiet streets, and as I came to Walton Street, I caught the echo of footsteps behind me.

The man in the bowler. Waiting for me at the station to follow me? Was there any sense in trying to outpace him? He knew where I lived, no doubt where I worked too. I could give him the book but I hadn't glued the endpapers back down. Would he notice or care? These were old books, prone to damage. If he asked, I would say it was how I acquired it.

The footsteps grew closer.

I was tired of being afraid. The girl's defiance had bolstered my own.

I stopped and spun around. 'Stop—'

My voice caught. A young man stood behind me, shocked at my sudden halt. 'My apologies, ma'am.'

He hurried past me and the wall I'd built up to face the bowler-hat man crumbled. I stood alone on Walton Street, breath misting in sharp bursts. My hands shook. Anger had masked my fear and now it showed itself fully.

I made it home with no footsteps following and no cigarette flares in the shadows. I had not realised, until I saw the door to the bookshop, how tired I was, how long the day, and those last steps were like climbing a sand dune.

It was nearly eight o'clock when I opened the door expecting to find my father alone in his office, reading or fretting, but instead he was in the main shop with a guest. The man with him was in a garish waistcoat and had a moustache too long for his face. He looked at me with little regard.

'Ah, Lilian, you're back,' my father said, and did not look happy about it; in fact he looked sheepish, caught in an act he should not be doing.

'Hello, Father, who is this?'

He gestured to the man who gave a curt nod. 'This is Mr Goff. We were just finishing our discussion.'

The man nodded to me but seemed to barely see me. He had the air of a salesman about him, a slight unkindness in the way he glanced around the room. 'We'll talk again. I'm interested. It's a good enough space.'

They shook hands and my father saw Mr Goff to the door. Once he was gone, my father's sprightly demeanour deflated. His shoulders sagged and as he returned to me, he was seized by a terrible cough. I held his arm and led him into the office. He dropped into his chair, the cough deep in his chest and showing little sign of abating, so I rushed to the kitchen for a glass of water.

When finally my father stilled, he was a defeated man. Too tired almost to raise his head.

'What did that man mean, he was interested?' I asked.

'In the shop.' His voice was thin, cracked like early ice.

'I don't understand.'

'Goff is interested in buying the shop.'

The air went out of me. 'You're selling our home?'

He opened a drawer and took out letters. Every movement was slow and seemed to pain him. He dropped the letters on the desk. I'd seen them before, the ones from the London and County Bank, but there were more.

'How bad is it?' I asked, picking up a letter from a second bank.

'Bad enough.'

The walls of my life tightened around me.

'Why didn't you tell me?' I asked.

He huffed and took the letter from me. 'It's not your business. It's my mess and I'll get us out of it.'

'You're doing a fine job,' I sniped and immediately regretted it. 'I'm sorry. That was unkind but I'm no longer a child. I can help. How much is the debt?'

My father's eyes danced over the letters, then over the books around him. His face was drawn, hollow. He had never been a robust man but he'd always had in him an energy born of passion that propelled him through the days. That energy was all but gone but the passion still clung to him, like the scent of smoke after a fire.

'Father, how much?'

'Just a hair over two thousand pounds.'

I let the shock pass, for it was quick and blunt, and anger took its place. I ran through a dozen responses in my mind, from 'how could you, you old fool' to 'what did you spend it on' and finally settled on something more useful.

'Why . . . how did you get in such a situation?'

'You are still a child, Lilian, and know nothing of what it takes to maintain a business. Do you see these books?' he said and took up a nearby volume, shaking it in his fist. 'Nobody wants them. Not from me, not since your mother . . .' His voice trailed off and he dropped the book. I'd never seen my father cry until then. He broke into sobs and covered his face with his wizened, crooked hands. I went to him, knelt on the floor beside his chair and took his hand.

'I'm sorry, Lily, I'm sorry.' He wept and I held his hand and we stayed like that for a time until all his tears were spent and he sat, a man defeated by his life.

'Don't sell to that man. I will find a way to resolve the debt,' I said and he nodded slowly, though I didn't think he actually believed I could.

I made him eat then put him to bed. I could not think of sleep so I repaired the *Orpheus in the Tower* endpapers and reread the pages. I could avoid rest no longer and, as I lay in my bed, eyes wide in the dark, I tried to find a solution to the problem. A job that paid better, another loan to cover the first, endless auctions on our inventory, but eventually only one path appeared to me. A path I did not want to travel but I saw no other way.

I just had to wait for the man in the bowler to find me and pray he would not kill me before I had a chance to speak.

22.

The bindery was cold so early, where frost crunched on the steps outside. I arrived before Mr Caxton and started lighting the fires, hands aching in the chill. I had barely slept for worrying and, when I did, snatches of cruel dreams came to me. I was the girl in her bed, heavy with child, watching her father approach with violence in his eyes. I was her kneeling, cradling her lover's head in her lap, seething rage spreading through me like a plague. Then I was myself, standing before the bowler man's blade, awaiting the cut that would end it all.

I was so consumed by those thoughts that I did not hear the door open and Mr Caxton enter.

'Back to the land of the living I see,' he said and I startled, dropped the stove wood I was holding.

'Yes,' I said only and picked up the wood, put it into the growing flames and latched the stove door.

He set down his bag and took off his coat. 'Are you well?'

'Much improved. Thank you.'

I went to my desk and found upon it a stack of letters. I took to sorting them as Mr Caxton hated it when the post piled up. Then I moved on to a package, wrapped in brown paper. It was the unsewn pages of a new book, fresh from the printer's. The paper still smelled of the machine that printed it. I felt a great ease come over me as I examined it. Paper and ink and the process of binding, a world I knew and loved and could lose myself in, away from the concerns of the day. This one was a new printing of Hardy's *Jude the Obscure*, a popular title, especially in Oxford, and not the first time I'd bound a copy. This was for a professor of English at the university, one of Mr Caxton's old friends, and I knew if I was to make amends for my absence, it would need to be flawless.

I took a block of beeswax and spool of linen thread and began waxing the thread so it would not fray in the sewing. I laid each of the folded page bundles – the signatures – flat and pierced them with an awl. Then I took the sewing frame, set up the first of the signatures upon it, and began to sew. I felt a silence in the room and when I looked up from my work, Mr Caxton was staring at me.

'What is it?' I asked.

A strange, sad look overcame him and he looked away. 'You have soot on your face.'

'What?' I went to rub it away but at Mr Caxton's laugh, I realised the trick. 'One day I will tire of your jokes.'

'But not today, my dear.'

He held that sadness in his voice and I felt it creep into me. He knew, I was sure, that I'd lied to him. He had offered me everything he had and I had repaid him with deceit and distraction.

I set down my needle and went to his desk. He was reading a letter and didn't set it down when I stood before him.

'I am very busy, Miss Delaney. Can you not see me perusing my correspondence?'

'That is a fashion circular from Whiteley's.'

He coughed and squinted at the paper. 'So it is. What do you want?'

'To explain.'

His jovial manner turned serious at once and he set down the paper. I pulled up a chair and sat for a moment to order my thoughts. I could not speak of the burned book and what it contained, nor my flights across London, the theft, or the threats against me. Mr Caxton had asked me to stop, had gained my assurance that I would and I was already sore enough that I'd broken my promise.

'I am an old man,' Mr Caxton said gently, 'on the verge of expiration. A little haste if you please.'

I took a breath and began the other truth that hung above me like a sword on a thread.

'My father is unwell, so unwell in fact I fear he will not see out the year.'

'Oh, my dear, I am sorry.'

I avoided his eyes and tried not to hear the sorrow in his voice. If I thought too long about it, what it meant, I would be sobbing through the rest of this tale.

'But that is not the worst,' I carried on. 'He has accrued debts of some two thousand pounds and must sell the shop and our home, to clear them. I have been trying to figure out a way to free us from the debts. That is why I have been so absent.'

Mr Caxton shook his head. 'I knew the situation was bad but not that bad.'

'The worst is that I don't know *why*. Why he even needed loans that size.'

He looked down at his hands and appeared to be deciding

what to tell me. 'When your mother died, God rest her soul, your father went to a dark place. He began to drink and he neglected his business. For a long time, he barely sold a book, though he kept buying them. He became obsessed with finding rare volumes, believing books would solve his problems.' As Mr Caxton spoke, shame at the similarities between myself and my father grew. 'As the drinking got worse, the decisions got worse. He came to me for a loan once but I denied him. I hoped he would see sense then, but it appears the banks are not as responsible as I.'

I sat with the information for a while, that Mr Caxton had known my father's decline but not told me, yet who was I to judge someone for keeping secrets?

'I'm sorry I didn't tell you sooner,' I said.

Mr Caxton reached for my hand. 'And I you. Perhaps I should have, but it is a lot for such young shoulders to bear.'

'I believe I have found a way out of it.'

'What would that be?'

'I must sell something precious,' I said carefully and he narrowed his eyes in the way he did when he knew there was more I was not saying.

'What do you have worth that sum?'

I wondered for a moment if he thought I would be selling myself. 'A book, of course. Several, in fact.'

His eyes narrowed further. 'Very well.'

He went to say something else when a fierce knock came at the door. Mr Caxton checked his watch. 'Not time for the post.'

As I stood, the sharp sound still ringing in my ears, I felt a coldness settle inside me.

I opened the door and Mr Caxton called, 'Who is it?'

Nobody stood at the threshold, but a man leaned against a tree some twenty paces away. He wore a smart brown suit and a matching bowler and he looked right at me. He tipped his hat and that coldness turned to ice. I nodded to him and closed the door.

'Nobody, a kid playing knock.' I tried to keep my voice steady. 'After all that seriousness, how about a pastry from the café?'

'A fine idea. Get several,' he said and gave me some coins.

He rarely gave me money to buy lunch or treats and I felt a wave of pity for myself, though I knew Mr Caxton did not intend it.

On the street, the man in the bowler waited. St Giles was busy at this hour, with students, professors and the regular folk of Oxford making their way about town. The man looked no more out of place than any other gentleman looking for a new suit but I saw him for the ruffian he was, a great red flag perched high above him warning others, except no other could see it. Just by being near him, I felt eyes and their owners' judgement upon me.

'Good morning, Miss Delaney,' he said as I drew close. 'I trust you are well.'

I forced my jaw to unclench. 'I was.'

'I won't take that personally. And your dear father, how does he fare?'

'You didn't come here to talk about my father. I have what you want.'

A wolf's smile split his face. 'Give it quickly and we'll both be about our days.'

I glanced around. Too busy and too close. I imagined Mr Caxton peeling back the paper on the front windows and watching me. I checked, even, but the paper was intact.

'Not here.'

I walked towards Gloucester Green where I knew it would be quieter, it not being market day, and he followed a few steps behind.

I stopped on the far side, beyond the empty cattle pens, and although not deserted, it offered a degree of privacy.

'Hurry now, I don't have all day,' he said.

'I found another book,' I said and he held out his hand. 'But I don't have it with me.'

'And where might it be?'

'Hidden.' I spoke quickly so my fear would not have time to take hold. 'I will give it to you and your buyer, for a price.'

He cocked an eyebrow. 'You're in no position to make demands.'

'You want something I have, it's only fair you should pay for it.'

He laughed but it was sour and I smelt the tobacco on his breath. 'Give me the book, Miss Delaney.'

'No.'

His cheek twitched and he closed the gap between us. His hand went to his pocket and I knew the knife lay within. 'I won't ask again.'

'The book is hidden and nobody else knows where it is. You'll never find it without me.'

He sucked on his teeth. 'You are testing my patience.'

'And you mine. You can have it, if you pay.'

'How much?'

'Four thousand pounds.'

His face twisted and he withdrew the blade from his pocket, made sure I saw it. I tried to breathe. I needed to keep the steel in my spine for just a little longer.

'Four thousand pounds,' he repeated slowly.

'Half now and the rest when I find the other books for you.'

He made a show of thinking it over. 'How about I pay a visit to your dad instead? Or that nice young man who works in the Turf?'

'If you hurt me or my family, I'll throw the book in the river. Then I'll find the others and burn them. Your buyer will never have them.'

'And if I kill you before you can find them?'

I felt the knife press against my side. Every fibre in my body wanted to run, to give him what he wanted and be rid of him. My chin trembled and I forced back terrified tears.

'Are these books worth killing for?' I asked.

His sneer grew. 'Are they worth dying for?'

Not the books but what was within. The hidden story of a woman who could not live her life as she wished, could not love whom she chose. Finding it, knowing it, was that worth risking death? If I'd been asked the question when I first found the burned book, I would have laughed but now? Now she, this nameless woman, was part of me. I needed to know how her tale ended, to give her and myself peace. The torture of the unfinished story would consume me if I did not.

I leaned closer to him, felt the point of the blade press deeper into my stomach. 'Four thousand pounds.'

I held like that, keeping my nerve. Acid rose in my throat

and the thought entered my head that he may just kill me. Right there in the mid-morning hush.

But he withdrew. The pressure left my stomach and the blade disappeared into his pocket once more.

My breath left me and stars spotted my vision.

'I'll take your offer to my employer,' he said, reluctance staining his voice. 'Expect a swift answer.'

He backed away, tipped his hat to me so any looker-on would see a friendly parting and then he was gone around a corner.

My legs went from under me and I clung to the wall to stop from falling. It had been mere minutes in his loathed company but the sky had turned from blue to grey and a cold rain began to fall.

I composed myself, breathed away the fear until I stopped shaking. It took some time. Upon my return to the workshop, Mr Caxton accepted the apricot Danish with a comment about his new waistcoat not fitting any longer and all was normal again. I sewed *Jude*, Mr Caxton gilded a book on Roman history and the day went on as any other.

But the string above my head, holding my doom aloft, began to fray.

23.

My world quietened. The threat had retreated for now and my father's health seemed to improve with his burden shared. Mr Caxton returned to his jovial, mischievous self, and I began, after several uneventful days, to relax. I was confident the person looking for the Bell books would want them enough to pay a considerable sum for them. Perhaps they would want to haggle, for I had asked for more than I needed with that expectation. So it was with a lighter heart that I met Harry for dinner in the Bear.

I was relaxed but not reckless and checked for onlookers before asking him about the pages I gave him.

'Safe and sound. I put them—'

'Don't tell me. I need only know they're safe.'

He gave a concerned look. 'Are you in trouble?'

'Yes,' I said and he took my hand across the table. 'But I hope to be out of it very soon.'

'You really know how to worry a man.'

I smiled. 'You don't need to worry over me.'

'And yet, it's all I seem to do,' he said and after a moment, added, 'I spoke to your father.'

'Oh?' I'd all but forgotten his desire to court me like a gentleman.

'He told me I was talking to the wrong person and that he could no sooner tell you who to see than he could make horses fly.'

I laughed. 'That sounds like him.'

'I took that to mean he approved,' Harry said and seemed, all of a sudden, nervous. 'I found a new job too.'

'You did?'

'At the university press. Setting type for now, but on course to be a printer. Pay's better than the Turf and hours are good. I start on Monday.'

'Harry, that's wonderful,' I said and squeezed his hand.

We parted as our food arrived and after the waiter had left, Harry grew quiet.

'What is it?' I asked, for he just moved his chop around with his fork instead of eating.

'I did it for you,' he said. 'The job. I've got a career ahead of me now and it's in books. You love books. I wanted to know your world a little better before . . . you know.'

I didn't know what to say. I was struck with a dizzying sense of what might be coming and I wasn't at all ready to hear it.

'You did that for me?'

He took on a stern countenance. 'I intend to marry you, Lily.'

The air fled the room and I was suddenly gasping. 'You do?'

He took my hands. The strength and tenderness in them moored me. 'I'm not a fool. I know you're into something dangerous. Hell, it's rare you aren't, and I'll help you all I can until it's done. But it's always been you for me, Lily.'

I could not say the same, for in an instant I was back in Charlie's room over the bookshop, in his bed, wrapped in sweat and him. I wanted to tell Harry. I should have told him. But I couldn't. I didn't regret my actions until that moment but now the shame crept up on me.

'I don't deserve you,' I said.

'That's true.'

I let out a quiet laugh but it died quickly. 'We've been here before,' I said. 'The cusp of a proposal.'

'This is different.'

'How?'

'We're not seventeen. We're not reckless idiots anymore.'

'Speak for yourself,' I said and tried to smile but I saw again the anger in him when I'd told him I couldn't marry him all those years ago. When I told him I didn't love him to hurt him so much he'd realise I was no good. When I did the unthinkable to prove it.

I could do it again. Tell him about Charlie. It would break his heart and I couldn't bear that, to see the love in his eyes turn to hate once more.

'I love you, Lily. Always have.'

I brought his hand to my cheek. 'Me too.'

'Then marry me.'

I closed my eyes against his words and felt the tears.

'Harry . . .'

'What's stopping you?'

'I'm scared I'll hurt you again. That the devil on my shoulder will win out and you'll suffer for it.'

'I'm not fragile.'

Blood rushed in my ears and a dozen thoughts and memories ran with it. I saw that terrible day when we were seventeen play out in a blink. I imagined telling him of Charlie and seeing his world crash around him. I felt the point of the blade in my chin, in my stomach, imagined it plunged into Harry's chest. Too much. It was all too much, too fast.

The blood quietened and resolved into a solid thought.

'There are things you need to know about me. Things I've done,' I said slowly. 'I'll tell you, I promise, but after this business with the books is finished. If you still wish to marry me when you hear what I have to tell you then I'll say yes. If you don't . . .' My voice cracked. 'Well, that's that.'

'There's nothing you could say that would change my feelings.'

'I thought the same once but look how we ended up.'

He held my eyes. I could almost read his thoughts. What could I have done? Was this something he wanted to hear? How long would this business take? Was I worth it?

I expected him to press me, try to pull the truth out of me before it was ready to come as he had done back then. But he only held my hand and said, 'I'll wait.'

Then he smiled and took up his knife and fork while I looked on.

'Stop staring at me and eat,' he said.

Slowly, I began to relax and realised he wasn't going anywhere. Not yet anyway, and for now, that was enough.

*

Harry walked me home and I felt both light and heavy at once. I was an iron feather falling, and I didn't know who would end up catching me. Or if I wanted them to. The idea of marriage played on my mind as we walked, making idle talk. From what

I remember of my mother, she'd been a tired, mostly happy woman but I knew she'd dreamed of more. She'd given up her position as a housekeeper, a well-paid one, to support my father's dreams of a bookshop. Then a child came and locked the door on her soft prison.

I wanted freedom, choice. I wanted to run the bindery, be my own master. My notion of marriage would not allow that, but my notion of Harry might. Yet which was right? Would he expect of me a wife to fetch and carry for him or would he have me as I am? I thought of the few memories I had of my parents together before my mother died. I was ten when she died and the years before were a collage of disparate scenes I couldn't give a year to. But I knew they had been happy. Loved. I remember how they danced in the shop after hours. How she would laugh. I imagined myself doing the same with Harry but the picture was blurred.

Victor Street was hushed, as if holding its breath. The lamps lit at either end cast a great shadow in the centre. I still imagined the man in the bowler hidden within those shadows, waiting for me, so held tight to Harry and allowed him to walk me to my door.

His grip on my hand tightened and I quickly saw why.

The door stood ajar. All thoughts of proposals and the conversations of the evening disappeared at once.

Harry and I shared a look and edged closer.

The glass in the door was shot through with spidery cracks. He pushed and it swung open with an ill-sounding creak. I peered around Harry and saw chaos. Books covered the floor, a shelf was toppled, the lights were out.

'Stay here,' Harry said and stepped inside.

I did not stay. I couldn't. For my father was in there some-where and the shop, the rooms above, were horribly quiet.

Light from the streetlamps cast a sickly yellow glow through the large front windows. Harry picked his way across a carpet of books, each step tentative, listening. I rushed in behind him, ignored his pleas to stop, be careful, and was met with a scene of total disarray. The main room was strewn with broken books and ripped pages. Paper lay in drifts, dead and flat. Bindings were torn, irreparable. Books that had survived decades were dismembered, reduced to nothing but scraps.

I caught myself against the wall. Harry was at my shoulder.

'My God,' he murmured. 'Who would do this?'

I knew. I thought of him here, while I was fending off a proposal, he was tearing into my home. I didn't have words. Couldn't form thoughts beyond hate and horror.

'Father!' I called but no answer came. The world dipped in and out of focus and I pushed away from the wall, staggered over the dead books to the office.

The door was closed. The room beyond dark.

I gripped the handle and turned but the door wouldn't move. Something heavy lay against it. 'Harry, help me.'

He put his shoulder to the door and it moved an inch, then more, until the gap was wide enough for me to slip inside.

The room was utterly dark and smelled of tobacco and mint. My father never touched either.

'Father?' I asked the darkness. My heart beat so hard in my chest I could hear it.

He always kept a candle on the shelf to the right of the door. I moved to claim it and my foot hit something lying behind the door. I felt the floor and found fabric, a trouser, a leg within. Unmoving.

I reached for the candle, lit it, and as the light flared, I saw my father slumped behind the door.

'Harry!'

The next moments were a blur. I was at my father's side, pulling him from the door, then Harry was with me, his voice an echo in my head. He spoke of constables and hospitals and I heard none of it. I pressed my head to my father's chest and beyond the rushing of my own blood, I heard the faint drum of his heart.

Alive.

'He's alive,' I said and Harry was up and gone and I heard his running steps on the quiet street.

I hugged my father to me. He had no injuries, had not been beaten at least, no knife wounds or blood. Was this a robbery gone terribly wrong? I looked to the safe but it was closed.

A flash of white caught my eye. On the desk stood a folded piece of paper with my name written upon it. It was positioned so it would not be missed.

I laid my father gently down to the floor and shuffled to it on my knees. I lifted it with shaking hands. My name was not written in my father's hand, but a stranger's.

I wiped tears I didn't know I had cried and unfolded the note. Among a jumble of words, four struck me.

Your offer is declined.

I pressed my hand to my mouth. Rage and fear and agony stormed within me. I had done this. *I had done this.*

I balled the note in my fist and crawled to my father. I pressed my forehead against his, held his face in my hands.

'I'm sorry. I'm sorry.' I said it a hundred times. It would never be enough.

I felt his shallow, wheezing breath against my cheek. Barely there. He was barely there. Because of me.

Suddenly there were hands on my shoulders, lifting me and I was pulled into Harry's embrace. Lamps were lit. Men came, they checked my father and took him. Another man, so many of them, filled the office and stole the air from it as he spoke. He wore a police uniform. I was taken to my father's chair. A daze over me so heavy I felt I'd never break out, nor did I want to. Here my feelings were deadened; out there they were raw and raging.

'Miss Delaney,' came the policeman's muffled voice. 'Miss Delaney, can you explain what happened?'

But the words wouldn't come. I still held the note, crushed, in my fist. I stared at the spot on the floor where my father's body had lain. How long had he been there? He'd felt cool to touch. How much longer would he had lived if we had not come? I could not speak, for the questions and possibilities and shock of it all put my mind somewhere else.

Harry spoke for me, for he saw it all as I did and the police listened. Officer Bolton came. He knelt before me and spoke of my father, taken to the Radcliffe Infirmary. He was strong, Bolton said, he would be well. But his tone was unconvincing.

Finally, they were gone and Harry and I were left alone.

He held my hand, kissed it. 'Lily,' he said and his voice cut through the blur.

'I . . . I need to tidy this mess.' It was all I could think then. The books needed to be shelved, the shop righted.

'Not now,' Harry said gently.

But I didn't listen. I set about it. If I set it back to how it was, then all this would never have happened.

Only one shelf in the office was empty, the books scattered. I put them all back. Harry didn't try to stop me as I thought he might. It was all I could think to do. All I had power to do. I still had the note. My hand ached from holding it, the hard paper stabbing my palm. I put it in my pocket, couldn't bear for Harry to see it, ask me about it, have to explain it and how all of this was my fault.

In the main shop, the lamps now lit, I saw the extent of the damage.

About a third of the shelves were empty, as if someone – I knew exactly which someone of course – had swept the books free with one arm. They lay in heaps, their torn pages blanketing the floor like snowfall.

I dropped to my knees and let out a pained sob at the sight. I started trying to tidy them but where would I begin? So much destruction of so much beauty. My home was desecrated. The books punished to punish me. Hate burned in me the like of which I'd never experienced. I didn't know how my body could contain it.

Harry knelt beside me and took a ripped piece of paper from my hand. 'Not tonight. We will fix this tomorrow.'

I nodded mutely and let him lift me. Let him guide me out and into the air. He closed the door but the lock was broken so we left it open.

Harry led me to his house on the Botley Road and roused

his mother. She made me sweet tea while still in her nightgown and hugged me as if I was her own. Harry put me to bed in his room and took a blanket for himself. He went to leave but I grabbed his hand.

'Stay.' I didn't know my own voice.

He made himself a bed on the floor. I closed my eyes and saw my father's face, slack and grey. In my mind he was dead and the bowler man stood over him, laughing. I saw the girl too, from the pages, confined and reaching out for me, her belly heavy with child, being pulled away by her father into the darkness. I woke crying and Harry was there. Harry was always there. Would always be.

I shuffled to the far side of the bed and, wordlessly, he climbed in with me. I put my head on his chest and wrapped myself around him. His warmth and his life, I clung to it as if I would be pulled into the darkness too and he was my salvation. He kissed my hair and I felt my heart unclench. In his arms, chaste and proper, I fell to sleep.

24.

I sat at my father's bedside as the doctor spoke of his weak heart and the shock of the break-in. I wasn't listening. He hadn't woken up yet and the doctor seemed uncertain when, or if, he would. I held his hand, so small in mine where once these hands had seemed so strong. His bones felt like those of a bird, eminently fragile and ready to snap with a tight grip. After questions about his diet, how much of a drinker he was, and did he have any stresses in his life, the doctor finally left.

We were in the Frewin ward, a large room of ten beds, five to a side, with high windows letting in the watery morning light. Outside, the rain came down in sheets. Inside, six beds were occupied by sleeping men. They had all manner of ailments. One had his whole leg in white plaster, elevated so high it looked uncomfortable for him. Another young man had bandages around his head and hands and looked so downcast I almost sat with him to cheer him up. At the ends of the beds were tables on castors for meals and cards. The linens were bright white, the windows opened a crack to allow the air to move, and the place had a sweet aseptic smell I took to be carbolic acid.

I had never been in a hospital before, nor had, as far as I knew, my father. The beds were small and narrow but he looked smaller still upon it.

'I'm sorry, Father,' I whispered close to his ear. I had hoped he would stir, turn to look at me and tell me it wasn't my fault, but he did not. He was still, his breathing even but shallow.

I released his hand and took the crumpled note from my pocket. I had barely seen what else it said the night before, focusing only on the terrible phrase: *Your offer is declined*. But now, in the light of a new day, I read the rest.

Your offer is declined.

You have two weeks to find the remaining books.

There was no threat, no 'or else' because he didn't need one. The man in the bowler, by direction of his employer, had ransacked my home and scared my father so deeply he lay here, now, halfway between life and death. There would be worse. He knew of Harry. He knew of Mr Caxton. He would destroy everything I had if I did not find them. But two weeks. To find three books when I had no notion of where even one might be.

My satchel rested against my leg. I reached inside and felt the outline of the pages from *Orpheus in the Tower* within the lining. Safe, for now.

I raised my father's hand and kissed it. 'I'll be back soon.'

I left the hospital with a weight in my chest. Every step seemed to drag and my legs, my back, my head, my heart, ached deeply and unrelentingly.

At the bindery door, I stopped, tried to compose myself best I could to face Mr Caxton. It was late in the morning and I wasn't sure if he knew of my father's predicament. I turned the handle but the door didn't move. It was locked. In my dazed state I tried again, and a third time before believing it.

I knocked but no answer came. I went to the window, to the corner where the paper had started to peel. The workshop was dark, the fires unlit.

Panic rushed at me. I couldn't recall a time Mr Caxton had not been at his desk by half past eight nor left it before six. He'd never been sick, nor taken a holiday much beyond the occasional Friday for a trip to Brighton. Had the bowler man found him at home?

Of course not. There would be no sense in that. No further leverage for me beyond Harry if I refused to find the books. And Harry was no helpless old man.

I walked back to the bookshop, where the spectre of debt hung over it and the size of the task ahead all but brought me to my knees. There would need to be a new door, the books tidied, sorted into anything that could be salvaged or repaired. I needed to scrub the smell of tobacco and mint from the boards and attempt to find a solution for the moneylenders. I felt I would shatter under the weight of it all.

When I neared the shop, the door was not as we left it the previous night. There stood a gaping hole in my home. Had he come back for another round? What else could he take from me? My anger overrode my good sense and I strode to the door, fists clenched.

But Harry stepped out, staring up at the bare hinges. He

had taken the door off and behind him, resting against the wall, was a new, unbroken replacement.

'Harry?' He smiled when he saw me. 'What's going on?'

He kissed my cheek as I reached him. That small act of intimacy brought me such comfort. 'Repairs is all. How's your dad?'

'Sleeping. He hasn't woken and the doctor isn't sure when he will.'

'But he will, that's what matters.'

I didn't have the strength to see the pity in him should I speak the truth. He might not wake, said the doctor with a dour look.

'Is that Miss Delaney?' came a shout from within. 'She's late!'

Mr Caxton sat on the floor of the shop, surrounded by piles of books and torn paper. The relief hit me so hard I had to take a breath upon seeing him.

'I went by the workshop but it was locked up. I was worried,' I said and knelt close to him. 'What are you doing here? Surely the bindery . . .'

'It can wait,' he said. He picked up a volume with minimal damage and checked the spine, put it in a pile. 'Your busybody neighbour Mrs Hawes came to tell me what happened first thing this morning. I found the door ajar and this mess. How is your father faring?'

I could not answer, and for Mr Caxton, that was answer enough.

He picked up another book, this one's cover was damaged and hanging off as if someone had ripped it on purpose. Mr Caxton shook his head, solemn in his grief for the broken books.

'Philistines,' he muttered and put the book on another pile.

Tears strung my eyes. 'Thank you,' I said and the word caught in my throat.

Mr Caxton took my hand in both of his. 'Your father will be well and when he returns from the Radcliffe, this place must be shipshape.'

I glanced behind me and saw Harry, a pencil behind his ear, lumbering the new door into place. Before me, Mr Caxton sorted the fallen books. I sat between them, gratitude welling up inside me.

The next hour was spent righting the shop. Harry hung the door and between Mr Caxton and I, we cleared the floor of books. There was a pile of perhaps twenty that could be saved with some glue and binding, but another ten or so were beyond our help. Thankfully none of significant value. The rest needed to be reshelved in order but before taking that on, I made us all tea.

I still couldn't face going into my father's office. The image of him lying there, the weight of his body against the door, it was too raw. So, we three sat in the middle of the shop on mismatched chairs from the parlour upstairs.

I did not join in the conversation between Harry and Mr Caxton about what else was left to do, how well it was going. The guilt settled too heavy on my shoulders. I thought about telling them both what was happening, from beginning to end. But that would only put them in danger. The less they knew, the safer they would be.

I hated the lies between us. I looked at Mr Caxton, checking over a valuable edition of Coleridge's poems, and thought of the shame and mistrust he would feel if he knew the truth.

Then at Harry, gesturing to the door, telling of how the original was busted open, probably with a bar. My tryst with Charlie put an invisible cage around me, one I was sure Harry would lock tight once he knew, and he must know eventually. But not now. Neither could know their truths now. I had two weeks and little to go on.

A knock came at the door and Harry got up to answer it. He returned quickly with a letter for my father, handed it to me.

I opened it and within caught sight of the London and County Bank's letterhead. I drew out the letter with a stone lodged in my heart.

A final demand for payment within a month or the shop and its contents would be foreclosed on. My father's mismanagement and secrecy set us down a doomed path and my dangerous gamble had failed. We would be homeless in a month.

I closed my eyes.

I felt Harry's hand on my arm. 'Lily?'

The letter dropped to the floor and I pressed my hands against my face, forcing back the tears, holding myself together, for I feared one moment, one breath where I let in the enormity of my situation, would break me entirely. Blood rushed in my ears and muffled the sounds of the men around me. Two weeks to find the books. One month to find the money. Else I would lose my home, my family, my future. Everything.

I forced myself to breathe. I heard someone pick up the letter, then drop it again. I felt Harry's hand on my shoulder. Then Mr Caxton beside me. I ignored them both. I would not be beaten so easily. I had endured more than the bowler man and his overlord knew. I would not let them win. Rage replaced fear. Determination pushed out sorrow. I knew what

I had to do and as much as it broke my heart to do it, I could see no other way.

I stood up and turned to Mr Caxton. I spoke quickly, for I knew if I lingered, I would falter. 'Sir, it is with great regret that I must tender my resignation.'

'Lily!' Harry cried but I did not take my eyes from Mr Caxton.

Mr Caxton drew in a breath. 'Lilian, I understand this is difficult—'

'You deserve someone fully committed to her work and I am not right now, nor can I guarantee I will be again anytime soon.' My voice cracked. 'I am sorry.'

He shook his head. 'I do not accept.'

'You must,' I said. 'If you care for me at all, you will let me go and wish me well.'

He was silent, his cheeks puffing out, his mouth working as if testing what to say before he said it. Eventually, he adjusted his glasses and appeared to calm.

'As you wish.' He turned away from me and it took all I had left in me to not take back my words. He picked up the volume with the torn cover. 'I'll fix this and return it. It's an early Milton, worth a bit. If you don't mind, I'll be on my way.'

He moved past me to the hat stand and unhooked his coat. He paused at the newly fitted door, almost as if he was going to say something, but did not. He left and I could not believe what I had just done.

I found my chair and fell into it.

'Why did you do that?' Harry asked, mouth agape. 'You love your job and him.'

'I had to.'

'I don't understand.'

'You don't have to. You just have to trust me.'

I heard him sigh. That puff of air through his nose that used to irritate me but now I deserved it. I couldn't explain, not without putting him in danger.

'I trust you,' he said quietly, though he did not sound particularly happy about it.

I reached for Harry's hand and pulled him close. I leaned into him, my head on his stomach, and wrapped my arms around him. He bent, kissed my head, and we remained like that for a while.

Tell him, spoke a voice inside my head. But I could not face losing another man I held so dear. I resolved to tell him after all this business was put to bed. I had two weeks to find three books. I had found three already. How hard could it be?

'I have to go,' I said and held on to Harry's waist for another moment before releasing him.

'Where to?'

'Manchester.'

'What? Why?'

'To visit a publisher.'

'I don't understand. Your father is in hospital and you're off halfway up the country to a publisher?'

I hated the accusation in his tone. I stood up and pushed away from him. 'You think I would go if I had a choice? You think I would give up my career if I had a choice?'

'I don't know,' he cried and threw his arms up. 'I don't know, Lily, because you're not telling me anything. Someone broke into your home and scared your father so bad he's in the hospital. But you don't seem all that worried.'

I rounded on him, my ire up and my patience gone. 'How dare you tell me how I feel. You want the truth? The person who broke in was looking for me. For those books and the pages they contained. The ones I asked you to hide. So you see, this is my fault. My father could have died, may still die, because of *me*. I have to carry that with me for the rest of my life. You say how could I; you say I don't seem worried. To hell with you for that.'

I didn't realise I was crying until Harry reached for me and wiped the tears away with his thumb. Then he wrapped me in a hug and held on, even as I tried, half-heartedly to push him away.

'It's not your fault,' he murmured.

But it was. All of it. 'I have to fix it.'

He released me and I looked up into his eyes. He hadn't erupted at me as he once would have after an outburst like that. Years ago, we would have shouted ourselves hoarse and stormed away. We would have seethed for days and eventually reconciled with angry congress. But Harry was different now, a gentleman he said, and his inner storm had calmed to a breeze where mine still raged.

I pulled his head to mine and kissed him. His arms circled my waist and lifted me to the tips of my toes. He tasted of coffee and that particular sweetness that was all him. I wanted him then more than I had wanted anyone or anything for so long. His kiss was as fierce as mine and I felt his strength, his kindness, the change in him since we were young. My confusion at the future, at the tick-tock in my head between him and Charlie, began to clear. Today, it was all Harry.

I began to guide him towards the stairs, towards a bed and

a few hours of forgetting, but after a few steps, he stopped, pulled away.

'I can't. Not now, not like this.' I could see it pained him to say it as much as it pained me to hear it.

Shame flared in me. Who was I, that I would take a man to my bed so readily? Or that I would join a man in his though I barely knew him? I put my hand to my mouth and nodded, stepped away from him. 'I need to go.'

'Lily, wait.'

'I need to go now. To Manchester. To fix all this.'

'I'll go with you.'

'No,' I said and the sharpness in my tone made him flinch. 'I'm sorry. I need to go alone . . . Will you look after my father? I don't want him to wake up to strangers.'

Harry only nodded.

'And keep those pages safe. Please.'

'I will.'

I moved past him, to the office. I stood outside the door for a moment, took a breath and walked in. Without looking at the spot on the floor where my father had lain, I went to the safe and spun the combination.

'You're leaving right now?' Harry said from the door.

'I have to.'

From inside the safe, I took what little money there was for my train fare and closed it again. I pushed past Harry and went upstairs to wash the tears from my face and tidy my hair.

When I got back downstairs, Harry was at the books, shelving the undamaged volumes.

'I'll do that when I get back.'

'It's no trouble. Here.' He took a key from his pocket and

indicated to the front door. 'Don't want you having to break in.'

I put the key in my satchel and wrapped a scarf around my neck. 'Thank you.'

He gave me a tight smile. The heat of our kiss still lingered between us and I almost stepped to him again.

'I'll be back in a day or two.'

'Goodbye, Lily,' he said in a sad tone that made me think, suddenly, that this would be the last time I ever saw him.

I swallowed back the fear and tried to smile. Then I stepped out into the fresh air and drizzle and walked fast to the station.

25.

The afternoon train to Manchester was no quick jaunt to the north. It would take the better part of a day. The carriage was reasonably quiet, with a pleasant buzz of conversation. Passengers were unwrapping sandwiches and opening bottles of cider but I could give no thought to food. I tried to focus my mind on what lay ahead rather than behind me. I had left such a mess in my wake but if could just get through this, find the books, I was sure I could make amends on my return. I held on to that belief as the train passed through gentle fields, edged with bare trees and a lingering mist.

I had little to occupy myself so I read again the hidden pages from *Orpheus in the Tower*. And again, I was breathless at its end. It only deepened my resolve to find these books, as if the threats against me weren't enough.

I put the pages back in the lining of my satchel and took out the *Orpheus*. I had forgotten to hide it somewhere, but now I was glad of it. As much as I had studied these books, I had not read a word of them beyond the title page. I adored books but wasn't what you'd call a critical reader, nor a regular one. Everyone who had contact with these books or had heard of the author said Bell was a writer of worthless pulp so, with nothing else to occupy the seemingly endless hours until I had to change trains in Wolverhampton, I opened the book at chapter one and began with low expectations.

Orpheus in the Tower began, strangely enough, with a voyage at sea.

I have been asked to write down all I remember from the fated voyage of 1717. Every man aboard the vessel, *The Devil's Destiny*, is now dead or mad and I am the only one sane enough to hold a pencil. The men seated before me ask and ask for my tale and, herein, I confide it that I may finally be free of it.

It begins at Liverpool docks some years past, where I, a boy of fourteen, and Genny, a girl of my acquaintance and admiration, did steal a leg of mutton.

We mistook who we stole from and did not account for the three young brothers who stood nearby their father's market stall. Genny and I were chased through the docks.

'Drop the mutton,' said I but Genny would not and it was a fine thing she kept a grip on it.

We hid finally in the hold of a ship. Genny breathed hard and held that mutton to her chest. We heard the three brothers on the deck and hid ourselves under sacking and behind barrels of salt pork.

Genny and I ended up falling asleep in that den we had made and next we knew we were being hauled up by the collars by a rough-looking man with a gold tooth and nut-brown skin. His greased hair fell over his eyes and the collar of his soiled shirt.

We had found ourselves on a ship of pirates and what

brutes they were! Fierce growlings and drawn swords accompanied our ascent to the upper deck where the captain, a man in a long blue coat and wide-brimmed hat stuck with feathers, waited.

I had said it was fortunate we kept hold of the mutton, for when Genny offered it to the captain to spare our lives, he accepted, saying he had a fondness for the meat.

So it was, Genny and I came to be crew on *The Devil's Destiny*, the most notorious ship of the pirate fleet.

I set down the book. I had been expecting a romance, two lovers, separated, one perhaps even trapped in a tower as the title suggested. This was a tale of adventure and derring-do, of pirates of all things. Perhaps the romance would come between our narrator and Genny, though how a girl was allowed to stay aboard a ship without being cast overboard as a bad omen escaped me. I supposed realism did not matter too much to this writer.

Nonetheless, I found myself gripped by the story. I read on, to their adventures in the Caribbean, the cut-throat town of Nassau, of a dalliance between Genny and a young member of the crew. The tale wove through the years until finally it swerved into a ghost story where the *Destiny* was stuck in the doldrums and out of the mist came a long-sunk ship with a skeleton crew.

I read it from beginning to end with only a brief pause in the middle to change trains. I turned the final page with some time to spare before arriving in Manchester, for the train had to stop in Wellington to decouple a carriage. The author did not tie up the confession, nor the conceit that Nathaniel was telling his story to a room of men, perhaps at a trial. But it did not matter. The tale rollicked on and I could see why William Heathfield had enjoyed the stories.

But why did the title not match the story? I flicked back to the first page. There was the title, author, publisher, date. Same as the other books I'd found, though this one had heavier foxing on it. I examined every inch of the page, and there, at the spine, I spotted it. An almost invisible line at the spine edge of the title page. I angled the book to catch the lamplight and saw it clearer.

The title page was tipped in. Not part of the original printing. It was expertly done, as if to conceal it entirely, but some time in its history, water had found its way into the paper, dissolved the glue, and ever so slightly, almost imperceptibly, lifted the errant page. I had not seen similar on the *Knave* for the fire had damaged so much, and on the *Devotion*, I had not even looked. Now that book was gone and I could not. The skill to tip in the page and conceal the join so well spoke of a talent beyond that of the binding.

Mr Chand had said the book did not appear in the publisher's listings and I had a suspicion that all of the books found thus far would not appear in the catalogue either. So the girl had chosen these books, perhaps changed the titles and hidden her story within them to give to William. But why? My mind turned over the questions, for there were so many, until my head ached and I was still without answers.

It was close to midnight when the train arrived, dark and cold with a swift wind rushing through the streets. I found a lodging house close to the station and, with a baked potato from a cart nearby, I settled in for the evening and awaited the day ahead.

After a quick breakfast, I made my way into Manchester. I'd never been before and what struck me first was how busy the city was. The streets thronged with people moving in quick step. The roads were thick with carriages, some carrying people, others carrying carts laden with heavy loads. Horse-drawn omnibuses, large enough to seat dozens, rushed alongside nimble traps and hansoms. It was a city of stark lines, of poverty and industry jostling shoulder to shoulder with opulence. After gentle Oxford, and then London, a city used to its size and population, Manchester felt fit to burst.

I pushed my way through the endless crowds, up Piccadilly and Market Street and into the warren of streets surrounding King Street. At a junction, a single, brave policeman stood in the centre of the road, carriages rushing either side of him as he attempted to form some order in their chaos.

Eventually, after asking a few locals for directions, I found my way to a bookshop. If anyone knew where a publisher would have its office, it was its customer.

A bell rang as I entered and a friendly face looked up from the counter at the far end. This was not a den of antiquarian and dusty tomes but a bright shop of newly printed, mass-produced titles. Several other people browsed the shelves and I could not help but join them. New titles by authors I'd not heard of, latest books by those I had. The place had a smell of leather and paper, without the musty, sour notes given off by aged tomes. It was woody and pleasant and I inhaled it deeply. I spotted a novel written by someone called only Colette, two new ones alongside old favourites by Jules Verne and H.G.

Wells, and I was happy to see Jerome's latest *Three Men on the Bummel,* in beautiful red morocco with an elaborate but small blind-tooled frame in the upper left corner bearing the title and author's name.

There! On a high shelf, the name Bell jumped at me. Bell's books filled half the shelf, all slim volumes quickly written and printed. At a glance, the bindings were in vibrant leathers, but one at the end was darker. A shade of purple. I pulled it down and saw quickly it was not the same binding. The book was a series of short tales, ranging, it seemed by the titles, from horrors of the London East End to love in the saddles of the American West. The date, however, gave me hope, for it was published just two years prior, in 1899. It was likely Bell still lived and the publisher was most definitely still in business.

'That's a good one.' Beside me, a woman nodded to the book in my hand. She reached for another from the same shelf. 'This one is my favourite. It's an early Bell but I do love it.'

She showed me the cover. *The Devil's Destiny.* I took the book from her and checked the date: 1848, not 1851. Almost everything on the title page of the *Orpheus in the Tower* had been false, and I could assume the same of other books too.

'Would you believe I read that one just yesterday?' I said and the woman brightened further. She was a short, slim lady in a smart blue jacket and dress and had such a light demeanour I could not help but return her smile. She spoke with a faint local accent I found myself warming to further.

'Do you know much of the author?' I asked.

'Precious little is known of Abel Bell.'

'What do you mean?'

She leaned closer as if imparting a secret. 'The rumour

among Bell readers, of which we are many, is he lives just outside Manchester and is a recluse of the highest order. He delivers his pages to his publisher by courier. Nobody has ever seen him in person.'

'Leave the poor lady alone, Elsie,' came a voice from behind. At the counter, an older woman stood with her arms crossed.

'She's read Bell too!' Elsie said.

The older woman shook her head. 'She's a customer and I'll ask you to let her browse.'

Elsie gave me a guilty smile and stepped away.

'Is it true?' I asked them both. 'That nobody has met Abel Bell?'

Elsie nodded and, as she went to speak, the other woman got there first. 'He doesn't like the limelight – that's all. There isn't anything sinister in it. He writes his books and we sell them. That's all I need to know.'

'But he's been writing for more than sixty years!' Elsie cried. 'How could nobody have seen him for sixty years!'

'I just don't know,' the other woman said in mock excitement. 'And I don't care a fig.'

'Oh, you grouch, Bess,' Elsie said then turned to me. 'I must go but this was a pleasure.' She shook my hand and shot a jovial glance to Bess who waved her away.

The bell tinkled and fell still as Elsie left and Bess let out a sigh. 'Sorry about that, miss. She's . . . well . . . she's Elsie.'

'It's quite all right.'

'May I help you find something?'

I put *The Devil's Destiny* back on the shelf and went to the counter. 'Actually, I'm a bookbinder by trade, and my father owns a bookshop,' I said and the woman softened somewhat. 'I have a meeting with Montague and Cliff and I lost the address.'

My life was filled with small lies.

'So, you came here?' she asked.

'I'm new to the city and I found myself rather turned around. I thought if anyone might have the address it would be a bookseller. You can imagine my relief when I saw so many Bell books on the shelf.'

'I see. And you say you have arranged to meet them?'

'Yes, I'm hoping to gain a commission from them for new fine bindings.'

Reasonable and rational. Lies shrouded in truth. The best kind. This woman was clearly not to be taken for a fool and I hoped my earnest approach would work.

She regarded me a moment, then a moment more, and eventually, she said, 'I appreciate an enterprising young woman. We should all be more like it. When my husband left me this shop, everyone thought I should sell, but I wouldn't and would you believe I've turned it from a penny-profit business into three shops across the city.'

'That's wonderful. I am always happy to hear more book-shops exist, especially those run by women.'

She nodded, puffed up with pride and took a piece of paper and a pencil. She scribbled down an address. 'This is Montague's office.'

The address might as well have been written in a different language for all I knew where it was. She noticed my confusion immediately and offered to draw me a map, for it was not far.

26.

A twenty-minute walk across the city found me at the door of Montague and Cliff, publishers. It was a plain building with nothing but a brass number by the door to announce itself.

I rang the bell and waited. The door did not open for quite some time so I rang again, for longer. From inside I heard a thudding of feet on stairs and the door was flung open to reveal a small angry man who had about him the air of a rodent. He fastened a pair of spectacles to his nose and looked at me.

'You delivering something?'

'No, sir. I'm here to see Mr Montague or Mr Cliff.'

His eyebrow rose and he immediately straightened his back and tugged on his braces, which he wore over a pale green shirt. 'I am Montague. Cliff is dead.'

'Oh. I am sorry.'

'Don't be. He was an arse.'

My eyebrows shot up at his language and he showed no sign that he'd spoken out of turn and made no move to apologise.

'What can I do for you, Miss . . . ?'

'Delaney. Might I come in?'

He blinked and looked around as if surprised we were still on his doorstep. 'Yes, yes, follow me.'

Montague led me into a cramped, dim entry hall. Two closed doors stood on either side and ahead, a staircase. On the stairs were piles of books and small boxes and I had to pick my way up painfully slowly while Montague skipped up like a mountain goat. That he didn't break an ankle or his neck astounded me.

At the top, a corridor led deeper in the buildings, punctuated now and then with doors. Each had a plaque beside it with a different name and I understood quickly that Montague and Cliff were but a small outfit in a nest of other similar-sized businesses.

At one of the doors, he paused. 'What you see within these walls must not be spoken of outside them. I won't have Pearson getting wind of my dealings, you hear?'

I nodded and the eccentric little man ushered me inside.

Chaos! Had I not seen the calm look on my host's face I would have thought the place burgled twice over. Paper and books covered every surface in high, teetering piles. I believe there were three desks, each walled up with typescripts like castle ramparts. One would have to stand to be seen over them. Two windows let in a dreary light, for they were covered in yellowed paper and a fug of pipe smoke hung at the ceiling. A door stood on either side, perhaps leading to a kitchen or bathroom area and on the walls were overfilled bookshelves, the wood bowing beneath the weight. From within the cocoon of one of these desks came puffs of smoke and the tapping of typewriter keys.

'Dotty!' Montague squawked and a woman popped up, pipe clenched in her teeth.

'What?' She was elderly and bent but her cheeks were plump

214

and coloured with rouge. She saw me and pushed her glasses up her nose. Then smiled. 'A visitor?'

'Get some tea would you?'

'I'm not your servant, Henry.'

'But you are my secretary. Hop to it, woman, or you'll be out on your ear.'

'No such luck,' she muttered and I immediately got the sense this was a friendly snapping rather than an angry one. Dotty moved slowly. I suspected more to annoy Montague than out of necessity.

It reminded me somewhat of myself and Mr Caxton, and with a pang of guilt, I remembered what I had done.

'Come, sit.' Montague waved me towards his own desk. He gathered a pile of manuscripts from a chair I had not even seen and dumped them carelessly in the corner. The pile wavered, then fell, the contents splaying across one of the only clear sections of floor. Montague watched it happen and when the papers came to a rest, he did not go to tidy them, only shoved them out of the way with the side of his foot. Then he took his own seat, moving aside another pile of manuscripts from the desk so we could see one another.

He coughed, straightened himself and put on a professional air. 'How may I help you, Miss Delaney?'

I felt like laughing at the whole thing. 'I am after some information.'

His eyelids drooped somewhat and his voice took on a monotone. 'I don't accept poetry or plays. I publish only the finest novels and I pay nothing upfront. You will receive royalties once a year and only after my costs are recovered. I am a stringent editor, Miss Delaney; I shan't spare your blushes if I believe a text must be improved. Hmm. Delaney. Not very exciting. We'll have to change that. Have you a manuscript for me?'

I was taken aback by his speech and took a moment to recover myself. Just as I was about to speak, Dotty returned with two cups and no pot. She set them down unceremoniously. Each cup had a brown ring around the rim and was filled with a similarly coloured liquid. It smelled strong and sweet and not at all unpleasant.

'Tea,' she said and went back to her desk, disappearing behind the stacks.

'Come on now, Miss Delaney. What have you written?'

'She ain't a writer, Henry,' said Dotty without reappearing. 'Can't you tell?'

Montague looked me over once more, shifted his glasses and made a *humph* noise. 'You're not?'

'No, sir. I'm a bookbinder and I'd like to know about Abel Bell.'

'Are you one of them?'

'One of who?'

He sat back. 'One of them Bell fanciers. Women obsessed with him come around here knocking on my door for new books, wanting to meet him.' He took a gulp of the still-steaming tea and winced.

'I promise I'm not. But I have come into possession of a book.' I took the *Orpheus* from my bag and handed it to him.

'This isn't our binding.'

'The title page is false also.'

He looked inside and frowned. He flicked through the pages and within a few moments of reading one he said, 'This is *Devil's Destiny*. Explain yourself, miss.'

'I have come into possession of three such books. Can you tell me, did Bell write the novels *A Song for a Knave* and *He Sings His Devotion*? It would have been in the Fifties or earlier.'

He snorted. 'Terrible titles. I'd never publish that. But my father was running the place back then.' He went to a shelf, pulled a ledger-type volume from the lowest shelf and returned.

Montague set the large book on his desk and flipped it open. Within were dense lines of handwriting. He turned the pages until he reached the right one. At the top, the heading *Bell, Abel* and below, a list of titles. He ran his finger down them, flipped the page and continued, until he came to the end. The last dozen entries looked fresher, as if added recently.

'Neither title exists and our records are meticulous. We're known for it.'

I glanced at the chaos and clutter around me and decided not to question it. 'Can you think of why someone would change the titles on these books?'

'Fraud of course!'

A sigh came from behind the stacks of manuscripts around Dotty's desk.

'I can't see the fraud, here,' I said. 'They note the author, the publisher. It would be easy enough to check the authenticity.'

'Unscrupulous vagabonds trying to sell an old Bell as a new one of course.'

'I suppose. Have you come across any others?'

He sniffed and took another mouthful of tea. I sipped mine to appear polite.

'No,' he said and my heart sank. 'And I would burn any I had.'

'Ha!' cried Dotty. 'You filthy liar, Henry Montague.'

'Quiet, harridan!'

She appeared from around the stacks. 'Your father would be turning in his grave to hear you lying to the poor girl like that.'

'You mean to say you have heard of another book?' I asked, trying to hide my eagerness.

Montague huffed and crossed his arms, taking himself out of the conversation like a petulant child.

Dotty perched on the edge of the desk. 'This must have been, oh, what was it, Henry? Five years ago? Six?' By way of an answer, he huffed again and looked away. She shot him with a searing look. '*Turning in his grave*, Henry.' She pulled on her pipe and blew a column of smoke up into the hanging fog. 'We had a letter from a book collector we're acquainted with who came across a Bell book with a *froufrou* title like yours. Sometime about singing love or loving arias. Some nonsense. He was convinced it was a lost Bell and worth hundreds and we were lying to him.'

'He was an arse too,' Montague piped up and went back into his sulk.

'Who was he?' I asked.

'Now, miss, we don't share names of clients.'

'Even clients like him?'

Dotty narrowed her eyes at me. 'Why are you looking for these books?'

'Honestly?' She nodded and Montague side-eyed me. 'My father is a bookseller. He was attacked by someone looking for these books and I need to find the rest before that person comes back to finish him off.'

Another sharp stab of guilt for leaving so much unattended

and unfinished in Oxford. I wondered if my father had woken yet. If he had been alone or if he still slept. I put the worry away, locked it in a box inside my heart and focused, for nothing now was more important than the books.

'Lord!' Dotty said and she and Montague shared a look. I had suspected they were a pair who enjoyed the salacious and melodramatic and I had been right.

'Attacked, you say?' Montague leaned forward across his desk.

I nodded. 'He is in the hospital as we speak.'

'Life and death, ay?' Dotty said to Montague. 'Your father would approve if you chose to.'

These two spoke as if half the conversation was going on within their heads, such was the closeness of their relationship. I suspected Dotty had been around since the father's days and was something of an aunt to the young Montague (though he was far from young, of course).

'Fane,' Montague said and the name was not unfamiliar to me.

'Ambrose Fane,' Dotty added. 'A nasty man I'd caution you to avoid, miss.'

'Fane, who has the Burford Collection?' I asked. Mr Caxton had also told me to avoid that collection, for it contained works deemed improper for ladies and gentlemen alike.

Another look shared between the odd couple before me.

'The same,' Montague replied. 'After we stopped answering his letters, Fane came here demanding to see our catalogues. An idiot in another office let him into the building and he all but kicked down our door. Scared Dotty half out of her bloomers.'

'That's not how I remember it,' she added drily, and took another puff on her pipe.

'What did he say?' I asked.

Henry drained his cup. 'He claimed to have a book written by Bell that nobody had ever heard of, same as you. He wanted a letter of authentication from us saying it was real and worth a fortune. We wouldn't give it of course.'

'He left vowing to ruin us,' Dotty added. 'But it's been years and we're still here. Never heard from him again.'

'Do you know where he lives?'

Another look. Another pause.

'You shouldn't. He is not a nice man,' Montague said, disdain dripping from every word.

'I have dealt with plenty of not-nice men in my life and I suspect he'll be little trouble,' I tried. I was so close my impatience was beginning to show.

'He's in Birmingham,' Dotty said and disappeared again behind her desk. She rustled about for a while, banging around in drawers. When she returned, she held a letter, opened. 'This was the last letter we had from him. I don't feel an ounce of guilt in sharing this with you. That man can hang for all I care.'

I took it and read the return address. 'You kept this?'

'Oh, we don't throw much away,' she said.

'Thank you, this is more helpful than you can imagine,' I said. 'I should leave you to your day.'

'We are very busy,' Montague said and picked up some papers as if to illustrate the point.

Dotty rolled her eyes.

I put the *Orpheus* back in my satchel and stood to leave. Neither moved to show me out but at the door, I paused.

'Abel Bell. Who is he?' I asked.

'Ain't that the question,' Dotty said.

'I knew you were one of the fanciers!' cried Montague, standing. 'A man deserves his privacy.'

Dotty reached as if to clip his ear but missed. 'Hush up, you old fool.'

I smiled. 'If I wanted to contact him, would you pass on a letter?'

'For the sake of your father, we'd try,' Dotty said. 'Can't promise you'll get an answer though.'

'I appreciate it,' I said and left the office. I hadn't realised how thick the air in there was until I stepped into the corridor, and how dim the building until I emerged onto the street, blinking, clutching the letter.

I walked back to the train station, only getting lost twice, and found myself enjoying the stroll. The people here had been more helpful than I hoped and I felt a sudden kinship with the city. I resolved to visit again when circumstances allowed.

I had to wait several hours before a Birmingham train was due to leave and by the time I boarded, it was the middle of the afternoon. I asked the conductor how long the travel time was and my stomach sank when he said three and a half hours, give or take, on a good day with the wind behind her.

'More likely four,' he said and wandered away.

I would not arrive until the early evening and I wasn't sure I had enough money for a hotel. I took my seat and tried to keep my mind from the worry growing within. My father. Mr Caxton. Harry. My own safety over the coming day. The strange pair that was Montague and Dotty warned me strongly against this man, Fane, as had Mr Caxton. The bravado I had affected while in their company was all that. And now I was alone, it was gone and pure, icy fear took its place.

The train lurched out of the Manchester station and I had little to occupy myself. I could not bring myself to read the *Orpheus* again so I took out Fane's letter. It was all froth and threat, written in an arch, silly style. I wondered at the sanity of the man on the other end. The handwriting was spidery and deeply cut into the paper, written angry in black ink, and lacked any common courtesy.

Montague, you charlatan! I'll see your name blackened from shore to shore. I'll see you and your harpy wrecked on the rocks of your own arrogance. I will have my satisfaction, sir, and you will weep when you think of me, Ambrose Fane, holding lofty court above you. Grovel to me and repent. Bring me the authentication of the book and I will forgive your sins as the charitable man I am.

In reading, a terrifying idea occurred. Fane may be the one employing the bowler-hat man. He clearly carried an obsession, a fierce temper, and had the means to pay. The Burford Collection was known as one of the most valuable in the country though was not held in high esteem, for the books themselves were lurid and carnal in nature, and certain volumes were considered overtly blasphemous. It was rumoured he had a 1494 Koberger edition of Kramer's *Malleus Maleficarum*, the famed and horrific witch-hunting manual. Some even say Fane kept it by his bedside. Few people outside certain circles were permitted entry to the collection, but Fane's reputation as an unscrupulous collector stretched far wider.

I shrank in my seat and wanted to go home. Wanted to run away from it all and return to the quiet, safe, limestone walls of Oxford. But of course, they weren't safe and would never be again until this business was finished. Was this what Grieves had felt when he was searching for the books? Charlie had said the buyer had hurt someone Grieves cared for. At the time, I had thought it coincidence and thought Grieves dramatic and cruel, but now I knew what he'd said was true. I was on the verge of losing someone I loved to these books, perhaps I already had and would return home to awful news.

I closed my eyes against the light and told myself to stop. All was as I left it. All would be well. I would find the books, know the girl's fate, and be rid of them all. If Fane wanted these books so badly, he was welcome to them, but the story within would be mine.

27.

Ambrose Fane's home was set back from the street behind tall iron gates. A wall topped with black iron spikes ringed the property and the only other entrance was a firmly locked wooden service door in the back. I had walked around several times before working up the courage to enter. The cab ride from the station had stripped me of almost all my money, for the driver had taken me on a roundabout route and made me pay for the privilege, threatening constables if I didn't. I had enough for the train fare home and only a few pennies more for something to eat. A boarding house was out of the question and so, at past seven o'clock, I came to Fane's door. Propriety be damned, when he saw I had a Bell book, I was sure he would let me in.

A few lights were on in the lower floors of the house though that did little to help the building's grim, foreboding countenance. It seemed darker than the other houses on the wide, tree-lined street, each their own kingdom behind walls and high gates.

The gate was unlocked, to allow for callers. I imagined a butler would lock them when the hour grew late enough. I entered and walked the short path to the front door. The gardens, lit only by the gaslights on the street and the lights within the house, seemed well kept and mature, though full of strange shadows. The box plants were trimmed into odd shapes and there seemed to be the hint of a labyrinth on the lawn. The gardens appeared to stretch further than the walls of the property would allow, though I put that down to tricks of shadow. Still, I dreaded the thought of straying from the path.

At the door I rang the bell and a deep chime sounded within.

The door opened and a red-cheeked man, perhaps in his forties, stood at the threshold. He regarded me for a moment, and the strangest thing happened. Without a word of announcement, he suppressed a sigh, then stepped aside and let me in.

'Sir?' I asked.

'He is in the parlour,' the man, I assumed a butler, said in a weary tone.

'The parlour,' I repeated, in my shock.

Another long sigh and the tone grew wearier. 'This way.'

I was struck dumb by the interaction and followed the man into the house. And what a house it was. The front door opened to a grand hall clad in shining black marble. White and gold statues formed an avenue, urging one to follow deeper into the house. Tall, golden candelabras between the statues turned the hall from a stark, cold room into an esoteric chamber. The statues, as I noticed when passing closer, were in the classic style. Roman satyrs and horned creatures cavorted alongside beautiful men and women. Above, in recesses lining the hall, stood statues of the Roman gods and at the head, where the staircase wound up into the house, was Jupiter, proudly unclad and to attention.

I did not attempt to hide my blush, for I was too distracted by the whole situation. I was led into a room – the parlour, I assumed. This was just as grand and ornate. The walls were flocked red paper with a black pattern, a chandelier hung from the ceiling and huge exotic plants I'd never seen occupied the corners and tables. More statues, smaller this time, and on tall pedestals. Lacquered boxes in the Chinese style. Red velvet drapery. The scent of incense and a sweet, tobacco-like smoke I'd never encountered. A huge, golden clock, its face held in the buxom embrace of two nymphs, ticked on the mantel and a fire crackled in the grate.

On one of the many plump chaises, reclined a rakish man in a loose collar. His recline was awkward and looked uncomfortable, and he held in one hand a small volume that he, I realised, was pretending to read, for it was upside down.

'Your guest, sir,' the butler announced and deposited me in the room with little fanfare.

The man, languorous yet gangly, a soft attempt at sensuality in his smile, lowered his book and looked at me. The smile immediately faded.

'You're not who I ordered. Bentham! Who is—' But the butler was already gone and the door closed behind him.

Fane muttered something under his breath and swung his legs off the chaise. 'I am sorry, madam, but you have come to the wrong house and must leave.'

He went to ring a bell by the fireplace and my shock suddenly wore off.

'You're Ambrose Fane.'

'And you're not who I ordered.'

'I believe you'll want to hear what I have to tell you.'

Fane paused, his hand outstretched to the bell pull. He was

an odd one. Younger than I expected, only in his thirties at a guess, and was thin, with little in the way to recommend him physically. His face was clean-shaven, though I doubted a beard would grow even if he let it, and his hair was long and curled, tied back in a black ribbon. His shirt was untucked and he wore old-fashioned breeches and stockings the like of which a gentleman would have worn a century ago.

'Curious,' he said and folded his arms. 'Who are you?'

'My name is Lilian Delaney and I'm a bookbinder from Oxford.' I watched for a flash of recognition to pass over his features but none came and my thought that he was the buyer behind this whole mess wavered. 'I have come into possession of a volume I believe will be of interest to you.'

He cocked an eyebrow. 'Oh? What volume is that?'

'I will show it to you, on a condition.'

At this, he smiled. 'What condition is that?'

'If I show you mine, you show me yours.'

He arched an eyebrow and a lascivious glint came into his eye. 'Curiouser.'

He returned to his chaise and gestured for me to sit in the chair opposite. On the table between us was a decanter of red wine and two glasses. I hoped his company would be late enough that we would not be interrupted.

He had a slightly effeminate air about him, and for all his reputation and the unusual circumstances, I did not feel threatened, though a little self-conscious as he appraised my appearance.

Fane poured the wine and offered me a glass. I had not realised I was trembling and the wine, rich as butter, went down far too easily.

'How odd you are to come to my house unannounced and speak of books,' he said, sipping the wine. It left a blood-red stain on his lips and for a brief moment, he turned vampiric.

'I do apologise for the intrusion. I am in something of a strange situation where I need information and can offer little in return.'

'What information do you seek? And what is this volume you have that carries a condition?'

I reached into my satchel and pulled out the *Orpheus*. He took it with an amused look but upon seeing the author's name, he looked at me and the rake gave way to the collector.

'A Bell.'

'A Bell that should not exist,' I added.

He opened the cover with an almost reverent care. '*Orpheus in the Tower*. But this text, it is the pirate story.'

I nodded. '*The Devil's Destiny*. This title is not in the publisher's catalogue. And see, here . . .' I shuffled to the edge of my seat and pointed to the lower corner of the spine where the title page was lifting. 'It was tipped in. Someone created this book on purpose. The binder goes by the initials FFG but I've not found any binder to match.'

'How did you come by this?'

'This . . .' I said and took a chance at honesty. 'This, I stole.'

'You shock me, madam.'

'I doubt that.'

He gave a small laugh. 'Touché. And why would you come to me with this?'

'Because you have, or used to have, a similar Bell book.'

'You have done your research. I suppose you visited Montague.'

I nodded and took the letter from my bag. 'He gave me this. It's how I found you.'

Fane made no move to take the letter. He leaned back in his chaise, flicking through the book, examining the spine and running his hands over the covers as one would a lover's body. I almost averted my gaze but I didn't want to lose sight of the book.

'You have seen mine, now it is your turn. I wish to examine your Bell. Do you still have it?'

'I do . . .' He glanced at me from the corner of his eye. 'That's all you want?'

'Not entirely. I wish to keep what I find.'

He frowned. 'I will not part with it.'

'Nor I with mine. But I keep what I find. Do we have an agreement?'

Fane held my gaze for a moment, then he licked his thin top lip. 'What do I get out of this agreement?'

'The knowledge that you were right and Montague wrong. There is a series of mistitled Bell books out there. I believe there are six, in fact, and I have discovered three thus far.'

He leaned forward and poured more wine. 'Six? Are you certain? Where are they?'

'The two besides this one were taken from me.'

'Taken?'

He was as enthralled as I in the tale and perhaps it was the wine – for I'd drank half the second glass in one mouthful – but I found myself telling him. Ambrose Fane was a louche man, enjoying the free morality and sensual pursuits one gains with endless family money, but he was a booklover at heart. I imagined him an admirer of Oscar Wilde, for he attempted a Dorian Gray-like decadency yet lacked the charm. As I spoke of my situation, of the books and the bowler man, my father in the hospital and what it meant to me to find these books, I did not mention the story within the binding, for that was mine. I watched for his mask to slip, to reveal himself the man behind it all, but it never did. As I finished my tale, I drained the rest of the wine from my glass and he immediately refilled it.

'And so, I am here and while I do need the book you have, I have no means to convince you to give it to me and no funds to offer to buy it.'

'Indeed,' he said, and tapped his finger against his lips.

More wine. My head swam in a pleasant, warm sea.

The quiet stretched on as Fane contemplated my story and me and as he was about to speak, a sharp knock came at the door.

I jumped. My wine spilled on the rug but the stain was lost among the pattern.

'What?' Fane barked and the door opened to the butler, Bentham.

'Your . . . other guest, waits in the hall, sir.'

Fane glowered. 'Ask them to wait.'

The butler left without a bow or nod and I sensed he did not approve of his master's lifestyle.

'Will you return tomorrow?' Fane asked. 'I will show you the book. Where are you staying? I'll send a carriage.'

A wash of shame came over me. 'I have no lodgings. I hoped we could conclude our business tonight then I would sleep in the station until the first train back south.'

He looked horrified. 'Good Lord. No, no, no. You must stay here.'

'I couldn't . . .' The idea was both exciting and revolting.

'I insist. There are a dozen rooms rarely used in this house. All I'd ask is you remain in yours, no matter what you hear. Do you have any clothes? Night things?' I shook my head and he pursed his lips. 'We have spares. Bentham will attend you.'

'That's too kind but really, you don't—' I tried not to dwell on what he might mean by 'no matter what you hear'.

He held up his hand. 'I am many things, madam, but none may call me a poor host. You will stay here and tomorrow we will continue this discussion.'

I nodded, more grateful than I imagined, for the idea of sleeping on a bench inside Birmingham train station filled me with dread. I followed Fane to the door and he ushered me through it. He hung back a moment and, in a mirror nearby, adjusted his shirt and hair.

Bentham stood a respectable distance from the parlour door, picking at a fingernail.

'Bentham,' Fane said and the man looked up but did not snap to attention as one might expect. 'Miss Delaney is staying with us tonight. See she gets a meal and some clothes. Put her in the Dee Room.' Fane took my hand and kissed it. 'Until tomorrow.'

I forced a smile, for the feel of his lips on my skin turned my stomach.

Bentham gestured to me. 'This way, miss.'

Fane went on ahead, swaying his hips, the rake returned.

I followed the butler into the entrance hall and caught a glimpse of Fane and his guest – a man in a purple robe – disappear down a hallway. Their laughter echoed over the marble.

Bentham led me up the grand staircase. The handrail was supported by fat cherubs and rampant imps. At the top, where the stairs split and swept to each side, the statue of Jupiter stood erect. I stared for a moment at the god's anatomy, the wine having stripped me of my shame. I was amazed anyone would sculpt it, but for enough money, I supposed anything could be bought.

I followed Bentham to the first floor, where a balcony ringed the entire entrance hall. Corridors and doors ran off it and more statues of gods and goddesses, satyrs and nymphs, graced the alcoves. The carpet was soft and we made no sound as we walked. Narrow tables were dotted here and there and upon them, statues of odd esoteric symbols – a golden calf, an ouroboros carved from black stone, a pyramid with an eye atop it, and on the table nearest my door, an intricate seven-pointed star mounted on a tall, thin pedestal. It was carved all over with runes and symbols I did not recognise, but it gave me a chill to look at it.

The occult and the carnal skipped hand in hand through this house and I could well imagine masked rituals and bacchanals taking place with members of high society.

We came to the door of the room I was to sleep in and with a shiver I saw a symbol carved in the wood and inlaid with gold. It was made up of simple lines and I recognised it immediately as John Dee's Monad, his mystical glyph. It resembled a human figure with a circular head and horns. A memory stirred. In my early days learning the bookbinder's trade, I had helped Mr Caxton sew a volume of Dee's works for a scholar of the mystic arts and although Mr Caxton held no affection for mysticism, he was an admirer of Dee's poetry and would read great swathes of it aloud in the workshop, no matter how much I protested.

'Miss?' Bentham had opened the door and waited for me to enter.

'Sorry,' I murmured and went inside, a fog growing in my mind from the length of the day and the richness of the wine.

Bentham lit a lamp. 'There are nightgowns in the armoire and I'll have the cook prepare you something to eat.'

'Thank you, I'm very grateful.' But he was closing the door before I finished speaking.

The lamp filled the room with a pleasant glow. After the aesthetic of the rest of the house, I had expected a den of perversion in the bedrooms but there was nothing too remarkable about it. The walls were covered in one of Morris's simpler papers, a beautiful pattern of carnations and smaller flowers on a red background. The bed was ornately carved from a marble-like wood I couldn't name, and the lacquer shone in the golden light. The armoire and dressing table matched. On the walls hung paintings of pale women in rich, colourful gowns, framed by arching palm plants in elaborate brass pots.

A girl knocked on my door and deposited a tray of sandwiches and fruit. She was a meek one and didn't dare look at me, scurrying off as quick as she came. It made me wonder what went on in this house after dark.

It wasn't late, perhaps only half past eight by the time I finished eating. The warmth of the room and of the wine worked on me and I found myself weary enough to sleep. In the armoire I found several nightgowns, all clean and freshly laundered, a silk dressing gown, and at the end, three black robes. I took one out. It was large, with a deep hood and long arms and I supposed it was intended to cover the wearer entirely. Fane had said to stay in the room no matter what I heard. I shuddered and put the robe back quickly.

In a borrowed nightgown, I slid into bed and sank, deliciously, beneath the eiderdown. It was, by far, the most comfortable bed I had ever slept in and it was minutes before the wine, the day and all the days preceding, caught up with me. My eyes drooped and I was taken by sleep.

I woke to screaming. A man's screams from somewhere in the house.

I shot up, rushed to the door and flung it open. The corridor beyond was dark and full of strange shadows. I dared not step out.

No matter what I heard, Fane had said. As much as I itched to seek out the sound – what if my host was being murdered? – I forced myself to only listen. The screams seemed to rise and fall like breath, but whoever was screaming was not asking for their torment to end. No shouts of stop or don't, just wailing.

I faltered on the threshold. What was I doing here? Were the books really worth this? And I saw again in my mind the picture of my father in the hospital bed. I would not have that replaced with him in a casket.

I closed the door quietly. The carriage clock on the mantel ticked past midnight and the screaming cut off. The silence pressed against my ears and then came a maniacal laugh, echoing through the house. I rushed back to bed, hid myself beneath the cover.

I heard no further sounds but sleep did not come as easily a second time.

28.

I woke and the room was dim. The curtains let in slivers of light where I hadn't closed them fully. My bleary eyes found the clock. It was past ten. I had slept so long! I hurried up, dressed, splashed my face with water from the basin on the nightstand and opened the door.

The meek girl who had brought my food the night before dozed, standing, against one of the statues and I wondered how long she had been there.

The rush of panic in me subsided and I cleared my throat to wake her.

She startled, her eyes went wide as saucers. 'Apologies, miss. I came over all faint for a moment there.' Her accent was local and rather pleasant.

'I'm sorry to sleep so late. I didn't know how tired I was.'

She gave a weak smile. 'I'm to take you to breakfast.'

I followed her back through the house. Clearly Fane didn't want anyone wandering around this place, for what might they find in the dark corners?

'Did you hear screams last night?' I asked the girl.

She looked suddenly uncomfortable. 'We're not supposed to talk about it, miss.'

I suspected as much. Fane clearly enjoyed his privacy and the discretion of his staff was paramount. I wondered, given his reputation, how many of the stories came from his guests and how many from former servants.

I was led into the dining room where two places were set at the table. My host was not there and both plates were clean and untouched.

'His Lordship is not yet up,' said the girl, pre-empting my question.

Bentham stood beside a long table covered in silver serving dishes, and bowls piled high with chopped fruit. He stifled a yawn and nodded to me in greeting.

The girl bobbed on her heel and left.

I was stuck on the spot, for I'd never been presented with a breakfast like this and I had no idea how to act. I could smell the salt-sweet scent of bacon and my stomach ached. I went to one of the place settings and wondered if Bentham was to serve me, but I hated the presumption so I took a step towards the food but then a step away, for what if I was thought improper?

Bentham saw my confusion and gestured to the buffet. 'Please help yourself, Miss Delaney.'

'Thank you,' I said, relieved, and went to pick up my plate from the table. Bentham nodded.

He kindly lifted the first cloche and within, steaming strips of bacon. He indicated to a pair of silver tongs and I filled my plate with a few more than was proper. The next dish held links of fat, glistening sausages. The next, a bowl of scrambled eggs so plump and buttery they were like gold nuggets. Then more still – kippers, sweet porridge, kidneys swimming in sauce, three types of bread, a cheese board, endless fruit, an array of jams and marmalades and honey. I was used to pottage and toast. This was plain indulgence and although I felt totally out of place, I decided to enjoy it, for I had no idea what may come when my host awoke.

I took my plate to the table.

Bentham appeared beside me as I sat. 'Tea or coffee, miss?'

'Coffee, please.'

Bentham reached for a tall silver pot with a long, curved spout. He set it before me, along with a jug of milk or cream, and pot of brown sugar. Then he stepped away, back to his spot by the table, and left me to it.

I was nearly finished with my breakfast and on my second cup of coffee when Fane arrived. He swept into the room, saw me, and jumped.

'Oh!' he cried and pressed his hand to his chest. 'I'd completely forgotten you were here, Miss Delaney.'

I spoke through a mouthful of bacon. 'I am not sure how to respond to that.'

He laughed and took the empty seat opposite me. He was in a state of undress. In a silk robe in the Japanese style, printed with cranes and bamboo forests. Below that, an untucked shirt and pantaloons. His hair was loose and rested past his shoulders in a pronounced wave. His eyes were darker, as if he had not had enough sleep the night before, which I was sure he hadn't. He yawned and raised his hand to Bentham.

The butler poured him coffee and brought over a plate of fruit. Fane picked at a grape but did not eat.

'I do hope you slept well,' he said and eyed me as if to test my character by my response.

'I did, slept right through. I hope the same can be said of your other guest. Will he be joining us?'

He smiled and I wondered if I'd passed. 'Not this morning.'

'Thank you for your hospitality, Mr Fane—'

He stopped me with a wave. 'You must call me Ambrose.'

'Ambrose. I don't wish to seem ungracious but . . .'

'But you are aching to see my book.' The innuendo dripped from his words. He was trying to shock me, but it would take more than a leering gaze and choice language to do that.

'Indeed. I must get back to Oxford, to my father.'

He popped the grape in his mouth and, coffee in hand, rose from the table. 'Let us be away, miss.'

Ambrose swept from the room in a flourish of arms and hair and I scrambled to follow.

He led me through the wide corridors into the back of the house, his silk robe billowing behind him. Every inch of space was given over to something exquisite. The walls were papered in bright patterns of the most intricate designs. Statues of all sizes, on Roman-inspired plinths and pedestals, in white and black marble or alabaster were everywhere. Candelabras held half-burned candles; every surface held curios: a scrimshaw whalebone, a carved symbol of a snake coiled around a woman, a mask adorned with deer antlers, a mirror that seemed not to reflect anything. This house was stuffed and claustrophobic despite being so large. Ambrose Fane had taken the tenets of the aesthetic movement and pushed them to a fecund extreme.

'You have quite a home here,' I said.

'I collect beauty in all forms. I do not judge what form that takes.'

I could tell, for how one could find beauty in a mummified

hand, as we had just passed, was beyond me. He looked back at me and grinned. There was something wolfish in his eyes and I was suddenly not sure he was as harmless as he had seemed.

We came, finally, to a set of doors. We were in the back of the house, far from where I would expect a library to be, but Ambrose did not seem to adhere to expectation. The doors were clad in gold with a detailed scene hammered into the metal. It was a classic depiction of the gates of heaven, a stair leading up, a sunburst behind welcoming souls and St Peter waiting, except he was horned and carried a blade instead of a quill. The souls, flying or floating, some walking, were screaming. One tore at his face. Another tried to cast herself from the steps. Another stood straight and still and wore a bowler hat. A chill ran down my spine. As I looked closer, the figure appeared to turn towards me, look right at me, and his face was the bowler man's face. The hungry eyes. The promise of death.

A hand on my shoulder made me jump back.

'Are you all right, Lilian?' Ambrose asked with a furrow of confusion in his brow.

I caught my breath and looked again at the figure. It was just a man, no hat, no hunger. 'I'm sorry.'

'What did you see?' His tone implied I was not the first to have seen something in these doors.

I shook my head. 'Nothing. Nothing at all.'

'These are the Baleful Doors. Taken from a church in Germany said to worship the Devil himself.'

'They are blasphemous. And beautiful,' I said, forcing the words, for I could no longer see beauty in those things.

'They are cursed,' he said with a thrill in his voice. 'Said to show a person's fears and, for the lucky ones, their future. Oscar told me, a few years before his arrest, that he saw bars across the gates.'

'You have the most interesting possessions. But really, I care for only one.'

'All business, I see. This way.'

He pushed on the doors and they swung open with a heavy sigh. Within, the space was expansive and unlike any library I had ever seen. Books lined the walls, some behind glass, others free. One section of books, I saw with knot in my stomach, were chained. The centre of the room was given over to a large, square dais, two steps up and big enough to hold a dozen people. On either side were tall candelabras with a dozen candles each. At the back corners of the platform were colossal statues of rearing horses, easily as big as their real-life counterparts. A blood-red carpet led from the door to the centre of the platform which, I realised, had the feeling of an altar.

'This is . . .'

'Don't be alarmed, Lilian,' he said. 'This is purely a meeting space for those of like mind. Sometimes we like to dress up, for the spectacle of it, but it is purely academic.'

I forced a smile as I followed him inside. Most of the time, when I entered a library, a feeling of calm washed over me, for I was in a place of comfort with objects I understood. But this library did the opposite. I wanted to run. There existed in that room a strange energy, a fizzing of the air as if a storm approached. It set a shiver in me though it was far from cold. The image on the door haunted me, but if I didn't want that in my future, I needed to focus.

'This is the Burford Collection,' I said. 'I have read about it.'

'What did you read?'

'That you hold one of the only known copies of the first printing of the *Malleus Maleficarum* and a first edition of Nider's *Formicarius*.'

Ambrose waved his hand and seemed disgusted. 'My father's books. He had a strange obsession with witches. I wonder if he thought he could conjure the Devil to save him from his bad investments. I am more interested in the earthly delights.'

He led me to one of the bookcases and pulled out a slim volume.

'The *I Modi*. Veneziano edition,' he said, as if I would be familiar.

It was old, 1500s, bound in pale skin. I opened it and was assaulted by graphic engravings of coitus. A blush rose in my cheeks and I closed the book. He took it from me and set it back in its place.

He looked pleased to have shocked me and began to stroll about the shelves, waving a hand at mention of other titles. 'I have a first edition of *Fanny Hill*, the 1683 translation of *Venus in the Cloister*, four different editions of the *Decameron* and a beautiful copy of the *Satyricon*. It's incomplete of course, being Roman and half lost, but it's fascinating – all about an impotent man and his catamite. Have you heard of it?'

As his excitement grew, so did my discomfort. I was not a prudish sort but this taxed even my limits. 'I'm sorry, sir, to be impatient but the Bell?'

He narrowed his eyes, the first time I had seen him approaching annoyance so far. A collector likes nothing more than to show off their collection.

'Indulge me, a moment longer, will you? It's not so often I have a fellow bibliophile in my sanctum.'

Across the room, Ambrose climbed a ladder to a high shelf and ran his finger along several spines before finding the right one. He pulled out the volume and climbed down to me.

He handed it to me and waited.

It was bound in dark red morocco, with simple gold tooling and a banded spine.

'Nathanial Hawthorne,' I said. '*The Scarlet Letter.*'

'Are you familiar?'

'I have read it, yes. But I don't understand . . .'

He took the book from me and opened the back cover. 'This is a newer edition. From the Sixties.' He spun the book around to me, his finger on the lower corner of the cover. 'Here.'

I angled the book for better light and saw it. The binder's initials, blind-tooled inside a box. Identical to the Bell books.

'It's the same binder,' I said.

'When you mentioned it last night the initials rang a bell, but I was four glasses deep into the evening and I could remember nothing further. But now, in the cold light of day, I do. My father used that binder for several of his books. Dozens in this library. Father said he liked the "understated style", which I find abhorrent of course.'

'Do you know who it is?'

'I believe his name is Felix.' Ambrose frowned in thought. 'Grouch or Gauch. Yes. Gauch. That's it.' His eyes brightened as he recalled the name. 'Felix Fidelius Gauch. My father and he were friends, as much as one could be with a tradesperson.'

'Do you know where I can find him?'

'That man was ancient when I was a babe. He'll be dust

and ash. But I believe he worked with a bindery in London. Had all sorts of unimaginative clients with deep pockets in the Forties and Fifties.'

'Do you know which?'

He shook his head.

'Would your father?' I was becoming desperate.

'Dust and ash, I'm afraid.'

'But his papers, perhaps there is correspondence?'

I had overstepped, I could see it in Ambrose's face. His frown deepened. 'My father's office has been sealed since his death. I won't go in there.' His eyes flicked to a door on the far side of the library.

'May I?'

He recoiled in shock. 'You are quite impertinent, aren't you, Miss Delaney?'

'I have been called that before, yes, and worse. I am merely desperate. My father's life, and the lives of those I care about depend on me finding these books.'

'I do not know what to make of you,' he said.

'I have heard that before also.' I attempted a smile and he began to soften.

'I suppose you would like to see my Bell.'

'Very much so.'

I rose from the floor, put the *Orpheus* back in my satchel and followed him to yet another corner of the library. This one seemed to be for the more modern works. The spines more colourful, not yet faded by age, and the gold lettering shone. I scanned the titles as I passed. Novels of Dickens, Haggard, and Twain. Poetry by Rilke, Whitman, and Wilde. Then came a shelf of Bells. Twenty, maybe more, slim volumes in red binding, the same as I'd seen on a table outside Watkin's in Cecil Court.

'So many,' I murmured, absently running my hand along the spines.

'And yet not enough. I read these as a child. I know they are not exactly food for the mind, but they are sugar for the soul.'

At the end of the shelf there was a slightly larger volume in that all too familiar deep purple leather. A thrill went through me and I had to stop myself from snatching it away.

Ambrose took it from the shelf and held it for a moment, as if unwilling to part with it. But eventually, he handed it to me and indicated a desk nearby I could use. Holding the book as if holding a cracked vase that was ready to shatter any moment, I sat at the desk and tried to calm my breathing.

I checked the book as I had the others. The title, *Love's Last Aria*, the year 1851. At the back, the dots.

* *
*
* *

The fourth book. It was only now the second and the sixth I was yet to find. I felt tantalisingly close to being free of this mess and in possession of the truth.

I felt Ambrose's gaze on me. He watched my every movement, leaning closer over my shoulder each time I seemed to discover something.

On the inside front cover, there was the slight raised edge beneath the endpaper, which spoke to the pages within.

I could not begin to cut into the book with Ambrose present, for I had not told him of the pages and he would not take his eyes from me or his book. The book was in fine condition but not quite as good as the *Orpheus*. There was a great deal of foxing over the pages and the join of the faked title page, when one strained the spine, was more visible. I turned back to the endpaper, ran my finger along the edge of it. This one seemed to have no thicker areas or lumps of glue as the others had. With my nail, I tested the strength of the join. The corner of the paper peeled easily and with it came the flakes of dried glue. I was confident the paper would lift easily and swiftly, if only I could have a few moments alone with it.

'I trust you have what you need,' Ambrose said with a yawn.

My mind raced. How could I engineer time alone with the book? I looked about the desk for something – anything – that might assist and lit upon the sharpened horns of a small brass stature of a bull. I swallowed and flexed my hand to ready myself.

'I have, thank you,' I said and he swiftly took up the book, closed it and wandered back to the shelf.

With his back turned, I reached for the statue. I had moments. 'What a beautiful library,' I said, too loud, too forced. I hoped he wouldn't notice. 'And this statue! Is it a Colchis bull?'

I raised my left hand and slammed it down. The pointed horn stabbed into the meaty part of my palm and pain shot through me.

I gasped. My eyes, for a moment, filled with stars.

'Another of my father's oddities,' Ambrose said, over his shoulder. He'd reached the shelf and was slotting the Bell back into its home.

'Oh!' I cried, teeth gritted against the throbbing in my hand. I made a fist to stem the bleeding but I could feel the hot slick blood begin to flow.

Ambrose turned and his eyes widened. 'What has happened?' He rushed over and, as if he had a string pulled in his back, recoiled when he saw my hand and the thin line of blood edging down my wrist.

'I was admiring the statue when I accidentally knocked it. I went to catch it before it fell and . . . well . . . might you get me a bandage and perhaps a brandy for my nerves?'

He stood with his hand over his mouth and looked like he was about to vomit.

'Sir?' I said and his gaze snapped from my hand to me.

He began to nod, as if speaking would be too much, and backed away a step.

I opened my hand, wincing, to see the extent of the damage.

It was then I heard a muffled thud and looked up to see Ambrose Fane sprawled on the floor in a dead faint.

I didn't move for a moment, such was the shock of his sudden fall, but then I was up. My hand hurt, the wound deep and pulsing. Blood ran down my arm and began to itch. I held my hand aloft and moved fast. From my satchel, I found a handkerchief and wrapped it around my palm. I also took out the paring knife and made for the bookshelf.

I slipped the Bell from its place and hurried back to the desk. How long this faint would last, I had no idea – could be hours, could be moments. All I knew was I had to be swift.

I used the back of my left hand to awkwardly hold the book still and I slid the point of the knife beneath the front endpaper. As I'd hoped, it came away quickly and in seconds, I had freed the lower join.

Ambrose groaned. I froze, knife poised. My heartbeat sounded in my ears and I felt it in my ruined palm.

He did not wake. The breath went out of me and I went back to the book. Another half a minute and the vertical edge was free. I slid the pages from their place, folded them without looking and slid them into the lining of my satchel.

Then I began to panic, for how could I restore the cover with no fresh glue. I checked the two shallow drawers in the desk but both were empty of anything useful. Ambrose groaned again. There was only one way I knew. I licked the edges of the cover like it was an envelope. The old glue tasted sour and gritty but my spit was enough to soften it. With one hand, I pressed the paper flat, closed the book and put my weight on it to set my fix.

I considered taking it. I could just put it in my bag and walk out of the house. The bowler-hat man wanted the books, after all. But Fane would know, immediately, that I had stolen from him. He knew my name, my profession, and where I lived. I would have police or worse, hired thugs, waiting for me when I returned to Oxford. I did not need another enemy.

With reluctance, I put the book back on the shelf, found the bell pull and rang for Bentham.

My hand ached fiercely. It felt as if the bull's horn had scraped my bone or pierced something important. The pain kept growing and the blood had now soaked my handkerchief. I tightened my hand to a fist and held it upright, trying to ignore the constant, sickening throb.

I knelt beside Ambrose and spoke his name. He was out

cold. I shook his shoulder and he did not move. I shook harder, spoke louder. 'Ambrose.'

He stirred as the door opened and Bentham entered. The butler saw immediately what had happened and appeared to roll his eyes.

'I'll get the salts.'

Bentham was gone a few moments before returning with a small, stoppered green bottle. He wafted it under his master's nose and Ambrose groaned again. His eyes flickered open then closed.

'He'll be all right,' the butler said with something approaching affection. He nodded to my hand. 'We should take a look at that.'

I did not argue.

He looped the insensible lord's arm around his neck and lifted him. 'I'll take His Lordship to bed and we'll sort you out before he sees it and faints again.'

'Thank you.'

'Follow me to the kitchen.'

I did as he asked and, when we reached the kitchen, he told me to take a seat at the servants' table. A woman in aprons I took to be the cook looked up from her task of butchering a lamb leg, and saw her master in Bentham's arms.

'Blood?' she asked and I held up my hand.

'Patch her up will you, Mrs Porter?' Bentham nodded to me and hefted Ambrose in his arms to get a better hold. The rakish lord looked like a child in his father's arms, tired out after a long day of play.

Mrs Porter indicated for me to sit, then washed her hands and dried them on her apron. She filled a bowl with water from the kettle and a shake of what I took to be salt, then sat opposite me and took my hand.

I drew in a sharp breath as she unwrapped my makeshift bandage.

'That's for the fire,' she said of the handkerchief and tossed it to the side. She examined my hand. 'Nasty but you'll do fine.'

She cleaned away the blood in silence and I was glad for it, for I had no talk left in me. My mind still raced from the ruse and the thought that at any moment, Ambrose would storm through the doors, know what I had done, and demand the pages.

But he did not.

Soon, Bentham returned and in an affected formal tone, as if he was flatly reeling off lines in a play, he said, 'His Lordship regrets that he is indisposed and will no longer be able to see you. I'm to ensure you're well and then you may have use of the carriage.'

'Of course. I do hope he recovers.'

The cook snorted. 'There's no cure for what ails him.'

'Mrs Porter,' Bentham said with a warning in his tone.

The woman wound a strip of clean cloth around my hand and tied it neatly. 'There you go, miss.'

It felt better, the throbbing easing already. 'Thank you. Both of you.'

I was escorted from the house to the waiting carriage and Bentham directed the driver, upon my request, to the train station. I felt a great weight lift off me and another one settle. I had the pages but not the book. Oxford was not the safe, secure home I had left. I had no job and no further leads on the last two books, and my father . . . I dared not think of what might have happened to him.

I sat on an uncomfortable train seat and waited for departure. It would be a long journey home and I had only one thing to occupy me.

29.

much to my annoyance, father accompanied me to Henley. Usually, it was a maid and a maiden aunt on my mother's side but this day, of all days, my father had come.

Do you remember the weather? How unpleasantly warm it was and yet the day was broken with bursts of rain so heavy they paused the races each time the clouds opened. The wide-eyed debutantes in their lace, holding useless parasols, were soaked and the men hid beneath their jackets, making them look little better than moles. You let the rain hit you. 'What was the harm in a little water?' you said.

I looked for you the moment I arrived. I took my father's arm as we walked through the crowds. He nodded and shook hands with men he knew while they looked on me appreciatively, bowing and offering little more than a polite greeting. I knew one or two from their visits to court me but none spoke to me, only to my father. I was little more than a trinket to him, to be traded away to the highest bidder.

Every man was dressed well, as they should be, in frock coats or linen suits. Every woman in the dress her age and standing required. My father engaged himself in talk of business and Daisy and I strolled alone.

'Do you see him?' I asked her.

'It's not proper, miss,' she said but I saw her glancing for you.

I cared little for the races but my father was an Oxford man and took his support seriously. I looked for you but found instead my cousin, Julian, and a cohort of his bootlickers. Julian was of a vicious mind, had been since we were children. He would pull the wings off flies and laugh as I chided him. He had sharp features that made him handsome but I saw only how he would use that for cruelty. Daisy heard a rumour from Uncle's housemaid that Julian was known to bed girls of good standing, promising marriage into his wealthy family, but would leave them ruined. One even ended up with child. What he did with paid company, however, was much worse. If he was here, it meant Uncle was too and I soon saw him and my father in discussion across the lawn.

I steered Daisy away, towards the boats and grandstand. Then I saw you. Sitting on one of the few punts still moored, relaxing as if you were on a chaise. You had a book in your lap and in one hand a paper and in the other, tapped a pencil against your top lip. I was close enough to read the spine of the book, another Abel Bell novel, before you noticed me.

'Is this seat taken?'

You tore your eyes from your paper. A smile drew across your face. 'It is reserved for you, my lady.'

My smile matched yours and I heard a huffing from Daisy. You put the book in your inner jacket pocket, along with the paper and pencil, and stood, bowing graciously.

The river was busy with punts and parasols, the racers downstream at Temple Island, we at the finish line near Henley Bridge.

'Would you care for a sail?' you asked, holding out your hand to help me into the punt. You did the same for Daisy, who sat in the front muttering. You untied the rope and took up the pole.

The sun glared above us but I did not extend my shade, for it would block you from my sight. I squinted up at you as you piloted us out onto the water where a breeze cooled the worst of the heat. We glided downstream, towards the Fawley bank where picnics were laid and photographers and haymakers bothered their occupiers. Houseboats drifted, their roofs and rails covered in spectators. We passed between them, your deft hand at the pole as if you were born upon the river.

'You are here alone?' I asked.

'I came alone, in hope of finding company.'

A curl of blond hair fell over your eye and I wished to stand and brush it away. A blush covered my cheeks. Did you see it? I always wondered.

'Tell me of your family,' I said. 'And why they did not accompany you.'

You looked at Daisy, checking she was not paying attention. 'I have little by way of family left. My father died when I was young and my mother remarried an indifferent man who cared little for me. They went on to have more children and I turned into a stranger in my own home. I have an allowance and a military career ahead.'

'Military,' I said, for in my selfish mind, despite your hardships, that struck me hardest. For it would take you away from me even though you were far from mine.

'I am to take up my post in a few months.'

'My congratulations,' I said, but I was heartbroken inside.

'In truth, I would sooner give it up. It was my stepfather's arrangement.'

'Perhaps you will find a reason to. I shouldn't like it if you were half a world away.'

You crouched so our faces were almost level. Your smile radiated heat. 'Why is that, my lady?'

'You would have me say it? I thought you were a gentleman.'

Your hand found mine where it rested against the stern. 'I am. A true gentleman.'

'Miss!' Daisy cried and, in that moment, the heavens opened and the river thrummed with rain.

I put up my parasol, what little good it did, and Daisy did the same. Parasols and umbrellas shot up across the banks and spectator boats. You let the rain soak you. It turned your blond hair dark and flattened it over your forehead. You sheltered with me. Beneath my parasol, behind the roaring of the rain, we were in our own tiny world for the briefest time.

You were but inches from me. Our breath became one.

I reached for you, our lips brushed together and it was as if the sun burst inside me.

But as quickly as the rain came, it stopped.

Laughter and life returned to our quiet moment and broke it apart. Everything was as it had been minutes before but I was changed.

Daisy made a disapproving sound at our closeness and you, being the gentleman, nodded to her and stood tall again, piloting us to the river's edge.

You jumped from the punt to the bank and helped me, then Daisy, onto Fawley Meadow.

'A walk?' you asked, rain dripping from your hair, and I put my arm through yours. Daisy trailed, my constant, irritating shadow.

The first gun went off for the diamond sculls, the signal for boats to come to the start.

'Oh, miss,' Daisy said, wringing her hands. 'Might we stay and watch?'

I saw in her a conflict raging. And an opportunity. 'Of course.'

You looked at me strangely.

The red flag must have gone up by the start line, for a few moments later, the second gun went off to signal the spectators to clear the course. The sculls were a slower race than the eights and fours, so I knew what time I had.

Daisy, along with every person along the bank turned their attention to the river.

You saw the chance as I did and took my hand. We ran away from the crowd and walked together across the meadow.

'What were you doing when I saw you in the boat?' I asked as we walked. 'The paper and pencil. You looked so intent.'

You smiled and pulled the paper from your inner pocket, handed it to me. It was a set of instructions. I believe they read something like – The initials of the following objects form the name of a city and the finals, read upward, the river that runs through it. Then came a list of clues and, beside them, the makings of a grid of letters.

'It is a double acrostic puzzle,' you said with a touch of shyness. 'I enjoy word games. They are diverting.'

'You have not finished it.'

'I was stuck and then I was interrupted.' You pointed to a clue.

'Fetched in the dark, banished in the light. What am I?' I read aloud.

'I thought it the moon but it does not fit the square.'

It came to me quickly. 'It's the stars,' I said and handed you back the paper. You took out your pencil and filled in the letters. I saw the answer, half complete, as you still had a few clues to guess.

'Paris and the Seine,' I said and you looked at me with surprise, then smiled.

'Yes, but the clues are not complete. When they are, the puzzle will truly be solved.'

'Even though you know the answer, you still wish to do the work of solving the clues?'

You looked at me then as if I'd said something so foreign. 'Of course. I am not a man who shirks work, nor does the idea of a challenge deter me.'

You said the last as you looked into my eyes. I was the challenge for you. You for me too. Writing this, reliving our moments, gives me hope again after so long away from you.

Your hand played in mine. You lifted my hand to kiss it. 'I will ask for your father's blessing.'

'You might want to ask for my own first, knave.'

'What would you say if I did?'

The question struck me, for I had so long avoided answering the question of marriage that I had all but put the notion from my heart. But you were a young man with a career ahead and a family name that may not have come with a title and a large estate but did come with respect for me and perhaps even love. Could my father deny me that?

What a question to ask myself now.

'I would say you must find out for yourself. My father is not an easy man but I would hope he would see my happiness ahead of his interests.'

Love's first blush had softened the truth of my life to a fool's dream.

'Now then, let us go.' We found Daisy looking for us. We were giddy and she worried. I do not blame her. There would be scandal if we were caught. But then I didn't care. All I wanted was you.

We found my father on the lawn of the Red Lion. You were nervous, your cheeks red. You brushed your wet hair from your forehead and straightened your jacket and collar.

He greeted you politely but without interest until he saw me beside you.

'What is this?' he asked.

'Sir, my name is William Heathfield. My family own an estate in Cornwall, in the business of shipping, formerly mining. I am a gentleman of some means and I have come to know your daughter. I wish to ask for your permission.'

'Permission for what?'

'To marry her, sir.'

My father laughed. His cohort of old men laughed with him. 'Run along, boy.'

'Father, please,' I said. 'I wish to marry him.'

His cheek twitched and I knew what was coming. 'You are not fit to make that decision, daughter. Young man, I applaud your ambition but the Heathfields are a destitute family on the fringe of society. I knew your father and he had no head for business and too much of a liking for gin and whores. I shan't have my daughter carry that name.'

'Sir Malcolm,' you tried. 'I am a gentleman and my father's follies are not mine. I would urge you to reconsider.'

Father turned away and signalled to someone.

My heart sank when Julian and two of his lackeys appeared. My father departed into the crowds, his business complete. I wished to run after him, beg him if that's what it took, but Julian took my arm, pulled me to him. He looked you head to toe and did not hide his sneer. 'You heard him, come away from this rubbish, Cousin.'

I tried to free myself but his grip was too strong.

'She said to let her go.' You stepped up to him and seemed so tall, so strong. 'This is not your concern.'

Julian was always quick to temper. He pushed you and I could

257

see the restraint in you, the wish to turn your fists to him, but you didn't. The crowd gasped and moved away.

He pushed you again. Goaded you. I don't remember the barbs that flew from him to you. He criticised your standing, the cut of your jacket, our familiarity. Then he threw a punch and your nose was bleeding. The two bootlickers laughed. The spectators gossiped. This would be the talk of the society pages come the weekend.

Julian grabbed me and pulled me away from you. 'Come now.'

I wrenched my arm free and ran to you. You held me for a moment and whispered in my ear. 'I'll write to you.'

Then you departed me. Stepping away with your hands raised and your face smeared in blood. Your eyes were on mine and they imparted their meaning. Then you were gone in the crowd as the next race began.

The next day was a tense blur. I thought constantly of the moment when our lips touched, when our hands met, when we spoke of marriage. I barely knew you but I felt I knew your heart and you mine and that was more than enough for me.

It all came crashing down that evening when my father summoned me.

'I have arranged your engagement,' he said, as if it was nothing more than a transaction. 'Lord Morton Beauchamp has asked and I have accepted. You are to marry him in October. We will travel to his estate and do it there so he does not have to miss the shoot.'

My head spun. 'I won't. He is old, has had three wives already. He is disgusting! I shan't marry him. I love William.'

Father would not even look at me, not even look up from his papers. 'You will never see that boy again, do you understand? Beauchamp is a better match than you could hope for. You will marry him.'

258

'Father, please!'

He looked then and the rage in his eyes silenced me.

I fled to my room where I wept until my body was empty of tears.

We wrote every day, the notes passed through an ever-judgemental Daisy. Our letters spoke of ways to convince my father, of my impending marriage, of ways we could sneak a meeting, of our families, our dreams, our loves and agonies. I even wrote you a riddle and you wrote one back.

It was another week before I saw you again, giddy with missing you.

That evening my father was absent at a dinner. I snuck out, leaving a note in my room with a few coins to buy Daisy's silence.

I took a cab to the theatre where we'd first met and found you there.

You took me in your arms and I'd never felt so happy and so wretched at the same time. I couldn't recall the last time anyone had embraced me, perhaps not even since my mother died, and you immediately felt like home.

We moved into the shadows between the buildings where we could not be seen.

'You came,' you said, breathless. Your hands found my face. I pressed my cheek to your palm and let my tears fall.

'What will we do? Father is intent on the marriage to that awful man. He would not be moved.'

'Do you wish to marry him?'

'Of course not,' I cried. 'I wish to marry you. Have my letters not made that plain?'

You pressed your forehead to mine. 'We could elope. Once married, they cannot deny us.'

I pulled back from you. The shock of the suggestion. The scandal. 'Elope?'

'Gretna Green. Scotland. We can go in a matter of days. We could even go now.'

'Now? Tonight?'

'Why not?'

'You are mad. If my father found out, he would have you thrown in gaol, or worse.'

That tempered your excitement, for we both knew it was true. We stood for a moment, in each other's arms and the idea came to me.

'My father is away to France a week from now. We could go then. It will be days before he discovers we're gone.'

Your smile grew and mine with it. 'Yes. A week.'

'A week,' I said and felt my body tremble.

You kissed me then. Do you remember? Our first true kiss. I was so in love with you, my knave. I still am, despite all that came after.

When I returned home, Daisy was fretting in my room. She gave me back the money and said she could not condone my behaviour. I feel bad for it now, but I threatened her dismissal and no reference and she soon put aside her judgement.

The week turned. Father left on his trip and I packed a bag. Again, I threatened Daisy with dismissal should she tell a soul and she agreed to keep her tongue. To the staff, I was visiting an aunt in Yorkshire for several days. Only Daisy knew that was not true, though she did not know the extent of it. I did not know if her silence would last, but that day nothing else mattered but getting to you.

We had written to one another with the arrangements under a code of acrostic puzzles. Father and the housekeeper checked my letters and this looked like nothing but a mailing from a magazine.

The place we were to meet was a riddle, the time a number square to be solved. And so I did. We met at Euston station where we took *train after train, over two days, to Newcastle. Then another rail line to Carlisle and from there, a carriage to Gretna Green.*

You were a gentleman the whole way. We laughed almost constantly, talked of what our life would be together, of what our marriage would mean. It would never be accepted by my family, nor by society if my father had anything to do with it. But those were worries for another day.

We reached Gretna and stayed in an inn. We were married the next morning at the anvil, the blacksmith gave the blessing and the innkeeper's wife, so used to such a spectacle, threw dried flower petals over us. Our rings were plain gold bands, for we needed no jewels to show our love. That ring hangs around my neck, hidden next to my heart as you are.

I almost hate to remember it now, such a happy day tarnished by what came after. But I will try, for both our sakes.

That night, lawfully man and wife, blessed in the eyes of God, you took me to your bed.

You remember it, don't you? I do not need to recount it, that I may save my blushes and those of my witnesses.

The morning after, we made our decisions. We would travel to the Americas but we had to first find enough money to buy passage and enough to start a home when we arrived. You had some saved from your allowance, but it was not enough. We needed time. Which meant

I sat back in shock. They had been married, which meant the child she carried was conceived in wedlock. A legitimate heir, should it survive her father's attack. I lowered the pages and was still for a moment, holding that thought in my mind. Did the baby live? The girl did, at least long enough to write and deliver this confession. If her child was a boy, he would inherit the fortune the girl's father wanted kept from her.

A thought occurred. If the baby survived, it could still be alive. I could find them, give this to them, this story of their parents, proof perhaps of an inheritance they may not know about.

I shook my head and garnered a strange look from a fellow passenger.

Reuniting this story with the child was a romantic notion but surely not one based in reality. Yet the idea stuck and felt right, inevitable almost. I just had to find the last two books. The sixth book must hold the fate of the child, for good or ill. I almost didn't want to know, for I was sure it would break my heart, as a similar story had once before.

30.

I dreaded what awaited me in Oxford. So much so I dawdled at the station and took a long route towards the Radcliffe. I was in no rush to hear my father was worse and every step I took closer to the hospital convinced me of that outcome.

I sat by my father's bedside, holding his hand, while a nurse busied herself around me. His cheeks were sunken and grey, with dark rings around his eyes. He didn't look like my father anymore but a copy made of clay. I felt if I put my finger on his cheek, it would sink and never spring back.

The nurse finished her duties and, when she was gone, a doctor came in in his white coat.

'Good news and bad news, I'm afraid,' he said in such a nonchalant tone I wanted to rise and slap him.

'Tell me the good.'

'He retains some function. His pupils contract and nurses have reported him blinking. He is also breathing steadily on his own. All of these are good signs.'

I did not take my eyes from my father. 'And the bad?'

The doctor sighed. 'We believe he has suffered from apoplexy and given he is unable to eat or drink, we fear he will deteriorate quickly.'

My heart shrank inside me. I could not conceive of a world without my father. I would not.

'Is there nothing you can do?' I felt the tears forming, pressing painfully against my eyes.

The doctor was silent and I wondered for a moment if he had left. I turned and looked up at him. 'Is there nothing?'

'There is something we can try. It is not without risk.'

'Go on.'

'There is pressure on his brain and we need to relieve it. We must drill a hole in his skull and allow the brain room.'

Horror filled me. 'Trepanning? That's barbaric.'

The doctor's face took on a sympathetic mask which I, in my state of despair, saw as condescension. 'It is a well-used modern medical procedure. There is a risk of infection, as with any surgery, and some risk of decreased brain function but three-quarters or more of patients survive and recover.'

I sat with that for a moment, watching my father. His eyes moved beneath their lids like he was simply dreaming and one shake could wake him. But it wouldn't. Perhaps never would again.

'He will die without this?'

The doctor said nothing, only gave a slight nod.

'And he could wake up if it works?'

'It's possible.'

He had to live. It was all I could think of. 'Do it then.'

The doctor nodded. 'We'll prepare him for surgery in the morning.'

Then he left and I was finally alone with my father. I raised his hand to my face and held his palm against my cheek.

His skin was cool but soft. His hands smelled of old paper and I breathed him in.

'I hope I'm doing the right thing,' I said quietly to him.

I imagined him opening his eyes a dozen times. Every second I thought he would, every time I glanced away I imagined turning back to find him watching me. But he was still. Sleeping so deeply nothing could wake him.

'You can't go yet,' I said at his ear. 'I still need you.'

A nurse touched my shoulder and said in a soft voice, 'Visiting time is up, my dear.'

I blinked back tears and nodded.

She had a kind face and saw my grief writ deep on mine. 'We'll take care of him,' she said.

All I could manage was a choked 'thank you'.

I kissed my father's forehead, something I had never done before, and left.

Sharp winter rain pelted down upon me as I stood, numb and dazed, outside the hospital. I did not know which way to turn. Frigid water soaked into my shoes, biting my skin, forcing me to walk. I found my way home and when I entered, I was met with a profound and terrible silence. The bookshop was dark and chilled, no lights shone in the office or upstairs. The books were dead things on the walls not the warm circling embrace they had been. I lingered at my father's bedroom door as if listening for him.

In my own room, I lit a lamp, took off my wet clothes, and lay in bed. Sleep would not come. The house was too quiet. Too empty. Every second I spent lying there my heart tensed further and further until I had to move.

I took the pages and the *Orpheus* from my satchel and laid

them on my desk. The story was almost complete yet I feared there was much more to the tale of the young lovers than what was written here.

But the thought of it, of the next book, of the bowler-hat man, of the darkness encroaching upon me, so overwhelmed me I could not breathe.

I rushed downstairs in my nightdress, a candle in hand, and in my father's office found a half-full bottle of whisky. I slumped down on his chair and in the dim candlelit gloom, began to drink. I did not stop until the bottle was empty and the spiked thoughts in my brain quietened.

It was only then, in a stupor, that I was able to sleep.

*

When I woke it was to commotion downstairs. The clock read past eleven and as soon as I moved, a dizzying pain flared in my head. The room swam and I with it, and below the commotion grew louder.

I staggered from my bed and, upright, blood rushing the way it should, the world righted itself. I blinked away white spots in my vision and pulled on a dressing gown, tied it at the waist and made my way downstairs.

Immediately, I saw Harry at the door. But inside, in the hallway, his arms planted firmly on either side of the doorframe. Beyond him, were two men in brown tweed.

'What's going on?' I asked and Harry turned.

One of the men tried to push in but Harry held firm.

'These men are trying to steal from you,' Harry called over his shoulder.

'Are you Delaney?' one of the men, the taller and older, said in a gruff, impatient voice.

'Are you a mannerless thug?' I shot back and his friend paused his pushing.

The taller huffed and the smaller backed away a step. Harry relaxed his shoulders for a moment but did not lower his arms.

'Are you Miss Delaney?' the taller asked in a more civilised tone. He had a town accent. Harsh about the edges.

'I am.'

He stood straighter. 'We're representatives of London and County Bank.' Something heavy sank into my gut. When I didn't immediately respond, he carried on. 'We're here to collect on a debt, Miss Delaney. We require immediate payment or we're to take assets to the same value.'

'Let them in, Harry,' I said as an idea seized me. I looked at the tall one. 'There are books in here worth twice my father's debt and more. See if you can find them.'

I spoke with more disdain than I should have, for the taller man's cracked, leathery face broke into a sneer. The smaller just looked up at his companion, possibly his boss, and waited for his nod to enter.

Inside, the men filled the small shop with their unwelcome presence, as if the very walls were rejecting them. Harry stuck close to me and I leaned, arms folded, against a shelf. The two bailiffs wandered, lost, pulling out books, looking to me as if I'd give them the clues to rob me, then put the books back.

'Look, miss, we're just doing our job,' the taller said as the smaller touched every spine he passed.

'Your job is abhorrent,' I replied.

'Maybe. But it keeps my children fed. So if you could oblige us with some assistance, we'll be on our way. Or we get a cart, take every book in this place to get valued and if it doesn't cover the debt, the bank will take the building.'

I tried not to show my fear at that outcome. I already had so little, I could not lose my home as well. 'Fine.'

'Lily . . .' Harry said in a whisper, 'you can't.'

I put my hand on his. 'I must.'

I went to the office and the bailiffs followed a step behind. This was where the valuable books were but not all were worth as much as I was about to tell them.

I pulled several from the shelves and handed them one by one to the bailiff. 'Lord Byron, worth around two hundred pounds, Shakespeare first folio, five hundred.' It wasn't a first folio of course, but I chanced my arm anyway and neither questioned it. 'First-edition Milton, six hundred. Are you writing this down? Bunyan, Bacon, and Cervantes.' I dumped a trio of fine and beautiful but not all that valuable editions on their pile, and moved to the other side of the room. 'Two Defoes – *Robinson Crusoe* and *Moll Flanders* – a matching pair, three hundred and fifty together. A first-edition Voltaire, another five hundred. And here, *Gulliver's Travels*, for your kids.' I all but threw the final volume at him. 'Is that enough?'

The smaller one, who had been keeping a tally, looked up at his boss and nodded.

The taller sniffed, straightened. 'We appreciate your cooperation.'

'Good. Now leave,' I said.

The sneer returned and I saw violence in this man who, had I not allowed him in, would no doubt have knocked down Harry and taken anything he liked.

At the front door, the taller man turned to me, while his associate struggled with the books.

'These will be valued by a bank-appointed official and taken to an auction. Should they raise sufficient funds, the matter will be closed. Should they be found lacking, we'll be back for the keys.'

'And if they raise more than the debt?'

'Then we get a bonus,' he said with a little too much glee.

I closed the door on his sneering face and let the air out of my lungs. Harry waited by the office and I folded myself into his arms. He smelled so clean, of sweet soap and lilac, a scent favoured by his mother. His shirt was soft against my cheek and I felt him kiss my head.

'You didn't have to give them so much,' he said, into my hair.

'My father built up a substantial debt.'

I should have given them more. I'd chosen substandard and mass-produced editions worth perhaps a third of the overall debt. I couldn't bring myself to tell Harry. It would come back to bite me, I knew, but not today. I did not know how I was going to escape this debt and, like my father, I was making it a problem for another day.

I pushed away from Harry. 'Why are you here?' He looked a little stung by my bluntness so I smiled. 'I mean, well, I don't often wake up late to find you downstairs barricading my door.'

He gave a small laugh. 'I wanted to see if you were back. I've been looking in on your dad but they wouldn't tell me much.'

My smile faded. 'He needs surgery. On his skull.'

'Christ. I'm sorry, Lily. He'll get through it though, I'm sure.'

'Let's talk of happier things. And eat – I'm starving.'

Harry made some tea and found some bread and jam in the pantry. We ate upstairs in the small sitting room.

'How was Manchester?' he asked, through a mouthful of bread.

'Useful.'

'Will you tell me now? About those pages you had me hide?'

'It's complicated. I don't want to put you in danger.'

He set down the bread and took my hand. 'Remember the canal? The Christchurch porter? If you're in danger, I'm in danger.'

I knew he meant it too. 'You remember I told you about the letter I found in a burned book. And a man who attacked me.' He nodded. 'That was only the beginning.' I told him everything, about the books, the pages within, the reasons I had to act as I did, to leave Mr Caxton and my father, and he listened to it all, holding my hand. 'So you see I have to find the books, else this man will come back and I don't know what he'll do. He already scared my father half to death, I won't have him come near you.'

Harry was quiet for a moment and I could see the knit in his brow that told me he wasn't sure if he should say something.

'What is it?' I asked.

'This man. He wears a brown bowler right? About yay tall, dark hair?'

A knot formed in my stomach. 'Yes.'

'He's been following me. For a few days now.'

All the fight went out of me. I put my head in my hands. 'Don't go near him; he's dangerous. I'm sorry, Harry, so sorry.'

Then Harry was off his chair, on his knees before me, pulling my hands from my face. 'This isn't your fault.'

'It is. If I'd just let it go, given them what they wanted, this would never have happened.'

'You don't know that. Besides, you're Lilian Delaney, you don't give up, never have.'

'I did once,' I said quietly and held his hand tighter.

Harry sighed and wrapped his arms around me. The past was still raw for us both, despite the years separating who I was then, and what I did. Maybe I was still that selfish person. Still putting my own desires and needs above all others, even those I loved the most.

'A letter came for you,' Harry said, lightening the moment.

'A letter?'

He nodded, stood up. 'Before those men came, there were a few letters.' He went downstairs, I guessed to the office, and returned a few minutes later with three envelopes.

Two were addressed to my father, which I set aside, but the last was for me. I didn't know the handwriting and there was no return address.

I opened it and took out the single sheet.

Dear Miss Delaney,

After your visit to the Looker-On, *I asked about for your missing man, William Heathfield. Nobody knows of him or his family. An acquaintance of my mother's, an elderly man who used to write for the Gazette, remembers a scandal at the time involving*

271

a young gentleman and the daughter of a lord, which ended in a duel. It appears she was also removed from the archives and he does not recall her name. I'm sorry I could not be of more help.

Yours,
Evelyn

My excitement at the first line had turned to despair by the last. Evelyn could tell me nothing I did not already know. A dark weight settled on me. I had no leads to the last two books, no idea who the confession within belonged to, a career in tatters, men who would return soon to take my home and a father a step away from death.

My thoughts turned to him. He would be in surgery. Perhaps already out. Perhaps already dead. 'I need to go to the Radcliffe.'

'I'll go with you.'

At first I wanted to stop him but then, if it was bad news, if my father had not survived, I didn't want to be alone. 'Thank you.'

I dressed while Harry tidied away the empty plates and tea, and then we were away.

*

'The surgery went as well as can be expected,' said the doctor as I stood by my father's bedside. 'But we'll not know for sure until he wakes up.'

'When will that be?'

272

The doctor pursed his lips and did not answer. 'We've got him on fluids so we're hopeful.'

They'd put a needle in his arm. From it, a rubber tube led to a glass bottle of clear liquid. 'Is that safe?' I asked.

'Oh yes, very safe and effective,' the doctor said and I wasn't sure I believed him.

My father looked even smaller now, his head wrapped in thick white bandages, a tube running out of him. His body still but for his breathing.

The doctor left and Harry put his hand on my shoulder. 'He'll be okay.'

'Hello there,' came a familiar voice from behind.

I turned to see Mr Caxton and my heart all but broke. 'You're late,' I tried to joke but instead the tears came fast.

Mr Caxton came close, put his hand on my cheek and wiped a tear. He saw the state of my father, shared a sad look with Harry, then looked back to me. 'Oh, my dear. I am sorry.'

I held his hand to my cheek. 'It's all going so wrong.'

'Life has that way about it.'

'I don't know what to do. The debt, the books, everything – it's too much.'

People in the ward were staring, pity in their looks, but I didn't care. I was breaking and once the cracks had started to open, I could not bring them back together.

'I know, dear. But you will endure. You must, for his sake. He will need you at your strongest, for he will be at his weakest.'

Mr Caxton tipped my head up to look at him. His eyes glistened behind those round glasses. It had only been a few days but I did not realise how much I had missed him.

'These things have a way of working themselves out,' he said in a kind voice.

I wanted to believe him, desperately, but I simply could not. Too much was happening, had happened, would need to happen before my life could return to something approaching normal or safe. How I wished I'd never been asked to Dr Ashburn's house, never seen that burned book, nor taken it home. How I wished so many things of the last few weeks had not happened. Though if they had not . . . I looked up at Harry and gripped his hand . . . we would never have come back together.

'Now, Lilian,' said Mr Caxton in a brisk tone. 'I don't mean this cruelly but you look awful. Terrible, in fact. Your eyes are puffy and your hair dishevelled and I smell a certain favourite liquor upon your breath.' He paused and I reddened. 'Go home, wash, rest. I will look over your father, for he is my good friend after all and I've brought him a volume of Tennyson to read.'

I couldn't possibly leave him. What if he woke? What if he didn't? But when I went to object, Mr Caxton raised a hand.

'I will send word should anything change.'

'He's right, Lily,' Harry said gently.

I could see this battle was one I would not win against them both. 'You think I look terrible too?'

Harry's eyes widened in horror at offending me and I wondered if that's how I looked to Mr Caxton when he played his tricks. I couldn't help but smile.

'All right,' I said. I brought my father's hand to my face, kissed his thin, papery skin, and held tight. 'I have to go, Father, but I'll be back later.'

My father only lay there, unmoving as he had now for days.

I set his hand back and adjusted his blanket and fussed about until Harry took me by the shoulders and guided me away.

I glanced back as Mr Caxton took my seat beside my father and patted his hand. Mr Caxton opened the volume of poetry and began to read. My father loved Tennyson and his short, sharp lyrics, and if anything could coax him back from the darkness, it was the rhythmic chant of 'half a league, half a league, half a league onward'.

Harry and I left the hospital and wandered, aimlessly through the city for a time. The sun was bright but low, its beams cutting between the spires and towers of the colleges. We found our way to a café and a much-needed coffee, for the excess of whisky still swirling around my blood and lack of food barring two bites of bread, was beginning to make me sick.

We ate, though I don't recall what, and drank hot, bitter coffee, strong enough to wake a sailor the morning after shore leave. Harry talked of his new job at the university press, how nervous he was to start on Monday. He spoke of his mother working too hard and his sister in Kent, married to a factory foreman. I tried to listen but my thoughts were elsewhere.

Harry paid and walked me back to the bookshop. The mid-afternoon bustle of Oxford was strong and a crowd had formed at the base of Carfax tower. A speaker stood on a box, waving a pamphlet and talking of social reforms. Carriages rattled along Cornmarket Street and wide, white awnings flapped in the breeze. The Saxon tower loomed at the far end, so ancient and out of place against the more modern buildings surrounding it. Harry and I jostled for space on the pavement, for the sun had brought out the scholars and residents alike and all were making the most of it.

I walked through my city in a daze, every step a chore. I wanted to be home, behind walls, away from crowds and finally, after what felt like an age of struggling through a tide of people, we made it. The bookshop was as we had left it.

Harry made to enter with me but I put my hand on his chest. 'I think I need to be by myself for a while.'

His handsome face crinkled with concern. 'Are you sure? I'm worried about you being alone.'

'I'll be fine. It's been . . . a lot and I need time to work it all out. You understand?'

He nodded. 'I'll come check on you in a few hours.'

I felt suddenly constrained by his worry. 'Please, let me be for tonight. I'll call on you tomorrow.'

He tried to push, could see he was about to make another argument for my safety and frankly I was sick of worrying over my safety. He opened his mouth to speak.

'Please, Harry. I need you to go.'

He sighed. 'All right. But if you need me . . .'

'I know where you'll be.' I leaned forward and kissed his cheek and with a final, 'See you tomorrow,' he left.

I shut the door against the world and for a blissful moment, all was quiet, still, and safe.

I needed to gain some control over my situation, though what that might be, I wasn't sure. I began with the most pressing: my father's debt. I made myself comfortable in his office, a nip of gin at hand – for we had nothing better – and searched out every letter and demand from the various banks.

It was a few hours later, as the light waned, that I heard

the bell ring and realised I'd forgotten to lock the front door. I put the papers in a drawer and left the office, locking it behind me.

'May I help you find something?' I said as I was rounding the corner into the main shop.

'I hope so,' said a cold voice that stopped me in my tracks. The smell of tobacco wafted to me, that harsh, muddy smell I had grown to hate.

The man in the bowler hat lingered at a shelf, tapping his finger on the wood. 'It's much tidier than when I saw it last.'

'You mean when you attacked my father.'

He waved his finger like a metronome, tutting with every swing. 'Now, now, let's not cast aspersions on my good character.'

'Get out,' I said, my anger overtaking my sense.

His smug smile dropped. 'That's no way to treat a customer and by the look of things, you could use all the custom you can get.'

My teeth hurt from clenching them. I wanted to rush at him, rip his eyes out, scream until his eardrums burst.

'You said two weeks,' I said. 'It's been days. What do you want?'

'My employer has decided to alter your deadline.'

My anger gave way to shock and fear. 'What do you mean?'

He slowly slid the knife from his pocket and unfolded the blade. He pressed the tip into the pad of his finger. 'My employer is impatient and wants their goods sooner. One week. And oh, you've had half that time already so consider this a progress review.'

I backed away a step. 'You can't . . .'

He shot me a vicious look. 'I can. I have. Where are the books?'

I had to tell myself the books didn't matter. It was the pages, which were safe and hidden, though not well currently. 'I have one.'

The man took a sauntering step towards me, the knife to his lips. 'One.'

'It's only been a few days,' I said again.

'Give it to me.'

I went to my satchel by the office door and took hold of the *Orpheus*, spying with a bolt of fear, the pages peeking out from the slit in the silk lining. With a movement I hoped he didn't see, I pulled out the book while pushing the pages back inside. When I turned around, he was staring at my back, wolf eyes intent, knife glinting in the light.

He snatched it from me, checked the author's name and title. Finally a smile grew and he tucked it under his arm.

'There are three books missing, Miss Delaney.'

'I don't know where they are.'

In one swift movement, the man grabbed the book and whipped it across my face. The impact knocked me to my hands and knees. Warm, throbbing pain filled my cheek, turning sharp and jagged. Bright spots danced in my vision and I tasted the awful metallic tang of blood.

'Where are the books?' He stood over me, wiping my blood from the book cover with a pristine handkerchief.

My hand went to my cheek, already swelling. 'I don't . . .' I could barely speak through the pain. I worked my jaw and it gave a terrible clicking sound.

'You don't what, Miss Delaney? I'm sure you can't be about

to tell me you don't know. I'm sure you can't be about to tell me that your trips to Manchester and Birmingham were worthless?'

I closed my eyes and tried to breathe. He was watching me, or had others watch me. But Harry had said he was following him the last few days, maybe he had only seen which trains I'd boarded.

'You seem to know so much. Why can't you find the books yourself?' I asked, sitting back onto my heels.

He spread his hands, book in one, knife in the other. 'Unfortunately, my skills lie elsewhere.' He squatted before me and brought the knife to that same spot on my chin. I strained to get away from that blade, but he grabbed the back of my head and forced me close. His hot breath stung my cheek.

'I'll ask nicely one more time,' he said. 'Where are the other books?'

When I didn't answer immediately, he tightened his grip in my hair. The pain lanced through my skull as he ripped strand after strand from my scalp. At the same time, he pressed the knife harder. I knew he would kill me, kill Harry too for good measure, find some other poor soul to seek out the rest of the books. My father, should he live, would be alone.

'Ambrose Fane,' I blurted out. 'He has one. I couldn't get it from him.'

The pressure from the blade eased and his grip in my hair relaxed. 'There. That wasn't so hard, was it?'

He threw me backwards as he let go and my elbow cracked against the floorboard. I bit back a cry and added the new pain to the list.

'What of the others?' he asked.

Anger flared. *'It's only been a few days.* Give me a chance. I'll find the damned books.'

He smiled and I hated him. 'Good girl.'

He put the book under his arm and, as he walked out of the shop, began to whistle.

At the door he called back, 'I'll see you soon.' Then he was gone and the door swung closed with the soft sound of the bell.

The pain all but overwhelmed me. I wrapped my arms around my body and let out the terror of the last few minutes in great, heaving sobs. My eyes, my face, my head, were all swollen and tender. I ventured to touch my scalp and it stung, as if terribly sunburnt. I felt like one large bruise, both outside and in.

I stood up slowly but bright spots covered my vision and I swayed, caught myself against a shelf. A sick taste rose in my mouth and when I tried to swallow it down, it came back fiercely and urgently. I rushed to the kitchen, to the sink, and emptied my stomach against the porcelain. Blood-tinged bile splattered the white and slunk down the plughole. My chest shook, my stomach clenched and hardened. I felt around in my mouth and found a gash on the inside of my cheek. Hot blood oozed onto my tongue and my stomach heaved again.

I found a glass and filled it, sipped gently, swilling away the sour, metal taste.

I stayed beside the sink for what felt like hours, sitting on the floor, my head pressed against it. I clutched the glass to my chest, taking tiny sips, waiting for the nausea to pass and my stomach to relax. I had felt this low before but only once. The day I lost Harry, the day I told him what I'd done. At the hint of the memory, tears came.

I closed my eyes and saw that day again. Seven years had passed and yet I could see every detail, remembered every step I took, every scent in the air. I was eighteen and headstrong, had it in my mind I would work with books but not as a seller like my father.

Harry and I had been sweethearts for half a year and friends since childhood. The memory of that first shift from platonic love to romantic made me ache for those simpler times. A shared look in the sunshine, lying in the wildflowers of Port Meadow. Anything feels possible in the summer, especially falling in love. The kiss that followed so perfect and true and right it was as if written in a novel.

The months after were joyous, a summer love that only grew as the seasons changed. The cold weather, the snow and darkness of winter, did nothing to cool us. He was the calm centre of my storm but I broke us. I had begun working at the university press and saw before me a glittering career in bookbinding. One where I could escape my father but didn't have to go far. Where I could build a reputation for myself and learn skills I could lean on for life. We laughed, kissed, loved, felt like the city was ours for the taking, such is the arrogance of youth.

We did not wait for marriage, as young, hungry new adults outside the stuffy upper classes rarely do, and it was nearly two months before I realised my condition. Harry was thrilled. He spun me around and talked of marriage. He yearned for a family, for many mouths, fat and wanting like a nest of baby birds. He made plans for a wedding, for a house, for how I was to look after myself now I was more than just me. I was now a vessel, a host for a growing thing.

But I want a career, I'd said.

You'll have the most important career of them all. You'll be a mother, he'd said, grinning, as if that was all any women should want.

But I didn't want it. I didn't want any of it. For weeks I lay awake in panic. Weeks feeling this creature grow within me that I felt nothing for. Sickness swirled about in my guts and every day I was ill. Every day was a step closer to a life I didn't want and could not escape from.

Yet . . . There was a way. A terrible way. But I could see no other. My life stretched out before me in a great line, the career, the freedom, the excitement of it, but that line then veered into childrearing, homemaking, a husband I wasn't ready for, my choices taken from me. I couldn't bear that. As much as I loved Harry, and I truly did, I could not lose myself for him.

I found a woman. A tidy house on the Iffley Road. She told me it would hurt. She told me I may never bear children. She asked if I was sure and I was. A swift, excruciating procedure. I cried every second and the woman hugged me at the end. Told me my decision was right for me.

I was pale and sick and would not leave my bed for days. Harry feared the worst and called his mother to my bedside. She took a look at me and knew the baby was gone. Saw too, I believed, the guilt in my eyes.

Harry was devastated. But he rallied quickly, for it was not his body nor his mind, and we could marry and try again. And again and again, until we had our family. Until the plans he'd made and the ideas he'd had came true.

No, I'd said. *I can't. I don't want that.*

You don't want what?

A child. I don't want a child. I don't want marriage or the life my mother had.

But, Lily, it's just the grief talking, a few weeks and you'll feel different.

I won't. I don't want a child. I never did. I may never. That's why . . .

And then he knew. By my face. My shame, my sorrow, my pain.

I'm sorry, Harry, I said but his heart was broken.

We fought for hours. Flung cruel insults at each other and tore open every wound, every tiny mistake, and irritation became a mountain we could not climb. He left past midnight and we didn't speak for weeks. Hearts torn asunder. A future changed and uncertain. A love dead too soon.

But I did not regret it. I refused to regret it. I made the right choice for me and would make it again.

31.

My father did not wake the day after his surgery, nor the day after that. The doctor said to be prepared; the nurses looked on me with pity. I sat beside him the hours I was allowed but more and more my grip on him slipped. He didn't look like my father anymore. His bandages changed his face; the bed shrank his body. He was cool to touch and the scent of paper and book dust had left him in favour of carbolic acid and sickness. It had been almost a week since he last ate and the fluids they pumped into his veins were not having much of an effect as far as I could tell.

I'd stopped asking for news. Stopped asking when he would wake because the doctor would only give a pitying smile and say they were doing everything they could.

I was helpless, and useless, and when I wasn't in the hospital, I was in my bed, for I saw little reason to leave it.

Harry brought me food and tried to coax me outside but I refused. He didn't stop trying but his efforts lessened and he took to just being beside me until I asked him to go.

I had bought myself some time with the bank but the man in the bowler would return soon and I didn't think he would accept I did not have the books. But I had no way to find them. No clues. No ideas. The only avenue open to me was the binder, Felix Fidelius Gauch, and a vague notion he had a bindery in London. But that man was no doubt long dead and binderies could open and close as easy as curtains.

My wallowing lasted through the night, when I barely slept, until the morning brought with it a new problem. The first post delivered a letter from Mr Caxton. I was hurt he would not come here himself to tell me whatever he needed to but I had resigned and he owed me nothing.

Dear Lilian,

I received the enclosed letter from Mr Ambrose Fane yesterday morning. He included a cover note to say he wished to engage you for a binding and the instructions were in his letter. As you know he is an unsavoury chap with a scandalous reputation but given you are no longer my apprentice and now captain of your own ship, I thought it the right thing to do to pass it on. He is in Oxford and wishes to meet.

I hope you are well under the circumstances. I will call in on your father this evening.

John Caxton

The note, still sealed, with Mr Caxton's letter read:

Lilian, you strange and intriguing creature. I have found you at last. Come to the Randolph Hotel for tea at one on Monday. We have much to discuss.

My heart beat wildly. Fane knew, he must, that I did something to his book. Had I put it back in the wrong place? Had he noticed the open endpaper? He had more money than scruples I was sure and would not be afraid to wield either.

I could not go, of course, but then I was certain he would find me either way and perhaps with less patience after I stood him up. If he found Mr Caxton, no doubt he found the book-shop too, for it bore my name.

I had to go. Maybe he would be reasonable, for there did seem to be a streak of kindness there, behind the debauchery.

I checked the clock. A few minutes past ten. I had time to prepare.

I looked in the mirror and did not recognise myself. My face was not mine, still puffed, eyes sunken with dark bags beneath them but that was far from the worst. The bruise on my face had bloomed black and purple, stretching across my right cheek and down to my jaw. It was as if I'd been attacked with ink and nothing I could do would wash it off. My hair was loose and ragged, unbrushed for days and thrown into a steadily messier bun for the hospital visits. I had avoided looking, for I knew a sight like this would greet me, but I knew if I was to set foot inside the Randolph, the haunt of the Oxford rich, I needed to sort myself out.

I bathed, brushed the knots from my hair and worked several layers of powder onto my face until I looked someway closer to my former self. Yet I felt anything but. I was hollowed out, with a constant gnawing in my gut that I feared would never leave me. I dressed in the best I had: a green skirt and jacket that buttoned a little too tight at my neck. I did my hair in a tall, neat chignon with some curls loose at the front to hide the still-livid cut on my forehead and distract from the powder, then checked myself in the mirror. It would have to do, for I had no better.

By the time I had righted myself, at least on the outside, it was close to one and I made my way to the Randolph. The Gothic-styled hotel stood proudly at the head of St Giles, across from the Martyrs' Memorial, and facing the neoclassical jewel of Oxford, the Ashmolean Museum. The Randolph was the grandest hotel in the city, so they say. It was an imposing building of golden stone and dozens of arched windows. Black iron balcony rails ran the width of two sides affixed with the hotel's name in tall white letters. Carriages waited outside, others dropped off, others picked up. People in fine dress milled about. The sounds of high tea floated through the open lower windows.

I felt distinctly out of place, which was confirmed as I approached. The doorman was dressed far better than I and looked over me with ill-concealed disdain. I did not have the energy to be offended. This was Oxford after all and the separation of town and gown was stark in every aspect. The young man took half a step in front of me as I made for the door.

'May I help you, madam?'

I sighed through my nose. 'I'm here to meet someone.'

He looked at me again, head to toe, not even trying to hide his appraisal. A moment passed and he must have decided it was not worth a guest's potential ire if he refused me. He opened the door and I thought he would let it hit me on the way in – it would be just my luck after all – but he did not.

Inside, the reception desk sat beyond a blue-painted arch,

and rising behind it, a staircase led up to the rooms. Heraldic banners hung on the papered walls, showing off red eagles and rearing lions, all manner of creature and colour. A man – slight and handsome in a pretty, elfin way – I took to be about my age stood behind the desk in a prim, neat uniform. The collar looked so tight I worried the poor man couldn't breathe.

'Welcome to the Randolph Hotel,' he said as I neared, unsure exactly where I was going. 'How may I help you today?'

'I am meeting a friend, Mr Ambrose Fane, but I am not sure where.'

His eyes brightened at the name. 'Of course. Mr Fane told me to expect a guest. He is in the lounge. Follow me.'

The man's back remained perfectly straight, his arms stiffly at his sides, as he walked me to the lounge.

At the entrance, he bowed slightly and indicated to the left side of the room. I saw Fane immediately. The receptionist left me and I made my way between tables of well-heeled men and few women, to a table near the window. I noticed a few tables of three – an older man and woman and a young man, always with a mop of brown hair, I guessed students with their parents. The mother always looked worried and the father disappointed, such was the way with students. The room itself was grand yet intimate, with vaulted ceilings and wood panelling, and yet more heraldic banners I took to be the symbols of the colleges.

Ambrose Fane was as out of place as I, yet for different reasons. He lounged as comfortably as he had at his own home, though this time he wore more clothes. A fine black jacket, cut in a different style to the more traditional garb of the other men. His hair was tied back but he made no effort to conceal its volume or length, and his collar was undone. One arm was thrown over the back of the chair and in the other he held a newspaper. He cut quite the figure in the fusty room.

'Hello again, Mr Fane,' I said and he looked up with a smile. Tea for two was already set upon the table.

'Miss Delaney, you are late.' He glanced at the clock on the wall, which read ten past the hour.

I was instantly reminded of Mr Caxton's frequent jibe and something in Fane's tone told me he meant it in as light-hearted a way as Mr Caxton had. I took a seat opposite him as he set down the paper.

Ambrose stared at me, eyes narrowed. 'You're different.'

'Am I?'

He waved his fingers around, indicating my face. 'Darker. Your father?'

'He lives, for now, but needed surgery. He's yet to wake.'

'I am sorry to hear that.'

The polite talk grated on me. 'How did you find me? Why I am here?'

'You're a lady bookbinder in a city of men. It was not hard to track you down.' He leaned closer, elbows on the table. 'What did you take from the book?'

I clenched my jaw. 'I don't know what you're talking about.'

He held my gaze for a moment then sat back, poured tea for us both. 'Well, if you won't tell me yours, I won't tell you mine.'

'You came all this way to play a game?'

He grinned. 'I love games. Can't you tell? Now, I apologise for my exit at our last meeting. It was not my best moment and I hope you can forgive it.'

I sensed a touch of embarrassment in him and the tension I'd carried since receiving his note began to ease. 'I barely recall it.'

'Good. In which case, to business,' he said, squeezing a slice of lemon into his tea, then licking his fingers. 'You did take something from my book. I found a smear of your blood on the endpaper and discovered it loose. Now, at first I was angry, nay *enraged*, that you would damage my property so, but the rage soon became curiosity. Intrigue. You intrigue me, Lilian, and so I wish to help you.'

'Help me?'

'I have some information you will want and, in exchange, I wish to know what you took and why. The truth of it.'

I stared at the specks of tea leaf in my cup. 'It's not safe.'

His eyebrow rose. 'Safe? Because of this behatted fellow you mentioned before?'

'He's dangerous.'

'Did he give you that stunning bruise you're so deftly hiding behind powder?' He spoke kindly, lowering his voice.

I put my fingertips to my cheek. Even the lightest touch brought pain. 'He almost killed my father.'

'I see. Well, then I feel I must tell you that I had a visit from him.'

I could barely speak for the shock. 'You . . . did he . . .'

Ambrose batted away my concern. 'You needn't worry. Bentham is a champion pugilist. But this man was cordial enough. His name by the by, is Devlin, a fallen gentleman putting his boarding school fencing and boxing lessons to good use. I suppose he quickly realised he could not bully me as he does you. He wanted to buy my book and named a frankly outrageous sum I only laughed at.'

My jaw hung open. 'Did you give it to him?'

'After I saw what you had done, I reasoned the value of the book was already taken from it, so I did give it to him. Does he know, do you think, about whatever secret the books are hiding?'

'I don't know. But now he has four of the six. And I have a week, at most, to find the others.'

He took a long sip of his tea. 'Then you'll be thrilled to hear that I know where one is.'

I almost knocked over my cup at his words. 'You do? Where? Please, Ambrose.'

'As I said, I will tell you in exchange for the secret you have uncovered.'

I regarded him for a moment, this rakish man with a hunger for games and intrigue. A bored man, no doubt, but he did not seem unkind, nor aggressive in his desire.

I let out a long sigh. He knew where one of the final two books was. That was worth sharing for and, beside that, I liked him and was coming to see he may even be trustworthy.

'There are handwritten pages hidden inside the books. The first I found was a letter from a woman to her lover. She called him her knave. The next book I found held five or six pages of . . . well, I don't know what else to call it but a confession. Each of these Bell books, all with fake titles, has hidden pages.'

'And what do the pages say?' He leaned closer, rapt.

'They are a love story between the daughter of a wealthy yet cruel lord and a young, penniless gentleman. They met by chance at a theatre, then again at Henley Regatta. They fell in love. There is mention of her inheritance, how she cannot claim it without a male heir. She is betrothed to an older man she despises. There are hints of a fatal duel, of her imprisonment by her father. The young lovers were married in secret and she fell pregnant, though the fate of the child remains unknown to me. His name is William Heathfield but hers is a mystery. She has an uncle named Silas and a cousin, Julian but without a family name, there is no finding her.'

A wide smile covered Ambrose's face. 'It sounds like a Bell novel. Are you certain it isn't just a fiction?'

'I'm certain.'

He narrowed his eyes. 'How can you be? This all sounds like a fancy concocted by a bored author and their publisher to attract sales.'

'Nobody would be willing to kill for a fancy,' I said coolly, 'and when I searched for William Heathfield in the archives of the *Looker-On*, I found nothing.'

'There you have it,' Ambrose said.

'Nothing because pages were ripped from the archive copies in several different issues. I knew him to be at Henley that year and all the weeks leading up to the event were present, talking excitedly about the regatta and showing the race times, but the actual weekend was removed. So were a few others through the next year. This man was ripped from society's memory and I want to know why. It is not a fiction, Ambrose.'

He ran his finger across his lips in contemplation for several moments before speaking again, and this time it was without the dismissive tone.

'Do you have the pages from all the books found thus far?'

'All but the letter. The bowler – Devlin – attacked me on the street and stole it from my bag.'

'Nasty little man,' he sneered. 'Where are you keeping them?'

I smiled. 'Nice try. But they are safe – that's all I can say.'

He matched my smile. 'Good. Very good.'

Then he sat straight, emptied his teacup in one mouthful and brushed an errant hair from his face.

'Very well, you have told me yours, now it is my turn,' he said and my heart suddenly leapt. 'I do have many questions but perhaps after you find the rest of the books, you will answer them for me. I don't see the harm in sharing this given that if I cannot acquire the book from them, I doubt very much you can. An auctioneer at Sotheby's I once bedded told me of a "lost" Bell they had in their listing a few years ago. It struck him as odd because he expected the book to go for a modest sum, a few pounds at most, but it didn't. Two buyers bid it up into the hundreds. It was a tennis match between them, back and forth until the victor named an astronomical sum and the loser conceded.'

I all but held my breath. 'Who bought it?'

'A collector I'd never heard of. Fahig Peal. A name so strange I could not forget it.' And nor would I.

'What did he look like? Where does he live?'

Fane shook his head. 'The man doing the bidding was an agent of the buyer. Nobody saw Peal and to my knowledge, he has not appeared at any auction since.'

'Who was the agent?'

'A bookseller. Edmund Grieves.'

The name hit me like a train. 'Grieves? Are you sure?'

'I've had dealings with the man in the past. I am sure.'

'Did you know Grieves was tasked with acquiring these Bell books?'

Ambrose raised an eyebrow. 'I did not.'

'He found three. Then something happened to him, some tragic event, and he refused to find any more. He scattered his three to the wind and that is how I came to find the first.'

'I did not know that but I know his tragedy. A few years ago, his lover was killed,' Ambrose said. 'Grieves did not believe it to be an accident.'

That poor man. No wonder he could not look upon the books with anything but hate.

'Devlin,' I said. 'It had to be.'

'Officially it was a break-in turned bad but perhaps you are right.'

'How do you know this?' I asked.

'As I said, Edmund and I have had dealings.'

Dealings enough to share something so personal . . . and Ambrose had said 'lover', not wife nor fiancée or sweetheart. 'His lover was a man?'

Ambrose gave a slight nod. 'They were together for more than a decade. This happened before this auction, you see. I suppose, if it was Devlin and whoever employs him that killed dear Percy, then Edmund would want the books as far away from them as possible.'

'That is why he acted the agent against them? Unless this Fahig Peal is Devlin's employer.'

He shook his head. 'I don't believe so. I wrote to him expressing an interest in his book, saying I had another like it, but he wrote back only to say he was not going to sell. No break-in or strong-arming followed to acquire my volume and so here we are.'

'You wrote to him? You have an address?'

'All conducted through Edmund, I'm afraid.'

I deflated somewhat in my chair. Finished my tea, poured another cup, and wished for something stronger.

I barely saw it but Ambrose indicated something to the waiter and in a few moments, a tray of tiny, exquisite sandwiches was placed on the table. When the waiter had departed, Ambrose checked for onlookers then pulled a silver hip flask from inside his jacket. He dropped a snifter of the spirit into his cup and before he could put it back, I held out my own cup to him.

A devilish smile curled his lip as he poured me a measure.

I drank deeply and felt the warmth of the whisky work its way to my stomach. 'Do you have any notion of who the other bidder was?'

'Afraid not.'

I sat with what I had learned, let it soak into me and hopefully make some sense. It was a solid lead on the next book but it meant going back to Grieves. Seeing Charlie again after I had left him so abruptly. The thought put a stone in my stomach.

'You will wrinkle if you think so hard all the time,' Ambrose said.

'I must go to London, yet I don't have a penny for the train. I must convince a man who hates me to share information and see another who I . . .'

'Who you what, dear?'

I sighed, shame creeping up on me. 'Who I dallied with. Despite my affection for another.'

'Well, well, quite the dark horse, aren't you? I dare say you'd be welcome at one of my soirees.'

I tried to smile. 'I politely decline.'

'You are in quite the predicament, aren't you?'

'That is a kind way of looking at it.'

He ran his finger across his lip again in a movement I now saw was a nervous habit. 'I will give you the train fare.'

'No. Thank you, Ambrose, but no. I won't accept charity.'

He gave an exaggerated frown. 'Charity! Do I seem the charitable type? No, Miss Delaney, I will employ you to deliver this –' he picked up the book of poetry from the table – 'to Edmund Grieves. I will also employ you to discover his titbit of this tale that I may know the truth of it. And lastly, before you decry charity by another name—' He held up his hand as I tried to object. 'When you find it and find the books, I will read these hidden pages. That is my stipulation. I am investing in your delivering to me this doomed romance that I may revel in it. I will be staying in Oxford for several days to ensure you complete your contract.'

My objection faded and a sense of protection came over me. I hadn't shown the pages to anyone, only the letter. It felt invasive, as if this story, which had been mine for so long, would now be shared and picked over and questioned. But without it, I could see no other way of finding the remaining two books.

'You would do that?' I asked.

'Call it a temporary patronage.'

'And that's all you want, to read them? Not to keep them?'

'To read and enjoy. You may do with the paper as you wish.'

But there was something off about all of this. I couldn't contain my confusion, my suspicion. 'Why are you doing this? Why are you here?'

'I can't resist a good story and ever since you walked into

my house unbidden, you have proved to be a good story. I truly don't wish anything of you, Lilian, but to know the ending.'

Perhaps I was naïve, or just desperate, but I believed him. There was sincerity in his eyes, despite his reputation and his unorthodox manner. He drew the eyes of the women in the room, and from the men he drew both curious and disparaging glances. Ambrose was the man he wished to be and had the money and name to ignore the looks and scandalous whispers of those around him. Oh, to be so free, I thought.

'All right,' I said. 'Against my better judgement, I will trust you and accept your patronage. For now.'

'Most wonderful news,' he said and shoved a cucumber sandwich in his mouth.

I felt light and heavy at once. Light that I had a lead and the money to follow it, but heavy in the expectation that brought. I was now answerable to two masters, one seemingly kind and the other outright dangerous. I only hoped my assumptions of the former turned out to be correct.

32.

Ambrose insisted I travel first class, for what other class was there, he said, and gave me enough money to do so. But I travelled third and kept the rest. I didn't know what awaited me and having a purse-full of coins and notes gave me a sense of security I'd been sorely missing.

I'd left a note at the shop for Harry, telling him I needed to go to London. I didn't tell him why. I would explain later and I hoped he would accept it. It felt like I was entering the final stages of this nightmare. I was like a book in the press. I'd been hammered and stitched and now I was to be squeezed until I could be freed and breathe again.

As the train chugged on, my thoughts turned to what might happen after I'd found the remaining books, after I'd learned the fate of William and the poor girl in the pages, after I'd handed over the last to Devlin and his employer. Would they leave me alone, my job complete? Or would they remove me entirely, a loose end and witness to their crimes?

I tried not to think about what was next, only what was in front of me now. That was Edmund Grieves and Charlie. I was both excited and dreading seeing Charlie again. It had only been a few weeks since our tryst but a lifetime had passed. So much had happened, I wondered if he would even recognise me, for I barely recognised myself.

I'd covered the blackening bruise on my cheek with more powder but I was not used to wearing make-up and found myself touching my face without thinking, brushing away the concealing dust until it flaked onto my hands and jacket. When a conductor came around to check for tickets as we neared London, he looked at me with alarm and asked if I was all right. I touched up the powder after that and sat on my hands.

I stared out of the window, at the flat fields rushing by. Frost turned the grass pale green and morning mist settled, like a wool blanket, over the land. The air was crisp, a snap of cold after a balmy day before. As the hours passed, the sun brightened and the mist began to steam away.

The train pulled into Paddington after midday and it was with some trepidation that I made my way to Cecil Court. I had all but run away from Charlie last time and Grieves had not exactly been forthcoming or friendly, so I was not at all sure what welcome I would receive from either. I'd be drawing blood from a stone while fending off a wolf.

Cecil Court was, as it always was, a haven of books and their sellers in the roaring mess of London. I glanced at every doorway and corner, expecting to see the man, Devlin, ready to rob me again. I passed the place he had attacked, where his elbow had crashed into my face, where onlookers had gasped but done nothing, except Charlie. Now I sported another bruise from him and, under the powder, it ached.

Grieves's shop was the same but entirely different now under my eyes. I recalled the naïve girl I had been walking in

there with the burned book and a barrage of questions. I had
been so appalled by Grieves's manner but now I understood it.
The books were cursed. They were dangerous. He was right
to warn me as I would now warn another to steer clear of
those titles. I only wish he had been more forthcoming with
the details.

Resigned to whatever grim reception awaited me, I pushed
open the door. No bell rang and the door swung closed with
a dusty sigh.

I didn't peruse the shelves, nor wait to be asked my business. I went straight for the counter where Charlie stood,
unpacking a delivery. I saw him before he saw me. He held
up the books, checking the spines in a manner that spoke of
failing eyesight.

'You need eyeglasses,' I said and he looked at me. His
handsome face broke into a wide smile.

'Well, look what the cat dragged in.'

'Hi, Charlie.'

'Miss Delaney, what can I do for you? Are you robbing
a library this time?'

I laughed. 'Not today. I'm here to see your employer.'

His smile faltered. 'Mr Grieves is unwell. He's at his home.'

'Oh . . . I'm sorry to hear that.' My plans, and hope of
a tidy resolution, crumbled. 'I don't suppose you will tell me
where he lives?'

Charlie pursed his lips. 'Sorry.'

I had one chance at this, or I had to wait until Grieves
recovered, which could be days. I did not have days.

I took a step closer to Charlie, stood on the opposite side
of the desk to him. 'I'm sorry for how I acted the last time

I saw you. Things have become more complicated than I'd expected.'

He shook his head. 'It's all right, Lilian.'

'It's not. I have not been a good person.' I reached for his hand. 'I am forever grateful to you. Both for helping me with the books, and for, well . . . our shared time.'

His thumb stroked my hand and a tremor went through me. A heat rose and I did all in my power to beat it back down.

'I don't want your gratitude for that,' he said softly.

It was lust only, this rising tide between us. It would grow and crash and disappear as a wave on the ocean. Charlie was a glorious moment, but Harry was the ocean.

'You have it, nonetheless. I don't regret it, know that, but I can't repeat it,' I said.

'I guessed.'

'But I do need to see Grieves. Today. So I must beg your help once more.' He sighed and moved to pull his hand away but I held him. 'I know the friend of his who died was not just a friend but a lover. And I know he did not just die. He was killed. By the same people who tried to kill my father.' My voice cracked at the edges. 'They might still succeed, for he has not woken for days and may never.'

Charlie came around the counter so there was nothing between us. 'I'm so sorry, Lilian.'

'These people . . . they won't stop hurting others until they have what they want. They'll destroy everything and everyone I love for these books and Grieves knows where I can find one. Please, Charlie, I'll do anything.'

He was quiet for a while, leaning against the counter, arms folded across his chest as if he were holding himself together.

'He has a flat around the corner.' Charlie took a scrap of paper and wrote down the address and a quick sketch of a map. 'I didn't give this to you.'

He looked me in the eye and I saw sadness there. I took the paper and my fingers lingered on his a little too long.

'Did it mean something, our night?' he asked.

'It meant more than you know.'

'But not enough.'

I shook my head. 'I'm sorry I can't give you what you deserve.'

He pulled his hand away and crossed his arms once more, but not in anger or impatience, in disappointment.

'You'd better hurry,' he said.

I nodded. 'Thank you.'

I left the bookshop, glancing through the window to see him back behind the counter, squinting at another spine. If he was heartbroken, he hid it well. It was for the best, though again, a part of me wished to run back in there, tell him I'd been wrong and it was him I wanted. Because I did want him. I wanted to let the wave take me where it wanted to go, to lose myself to the rise and swell of him. But it wouldn't last. Couldn't.

Could it?

I forced away the invasive, tangling thoughts. It was all distraction, this back and forth between men, when only one thing truly mattered right now.

I followed the map to St Martin's Lane and then into St Martin's Court. This short alley was bookended by theatres. The Wyndham at one end, and a new theatre still being built at the other. Between the Salisbury pub where I'd met with

Charlie once, and the bright red, newly painted façade of the J. Sheekey Restaurant, was a doorway. I checked the number against the paper. Grieves's flat was number nine in this building, a long block fronted with pale stone.

Inside the small entry was cool and had a taste of damp in the air. I climbed the staircase and began my search for his door. I found it on the second floor, midway along a corridor.

I stood before the dull, old-varnished wood, suddenly afraid of what reception might await me. If he remembered me at all, he would surely not let me in.

After a few deep breaths, I knocked.

'Who is it?' came a shout from within.

I did not answer but instead knocked again. Harder.

'*What is it?*'

I readied myself and knocked again.

Grieves swore and I heard the sound of his footfalls thudding on the boards. In a moment, the door was wrenched open and Grieves appeared, unshaven, glasses at an angle on his face as if shoved on in the dark, a blanket over his shoulders, glaring at me.

'What do you want?' He snarled the words through clenched teeth and then coughed into his arm.

'Mr Grieves,' I began and his deep frown cleared as he recognised me. 'I need to speak with you.'

'You . . . Get away!' He moved to shut the door but I jammed my foot in the way and put my shoulder to the wood.

'Please. It's important.'

He struggled against me, but my desperation gave me strength and I would not let him push me away.

'I know what happened to your friend!'

At that, his grip faltered and he collapsed into a fit of coughing. I took my chance and pushed into the room, closing the door behind me. Grieves scowled at me as he coughed, pulling a handkerchief from his sleeve, pressing it to his mouth.

His home was a few small gloomy rooms. The curtains were closed, not that they let in much light facing the back of a half-finished theatre. The room smelled of sickness and sweat and the source, the man once well kept and steely-eyed, was now a ragged creature. His eyes were red and full of hate and fire and perhaps a little fear. He slumped down in an armchair, the cough slowing, his breathing now a high-pitched wheeze.

I edged my way past him into the small kitchen and found a glass, filled it with water and brought it to him. He glared up at me but after a moment, took the glass and sipped.

'I want . . . you . . . to leave,' he said, as the cough eased and he drew in long, whistling breaths.

'I know. But I can't,' I said, backing away to a wall, shaking my head. 'Not without the information you have.'

He turned away in his chair. 'Come back when I'm well. Or dead.'

My whole body shook. 'By then it'll be too late.'

'I don't care.' Grieves coughed again.

'Please, Mr Grieves. Hear me out, if not for my sake then for the sake of your friend who died for this.'

He whirled around, fury in his eyes. '*How dare you?*' He stood, moved towards me with ill intent.

'I know your friend was not just a friend,' I said quickly and he kept coming. 'He was more than that. And the man, Devlin, the one looking for the books, he killed him because you refused to find more.'

Grieves stopped. His untrimmed moustache twitched at the edges.

'It's happening to me too. That man attacked my father. He hasn't woken for days. He may never, because of these books. *Please*, I am begging you. Help me.'

'I told you . . .' He broke into another wretched cough. 'The books are dangerous. You should have listened.'

The fight seemed to leave him and the illness overwhelmed. He dropped back into his chair.

'I wish I had,' I said.

Grieves reached past the glass of water to a small brown bottle and took a long drink. He winced against the taste. He raised the bottle, gesturing for me to speak, then took another mouthful.

I let myself breathe for a moment before beginning. 'Some time ago you acted as the agent for a buyer in an auction for a Bell book.'

'How did you come by this?'

'It doesn't matter. You won that auction for your client, didn't you?'

He cleared his throat. 'I've won a lot of auctions.'

'But that one was special. The book went for a huge sum, far more than its worth, because of a bidding war between your client and another.'

Grieves shrugged. 'I was glad of it. The commission paid for a new suit.'

His manner was beginning to grate but I did my best to keep my anger beneath the surface. 'Who was your client? Who has the book?'

'If you know all this, then I'm sure you know the client's name.'

'Fahig Peal. I suspect a fake name.'

'You suspect correctly. But do you know why it's fake? What it means?'

I frowned. 'What are you saying?'

'You have all the information you need, Miss Delaney. Now kindly leave.'

'I don't have any information!'

He stood with a groan, the brown bottle still in his hand. 'You have the name, should you care to find it. Books may hide truths but words are great tricksters.'

Words . . . 'You mean . . .' The name rolled around inside my head until the letters split and rearranged, but nothing formed.

'Get out, Miss Delaney, before I call for a constable.'

'But I don't understand.'

'Then I can't help you.'

He took me by the shoulder and pushed me to the door, then out of it into the hall.

'Mr Grieves,' I tried but he had already closed the door. A moment later, I heard the sound of a bolt being drawn.

Heat flooded my cheeks and it took all my will not to take my fists to the door. I clenched them, so hard my knuckles turned white and my palms hurt. This had been useless. I cursed Grieves's hard-headedness, his spite. He knew where at least four of these books had been and yet he had refused to hand them over to Devlin. And then refused to help me.

I stepped outside into the cool air. St Martin's Court was quiet but the world encroached at either end. I didn't know which way to turn, which stream of faceless people to join. Where could I even go?

I forced myself to calm, my fists to open, and replay what little Grieves had said. He said I had the name; I had everything I needed and words were tricksters. What utter dross! I had nothing and he was a cruel little man with no heart. I was no closer to an answer and ever closer to ruin.

33.

I took myself to a café and sat at a table in the back where it was quieter. I seethed at Grieves's manner, at the nothing he gave me, at the hopeless anger I couldn't shake.

'What can I get you, love?'

I looked up into the friendly face of a waitress. She had a slight accent I couldn't place, with ruddy cheeks and a loose mop of white hair. I levelled my voice, lest I snap at her too.

'A coffee please . . .' I spied a cake stand on the counter and realised I hadn't eaten all day. 'And a slice of that. A large slice.'

She winked at me. 'Coming up.'

'Oh,' I said as she was walking away, 'do you have any paper I could use?'

She frowned for a moment then said, 'I'll see what I can find.'

I drummed my fingers on the table while I waited and although it was only a few minutes, it felt like an age. The coffee pot arrived with a wisp of steam escaping the spout, alongside a thick slice of almond cake. The waitress handed me a sheet of baking parchment.

'All we got,' she said.

'Thank you, this is perfect.'

I took a large, unladylike bite of the cake and felt the sugar hit me, lift my body and spirits, and beyond it, the deep, heady taste of an almond liqueur. In three bites the cake was gone and I got to work.

Grieves had said words were tricksters and all I needed was the name.

At the head of the paper, I wrote in large letters FAHIG PEAL.

Then I began to jumble the letters.

half paige
felipa hag
fail phage
al half peg
heap if lag

And a dozen more nonsense phrases. I threw the pencil down. Nothing. I angrily drank my coffee, lukewarm now and bitter. What did this name mean? This stupid, fake name!

'Is it a puzzle?'

The waitress stood beside me. I hadn't even noticed her approach. She nodded to the paper.

'Yes. I suppose it is. It's a name that means something else but I can't figure it out.'

She bent slightly to look closer. 'Do you have any clues?'

I shook my head. 'None.'

'How funny. What kind of puzzle doesn't have clues? Let's see.' She pulled a pair of eyeglasses from her apron and perched them on her nose. 'Fahig Peal. Fahig isn't like any name I've heard before. Sounds foreign if you ask me. And Peal. Peal. Like the Peelers?'

I stared at the words. 'No, that's spelled differently . . . Peal like the ringing of a bell. But what does Fahig mean?'

'It's German, dear,' said a woman at the next table. She was an elderly lady in a rich purple gown. The map of lines on her face spoke of a life well lived. It was then I noticed the conversation in the café had died down and customers nearby were craning their necks to listen.

'German?'

The lady shifted in her chair to face me. 'My husband is Austrian and he speaks it to the staff. I pretend I don't understand so he will deal with them.'

'But you do understand?' I asked.

'I do.' She beamed, entirely pleased with herself and the ruse with her husband.

'What does it mean?'

Her forehead creased and she squinted as if searching the corners of the room for the answer. The rest of the café was pin-drop silent; the waitress and I shared a look.

'I believe, *fahig*,' she said it with a strong German accent, 'means "capable".'

'Capable . . .' I repeated and the realisation dawned. 'Or "able" maybe?'

The lady nodded. 'Yes. "Able" is also right.'

'Fahig Peal means able bell,' I said slowly and could not believe I hadn't seen it before.

Abel Bell. The author was the other bidder. He had the fifth book. I jumped up from my seat and grabbed my bag, the pencil, the paper. I grabbed the waitress in a hug and shook the lady's hand. The rest of the café began to titter and gossip but I didn't care.

'Thank you! Thank you both.'

'What's it mean?' asked the waitress as I threw down some coins, too many I was sure, but what did it matter now?

'It's an answer. I can't believe it,' I said, rushing for the door.

Outside, the London bustle barely touched me. I needed to write a letter, immediately. I raced along Charing Cross Road until I found a stationer's. A fine one, too rich for my purse had I not been carrying Ambrose Fane's money. I bought paper, stamps and two gummed envelopes, and on one of the tables, began to write.

Dear Mr Montague and Dotty,

You'll remember me as the visitor asking after Bell books that should not exist. I beg your help as I have good reason to believe Abel Bell himself owns one of these books and bought it under the name Fahig Peal. I must speak with him. It is life and death. Please could you forward on the enclosed letter as soon as you can.

Kind regards,
Lilian Delaney

On the next sheet, I penned the letter to Bell.

Dear Mr Bell,

I am a collector and bookbinder who has come into possession of several volumes of your work that are not listed in your publisher's catalogue. I have also been

victim of vicious attacks by a person wanting these
books for themselves. I know you have one, and I don't
wish to alarm you, but you may be in danger.

I faltered . . . how could I convince this reclusive, no doubt very elderly man to meet with me? The words failed and I drew annoyed looks from the stationer behind the counter.

I know you value your privacy and I can assure you,
with all I have within me, that I will not jeopardise that.
These books that bear erroneous titles, do you know
they all hide a secret? Do you know there are six and
within them, a story so dramatic it belongs in one of
your own fictions? Please, allow me to meet with you
and examine your book and I will explain it all.
I look forward to your letter.

Yours sincerely, and desperately,
Lilian Delaney

I wrote my address and sealed the envelope. I added a stamp, and the name *Fahig Peal* on the outside, with enough space for Montague to address it. Then I sealed it within the other envelope and addressed that to the publisher.

'Are you quite finished?' came the snippy voice of the stationer.

I barely heard him, such was my need to get this finished and sent, that I left without acknowledgement and found the nearest post box.

As I dropped the letter into the box, all my hopes and

excitement deflated. All I could do now was wait for a response that might not come. Panic took hold and I steadied myself against a nearby wall, pushing my way past a mass of pedestrians to stop myself falling among them. If Bell didn't write back, didn't say yes to meeting and parting with his book, then I didn't know what would happen. I didn't dare think past the next few days, for I wasn't at all sure if I even had a life beyond that. If those I loved did too. The thought made me shiver. I held my collar together at my throat as if protecting myself from a blade and could think of only one place to go. The last idea I had.

34.

Frank Karslake looked at first surprised and then pleased to see me in his office.

'Miss Delaney!' he cried, above the sound of hammering from the bindery.

The young girl who had shown me in and led me through to the office bobbed to Karslake and left us.

'It's good of you to see me,' I said, 'especially uninvited.'

He stood up from his desk and shook my hand. 'A talented bookbinder is always welcome in my humble workshop.'

He gestured for me to take a seat and as I did, I noticed the pile of finely bound books that had been here when I visited before, was half as high again and a second pile had been added beside it.

He noticed me looking. 'We have an exciting auction coming up. The girls are beside themselves.'

I smiled. 'The books are very beautiful. I'm sure they'll fetch a high sum.'

Karslake spread his hands. 'What may I do for you? Have you come to sign the paperwork to join us?'

I realised then that I'd never sent my polite rejection of his representation. I put on a demure smile, the best I could after all that had happened. 'Actually, I'm after some information about another bookbinder. An older gentleman, may be passed on.'

He seemed a little ruffled at my sidestep but recovered quickly. 'Who might this man be?'

'His name is Felix Fidelius Gauch. He signs his bindings FFG. I found a book of his from the Fifties.'

Karslake steepled his hands and pressed his fingers to his mouth for a moment before speaking. 'I know of Gauch.'

He said it in a strange way, as if this bookbinder had a certain reputation. 'Do you know where I can find him?'

'I'm afraid he passed many years ago. I met him once or twice when I was a young man starting out.'

'May I ask what you know of him?'

Karslake regarded me carefully, as if deciding what was appropriate to say. 'He was a good bookbinder. He had the technical ability but lacked imagination. A showboater. You know if you shout loud enough that something is valuable, at some point people will start believing you. Felix could shout loud indeed. New collectors or those with new money, they believed him when he said he could build a library for them with the finest, most modern bindings, when in fact, his designs were overly simple and derivative.'

'Do you know who he worked for?'

He blew out his cheeks. 'Plenty. He found his clients in unsavoury places. There was Brandling whose family money came from slavery, Lord Chatton, who had his hands in all number of rotten pies, Erskine who made a fortune in prisons and asylums. Who else . . . Dalrymple and Coins. Oh, and Aloysius Fane. I don't recall any others I'm afraid.'

None of those names lit a fire in my memory, except for Fane. Ambrose's father. This lead was rapidly turning into a dead end.

'Was there any client he worked with more than others?'

Karslake shrugged. 'I wouldn't know.'

'Does he have any family or a business partner, perhaps, I could speak with?'

'His business partner deserted him before Felix died and I don't believe he had any family.'

'How did he die?'

At this, Karslake's eyes took on a conspiratorial twinkle. 'He was murdered.'

'What?'

Karslake nodded at my shock. 'Murdered. Nobody knows why but – I have it on good authority, for at the time I was a young apprentice and it was the talk of the book world – he was killed for binding a series of books.'

A chill ran down my spine.

'Who would . . . why would anyone kill someone for binding a book?'

But I knew who would. His face appeared in my mind, his devilish eyes, his hat, his shadowy employer in the background, but Devlin was too young to have killed Gauch, if he died when Karslake was an apprentice.

'The rumours at the time, and this was thirty years ago so you'll forgive if my memory is a little moth-eaten. The rumour went that some time before, Felix had taken on a commission for the daughter of one of his clients. He didn't know it was for her – she had lied in her letters to him and they never spoke in person – but he did the work and when the lord or perhaps his brother, I can't recall, found out, Felix was beaten to within an inch of his life and thrown into the Thames.'

My hand went to my mouth. 'Dear God.'

'God had nothing to do with it. But that's not all. The poor man *survived* his swim, washed up in Southwark, took to his bed where, a week later, someone shot him in the head.'

I was almost too shocked to speak. A few weeks ago I wouldn't have believed someone would go to such lengths over books, but now I knew too well. 'That's . . . terrible.'

Karslake nodded. 'Someone wanted poor Felix dead and made sure of it.'

'It was never discovered who?'

He shook his head. 'Alas. It is those with the most despicable tendencies who have the deepest pockets and often a police commissioner or two on their payroll.'

I sat back in the chair. 'Was there any talk of who hired him? This lord's daughter?'

'Little more than that. When I met Felix the first time, he told of how she was a great beauty who had been locked away by her father. He didn't know why.'

I knew why. The marriage, the baby, her father's fury. This was her, the girl from the pages. She had asked Gauch to bind the six Bell books and this one act had got him killed around twenty years later. But why then, why wait so long? What could have triggered it? And who would have done it, if not Devlin? The employer, perhaps, had been looking for these books far longer than I expected. Every scrap of information I discovered about this mystery begat more questions and more after that. I feared it would never end, that I would never unravel it all in time. I was beginning to understand that the pages hidden within the books were only half the story.

'Thank you, Mr Karslake. I do appreciate your time and your candour.'

'I must confess, Miss Delaney,' he said with a smile, 'I do enjoy a gossip. I had forgotten almost entirely this period of my life but it has been, well, rather fun to relive it. A fine distraction on a chilly afternoon. Now, about your contract.'

'I am afraid I am taking a break from bookbinding and am no longer under Mr Caxton's employ.' It still hurt to say it, still couldn't quite believe it.

'Oh. Oh I am sorry to hear that. Should you change your mind, our door is open.'

'I appreciate that,' I said and, as much as I had thought little of Karslake's operation, his offer gave me a tiny spark of hope for what the future might bring, should I live to see it.

I returned to Oxford on the evening train. My life had become a series of trains and rushed journeys, a constant sense of panic as if my body was permanently ready to run or fight. My feet ached as I walked home from the station and I hated, again, that I had arrived back too late to visit my father.

The bookshop was dark and empty and I was grateful for it. The last thing I needed then, after the whirlwind of a day I'd had, was Harry waiting with questions or bad news. I went straight upstairs and lit a lamp. The house was eerie without my father's shuffling feet and grumblings at how long the kettle took to boil. I felt like a trespasser in my own home.

I sat at my desk, took the two sets of pages from the hidden pocket in my satchel and laid them out. I arranged them in order, first the pages from Ambrose's book, *Love's Last Aria*, and then from *Orpheus in the Tower*. I read them again and, again, the story pulled me in. I could not let this go until I knew. I thought of the poor bookbinder, Gauch, who ran afoul of this girl's father, or uncle, Karslake had said. Could either of those men be the ones behind Devlin? But the timing wasn't right. Too many years had passed. I was no closer to finding my answer, and the story of Gauch disturbed me greatly. I only hoped I would not share his fate.

35.

The morning brought heavy rain. Endless sheets of water turned the pavements slick and grey, filled the uneven cobbles and potholes. The sound of the city changes, every cartwheel and running footstep was magnified and accompanied by muttered complaints and the mechanical clicking of umbrellas.

I arrived at the Radcliffe soaked to my skin and shivering. The November cold bit hard as the winter barrelled ever onward. I drew sympathetic murmurings from the receptionists and indications of where to hang my coat.

I made my way to my father's ward and caught the eye of a nurse who I knew had tended him. I offered a smile but her face was grave and she hurried to me.

In a heartbeat I knew what had happened.

The nurse took me by the arm into a quiet area away from the main corridor.

She began to speak but I barely heard it. My mind had closed itself away because it knew. It knew what had happened the moment I heard the rain on the window that morning, the moment I'd stepped into the hospital and the air had felt different, and now that look. That sad, creased brow and downturned mouth, that pity and the nerves at what she needed to tell me.

'He slipped away in the night,' she said as if he'd snuck out. An image of him in his white gown, creeping through the corridors.

'What do you mean?' I said, for that was the only thought I had. That he'd left. He'd woken and left.

'Someone really should have sent for you.' She wrung her hands, fretted.

'But they didn't. What happened?'

She sighed. 'I'm so sorry, Miss Delaney, but your father passed away in the night. The nurse on duty reported it early this morning. It had been peaceful by her reckoning.'

The colour drained from my face, then from the world.

'Are . . .' my voice caught '. . . are you sure it was him?'

She nodded. 'Andrew Delaney. I tended him through the days.'

I couldn't think. Could barely breathe. My throat tightened around rising bile. 'Did he wake?'

The nurse shook her head and looked down at her clasped hands. 'I said a prayer for him when I found out.'

A sudden spike of anger pierced my daze. 'What good are your prayers now? My father is dead.' My legs buckled and the words came again. 'My father is dead. My father . . .'

'I am sorry, miss.'

Then her hands were around my shoulders, holding me as I rocked, as I repeated those terrible words, as I stared into nothing, as the pure white-hot anger built a wall inside me, burning away tears and sorrow and leaving only hate. For the man who did this and the other who told him to.

'Where . . . can I see . . . ?' I couldn't form the sentences but she knew my meaning.

'He's in the mortuary, miss. I'll take you.'

I felt her hands pulling me up and I let her. She had her arm around my shoulder, guiding me through the maze-like hospital, down to a lower floor and a long, cold corridor. A black-painted door stood at the far end and as I neared it, the walls seemed to warp and bend and I almost fell. The nurse held me. Led me.

The mortuary was cold, with white-painted brick walls and small, high windows letting in limited light. Lamps were lit, metal trolleys laid out in a grid, some occupied, most not. A man in a shirt, his sleeves rolled up, stood over a corpse at the far end of the room.

He looked up as we entered. 'You shouldn't be here.'

'This lady wishes to see her father. Delaney. He was brought down this morning.'

The man straightened. 'Oh. He's over here.' He walked to one of the trolleys, the shape thereon was covered in a white sheet. So small.

He pulled back the sheet to the shoulders and there was my father, the bandage still around his head. His skin grey, face slack. He looked relaxed. More so than I'd ever seen him in life. He was at once my father and not, and I didn't know how to put the two images together. The frail but fierce man who had moved around the bookshop like it was his kingdom, who had set me challenges to find the value in a pile of paper and board. And this. This cold, still, empty thing. I wanted to shake him. Tell him to wake up. Take him by the hand and lead him out of here, back home, back among his books.

'You may touch him, if you like,' the nurse said gently.

I lifted my hand to lay on his but couldn't. I knew what it would feel like and I didn't want that memory. I shook my head.

I don't know how long I looked at him. Moments probably. But enough. I had seen enough. I turned away and walked to the door. My legs didn't feel like my own. They trembled beneath me. I heard the nurse say something to the mortician but I didn't care to listen. I needed to be out of that room and I hated that my father had to stay inside it.

In the corridor, I leaned against the wall, feeling the cold against my cheek, staring into nothing. Then the nurse had me by the shoulders again and was leading me away. Then we were back in the bright hustle of the reception where visitors came and went, smiling, with flowers and bags of fruit. A pregnant woman was wheeled past in a chair, another woman wheeled the other way with a babe in arms.

'We'll release the body for burial in a day or two. You will need to make arrangements,' the nurse said and I could hear impatience in her voice.

'Yes,' I muttered.

I walked out of the Radcliffe, into the rain, and my feet took me where they knew I needed to go.

*

The door opened a few moments after my knock and Mr Caxton looked up at me first with surprise, then with concern.

'Lilian, whatever are you doing out in this weather?' He frowned. 'Where is your coat?'

'My father is dead.'

His face broke and, seeing it, a dam burst inside me. Tears mixed with rain and did not stop as Mr Caxton pulled me inside. The smell of the place hit me first and I didn't realise how much I had missed it. The paper, the leather, the glue, the fire. It was home when I needed it most.

'You'll have to come back another time,' said Mr Caxton and I thought for a moment he was talking about me but then I saw, sat in a chair opposite his desk, a young man with pink cheeks and a brown suit too big for him.

The boy stood up, clutching his cap in his hands. 'Uh . . . yes of course.' He stepped smartly to Mr Caxton and held out a hand to shake. 'I do hope you consider me for the position.'

My heart lurched. He was replacing me. Of course he was. He needed help and I had resigned. It was only a matter of time but I didn't think it would hurt so much.

Mr Caxton waved the boy away. 'See yourself out, please.'

He nodded, lingered a moment, no doubt taking in the state of me, dripping wet, hair plastered to my face, pale as a ghost, then he finally left.

Mr Caxton led me to the hearth where now just one arm-chair stood. He pulled over another and sat me down. 'Let's get you warmed up.'

I nodded slowly and within ten or so minutes, I had a blanket about my shoulders and a cup of tea in my hands. Mr Caxton sat opposite, on the edge of the chair.

'I'm sorry,' I said. My voice was a shade of itself. 'I interrupted your meeting.'

Mr Caxton frowned as if forgetting someone else was ever here. 'Don't you worry about that.'

I could see he was putting on a brave face. He tried to smile but it wouldn't stretch. He blinked over and over, forcing back his own tears while mine were drying in the heat of the fire.

'He's really . . . ?' Mr Caxton asked.

I nodded and a fresh wave of tears fell. I pressed a hand across my eyes as if I could keep the grief inside through sheer force.

'How did he go?'

I swallowed back a shuddering sob. 'Peaceful, they said. In his sleep.'

Mr Caxton's shoulders relaxed. 'That's all we can hope for.'

'There will be a funeral. I'll need to . . . the service, a priest.' Panic climbed up my throat and clawed at my voice. 'Oh God, the bank. They'll take the shop. I don't . . . I don't know what to do.' I put down the tea and leaned forward, hands over my face, my breath coming in short, sharp bursts. 'I don't . . . what do I do? What do I do?'

Mr Caxton put his hands over mine and pried them from my face.

'You find those books.'

I met his eyes and my breathing calmed. 'What?'

'You find the books and you get yourself free of this, whatever it takes. Don't worry about the funeral arrangements. I will handle them. I've buried a good many friends and family in my long life and I'd be honoured to help put dear Andrew to rest.'

I blinked. 'You would do that?'

He put his hand on my cheek. His skin smelled of paper, of home. 'You're family, Miss Delaney. Inside and outside these walls, even when you're acting a damned fool. I know you've got yourself tied in up something and it's been a regret these past days that I'd not been more understanding, given you the time you needed.' I began to shake my head, to stop him, but he kept going. 'But now, things are different. You understand, things are different.'

'It's my fault. This is all my fault. If I'd just listened to you . . .'

He gave a smile. 'My dear, the world would be a far greater place if more people listened to me, but alas, I am one small bookbinder making my way.' He squeezed my hands and his voice turned serious. 'You are not responsible for the actions of others. You didn't make that man attack your father; he chose to do that and he will pay for it.'

I stayed in that moment for as long as I could. Feeling kindness I didn't deserve from this man I had lied to and hurt.

'I wish I could take it back,' I said softly.

'Take what back?'

'My resignation. I didn't want to leave you but you see now why I had to. I didn't want you to be in any more danger than you already were. I . . . I need to fix this.'

Mr Caxton smiled. 'Then fix it, and when you have, let's discuss our partnership.'

My chin trembled and I couldn't speak. I only nodded.

Mr Caxton handed me the tea. 'Drink this. The next one will be Scotch. Stay as long as you like, my dear, and I'll send for Harry.'

'Thank you.' I sipped the tea as Mr Caxton returned to his desk and his binding. I stared at the fire and let the hours slip away. Sometimes I cried. Sometimes I was numb. I relived my memories, old and new, with my father. The time he whipped me for peeling back the leather of a 1780 *Don Quixote*, his surprised expression when I told him of the oppressed Shelley volume and then the pride in his eyes as he gave me my share of the proceeds. The way he and my mother laughed and danced and talked of books. The way he gave me poetry to read because he couldn't find the words himself.

And now he was gone. The memories I had of him were all the memories I would ever have and already so many were forgotten. If only I had a book of his life I could read again and again.

The sky darkened and I watched Mr Caxton light the lamps. He'd bring me tea, a biscuit or two, though my stomach was hard as stone and refused food, and the occasional Scotch. The alcohol filed off the sharp corners and the world took a step away from me. Or I from it.

Harry came just after five. I didn't have the energy to go through the telling again and Mr Caxton knew it, like he knew so much without it having to be said.

Harry made to rush to me but Mr Caxton stopped him by the door. I couldn't hear them and didn't want to. I fixed my gaze, swimming in Scotch, on the flames.

Harry came to my side. 'Let's get you home. Where is your coat?'

It was then I realised I'd left it in the hospital. I could only shake my head, so Harry took off his and draped it over me.

He walked me to the bookshop and I was thankful of the rain. It made it too hard to talk or think beyond the next step. I stood outside the door and could not move.

I raised my voice above the rain. 'I don't want to be here tonight.'

'We can go to mine,' Harry said.

I made to walk away with him then remembered. I'd left the pages out on my desk. I couldn't leave them here, exposed and so far from me.

'I need to get some clothes,' I said and didn't want for Harry to question it. I walked in and kept my eyes on the floor, on the stairs, refusing to look at anything, for fear of the memories it would conjure.

In my bedroom I went straight for the desk, for the pages. But they were gone.

My heart stopped, sank into my gut. 'Where . . .' Everything else seemed untouched. Except for one thing.

A cigar had been stubbed out on the wood. The smell of it was suddenly everywhere. I knew the smell, hated it. The man in the bowler had been here. In my room. In my space. And he'd taken the pages.

Rage overtook me. My breath turned short. Every muscle in my chest tightened. My heartbeat thundered in my ears. I wanted to destroy something. Him. And whoever paid him to do this. He had taken my father, now he had taken the pages. A fire lit in my heart so fierce I didn't know if it could ever be extinguished.

One thing became startlingly clear in the moments after I saw that cigar stub, saw the little evidences of someone else – the wardrobe ajar, the drawers not quite closed, the bedding piled oddly. One thought rang out against the throbbing in my head; they knew about the pages. They didn't care about the books themselves. They wanted the story hidden in the bindings. But why?

36.

I lived in a hot rage for days. I drank too much and pored over every auction listing and library catalogue I could get my hands on looking for a Bell that should not exist. I walked the streets of an evening looking for Devlin, for a fight that never came, despite my deadline passing.

News of my father's death spread and visitors came to the bookshop expressing their sympathies. Other bookmen came to offer false condolences and check out the stock in case of a sell-off. I locked the door and stopped answering the knocks.

I sent a letter to the Randolph telling Ambrose what had happened and, later that same day, he came to the bookshop.

He seemed too big, too grand, for the space though he was shorter than me. I expected him to look on the humble shop with ill-concealed disdain but he didn't. He was curious, walking the shelves, taking out titles that intrigued him.

'Do you want to talk about your father?' he asked, as he put a book back on the shelf. My father would know it by its placement but to me it was just another book.

'No.'

He nodded and turned to me. 'Good. Then tell me why I am here.'

'Devlin was here. He stole the pages I had. That means they know about them.'

'How inconvenient. I was hoping to read them myself.'

'I'm going to get them back.'

Ambrose nodded slowly. 'And how are you going to do that?'

'Find the next book and wait for them with a pistol.'

'Well, well, wouldn't that be a sight.' He sauntered about the room, as unconvinced by my bravado as I was. 'How goes the book hunt?'

'That auction you told me about. I found out who the buyer, Fahig Peal, really is.'

He raised an eyebrow. 'Bravo. Do tell.'

'It's Abel Bell.'

Ambrose frowned and as if working out the puzzle backwards from the solution, then rolled his eyes. 'Of course. German. I'm mortified I didn't see it before.'

'I wrote to Montague to pass on a letter but it's been days and there has been no reply.'

'Bell is quite the recluse.'

'I don't care. I need to see him. Do you know where he lives? Can you find out?'

'I've tried. Besides, you have more important things to focus on. Isn't the funeral tomorrow?'

I folded my arms across my chest. 'I said I didn't want to talk about it.'

'Fine, fine. But you could at least wash.' He waved his hand in front of his nose. 'I've been looking for Bell for a decade and never come close. What of the other book out there in the wind? Any ideas there?'

I sighed, more petulant than I intended. 'I have been looking through catalogues but so far nothing. No Bells at all.'

'Then we must wait. Or break into Montague's office and steal the address.' His eyes gleamed a little too brightly at the idea.

'And have the police after me too?'

'Pish! Police are as much use as a quim in a molly house.'

'Ambrose!'

He cocked his head and looked at me with a wry smile. 'Do spare me your blushes. I know you are no stranger to carnal delights; you told me as much yourself. But perhaps you are right. I will shake some trees of my own and see if an author falls out. Though it will take a few days.'

A few days I didn't have. Devlin would return, and this time I was sure he would not hesitate to make good on his threats.

*

My father was buried in St Giles churchyard on the last Monday in November. I stood by the graveside as the minister read his verses and spoke of a life. He told a tale of a jovial man, a lover of books, a storyteller. Those around me nodded, smiling, but that didn't match the man I knew. Harry held my hand, with Mr Caxton on the other side. Ambrose had left the city, talking of trees. I would catch Mr Caxton often bringing his handkerchief to his eyes. Mine remained dry, even as I threw the first handful of dirt on the casket.

As I stepped away, I saw Devlin at the edge of the churchyard. I gripped Harry's hand and he saw him too.

Harry met my eyes and whispered, 'Not today.'

As we left the churchyard, Devlin smirked at me and tipped his bowler.

I clenched my fists and my jaw and pressed down the fury. Not today.

The rest of the day passed in a blur. Mr Caxton had taken charge of everything as he'd promised. He'd hung a laurel wreath on the bookshop door, covered the mirrors and handed out biscuits wrapped in white paper. Harry was stoic and handsome in his blacks; people were kind and shook my hand and told me what a wonderful man my father had been. It all felt like it was happening to someone else. As if I was reading about it in a novel rather than living it. My thoughts were wholly occupied by what lengths I might have to go to, to find Bell and the remaining books. At that moment, there was little I wouldn't risk, for I had so little left to lose.

37.

The day after I buried my father, I boarded a train to Manchester with Ambrose's money. I had gone to Harry and retrieved the pages I'd had him hide. I felt better with them with me. Harry was safer too, without them. I hadn't told him where I was going and he knew better than to ask. He only kissed me goodbye and I hoped it would not be our last. I promised myself it would not and checked my bag for my paring knife. After the attack, I had carried it with me always and today was no different.

I arrived in the evening and took a cab straight to the offices of Montague and Cliff. Several lights still shone in the high windows and I could only hope theirs was one of them.

I climbed the stairs and found the door, the brass plaque declaring their name. I waited. Heard them talking within and smelled the floral tobacco scent of Dotty's pipe wafting beneath the door. I stood outside the door for a few seconds before working up the courage. I knew if I knocked they may not answer; if I announced myself they may turn me away and I couldn't risk that.

So, with a drumming in my heart and head and a few quick breaths to prepare myself, I opened the door and walked in.

Montague and Dotty both looked up from their desks. Dotty saw me and frowned and Montague gaped like a caught fish.

'Miss Delaney?' said Dotty, pipe hanging from her mouth.

'I need to know where Abel Bell lives. I need to see him,' I said, trying to keep my voice as steady as I could so they would not hear the tremble, see my fear.

'Bell doesn't want to see you,' Montague said, full of spite. He stood up and rounded his desk, pointing at me as if his finger was a gun. 'You get out. I passed on your letter and Bell said no. Don't come in here demanding!'

I clenched my jaw, my fists. 'I don't care. I'm not leaving without the address.'

Montague huffed. 'Dotty, get a constable, will you?'

Dotty hadn't taken her eyes off me and didn't make any move towards the door. 'Are you in mourning, dear?'

I looked down at my black dress and jacket, suddenly off balance. 'My . . . my father died last week.'

Dotty's face broke into the same expression every visitor and guest at the funeral wore when speaking with me. 'I'm sorry to hear that.'

Montague's cheeks had turned red. 'Yes. Well. Very sad. But still, that doesn't give you the right to barge in here making demands.'

'My father was killed because of these books,' I shot back at him. 'The author has another one and I need it. Do you understand? I *need it*.'

'It doesn't matter what you need. Get out of here!' Montague's voice had turned shrill and he rushed towards me.

I fumbled with the straps on my bag, hands shaking, but

got them open and pulled out my paring knife. I held it up at him and he stopped dead, hands raised.

Tears brimmed in my eyes. 'I need the address.'

'Dotty!' Montague shrieked. 'She's mad, get a constable.'

Dotty, standing now, sighed. 'Shut up, Henry. The girl is clearly upset. Give her the address.'

He looked at her with wide-eyed shock. 'Have you lost your mind? Send a dangerous, unhinged woman with a *knife* to the door of our bestselling author?'

'*Please*,' I said, tension and heat flooded my body, and my hand shook. I saw the fear in Montague's eyes. The same fear I had felt when the man in the bowler held a knife to me.

Is this what I had become? So desperate I was willing to threaten? To hurt? How far would it go? Was I to become them? I had said I would do anything for these books but this? Was I to kill for them?

Never.

I dropped the knife. It clattered on the floorboard.

Montague snatched it up and held it at me but I barely registered his movement. My eyes clouded with tears and I sank down the wall, head in hands.

'Please, I need the address,' I said in a small, strained voice, slowly feeling all hope drain away.

'Dotty, get a constable *now*!' I heard Montague move closer.

The fight was gone. The fury replaced with shame. How had I been reduced to this?

'Go get one yourself,' Dotty replied.

Montague huffed and I heard him dash past me, open the door and run down the hall.

'Miss Delaney.' I looked up and saw Dotty standing at her

desk, opening a drawer. She took out a letter. 'Henry is many things and a liar is the least. I'm afraid he never passed on your letter.'

My mouth fell open. All this waiting and he'd never even sent it.

'But I did,' Dotty said with a warm smile. She came to me, knelt before me. 'I'm ashamed to say that when Henry read your letter, he tore it up and threw it in the waste basket. I'm afraid I lost the envelope with your address on it but I pieced together the one to Bell. I sent it off and a few days later, Bell wrote back.'

She handed me the letter, addressed to me but sent here. Now it all made sense.

'He asked me if you were one of those fanciers, you know?' I nodded and Dotty's smile never wavered. 'When I told him you weren't, he wrote back with this. I haven't opened it.'

The letter was sealed with blue wax, with a rabbit of all things, or perhaps a hare, on the seal. It had a steely look in its eye, as if pre-emptively upset with the reader for breaking it. I slid my finger beneath the flap and the seal cracked, the rabbit beheaded. I pulled out the letter, a single sheet.

Dear Miss Delaney,

Your letter intrigued me. D says you are to be taken seriously and one does well to listen to her in all matters. Come for a visit when you're able. My address herewith, below. Do bring a treat, for I don't get out much and a caramel or two would endear me greatly.

Anon,

A.B.

I pressed my hand to my mouth and laughed and cried at once. 'Thank you.'

Dotty put her hand on mine and there came the piteous expression once more. 'Dear girl. I lost my father when I was eighteen and I would have done anything to avoid feeling it. Even run halfway across the country, like you are.'

'I'm feeling it.' I wiped away tears with the back of my hand.

'Good. That pain, sweetheart, is what keeps us breathing. You have to live *for* him now, not with him. That's a burden for some but I've a feeling you'll make the most of it.'

I met her eyes, this almost stranger, who had shown so much kindness when she had no reason to.

'My father always had a penny to spare for someone in need,' she said, as if by explanation. 'I try to keep that part of him alive best I can, even all these years later. Henry makes it damned hard sometimes but I do my best. I hope that letter was what you needed.'

I nodded, unable to speak through the rising emotion. I threw my arms around her and held her to me as if I was holding my father one more time. She didn't flinch or pull away and her scent, sweet tobacco and something else, the perfume of age and books and paper, filled my lungs. That was my father's smell, or as close to it as I'd ever experience again. I didn't know how, didn't question it, just took in every second I could.

I never wanted to let go but then the clattering feet of Henry Montague brought me crashing back to the world.

'Dotty! What in God's name! Is she strangling you?' he screamed.

Dotty let me go and we helped each other to our feet.

I concealed the letter behind me, lest he think I'd stolen from her.

Dotty faced Henry and sighed. 'Will you get a hold of yourself? The girl isn't dangerous; she's grieving and in trouble.'

'She meant to kill me!' Montague still held my knife but no constable accompanied him.

'I didn't,' I said, sniffing and tearful. 'I swear it.'

'See, there you go. Now take yourself back to your chair, sit down and be quiet. Our guest is just leaving. Give her back her property.'

He glared at Dotty. 'You are not serious, *madam*?'

Dotty raised an eyebrow and Montague knew at once he'd overstepped. He turned defiantly meek, like a chastised toddler, and handed back my knife.

'You'd best go, love. Henry and I are going to have a little chat.' Dotty patted my arm and smiled. Montague's cheeks reddened.

I needed no further encouragement and was glad to be out, in the hallway, the letter and a new hope in hand.

I read it again, standing outside the door, hearing Dotty's calm voice reprimand a diminishingly shrill Montague. I memorised Bell's address and, while so very glad to have it, my joy was dampened by the location. The Dorset coast, near Swanage. I had no idea how to get there, nor even which train stop I might need or how long it would take. But I had to keep moving forward, no matter what, for if I stopped, I feared the weight of the last few weeks would knock me down and I wouldn't have the strength to get up again.

I made my way back to the train station. It was busy at this time; clouds filled the far end where the trains waited, porters made their tips with fast legs and strong backs, guards blew their whistles, and the great metal machines disappeared into their own steam.

I queued for the ticket booth and, as I waited, counted the money I had remaining. Enough, I hoped. My turn came and I hurriedly put the money back in my pocket and stepped forward. The woman in the booth smiled as one does who deals with person after person, until they all become one blurred face over the hours of the day.

'I need to get to Swanage, in Dorset,' I said.

She raised her eyebrows. 'Swanage . . . that's a way.' She took a book from below her desk and flopped it open, for it was well used and the covers softened. I quickly saw it was a book of rail routes. With practised movements, she found the pages and traced the myriad of lines criss-crossing the shape of the country.

'You in a rush?' she asked.

'Yes.'

'Quickest is back to London then out on the Weymouth line, number sixty-eight, from Waterloo.' She brought the page closer to her eye. 'Get off at Wareham and take the branch line to Swanage.'

The scale of the route made me tired even thinking of it but at least it was possible. 'When is the next train to London?'

She checked the clock on her wall. 'About ten minutes. It's the slow one but there won't be a Weymouth train until the morning.'

'Thank you. I'll take a ticket.'

'I can give you one to Paddington, but you'll have to get the Weymouth ticket at Waterloo. Class?'

'How much for second?'

She named a figure I knew I could afford, and given it would be a slow train, I wanted a touch of comfort to see me through. 'One, please.'

She pulled a ticket from a book, stamped it and wrote the price, which I duly paid.

'Platform eight,' she said.

'Thank you.'

I boarded the train with no issue and was pleased to find little in the way of passengers in my carriage.

As the train pulled away and the rhythmic rocking of the journey began, the events of the last few days caught up with me at once and I fell into a heavy sleep.

38.

After a midnight dash across London, a cold cup of soup and an uncomfortable four hours on a bench in Waterloo station, among the pigeons and pickpockets, I boarded my hundredth train of the week, or so it felt, and was on my way to Weymouth. I promised myself that when this was over, I would not set foot on a train for the rest of my life.

I finally arrived in Swanage and found a local shop in which to buy caramels. When I asked for directions to Rosemark House, Bell's home, the shopkeeper looked at the caramels and smirked.

'You know this address?' I asked.

'Oh yes.' The shopkeeper said it in such a way as to make me a touch nervous at what I might find. He gave me directions, for it seemed the author, despite his reclusive nature, was well known locally for his sweet tooth.

The way to Bell's turned out to be an hour's walk along the cliffside. The cold was bracing but not unpleasantly so, and the wind off the sea brought a welcome salt tang to the air. It was good to stretch my legs and lungs after so long sitting and it gave me time to think on what I might say to Bell when I met him.

The directions I'd been given led me away from the town – quiet in the winter, bracing itself no doubt for the onslaught of summer – and into the countryside above. The views across the cliffs and sea were breathtaking and the stuffy yellow walls of Oxford seemed so far away.

The track turned out to be a driveway, crowded with densely grown trees, making it feel as if one was entering a tunnel and, with it, another world. As the sun broke through the clouds for a brief moment, the tunnel turned from a dreary, cold place, covered in the muck of last year's leaf fall, to a shifting kaleidoscope. The bare trees cut up the sunlight and scattered it like sequins across the ground. The clouds moved and as quick as it came, it was gone and the dim light seemed all the dimmer.

Finally, I emerged from the trees. The track continued up a hill and sitting atop, proudly above the treetops as if on an island, was the house. From the name, Rosemark House, I had expected a quaint little home, perhaps thatched, nestled in a well-kept garden, but this was a foreboding stone manor, rising up from the hilltop. I approached with a nervous step, for I wasn't at all sure what kind of man I'd find behind those doors.

The house was old, hundreds of years at a guess, at least parts of it. It was fronted with a formal garden left to deteriorate. Tall, pointed trees framed the garden and the walk to the house. The house itself was an imposing Tudor design, with two large gable ends on either side and a smaller, central one holding the front door. Slate roofs and lichen-kissed stone, scents of lemon balm, rotten and pungent, and evergreen rosemary at the borders. The windows were deeply recessed and narrow, with thick stone banding between, and I could see no movement within.

I approached the door, and, taking a deep breath, pulled on the bell.

A sonorous clang rang within and for a while nothing happened.

I shifted my weight and had a terrible thought that I'd come to the wrong house, or at the wrong time and nobody was home. The idea made me tremble, made my chin quiver as if there was nothing but tissue paper holding back a wave of tears. Even the smallest setback would be enough to pierce it and then I didn't know how I could hold anything back.

'Ho, there!' called a sweet voice from my left.

I stepped out of the porch and around the side of the house, between one of the tall trees and the stone, was a woman. She wore gardening gloves, one hand holding a pair of shears and the other a handful of weeds. She looked older than me but not by a lot.

'Hello,' I said, for I was a little taken aback.

'Are you the bookbinder?'

'Yes. I'm Lilian. I'm looking for Abel Bell.'

The woman smiled. 'You found her. Come round!'

Shock rendered me mute for a moment as I stepped over the border, crossed the lawn and followed the woman – surely not *the* Abel Bell! – beside the house. She looked over her shoulder at me, still smiling, as we walked around the outside of the house, through the gap in a border hedge and into a rear garden.

Here, it was apparent, was where the outdoor attention went, for it was a wide and expansive kitchen garden. Rows of winter vegetables, a glasshouse, a stand of apple trees, and all the tools and equipment one would need to manage it. Another woman, her head wrapped in a scarf, was on her knees pulling bindweed from a trailing pumpkin vine.

'Did you bring the caramels?' said this other woman. She was older, easily sixty and change, but she beamed as she looked up at me from the mud. Her breath misted as she talked and the cold seemed not to bother either of them.

I nodded.

The younger woman went to the older and helped her to her feet. 'She expected a man, Mams.'

The older laughed. 'They always do.'

'I'm sorry,' I said, my voice finally returned. 'I admit, I am confused.'

'Let's have something to drink and we'll explain,' the older said, always smiling. Her deeply lined face spoke of a lifetime of such.

They took off their gloves, dusted themselves off. They were both wearing men's overalls and boots. They led me to the house where large double doors were open, despite the chill in the air.

I followed further, into the kitchen where they both washed their hands at butler sinks and went about preparing a tray.

'We'll have to wait an age for the kettle,' said the younger woman. 'How about a warm cider instead? We make it from our own apples.'

'That sounds perfect,' I said.

Her smile widened to a grin and she stoked the fire in the stove and set a pan atop.

In the middle of the kitchen was a square table where the older woman now sat. At her indication, I took a seat beside

344

her. A loaf of bread, half covered in a cloth, was nearby and a bowl of apples on the far side.

'Now,' she said, 'I expect you're wondering just who Abel Bell is.'

'Very much so.'

'Good. That means our secret is kept. I am Abel Bell,' the older woman said and ripped a chunk of bread from the loaf.

But the younger had said the same. 'I'm sorry, but she said too . . .'

They laughed as one and, at the stove, the younger said, 'We are both Bell. Depending on the day. I am Agnes.'

'And I'm Deidre,' said the older.

'I'm so pleased to meet you both. But . . . Bell's books go back to before the Fifties and, forgive me, Deidre, you don't seem old enough.'

'You flatter me. Unfortunately, I am older than I look. The sea air and garden keeps me young. I am seventy-four and I began writing the books when I was eighteen. I took on the name because well, a young woman publishing adventure stories would not get very far back then.'

'I write them now my grandmother is too old,' said Agnes.

'Too old my eye!' Deidre cried and threw a piece of bread at her granddaughter.

Agnes laughed, and I realised I had not heard such constant laughter, seen so much joy, in such a long time.

Agnes set down gently steaming cups of cider before the three of us. The heady apple smell hit me and it felt like Christmas morning. The warmth of that thought was immediately dispelled by a sharp shot of grief. Now my father was gone, Christmas would not be the same ever again.

'Are you all right?' Deidre asked, putting her hand on my arm.

'Yes. Yes, it's just been a long road to get to you. To you both.'

They shared a look. Deidre patted my hand. 'Well now you are here, it seems we have some intrigues to discuss.'

Deidre looked at her granddaughter and the younger woman leaned against the counter, arms folded.

'You're surprised to find us?' Deidre asked.

I let myself relax enough to smile. 'Not much surprises me anymore.'

Deidre's eyes narrowed. Her face was so expressive, so many lines about her eyes and mouth, it read like a map of a happy life. 'That is a shame for one so young.'

I could not disagree with that, and despite my desire to find and know the story of the girl, I wished I'd never come across that burned book, for in truth, I knew no more now than I did then and yet had lost so much.

'You're a bookbinder, your letter said,' Deidre began, evidently seeing my discomfort and changing the subject. 'That must be fascinating.'

'There is little I love more than books and bringing them a new life. My father always said books endure as we do not and it is my little piece of immortality to have taken a hand to one or two of them.'

Deidre smiled, as she always seemed to. 'I know what it is like to love one's vocation. May we all be so blessed.'

Then came a few moments of strained silence where I itched to ask about their book, to hurry on this proceeding so I could bring the whole nasty mess to a close.

As if reading my thoughts, Agnes said, 'We have a book bearing our name but not our title. The text within is *The Curse of El Dorado*, one of Mam's early, best-loved stories. Forty-nine you wrote it, right?'

'Forty-eight, published in forty-nine,' Deidre said. 'But you knew the title didn't match the text, didn't you, Lilian? You spoke of a secret. Now it's time for you to share.'

I needed little encouragement for I was tired, desperate and for some reason, I was beginning to trust these women. I told them everything. There was no sense in keeping anything from them. I was so sick of half-truths and keeping track of who knew what and why. I felt like one of the books, the outside hiding the inside and the inside hiding more.

I told them of how I came to the first book, the man in the bowler hat, this mystery employer, my father, his death. Deidre took my hand at that, but neither interrupted. I recounted the bones of the story from within the book, of the lovers, their marriage and child, the girl's confinement and terrible father. I told of how I came to find each book. I left nothing out.

The sun had long set by the time I was done and we sat in gloomy candlelight. When I spoke the last words, I felt hollowed out, exhausted by the telling as much as the events themselves. I wiped my eyes and drank down the cold cider while I awaited Abel Bell's response.

When it came, it was not the response I was expecting, but then, nothing about this situation had been.

Deidre and Agnes shared a look. Agnes puffed out her cheeks and shrugged, as if some message had passed between them.

'Let's have one of the caramels, shall we?' Deidre said, her smile now not quite creasing her eyes.

I blinked and felt like a terrible guest. I took the box from my bag and put them on the table. Both women took one at once.

The kitchen was quiet but for the muffled clacking of hard sugar on teeth.

'Time for bed, I think.' Deidre stood up. 'We'll pick this up in the morning for, at my age, when the sun goes down, so must I.'

'But . . .' I tried but Agnes shook her head.

The younger woman stood too. 'I'll show you to the guest room.'

I gathered myself, feeling horribly exposed. I had laid my heart, bloody and beating, on their kitchen table and they had reached over it for the caramels. I wasn't at all sure what was going on but I numbly followed, satchel in hand.

Agnes led me upstairs with little in the way of conversation. The house was dark and she held only a candle. Ahead, a similar light bobbed as Deidre made her way to her bed. I saw nothing but what was in the halo of candlelight and that was covered in shadow. We turned down a corridor and soon came to a door. Agnes handed me the candle.

'Did I . . . offend your grandmother?' I asked, hushed.

Agnes smiled. 'Not much could offend her. She is deciding, is all.'

'Deciding?'

Agnes reached beyond me and opened the door. 'Sleep well, Lilian.' With that, she left and disappeared into the darkness. For a moment I stood there, listening to her footsteps on the carpet, before venturing into the room.

The first thing I saw was the windows. Large and wide,

348

despite the age of the house. The earlier clouds had blown away and pale moonlight shone through and lit the room in monochrome. I set down the candle and went to the window and the view, despite the darkness, was remarkable.

The trees were laid out below like a blanket and, beyond, the ground fell away to the sea – and the sea! The moon hung above it, a bright coin in a black night, shutting out even the stars with its light. The water sparkled, black and silver and ever shifting and never ending. It stretched beyond my sight, beyond the turn of the world, so open and vast it should have brought fear but it brought me nothing but calm. There was more to the world than the sharp edges and close walls of cities and their concerns. I felt so very far away from it all. I was hidden among the trees, among the vastness and for the first time in many, many weeks, I felt utterly safe.

I unlatched a window and felt the cold rush in, and with it the scent of the ocean, the sound of the waves and once I'd heard it among the quiet of this place, I could not think to shut it out. I slept that night to the sound of the sea, and I slept well.

39.

I found the women in a large, comfortable room full of chairs and chaises and cushions. A low fire burned in the grate, the windows were open to let in the fresh morning air and a tea set steamed on a small table. Books lined one wall. Most of them were the same size with a variation in cloth cover every dozen or so. I took these to be the authors' own copies of their books. A pair of dark-wood desks were set before the window; a typewriter on one and piles of papers and notebooks on the other, pushed together so their occupants could face one another. Agnes and Deidre chatted, tea in hand, as I entered.

They greeted me, as ever, with smiles.

'How did you sleep?' Deidre asked.

'Better than I have in a long time,' I replied, the fog of sleep lifting fast.

Agnes nodded to the tea. 'Help yourself.'

I did, gratefully, and wolfed down a biscuit too, for I had not eaten the night before. As I ate, and drank, the pair looked at each other.

'We have been deciding,' said Deidre and I caught Agnes's eye.

The younger woman gave me an 'I told you so' look. 'And we have decided to believe you.'

I stopped mid-chew. 'Believe me?'

Agnes picked up a familiar object from her desk and walked to me. My heartbeat quickened. Bound in dark purple, with scuffing on the edges, it was a Bell book. I almost fell out of my chair wanting to reach for it. Agnes handed it to me, taking an armchair opposite me as Deidre joined us.

I felt their eyes on me as mine were on the book. Neither spoke. I ran my hands over the cover, checked the spine. In fading gold letters was the title: *When Love Lies Unsung.* The title page bore the same and was ripped at the bottom of the spine edge to about a third of the way up. A neat rip, as if cut, right on the tip-in line.

I was itching to turn to the endpapers and tear them from their binding.

'Go ahead,' said Agnes. 'Look for it. We know you are dying to.'

I felt a blush come and forced my eyes to the book. I did as I had done with the others I had found and went straight to the back cover. To the dots. I angled the book to the sunlight – for it was shining today with not a hint of cloud so far – and found them.

* *

* *

*

This was the sixth book. My breath caught. The conclusion of the girl's story to which I did not yet have a beginning. There was only one more of these books out there. One more I needed to find before I could put this ordeal to bed. I felt a glimmer of hope in the back of my mind but was wary of letting it grow.

The women watched me and I turned the book over and opened the front cover. I ran my hand over the endpaper and frowned. Did it again. I could not feel the ridge that signalled the pages lay within. Fear took hold of me and I looked at Agnes and Deidre.

They were both smiling.

'Did you wonder, at all, why such reclusive authors such as ourselves would invite a perfect stranger to their home?' asked Deidre.

The fear grew. What had I walked into? 'In truth, I was too relieved to question it.'

'We found the pages years ago,' said Agnes.

'When you spoke of the girl's story in your letter, we knew you had no real interest in Abel Bell the author, but in those fraudulent books,' added Deidre. 'We were curious to meet you and hear the rest of this tale. For it would make an excellent novel, wouldn't it?'

I could only nod.

'What do you intend to do with the pages?' Agnes asked.

'Keep them from harm and I thought to return them to their owner. The girl, if she is still alive, or her lover, William, if he is. If I can't do that, then at least I will be someone who remembers them, and knows their story.'

They shared another look and Deidre gave a nod.

Agnes went to her grandmother's desk and returned with an envelope. She handed it to me. It was unsealed and inside, the pages, folded and many more than previous instalments, the neat black copperplate showing through the paper. The fear began to recede. I had them in my hands, at last. The relief was so strong, I thought I might cry from it.

'We are trusting you, Lilian the bookbinder,' said Deidre, 'because stories, while precious, should be shared. We cannot in good conscience keep a piece of this from you; however, we do ask that you return when you are safe and have the pages and let us read them. An unfinished story is as an unfinished meal: one feels forever hungry until it is complete.'

'I know that feeling too well,' I said and tightened my grip on the pages. 'Might I also take the book? The person threatening me, their employer, they want the books themselves.'

Another look between the women, a silent agreement, and Agnes nodded.

Devlin knew of the pages, but perhaps did not know where they were to be found. I hoped I could buy myself some time with another volume.

Now I had the pages, it took all my will to not read them immediately. But there was another matter I needed to discuss.

'Might I ask for your help once more?'

'Go on,' Deidre said.

'The auction where you acquired this,' I began and both women reacted with nods and huffs, a sore point clearly, 'I was told it was a bidding war.'

'That auction! Cost us *three hundred* pounds to acquire a fake copy of one of our own books. Can you imagine it?' Deidre shook her head and puffed out her cheeks.

Agnes, calmer but I could see the more business-like of the pair, added, 'It was a farce.'

'Might I ask, who was the other bidder?'

Deidre smiled, a spark in her eye at the intrigue of it all. 'I was sat at the back while our man Edmund did the bidding on our behalf. When I saw the other bidder was so vehement, I moved a little closer. I didn't believe it when I saw her. It was Silas Chatton's girl. Not a girl anymore of course, in her forties, but it was her.'

The name rang out like a bell. Uncle Silas was Silas Chatton.

'Do you know her name?'

Deidre frowned and looked at Agnes. 'Margaret? Meredith?'

Agnes made a face. 'Your memory is going, old woman. Her name is Julia.'

Julia . . . that name. Julian, Silas's son, and now Julia, his daughter.

'The Chattons . . . I've heard the name before, just once. The bookbinder who made these –' I tapped the cover of the Bell book – 'he worked for wealthy families, including the Chattons. It can't be a coincidence that Silas Chatton's daughter was after this book.' The realisation crashed down on me. 'She is looking for them all. She's the one who employed Devlin. She must be. Who else could it be?'

'That I couldn't tell you. But she is not a woman to be trifled with. Growing up in that family would not have been easy.'

I thought of the girl, held prisoner, her beaten lover presented before her, and caught a sudden chill. The girl was Julia Chatton's cousin. Maybe Julia was trying to help, to find these pages and bring about a kind of justice. I wanted that to be true so much but her methods, the threats, the attacks, left me in doubt.

'Will you tell me about them?' I asked.

Agnes rolled her eyes. 'Don't get her started on her youth; you'll be here for a week.'

'Hush, you, the girl has asked and as a storyteller, I must answer.' Deidre settled back in her chair. 'When I was a young woman, I lived in London thinking to make it as a writer. I thought being among the same streets as Dickens would confer me the same success but alas, here we are. I was obsessed with the society pages, for I believed the juiciest stories lay with those richest to live for experience rather than work. The Chattons were one such family. Rich beyond belief but not well liked. New money, you know? But it was money made from exploiting others.

'There were two brothers, Silas, the older by a few years, and Malcolm. Malcolm Chatton was the one with charm. He was handsome and well dressed, but he had no taste. He was all about power. He became a lord through connections and bribes and, if the rumours were true, blackmail. Silas was a toad by comparison. Had none of his brother's wit or looks. There was a cartoon in one of the gossip pages about him where he was depicted as a slavering pig beside his lion-like brother. That newspaper shut down two months later and I don't believe it was a coincidence.

'I don't know much about what happened to them but over the course of a year or so, they just fell apart, and – if the rumours are to be believed – it was all because of Malcolm's daughter. She entered society one year and almost immediately disappeared. She was due to marry all kinds of men but never did. For a while it seemed like a new engagement was announced for her every month. Was it the summer of fifty-one? She was seen, written about in various papers, but then poof! It was like she never was. Oh the rumours! It'd make your blood boil to hear them. They said she was syphilitic and lost her nose, she'd fallen pregnant by the garden or kitchen boy or, worse, her own father. It must have been terrible for the poor girl.

'I don't know much about what happened, nor the truth of it, for I believe Silas and Malcolm owned a lot of the newspapers so were able to tell their own version of the truth. That seemed to be that Malcolm and his daughter emigrated to America for a new start. Silas's son died and Silas was left by himself. He married sometime later and there came Julia but he was a sickly sort and retired too from public life.

'You're suggesting, Lilian, that those pages, are about the Chattons?'

I nodded. 'I believe so, after what you have said. There is mention in the rest of an Uncle Silas, of Julian. The book-binder was known to work for them. What you say about the daughter disappearing from public life, it was because she fell pregnant with William Heathfield's child, the man she loved. There is also talk in the other pages of Malcolm's will, the inheritance of his entire estate, how he changed it to cut her out in favour of a male heir, should she provide a legitimate one.'

Deidre shook her head. 'Men and their power. They hold too much, that's for sure.'

'Now is not the time, Mams,' Agnes chided, with a smile.

'Do you know her name, Malcolm's daughter?'

Deidre nodded. 'Isabel.'

Isabel Chatton. I.C. The initials at the foot of the pages. The confession was hers. I returned the smile for it felt, for the first time, that I was getting close to this girl, this forgotten, ill-treated girl.

'Thank you. Isabel Chatton wrote the pages. Of that I'm now certain. But her cousin, Julia, of her I am not,' I said. 'Do you know where I might find her?'

They both shook their heads and Deidre said, 'I'd advise you not to look. If she is anything like her father, she'll find you if she wants to.'

'From what Mams says, from the way that woman acted when she lost the auction . . . you'd best steer clear,' Agnes said.

I frowned. 'What did she do?'

'When the gavel hit, that woman brought down all manner of curses on poor Edmund. She was screaming in the auction hall, spouting all kinds of threats to him. Two men had to carry her out of there and she shouted the whole way.'

A temper and the means to enact it. Just the kind of woman to hire a thug to do her bidding, to attack me in the street, to intimidate me and scare my father to death.

'I don't think I'll be able to avoid her. I'm certain she's the one behind all of this.' I shook my head. 'The Chattons. I'd never heard of them.'

Deidre nodded. 'It was almost Roman, a great house cursed and ruined. I wrote about them back in the Sixties. *The Fall of the House of Octavius*. Of course I made some embellishments, as one does, for no story is wholly true or wholly false. Not one of my best, I'll grant you, but it sold a few.'

I sat with the information for a moment, for there was so much rushing around inside me that I struggled to order it. But I had names now. A ruined family, a girl caught up in the middle of it. Her only crime was loving the wrong man. And now she could be in America. So far away, yet it made sense. And what of William, of their child?

I looked down at the pages. 'The baby, does it live?'

Deidre wagged her finger. 'I shan't spoil it for you.'

'We'll go make some breakfast. Come to the kitchen when you're done,' Agnes said, standing and offering her grandmother a hand.

The older woman took it, and with a great effort – for the chairs were deep – she got to her feet. As Deidre passed me, she put a hand on my shoulder, squeezed and gave me a wink. What it meant, I wasn't sure, but I smiled nonetheless.

The door closed behind them and I was alone with the story, which now took on new depth, given the family involved. I took a breath, poured myself a fresh cup of tea and settled in to read.

40.

and I thought for certain myself and my child were to die but my father stopped himself. Perhaps it was because he could not bear to touch me. Or because he still saw in me a shadow of my mother, whom, despite his manner, he did love.

He did not strike me, did not cast me down the stairs but I had never seen him so angry. So fearsome. He called me wretched names again and stormed from my bedroom. On the landing, I heard him speaking to one of the servants.

'She will not leave this room until I declare it. Only I, your maid, and the doctor may enter. Do you understand?'

The servant, I didn't know who it might be, made a mumbled reply, then I heard my father's heavy steps on the stairs.

The servant's meek footsteps came to the door and it closed gently. Then locked.

I was trapped in my room, with only Daisy bringing me food and the doctor checking my health and the health of my unborn baby.

My father kept delaying Lord Beauchamp, for months, as I grew and swelled but finally the old toad grew bored and broke off the engagement when my father failed to produce me for inspection.

I was coming to the end of my pregnancy and despite tiredness, all was well. Daisy, when she could, brought me treats and news of the outside. Cakes and jellies wrapped in newspaper. And sometimes, a letter from you. I wrote to you when Daisy could smuggle me paper. I tore pages from my books and underlined words so you could piece together my meaning. You responded with your own puzzles. My only bright spots were those days when a letter would come. I felt our child wriggle around, desperate to be free. I thought it a boy at once, for I felt your heart beating there within me.

One day, Daisy brought grave news. 'I've been hearing His Lordship and your uncle talking.'

'They talk a lot.'

'But they're talking about you, miss. About your situation. Your uncle, miss, he wants to marry you to someone quickly to repair your standing and his in society.'

I recall feeling terribly sick in that moment. 'Who?'

Daisy looked at her feet, shuffled them around like a punished child.

'Tell me, Daisy.'

'Mr Julian, miss.'

The sickness rose and I grabbed for a basin. Daisy was quick and brought me a bowl, into which I emptied what little was in my stomach.

'Julian! But he is my cousin.'

Daisy set the bowl by the door. 'That's what they like about it, miss. It keeps it in the family, His Lordship said.'

Julian was a thug, as you know. A dirty young man with no morals and a cruel streak wider than my father's. To marry him would commit me to a life of pain and sorrow. I felt more hopeless than I ever had.

It was the next day my father came to see me and confirmed Daisy's news. I was to marry Julian in the summer, after the baby was born and could be hidden away, put in an orphanage some-where. We would maintain a show of innocence, no child ever existed, and that would be enough for society to forget, in a few years. The marriage to Julian would hasten that forgetting, for no one else would have me, even the lesser nobles saw me as damaged goods and the longer I remained a spinster, the worse for us all. Julian knew of my situation and had kindly agreed to save what was left of my reputation.

My father would not even look at me as he handed down my sentence.

Barely two days later the engagement announcement appeared in the **Looker-On**. Silas owned half the paper and had them write a glowing report about how in love we were to distract from the failure of my engagement to Beauchamp. Julian and I were to be married in July, after the baby would be born, and I would be free to go about society once more. The announcement said I was abroad, taking the air in France, planning the wedding, staying with an aunt who did not exist.

You saw the paper. You came to the house. I watched you standing below my window but it had been nailed shut and I could do nothing but stare. I had never seen you so unkempt, so beside yourself with worry. I held my heavy stomach as I watched you and thought of our child, of how I could get him to you, where he would be safe with his father.

You were beside yourself, pacing outside my house, shouting until the front door opened and you had to run.

I didn't hear from you for days and I could not think to relax. I begged Daisy for news but she had none. I wrote letter after letter but you did not reply.

I knew nothing of what happened in the next few days, only

that one night, perhaps a week after I saw you below my window, the pains began.

I'd never felt anything like it and my screams woke the house. Daisy was with me in an instant, even my father came. He immediately called for the doctor and took himself away.

The labour was slow and painful to begin with. Dr Ashburn arrived in the night, his eyes bleary from sleep. He checked me, gently as he could, and said it would be several hours. Those hours passed with crippled contractions every few minutes.

I slipped in and out of sleep and felt our child get ready to come into the world.

Dr Ashburn told me to push, Daisy held my hand, and the baby arrived before dawn.

The doctor smiled upon seeing him. For he was a boy. As I had known from the first. Ashburn handed him to Daisy who wrapped him in a blanket and then he came to me. I had never seen anything so beautiful. His puffy little face wrinkled and cried and I cooed at him, told him how much he was loved by both his parents.

Dr Ashburn looked on at us, wiping his hands. 'Where is the father?' he asked gently.

'Waiting for us.'

He nodded. And stepped outside to my father who was in the hallway.

I was in a cocoon of soft light and adoring eyes and this tiny bundle in my arms was everything I could wish for. I didn't hear the men talking. The voices rose.

Daisy's grip on my arm tightened. Her little voice whispered, 'Miss!'

I looked up to see Dr Ashburn and my father. The latter's face a mask of fury.

'Take it away,' he said to Ashburn. 'And kill it.'

The words were bullets.

'Sir, you cannot mean that,' Dr Ashburn tried. 'This is your grandson.'

'That is a bastard. Take it away, or I will dash it on the pavement.'

I had never seen such darkness in him. Such hate for one so innocent. I almost shouted that he was not a bastard but born in wedlock and conceived with love. But I knew that would make it worse. I would not let them take my baby. I wrapped my arms around him as tight as I could.

'Sir, it's best for the child to remain with his mother, at least at first.'

My father grabbed the doctor by the scruff. 'Kill it. Or I will and I won't be as gentle as you.'

Ashburn, wide-eyed with horror, could only nod. My father left then and Dr Ashburn turned to me.

'I'm sorry, I don't know what to do,' he said.

'You will not take him.'

'Where is his father?'

I looked at Daisy. 'I don't know,' I said. 'My father would kill William if he knew where he was.'

Dr Ashburn sat beside me on the bed and I tightened my grip on our child. He began to wail.

'Give him to me. I will see him away from here and you have my word as a physician that he will not be harmed.'

He held out his hands and the idea of handing over our child was abhorrent. But the alternative was worse. The doctor seemed as appalled by it as I was. I clung to our boy. I covered him in kisses and breathed him in.

'His name is Isaac. Isaac William,' I told the doctor.

'A fine name for a fine lad. This is not the end, Miss Chatton. You will see your son again.'

'Will you get him a certificate of birth? Promise me you will!'

He nodded. 'I'll see to it.'

I had no choice but to trust him, yet I did anyway and I still do, and you must too, my love. I handed him our child and cried so much I thought I would die.

'I will be back in a day or so to check on you and bring any news I have,' Ashburn said again.

I watched him take our boy, just hours old, and my heart shattered. I screamed and wailed and my arms were empty when they should have been full. Everything hurt and I resolved to do anything, everything I could to see us reunited. We would be a family.

I don't wish to dwell on that, for the pain was great and my heartbreak greater. I did not move or speak for days and I did not think it would ever get better. But somewhere deep within, I had a burning hate for my father, and that was the only thing keeping me alive.

Then came a letter from you, full of love, telling me where you were lodging.

Dr Ashburn returned and told me that Isaac was being cared for by his wife. Safe and well until he could arrange permanent care far away from my father and uncle. By then, I was resolved in what I had to do.

'Can I trust you, Dr Ashburn?'

He looked at me strangely. 'I believe so.'

'I wish a favour of you.'

'What is it?'

'I know where William is. Will you take Isaac to him? If my baby cannot be with me, I can live only knowing he is with his father.'

364

Dr Ashburn looked at me for a long moment. I could not read him, such was the physician in him, so used to giving terrible news with a soft smile. 'I will. I promise.'

'And something else.'

'Go on.'

'I wish for you to arrange a lawyer or notary, for two days hence. A man you trust. I need you and he to act as witnesses to my testimony, for I am not sure what will happen to me in this house. I will need a carriage too. At noon that day.'

'Miss Chatton, that is . . .'

'You have my son, doctor. You took him from my arms; you owe me so much.'

He hung his head, clearly ashamed of his part in this. 'I will see it done.'

I gave him your address and Dr Ashburn left. For the first time in days, a thin ray of hope broke through my darkness.

Isaac would inherit Father's fortune per the terms of his will, but I needed a way to prove it. I had hidden in my bedroom our marriage certificate, and as soon as there was a certificate of birth, and an account of our circumstances, I was certain that would be enough. But there were many obstacles. I was still confined to my room, though since the baby was born, Father often forgot to lock my door, but still I was watched and I had limited resources.

I should mention, of course, the matter of Julian.

His body was found one morning in Osterley Park. A gunshot to the abdomen but no pistols were found and nobody came forward to speak to his demise. Rumours flew about a duel but Silas used his newspaper connections to suppress any such attacks on his son's character. Silas was, of course, devastated. He flew into a rage so great, I thought he might tear the city down around him. My father tried to calm him each time he visited in those days but Silas grew more and more unhinged and spouted all manner of theories. The tension in the house grew and writhed, like a coiled snake, and upon the day Dr Ashburn gave his promise to me, it geared up to strike.

I had taken to staring out of the window at the farthest point I could and imagining myself there with you and our son, but that day, my eyes were on the street. An hour after Dr Ashburn left, a carriage pulled up outside. My uncle's carriage, with a driver I didn't recognise.

Silas climbed out onto the street and looked right up at me. His face was grim, eyes like the devil's. By instinct, I stepped away from the window, but I soon heard the door and Silas's fearsome shout.

I crept to my door and opened it a crack. His voice echoed through the hall and was soon joined by my father's.

I shan't recount their language, for it was foul but what happened during this one argument, changed everything.

'It was that boy,' Silas shouted. 'The cad who bedded your slut of a daughter.'

'You've no proof of it,' said my father.

'What more proof do I need? Their engagement was announced and then my son is killed. I will find him, you understand? I have men looking; they will find him.'

'If they do, you may kill him of course.' My father was infuriatingly calm and I could hear Silas grow more and more irate.

'I will kill anyone who knew. Anyone who helped.'

'Calm down, Si. You're overreacting. Have another child. What's the difference?'

'What's the difference? My son is dead, Malcolm!' he all but screamed.

'What do you care? You thought him an eel of a boy and he was. Barely good enough to carry our name.'

'How dare you! He would have inherited our fortune; he would have carried our name to the very top of society.'

My father made his greatest mistake then, and he laughed. 'He would not inherit. The money will stay in my line, as you know.'

'You line is dead. Your girl a whore.'

'She will breed. That is all she is needed for.'

'Not if she's dead.'

My blood turned cold and I gripped the door, ready to slam it.

'You won't touch her.'

'Maybe I'll put an heir in her, then. If I can't have my son, I'll have everything else. You won't stop me Malcolm!'

'Get a hold of yourself, Silas!' My father's voice rose and I thought I caught a hint of fear.

Then came strange sounds, grunts and scuffles, a dull thud of something hard hitting something soft. I snuck to the edge of the landing and peered through the banister rail.

Father had Silas around the neck but Silas twisted and drove punch after punch into my father's gut. Where Father may have the upper hand in mind, Silas was bigger, stronger, and had been a boxer in his youth. They growled and groaned like old lions.

Silas freed himself and struck my father in the face. He staggered, blood pouring from his lip.

My father pulled a small pistol from his jacket but he was not quick enough. Silas knocked it free and drove his shoulder into him, knocking him to the floor and showering him with punch after punch, screaming as he did so.

I looked on in horror as my father's face turned red with blood, as his body grew still, but Silas kept punching. Sickening wet slaps of flesh on flesh. He raged and struck more and more until my father was no longer there. His face no longer his. The sound of the fight brought the servants from their halls.

The housekeeper screamed and that snapped Silas back to reality. He looked down on what he'd done. At my father's body. At the witnesses around him. He looked up and saw me. I had never seen such hate in a person.

He fled the house and I rushed downstairs to my father.

He breathed for a moment, coughed out a spray of blood, then fell forever still.

The rest of the day was a blur. I was horrified yet relieved and even more terrified. My uncle had killed my father. I had seen it; so had the servants. News would spread fast.

Police came and took statements from me and the others who had seen it happen. We told them it was Silas. But at the name, the inspector and his constable looked at each other and stopped writing. 'We have enough,' they said, and the coroner took away the body. The servants washed the floor. My father's murder was cleared away in a matter of hours.

The servants fled that night, for fear of what Silas might do to them. Even Daisy left, though promised to return to help me. There are men outside the house, watching. They look up at my window and wave to me. They are Silas's men. I cannot leave without fear of being followed. That is why I don't come to you. I cannot lead them to you.

Dr Ashburn arranged the carriage as I asked. Silas's men followed me to the doctor's office where the notary was waiting.

Perhaps I have been too cautious. I could just put this in an envelope to you, but if Silas found it, if he found you and our son, he would kill you both. I needed a way to hide it from him but not *from you. I needed him to overlook it, should he find you before we can be away. I am paranoid perhaps but if it works, I won't care. During my confinement, I worked a puzzle just for you, so we may meet in secret. I have chosen to ring the bells, that you might know right away the source of the puzzle. Look out for it, my love. Dr Ashburn is looking after Isaac for us until we can sort this mess out.*

You can trust Dr Ashburn, my love, for now we have no choice.

I write these final words in the presence of Dr Ashburn, notary Harold Pierce of solicitors Pierce, Harrow, and Weald, who have initialled each page.

This will act as a statement against Silas should he ever see justice, though men like him rarely do. I fear for my life at what Silas might do to me and should I disappear, you must take this to the police. Knowing you have this gives me strength to see through what the next days or weeks may bring.

This is a legally binding document and the documents herein prove we are married and that our son, Isaac William Heathfield, born the 15th day of May, 1852, will inherit the Chatton fortune held in trust according to my father's will. Once his will is read, for the lawyers may not yet even know of his death, you and I will produce this and all our supporting documents and the law will be clear. Should you arrive where I have instructed, I will know we are free. I will wait for as long as it takes and when you come to me, I will take your name and be forever Mrs William Heathfield.

41.

I found Agnes and Deidre in the garden. They sat on a pair of lichen-crusted chairs, the wood weathered to the same grey as the flagstones. A jug sat on the table, with three glasses, within a clear liquid and black berries floating at the top. It was just past noon and the sun was warm but the air chilled. I inhaled the smell of soil and salt and the herbaceous scent of fir trees. I'd read the pages twice more and sat with them a while. I held them now, walking to the outdoor table, too afraid if I let them go, I would lose them forever.

Agnes set a glass before me and poured from the jug. A few berries fell into my glass. I took a sip and the gin and lemon smacked me in the mouth, along with a pleasant pine-needle flavour I took to be from the berries. I looked at Deidre and she winked and took a long drink herself.

'What do you make of the pages?' Deidre asked.

I coughed away the alcohol and set down my glass. 'Honestly, I don't know. That poor girl – Isabel. What she had to go through. What her uncle did.' I shook my head. 'I wish I knew what became of her.'

But, I thought, there is one person I could ask. One name that had screamed out at me from those pages: Dr Ashburn.

It could not be the same man I had met in Bath, for he would have been a child when these events took place. It had to have been his father. I knew my next destination, at least, and I was grateful I would not have to go back to Oxford and face what I knew would be a reckoning with the bank, with Harry, and with the grief I had run away from.

'You look puzzled,' Deidre said.

'This whole business is a puzzle. The pages spoke of a puzzle Isabel had created for William but I don't know it. I have in my mind this romantic notion that they escaped together, but then I would never have found these books. I want to know why William did not discover these pages. Though I suspect I know the answer, and I don't believe their love story will have a happy ending.'

'I imagine you're right,' said Deidre. She had the calmness of age, not a fidget within her, while Agnes scratched at a splinter on the table and rolled a stone around with her foot.

'It seems Julia Chatton is the one after these pages now, though I can't think why. Maybe to destroy them so she can inherit the fortune held in trust? Remove any evidence of the child?' I sighed. 'Whatever the reason, she will not stop until she has them and I have found myself in the middle of it all.'

And it all comes back to Dr Ashburn. The man who gave me the first book, the family who knew the Chattons intimately. I did not wish to tell Agnes and Deidre of Ashburn and his connection to all this. I felt the less they knew, the safer they would be. If Julia Chatton had the resources to hire Devlin and the lack of morals to use him, she would not hesitate to bring that wrath down upon these women. Too many people had been hurt by this and by me. I could not risk another.

Now I had a name, the spectre of Devlin's employer took shape in my mind and was not so terrifying. She was a person, an unscrupulous one yes, but still a daughter, maybe even a mother, maybe she was desperate for the money, their family name now a ruin. The fear I'd held of her and Devlin eased away and the anger flooded back.

'We like you, Lilian,' Agnes said and she smiled at me. 'And we want to help you. Take the pages, and the book too if it would help.'

'I believe it would. Thank you. Thank you both for your help, your hospitality. It's been a . . . difficult few months and being here is the closest I've come to feeling safe in such a long time.'

'We ask for one favour,' Deidre said, her smile creasing her eyes. 'You come back and tell us the ending.'

'I returned the smile. 'I will. Should I survive to see it.'

They laughed but I could not, for the fear was real. I could feel again Devlin's knife on my throat, against my stomach. He only needed an excuse and I was sure, once they had all the pages, that excuse would come swiftly.

I gathered my things and the two women hugged me and wished me luck. I hated to leave. This house was a port in a terrible storm, sheltered and hidden from the world, and I yearned to stay hidden, forget all this was happening. But life cannot be paused. It is a relentless march onward; only its path may be changed.

I walked the long road back to the town and to the train station.

The man in the ticket booth said I'd have to change at Poole and sold me a through ticket. I had been lucky with my timing and the train to Poole was due in a few minutes. I stepped out onto the platform. It was a small station and only a few people were waiting.

An old man tipped his hat to me and passed me by. As he moved, I caught a glimpse of a man wearing a brown bowler hat the far end of the platform. He was sat on a bench and had not yet seen me but I knew him instantly.

Devlin had found me. But how? Had he been following me this whole time? Did he go to Montague's? Threaten them? Worse? I could barely breathe for all the questions racing through my mind. I backed away to the wall, out of his line of sight, but so I could just catch the edge of him, my heart beating furiously in my chest.

A plume of steam came from down the track as the train approached.

Devlin stood and began to look around. If he moved further up the platform he would see me. I shuffled away, back to the wall, and stepped behind a woman and her trunk. From the gap between her hat and the wall, I could see Devlin eyeing the train rather than the station entrance. He didn't know I was already here.

The train pulled up with a loud hiss and cloud of steam obscuring my end of the platform. The carriage doors began to open. I rushed forward and leapt into a compartment as the first passenger disembarked. I barged past the next and pressed my back to the opposite door, breathing like I'd just run a mile.

I barely noticed the looks and tuts from other passengers in the compartment; my eyes were fixed on the windows. I couldn't see Devlin from where I was, which meant he could be anywhere. He could be on the train and I'd never know until he found me.

I exited the compartment and made my way along the corridor to the next carriage. I ducked down to see and there he was, looking frantically up and down the platform, then to the dozen or so passengers who had disembarked. He spotted a young woman and ran to her, pulled on her shoulder. But it wasn't me.

The train began to move.

''Scuse me,' said a man behind me wanting to get past and I had to step further into the carriage to get out of his way.

The station slid away and still Devlin looked for me. I edged further down the carriage and found a seat. I pressed down into it, lowering myself past the bottom of the windows so I could still see him.

He puffed on a cigarette, pinching it out of his mouth and squinting against the winter sun.

Then his eyes locked on mine as the train picked up speed.

He ran for a door but the train was moving too fast. My heart thundered and I strained to look down the platform. Could he jump on the end? I couldn't see. I pulled down the window and stuck my head out.

Devlin was sprinting through steam, dodging passengers. His hat tumbled off but he didn't stop.

The end of the train left the platform and Devlin stumbled to a halt, glaring at me. I waved and ducked back into the carriage. He had found me here, which I was sure meant he could find me anywhere, but at least I had a head start. There was not another train from that station to Poole for several hours but I had an image of him in my mind galloping down the coastal road on a horse, chasing the train and leaping on.

I closed my eyes and let the image fade. My life had become so sensational that even a horse-riding maniac felt possible.

Another train, another view of the countryside rushing past me. Shades of winter, browns and dark greens, bare trees, spindly limbs like witches' fingers spearing the sky. I wondered if I'd see spring and as the thought came, I pushed it away. No sense in worrying what someone else might do to me, not today at least. It also gave me comfort to know Devlin was here and not in Oxford with Harry or Mr Caxton.

I changed trains in Poole, hiding myself on the platform again while I waited in case Devlin had managed, somehow, to get here ahead of me.

But he was nowhere and I boarded the train to Bath without his shadow looming over me. When I arrived in Bath, I didn't dwell and I walked further from the station to find a taxi. I had a notion that Devlin would ask every cabman outside the station if he'd spotted a woman like me or given her a ride. In the centre of the city, I found one and asked him to take me to Dr Ashburn's estate.

Tynesdale House was as beautiful as I remembered. The Gothic arches and spires, the oriel windows that appeared to float. It was late afternoon and the sun was dipping, giving the pale Bath stone a golden lustre. I had no idea if I'd be welcomed but I couldn't entertain those thoughts, not when I was so close.

I went to the door and pulled the bell. I forced my hands into fists to stop them shaking. I tried to run through what I might say as I waited, but each version of the story felt farcical and outlandish. A man like Dr Ashburn would scarcely believe it. My reputation as a bookbinder was, I hoped, strong with him, but a madwoman ranting at his door about hidden messages and doomed romance was enough to shred that reputation. But I knew if I did not see this through, I would have no life left on the other side. What felt like a choice was not at all.

I heard the footfalls of an approaching man and readied myself.

The door opened revealing the butler. I can't recall his name but I remembered the way he looked at me.

His eyebrow arched. 'Might I help you, madam?'

I swallowed. 'I am here to see Dr Ashburn.'

'Patients are requested to make an appointment with His Lordship via his office in the city.' He went to close the door but I put my hand against it.

'I'm not a patient. I am a bookbinder. I was here some time ago, do you recall? My name is Lilian Delaney and I wish to see Dr Ashburn about a book he gave me.'

The butler stared down his nose at me. He gave the slightest bow and stood aside, allowing me entry.

He shut the door behind me. 'Wait here, please.'

I stood in the entrance hall as he stalked off, with no urgency, to his master. I spent the few minutes rehearsing what I might say. Finding a way into the conversation that Dr Ashburn would not balk at, from what little I knew of the man. At least I had met him before; at least I had some notion of him. I would not be surprised as I had been with the Bells.

The butler returned. 'His Lordship is in the library. Follow me.'

I stayed a few steps behind as he led me through the house on the same path as before. We came to the walnut doors, their brass inlays gleaming as if freshly polished. Inside, the green curtains were drawn against the afternoon gloom, the sun already lowering in the sky, and bright lamps provided the necessary light. The Ashburn Collection was as vast and remarkable as I remembered. The smell of the books calmed me as if I were breathing in a mother's perfume. To be among it again gave me a shiver. What a young, foolish girl I'd been then, afraid to speak too loud, afraid of saying the wrong thing or appearing too eager or not eager enough.

Dr Ashburn sat at the fireplace in one of the armchairs. He wore a pale suit, which didn't match the winter weather, and was reading a small book.

'Miss Lilian Delaney for you, sir.' The butler announced me and Dr Ashburn nodded without looking up from his page.

The butler left and I took a step towards Ashburn. 'Sir, thank—'

He lifted a finger to stop me, held it aloft for several seconds before finally looking up from the book.

'Miss Delaney, what a surprise to see you. Was there a problem with the bill?'

The question confused me for a moment. It had only been weeks since I delivered the newly bound *Botany* yet it felt like a lifetime ago.

'No, sir, no problem with the bill.'

He set down his book. 'Then what may I do for you?'

I stepped closer and he indicated, book in hand, for me to sit. I took a seat on the small, blue velvet settee opposite him.

'It is about that burned book you gave to me.'

'If you're here to return it, I'm afraid I won't be able to accept.'

I shook my head. 'I hope, sir, that my skill as a bookbinder, as you have seen, will carry some good favour with you in regard to what I'm about to say.'

377

He frowned. 'All right.'

'Within the book you gave me, I found a letter hidden under the binding. It was written in 1851 by a woman named Isabel Chatton, though I did not know her name at the time.'

A flicker of recognition passed his eyes. 'Chatton?'

I nodded. 'In this letter, written to a young man she fell in love with, she spoke of hiding their story in books. I found these books, at least all but one. There are six and each contains a part of their love story. It is quite sensational. There is of course romance, but also violence, murder, and a child set to inherit a vast fortune. There was even a suggestion of a duel, though that, unsurprisingly, does not feature in Isabel's confession. However, the last part mentions a Dr Ashburn who attended Isabel when she was pregnant. That doctor, who I believe to be your father, sir, spirited away the baby boy to save his life from Isabel's father and uncle who would see the boy killed. Did your father, if indeed it was him, ever speak of working for the Chattons?'

Dr Ashburn nodded slowly. 'He was their physician for several years, but he stopped after the death of Malcolm Chatton.'

'If Isabel's story is true, and your father put his initial to every page, then Malcolm Chatton was murdered by his brother, Silas.'

He spoke as if pulling from a memory that didn't want to come. 'That was the rumour at the time. I was ten or thereabouts. My father was troubled back then. I remember going to his office one afternoon and seeing him dishevelled, his face unshaven and his collar unbuttoned. My father was a fastidious man – one has to be as a doctor – so seeing him so unravelled stuck in my mind.'

'Did he ever mention what became of the child? Or of Isabel and her lover, William Heathfield?'

'Not to me, but then I was a child myself. Do you have any of this confession?'

I opened my satchel and handed him the pages Agnes and Deidre had given me. I waited while he read, eyeing the grandfather clock nearby as the afternoon ticked ever closer to evening.

Dr Ashburn handed them back when he was finished. 'That is quite the story. And I see you are telling the truth. The initials at the foot of the page are in my father's hand.' He took a breath and sighed it out. 'What do you hope to gain from this endeavour?'

I smiled, slowly, sadly. 'I have been asked that before and there is an answer I give, finding the girl, finding her child, reuniting them with William, but I am tired, sir. And I wish to know the truth that I may be done with it. There are others seeking these pages and they have caused me endless pain; they caused my father's death.' At that he gave a practised, sympathetic expression. 'I wish to be free of it and I cannot do that until the last book is found.'

He looked at me, silent, for several moments as if contemplating. 'Very well. I was not entirely truthful with you, for I wasn't sure of your intent, but you were right, your skill as a bookbinder has carried good favour. My wife, by the way, was thrilled with her book.'

I remembered that simple pleasure of a job well done. I could not wait to return to it. 'I am so glad.'

'I know of the Chattons. I know the story of the missing child. And I know the fate of William Heathfield.'

42.

Dr Ashburn led me through the house in silence. I was fizzing inside, wishing to hear the story, but the doctor would not be rushed. We reached a door and within was a study. It looked like it had not been touched for years and the smell of dust wafted out as we entered. Dr Ashburn lit two lamps and the small room came into focus. A wall lined with books I took on first glance to be medical texts; on the opposite wall was a fireplace and painting of a ship at sea; between them two large, curtained windows. In the centre of the room was an expansive, dark-wood desk with a neat pile of papers in a tray on one side and all the accoutrements one would expect – quill stand, inkpot, blotter, pencils, and blade.

'This is my father's study. He was fastidious, as I said, and he kept journals his entire life. He hoped it would make him a better physician being able to recall every detail of a patient's history and detect patterns. He never wanted to rely on his memory, for memory can be a savage, he would say. One must not trust it with anything important.'

Dr Ashburn went to the bookshelves; below them was a row of cupboards. I found I was holding my breath.

'When he died, I inherited several of his patients so I looked through his journals to find their histories and family histories. I ended up reading many, long into the night and the nights thereafter. I missed my father greatly, you see, and reading his words was, well, a comfort.'

He bent down and opened one of the cupboards. Within, I could just see a long row of slim journals, all the same, neat and uniform.

'I read his journals from recent years, but I was curious to know my father as a younger man and so I read them from the Forties, the Fifties. And that is when I came across the story you have also found.' He ran his finger along the journals and stopped at one, pulled it out.

He checked it, held it a moment as if holding something precious, then handed it to me. 'From about halfway through. I will wait for you in the library. Do you remember the way?'

I nodded. Dr Ashburn shut the door gently and I listened until his footsteps disappeared. I was alone in the office of the man I'd read about. The Dr Ashburn who had, I hoped, saved the child, and knew more of the story beyond the pages. I was almost afraid to read it.

I flipped open the journal, a simple notebook, bound in red cloth. On the first page it read, in a pleasing, looped cursive:

Dr Walter Ashburn ~ Notes
May ~ December 1852

I recognised the flourish on the A as it had appeared on the initials at the foot of the pages. A shiver ran up my back and I clutched the book in my hands, afraid I might drop it. I sat at the desk and brought a lamp close, turned up the light.

I skimmed the early pages, talk of other patients, quick staccato notes on symptoms and ailments, treatments offered and the fee charged. Then, as the doctor had said, about halfway through, the writing changed, the notes became sentences and the story began.

What have I done? What kind of doctor takes a child from its mother the day it's born?

I reconcile my actions with Sir Malcolm's threat. At least the child is alive today. My wife, an angel of a woman, understands and for now is caring for him. Little Isaac. A bonny lad, though he does cry. I can hear him now and I suppose it is my punishment. A reminder of what I have done to poor Isabel.

I return later today to check her recovery and provide her the child's birth certificate as I promised. She is a broken woman, as you'd expect, and it breaks me to know I have played a part in that. Isabel has always been a sweet girl. No trouble, no childhood illnesses beyond a bout of croup, a miracle after her siblings died so young. Yet her father never warmed to her, which I found a great shame, for she had wit and beauty and showed little fear at facing her life. I hope little Isaac inherits that trait, for he will need it.

*

News, at last. Isabel trusted me enough to give me the address of her lover and Isaac's father, William Heathfield. I wonder if he knows he has a son. I wish it was not me introducing them for the first time. Isabel supplied me a note to give to him, so he knows he may trust me.

I go in an hour. As much as Isabel begged me, I do not feel right taking the baby. I have not met this man nor seen his character or means and I cannot in good conscience leave a child with him without first knowing he is capable of caring for it. I do not know what I will find but I hope it is a young man with a sense of responsibility who will gladly accept his son. But I know little of him and littler still of his relationship with Isabel. She is a master of secrets. She has needed to be, with a father like Malcolm, so I wonder at the truth of this. I don't doubt she adores her son and the way she spoke of William, I believe that adoration of him to be real. I only hope she is right.

*

I am home after my visit to William. My son is asleep upstairs and I am more thankful for his health than I have ever been.

I visited William at his lodgings. A cramped two rooms in a boarding house in Brixton, wholly unsuitable for a child. He was shocked and suspicious to see me but when he read Isabel's note, he relaxed. He is a handsome young man, fair, with wide eyes. I can see him in little Isaac.

I told William of Isabel, that she is recovering well, except for her heartbreak. His concern was immediate. He spoke of saving her, taking her away from her father's house and living as a family. He asked after the child too, for he had known she was pregnant but not of the birth.

I told him I had the boy for his own safety. I told him Isaac's name and tears came to his eyes. He was distraught. My heart broke for them. He begged to see his son and for my help to free Isabel from her father. I said I would try.

I left him then with a promise to write with more news.

*

Malcolm Chatton is dead. Murdered in his home by intruders, if the rumours are to be believed. I was summoned by Sir Malcolm's butler that same evening to attend on Isabel. She was in shock, he said, and needed help to sleep.

When I saw her, she clung to me and asked for news. I told her of my visit and she told me the truth of her father's death. Not intruders but Silas Chatton, mad with grief at the loss of his son and suspecting William of Julian's murder.

I knew immediately what this meant. William was not safe, which meant neither Isabel nor Isaac would be safe with him. Not yet. If Silas killed his own brother in a fit of rage then I dreaded what he might do to William. The young man needed to flee.

I told Isabel I would help where I could but to be patient and gave her some drops to help her sleep.

As I was leaving, a messenger arrived. I was called, unexpectedly, to Silas's home.

It was with great trepidation that I made the carriage ride across town to his house. He was agitated, as one might expect, and paced his drawing room.

He asked me for something to focus him. I suggested something to calm him but he snapped at me and I ended up prescribing him a few doses of cocaine. He took one immediately and his demeanour relaxed, his eyes sharpened.

He tugged on his collar, opened a few buttons as if it was hot and I saw there on his skin, something far more troubling.

He allowed me to look. I examined his chest and abdomen. A cluster of foul-smelling pustules. I found swelling in his neck. Unmistakably syphilis. It was in its second stage.

I told him as much and he did not react. Did not seem to care. I prescribed mercury.

I dared not ask him about the blood and bruising on his knuckles, for I knew their cause.

He tongue loosened with the cocaine and he spoke of his son, his death, and how it was a blackguard named William Heathfield who was to blame.

I said nothing.

Silas had men looking for him. They thought he was somewhere south of the river, Brixton or Bermondsey perhaps. I tried to keep my face free of expression and in his state, Silas did not appear to notice.

I left there with a quick step and a deep fear for William's safety. I tore a page from my notepad and *wrote a note on it for him to run, then paid a messenger two shillings to deliver it.*

I must do all I can to help them.

*

Isabel's plan is coming to fruition. Her confession is written and she arrives with me any moment. I will sneak her from the back door of my office though she will not tell me where she goes. Silas has men following her. She cannot risk leading them to William, for I don't believe he has been found yet.

I hear her carriage.

*

William wrote to me. He wants to see Isaac but I said it was impossible, given the circumstances. The baby is as bonny as ever and has on him a delightful gurgle. I wrote back to William that Isaac was safe and well and he would do well to be patient and find a safer place to live.

I confess I was harsher than I should have been but I had begun to worry that my offices were being watched by Silas's men. Silas had engaged a new physician when I refused to give him more cocaine. I do not know the state of his mind and should he discover Isaac, he will surely kill him.

*

The fool came to the office! I saw him outside, moping around like a heartbroken pup. My staff told him to go, I was with a patient, but as he left, I saw two men peel away from a side street and follow.

*

I do not know what to write here. My hands shake and I still feel the blood beneath my fingernails no matter how much I scrub.

After I saw those men, I finished with my patients and went right to William's rooms. The door was ajar, the lock splintered.

Within, a scene of horror.

The rooms were ransacked, every item he owned pulled from its place. Torn or crushed and cast on the floor.

I found him near the fireplace, face down in his own blood. Books and papers scattered around him.

I rolled him onto his front. He was breathing, but barely. His eyes flickered open. His face was cut and swollen. To his chest he clutched a smouldering book. It looked like his last act was to pull it from the flames. Wisps of smoke rose from the corners and I prised it away. He clung to it but with some gentle words, he let it go. I put it to the side.

'Who did this?' I asked.

He coughed and blood filled his mouth.

I lifted his shirt and found boot and baton marks all over his chest, a mess of bruising and lacerations.

His abdomen was enlarged and I knew it was filled with blood.

'Silas,' he said.

I told him he would be all right but he would not. I pulled him onto my lap, tidied his shirt. The attack was vicious and meant to kill. I imagine they thought him dead when they left.

His voice was barely there and his last word was but a breath.

Isabel . . . or perhaps just bell.

He reached for my face but his hand did not make it that far. He fell limp and died in my arms.

I am no stranger to death. Many patients have taken their last walk with me holding their hands but this was not that. This boy did not deserve such a cruel end. He had done wrong, of course, but his first crime had only been to love a girl who loved him back.

Such waste.

I know I must tell Isabel, but I don't have the words. Isaac is in danger, for their marriage and his birth were legitimate and with Malcolm Chatton dead, the boy inherits a vast fortune I am sure Silas would claim as his own. I cannot let anything happen to him, so I am making an impossible decision. May God forgive me.

I set down the journal. My face was wet with tears. William was dead. The grief closed in on me as if he had been a friend or family. As if I had known him. I felt like I had. I felt like I knew them both and my heart was broken for them. Such young, hopeful love shattered by hate. William was a murderer and still she loved him. I thought of Harry for the first time in days and felt a great yearning to be near him, to hold him. We had a different love but the same too. I had done a terrible, necessary thing and still he loved me. I was finally starting to believe him. To believe I was worthy of it.

I wiped my face and blew out my cheeks. So many questions still rushed about inside me and there were only a few people left alive who may be able to answer them.

43.

I found Dr Ashburn, as he had said, in the library. He was reading the same book but set it down immediately when I entered.

'I had Carlisle bring some refreshments.'

I took my place on the settee. The same room, the same day, and yet I was changed, again, by the story I had read. I took two ham sandwiches but despite not eating since the morning, I could not bring myself to take a bite.

'I always suspected that William might not have survived but to see it written like that was awful.'

Dr Ashburn nodded. 'There is more to the story. As there always is. Are you prepared to hear it or would you like something for your nerves?'

I eyed the doctor and let myself smile. 'I don't need a prescription.'

'I was more thinking a brandy.'

I gave a small laugh. 'Thank you, but I should like to keep a clear head.'

'As you wish. Now, I imagine you are wondering over the fate of the boy, Isaac,' he said and I nodded. 'My father's "impossible decision" was to keep Isaac away from Isabel.

His priority was the boy's safety and given Silas had killed William, it was reasonable to assume Isabel and Isaac were in danger too. Now, this is supposition on my part because of what happened when I was a child. I recall having one older brother and then suddenly, one day, I had a younger one too. Isaac was taken in as my father's ward. We were told he was the son of a distant aunt who died in childbirth and the father was away in India. We didn't question it, my brother and I, and in truth, Isaac did not impact our lives that much. We grew up together and despite him being ten years my junior, we eventually became friends, though as people often do, we drifted apart as adulthood took over.'

'Is he alive?'

'He is alive, well, and – of course – a doctor.'

I did not know how to feel; relief and joy, yes, but also a strange colliding of worlds. For so long these people had remained in the books, their lives pressed into paper by a sure hand but no longer. This boy was real and grown to a man.

'Does he know his true parents?' I asked.

Dr Ashburn pursed his lips. 'That I am not sure of. If my father ever told him, Isaac did not tell me.'

'I cannot believe he is alive. Where is he? I would bring the pages to him so he knows the story of his parents.'

'I'm afraid that won't be possible. He is in New York, a doctor at the J. Hood Wright Memorial hospital. He has been for over ten years.'

I was brought swiftly back to earth. I could not see him, but I could write to him at least.

'It was so wrenching to read that your father had been beside the Bell books, all six of them, and did not know them.'

'Those books.' Dr Ashburn shook his head. 'According to his journals, for there was another, he did eventually tell Isabel the news of William's death. She was, of course, devastated. And when Father said it would be best if he kept the child, she had no heart left to fight him. She asked about the confession, about the books. He went back to William's house but it had been cleared out. When he asked the landlord of William's possessions, he said everything was auctioned off to pay outstanding rents. My father spent years and a small fortune looking for those books. He, eventually, found one.'

My eyes widened. 'One?'

Dr Ashburn nodded. 'I remember being home for summer when I was perhaps seventeen years old. My father had become a shell of himself, his obsession driving him mad. But he had this book. And he couldn't figure out what was so special about it. Eventually he gave up. When you turned up with those pages, talk of a book by Abel Bell, well, I went looking for it while you were reading his journal.'

Dr Ashburn stood and went to the small room off the main library where he had first received me as nothing but a bookbinder. Where I had first seen the burned book.

He returned a few minutes later with a book bound in dark purple. Excitement rushed though me. It was here the whole time and yet Dr Ashburn hadn't known. What strange twist of chance had brought two books into this house and then me to discover the thread that bound them together. Fate is a funny mistress but I could not think on it too long for Dr Ashburn was offering me the final book. I stood, reached for it and then it was in my hands. *The Lyre's Broken String.*

I flipped to the back cover and the dots said it was the second of the six. At the front, the endpapers were pristine.

'May I?' I asked and from my satchel, produced my paring knife.

Dr Ashburn nodded.

I was so practised at this now that within a few minutes, the endpaper was free and therein, were the last and most important of all the pages.

I lifted them out with something close to reverence. There were the familiar white pages, just two this time, and then two more. Isaac's birth certificate and Isabel and William's marriage certificate. These two pieces of paper were everything; they were proof of legitimacy and inheritance. Both so important and yet so fragile. I was almost afraid to hold them. The pages were in Isabel's neat copperplate.

A True And Full Account Of The Life
And Love Of Lady Isabel Chatton

Dated the Twentieth Day of May, 1852

This is a witnessed testimony, written wholly by Lady Isabel Chatton, daughter and sole surviving issue of Lord Malcolm Chatton, heir to the Chatton estate and all properties, monies and interests therein. It is noted that Lady Isabel Chatton has been examined and is hereby declared of sound mind and body and able to make this testimony. Witnessed by physician and man of good standing Dr Walter Ashburn, and by notary Harold Pierce of solicitors Pierce, Harrow, and Weald.

Herewith enclosed are documents proving the claims, namely one marriage certificate dated 29th August 1851 confirming the legally binding union of Mr William Heathfield and Lady Isabel Chatton. The second document is the birth certificate of one male child named as Isaac William Heathfield, born in wedlock on the 15th day of May, 1852, and thus the legitimate issue of Mr William Heathfield and Lady Isabel Chatton and sole heir to the Chatton estate under the terms of Lord Malcolm Chatton's will.

Signed:

Isabel Chatton   Dr Walter Ashburn   Harold Pierce

Here begins the testimony of Lady Isabel Chatton

My father died without a son, that much is widely known. It was his great shame, especially as my uncle often flaunted his own. I, being the only living child after the early deaths of two sisters and a brother who did not live past his first year, should have inherited all of his estate. But he was a cruel man of petty and insidious mind. He hated me by the end and made provision with his lawyers that I was his heir in name only and could not touch or benefit from his money, beyond a meagre allowance, until I bore a legitimate son to carry on his cursed name. Until such time, the fortune would lie in trust, abused by bankers and solicitors taking their fees, stripping my legacy a percentage at a time.

My confinement is an open secret within society, gossiped about by debutantes in corners. I am only twenty-two and yet my life is already over. Taken from me by a man who claims to know what is best for me. As if he could ever know.

He is dead now. That is all that brings me joy in this world. Though I fear for what may happen to me.

My uncle, Silas Chatton, the man who murdered my father in a rage over his lost son, has so far seen no justice. I doubt he ever will. Silas will attempt to claim the fortune for himself, so I hope those who drafted my father's will did so well, for that fortune must be my son's.

Silas means to take everything from me but I won't let him. I cannot, for the sake of you, William, and our boy.

The beginning then, for you and he, and your lawyers, and a judge should he see it, must know it from the start to understand.

My mother died a few months after I was born and I grew up with a series of nurses and

I handed the documents to Dr Ashburn who took a moment to read them. 'It is true then. Isaac really is heir to the Chatton fortune.' He handed me back the pages, shaking his head.

A dull sinking feeling came over me. 'He is in danger.'

Dr Ashburn looked up at me. 'What do you mean? He is on the other side of the world.'

'I don't think that matters to this woman. Julia Chatton, Silas's daughter,' I said and Dr Ashburn's frown deepened. 'She is looking for these pages. She is the one who ordered the man to attack my father. She wants these to secure her own claim on the fortune. If she kills Isaac, destroys these . . .'

'Then she is the sole surviving member of the Chatton line and can contest Malcolm's will.'

I nodded. 'Do you know what became of Isabel?'

Dr Ashburn sighed. 'I'm afraid not. After William's death, my father's journals do not speak of her again, just that she was no longer his patient. She disappeared. But Julia Chatton, she I do know.'

My eyes darted to his. 'You do?'

He sat forward, his elbows on his knees. 'She is a plague. A carbuncle of a woman. She came here some years ago, demanding to see my late father's journals. She came back several times talking about these books, to the point where I had to threaten to call the police. She clearly knew of my father's connection to the Chattons, perhaps Silas had told her, and she had in her head that certain books were more important than they appeared.'

'What happened?'

'Little. She did not come back after my threat but I had a man keep an eye on her. Her obsession with the books only grew. She even married a man in the book trade. A binder, I believe. An Indian fellow, by the name of Chand.'

My voice trembled as I spoke. 'Mohan Chand?'

'I believe so.'

The air went out of me and I sat back in the chair. Julia Chatton was Mrs Chand. My mind spiralled and everything, *everything*, fell into place.

44.

I sat with this new information for what felt like hours. Dr Ashburn watched me, his finger stroking his cheek in a thoughtful motion.

'You know her?' he asked.

I could only nod. 'I met her on a train after I left your home with the burned book. She joined me at my table as I was examining it.' Without invitation. Because she saw what I had and wanted it.

I could not believe it. That woman on the train, who had seemed so kind, who spoke to me of her husband and the *Knave* book, gave me advice to look beneath the leather for the binder's mark. That was the moment my life had changed. I had given her my name, she knew of my father's shop, and she had sent her man, Devlin, to follow me.

My heart sank deeper as I realised what I'd done in stealing *Orpheus in the Tower* from Mohan Chand. Grieves had sent him the book without knowing to whom he was sending it. Grieves had never known the identity of his employer, his tormenter who had taken so much from him. I doubted it would bring him solace now but I would tell him in a letter soon.

Mrs Chand must have found out what I had done in stealing from her and brought down her ire upon my father, for he was attacked soon after.

A rage burned up inside me so fierce it took my breath.

'Miss Delaney?'

I looked at Dr Ashburn, my eyes dry and jaw aching from clenching. 'I apologise. I . . .' An idea struck me. 'Might I borrow some paper?'

He led me to his desk and from a drawer pulled several sheets of cream paper, emblazoned with his letterhead. I sat at his chair, the last Bell book, *The Lyre's Broken String*, beside me.

'Sir,' I asked Dr Ashburn, 'where did Silas Chatton live?'

'Belgravia, I believe. I will find his address.'

He left, returned soon after with the address, and I worked quickly. I folded and cut the letterhead from the paper and began to write.

Dear Julia,

You and I hold half a story each. It's time to bring the pages together and with it, bring an end to our acquaintance.

Meet me, one day hence, at your father's house. Leave Devlin in his cage.

I slipped the letter beneath the endpaper and closed the book.

'Are you sure about this?' Dr Ashburn asked.

'This needs to end and I can think of only one way.'

'Why there? At his home?'

'It needs to be private. I don't want her in my house or

anywhere near what's left of my family. And . . .' I paused, feeling the rage build again '. . . I want her to know I know who she is and who her father is. I want her to be afraid.'

Dr Ashburn nodded, ran his finger over his cheek again. 'Very well. I will have a man deliver this in the morning.'

I stood and faced him. 'Thank you, Dr Ashburn, for everything.'

'You need not thank me yet. Do not underestimate this woman.'

He left with the book and I stayed in the quiet solitude of the library. I drew in the smell of the books and the worlds of knowledge they contained. How many of these books had stories hidden within them? Notes from printers and binders etched beneath the surface. Or tales of their owners, their provenance, curses and deaths over print and boards. Books were so much more than paper and words; they held magic within them and every hand they passed through was touched by that magic, forever changed, even if they did not know it.

I could have stayed in the embrace of those ancient books for hours but the hour was late and I was invited to stay for dinner. I could not refuse, for I was weary, hungry and did not want to be alone.

The meal was one of the best I'd had and Dr Ashburn and his wife were fine company. We spoke of his collection, how he had his eye on expanding to include volumes of Eastern medicine. She was overjoyed at the binding on the *Botany*, and assured me there would be more work for me as she expanded her library and he his.

A warmth spread through me as I saw the end of this Chatton ordeal and a possible future beyond it. I dared to look there for a moment, to see the brightness that future contained, a life of renown, no longer apprentice but my own master. And Harry there with me.

But the weight of what I had done in sending that letter closed in on me like storm clouds, shutting out the light and threatening endless rain.

When dinner was over and Dr Ashburn's wife bid me stay, I did not argue. One of his many servants led me to a guest room and I slept fitfully.

My dreams repeated that day on the train, the woman in the green dress. A kind stranger turned snake-like in my mind, darkness grew behind her and her eyes turned black and red at once. I saw in her how I imagined Silas, heard screams that weren't mine but sounded as I imagined Isabel. I heard a baby cry and then be silenced. I saw her, Mrs Chand, Julia Chatton, in the corner of my eye at every turn but when I looked, she was never there. But he was. The man in the bowler rushed at me, the silver flash of a knife in the dark and I woke, breathless.

Sunlight streamed through the open curtains.

Today was the day it would all end, one way or another.

45.

I stood on the street opposite Silas Chatton's townhouse in Belgravia. It was dark, the sun long set on these short winter days. Rain lashed at my face but I barely noticed. The cold bit at my edges but I did not let it in. Anger and apprehension kept me warm.

The house was large, with white walls and clean lines. A mask hiding the truth of the family. No lights shone in the windows and I feared that Julia had not come. Or she had not received the book or found my letter in time. I would wait, I thought, as long as it took. The pages I had, those from the second and sixth books, were in my satchel. The only insurance I had was the certificates I left with Dr Ashburn. I prayed it would be enough.

A light flared in a lower window.

She had come.

I gripped the strap of my satchel and crossed the street. The gate creaked when I opened it, the black paint flaking in my hand. The small garden was unkept and overgrown, left to seed, growing only shadows and weeds.

I pulled on the bell and within moments, the door opened.

Julia Chatton. Mrs Chand. Whoever she was, stood there.

She carried a candle that lit her face from below like a ghoul. A fitting picture.

She smiled and it was the same smile she'd shown on the train. Kind but false. A world of secrets hidden behind it.

'Miss Delaney.' Her voice was rich, like poisoned honey. 'How good to see you again. Please do come in.'

She stepped aside and I, with my stomach in knots, questioning every decision that led me here, entered the house.

I followed her and the single glow of the candle through the house. It was a dead place, the furniture covered in sheets, the stink of dust in the air. Her perfume trailed behind her, a spiced scent of cloves and orange that stuck in my throat. Corridors branched off either side of me; the staircase wound up into darkness, a thousand places for Devlin to hide and wait for his mistress's call.

I gripped my satchel and tried to calm my breathing.

Mrs Chand glanced over her shoulder at me and her lips slid into a smile. 'I was so pleased to receive your letter.'

Her voice was too loud in the empty house.

I watched her move, the sure, cat-like grace of good breeding. She was taller than me by half a head but it felt like more. She wore a dark dress. I could not tell the colour, just that it fit her slim frame well and was no doubt more expensive than anything I owned or ever hoped to. She fit the house well. Despite the gloom, the grandeur of it was apparent.

'You have surprised me, Miss Delaney,' she said.

'Is that a good thing?' I asked as we arrived at an open door. Light spilled from within.

She turned to me. 'No. It is not.'

I swallowed and remembered I had a knife.

She became the gracious host and ushered me into the room. It was a small library. A fire burned in the grate and candles were lit on the mantel. A mirror reflected the candlelight into the room.

The library was not well maintained. I could see that immediately. There were gaps in the shelves, books lying askew, piles on the floor and by a desk in the far corner. The desk was a mess of paper and what looked, at a glance, like stacks of catalogues.

'My father went mad in this room,' she said, still at the door. Then her eyes fixed on me. 'Let's not delay; you have what is mine.'

'I have what belongs to Isabel Chatton, not you.'

She scoffed and closed the door with a bang. 'What do you hope for, coming here like this? Asking to meet me in my father's house? Who do you think you are?'

'I might ask you the same, Mrs Chand. I know what your father did to his brother and to William Heathfield.'

Her lip twitched as she smiled. 'Quite the little investigator, aren't you?'

'I have discovered a lot about your family and its cruelty.'

'You know nothing of cruelty. My father did what he had to for his family. He was a great man.'

'Your father was a syphilitic murderer.'

Her eyes narrowed. 'You have been with Ashburn then. My father's condition was unfortunate but it did not stop him from his duties. It was her, that little tramp Isabel who sent him mad, not the disease. When he died, I found it all in his papers. He wrote everything down when his mind was failing. She taunted him with the existence of her child, her confession and proof of the boy's inheritance.'

'Did he kill her for it like he killed her father and her husband?'

'Oh no. He wanted her to live with her grief. He wanted her to suffer every day knowing he would take it all from her, that she would never see her beloved William again or see her child grow. He vowed to kill the boy when he found him. He scoured every orphanage and poor house. He found what was left of William's family and paid them for all the information he could on that man. Eventually, he found out about the Bell books, Isabel's little mystery. By then of course, Heathfield's belongings were long gone. He spent the rest of his life looking but he was not strong enough to see it through. I am.'

'You are as mad as he was.'

'I am what I need to be. For my son.'

'You have a son?' I knew immediately what that meant. He would be the Chatton heir, not her. Despite not being Malcolm's daughter, Julia would have the strongest claim to the fortune under the terms of Malcolm's will. A legitimate son to a legitimate daughter.

'He is four and the image of his uncle Julian,' she said. 'Not that I knew him of course. He was killed before I was born but his portrait hangs in the hall. My father married again and had me late in life. He knew an heir would be the surest way to contest the will but when I was born a girl, he ignored me. Tried for boys until it killed my mother. I didn't blame him of course. A parent does whatever they must for their children.' Her serpentine eyes found mine. 'Now you begin to understand the lengths I will go to.' She smiled a horrible smile and tilted her head in mock sympathy. 'Like with your father. Another debt-ridden fool better off in the ground.'

My anger rose. 'Don't you dare speak of him.'

'I dare!' She rounded on me, eyes blazing. 'You are nothing to me. Your life is nothing. Your father's even less. I will do what I must. Now give me the pages.' She held out her hand. Her pale bone-thin fingers reaching to me.

'Not until I see yours. The ones you took from my home.'

Her hand closed into a fist and she went to the desk, picked up a wad of paper. She held it up and I recognised it immediately.

'Your pages. Now.'

I handed them over and she turned away from me. Leafed through them. The fire popped in the grate and sent a spark onto the wooden floor. I watched as it died and left a black mark.

'Where are they?' she muttered, then spun to me. 'What have you done with them?'

I said nothing. Tried to maintain an air of confidence I did not feel. What had I done, walking into this place with the barest hint of a plan?

'Don't play the fool now, Miss Delaney.' She towered above me and I backed away. 'The documents. Proof of their marriage and the child.'

'I have them,' I lied. 'But I need some assurances first.'

The tension in her broke and she became the smug hostess once again. 'Oh, my dear. You are playing a losing hand.'

I straightened. 'Maybe. Where is Devlin?'

'He is keeping an eye on a friend of yours. Harry, was it? A handsome young man. I must congratulate you on that.'

'If he touches him, I swear those documents leave with me.'

She looked at me, surprised. 'My dear child, what makes you think I will let you leave?'

I clenched my fist to stop it from shaking and reached into my bag for the knife. I raised it to her.

'Give me back the confession and I won't use this,' I said.

Julia smiled. 'Is that why you came here? Arranged this little ruse with the book? Quite dramatic, I must say. Just like dear Isabel. It was all for these?' She held up all the pages in her fist.

'I want the pages and I want you to leave me alone. Forever. I know who you are, I know who Devlin is, and I know what you have both done to me and Mr Grieves. You leave me alone, call off your dog, and the police won't hear of this. We can both walk away.' I lifted the knife level with her throat. She was inches away from the tip of the blade but barely seemed to notice it.

'You are so young,' she said, almost wistful. Her mood shifted like sand, fierce one moment, sickly sweet the next. She brought her hands together and began to ball up the pages.

'What are you doing?'

'So very young,' she said with a sigh.

With barely a flick of her wrist, she threw the pages into the fire.

'No!' I cried out and instinctively rushed to save them.

The fire caught the thin paper and flared. I dropped to my knees before the grate but there was nothing left to reach for. Weeks of searching, of obsessing over these pages and in a heartbeat they were gone. Isabel and William's story turned to ash. I felt as if my insides had been ripped out.

I looked up, to see Julia standing over me. She struck me across the cheek and I collapsed. Bright sparks filled my vision and my cheek blazed. Hot blood flowed across my face. I blinked and saw in her hand a silver pistol, a smear of my blood on the barrel.

She pointed it at my head. 'The documents, Miss Delaney. This is your last chance.'

I pushed myself up, slowly, fury filling me. I would not be put down so easily. I gripped the knife and sliced upward, caught her arm.

She screamed and the gun clattered on the floor.

I struggled to my feet, but she was faster. She slapped me across my injured cheek with the back of her hand and pushed me back to the floor. My hand struck the grate and searing pain shot through my skin. She stepped on my wrist, pushed it hard on the hot metal. I cried out but couldn't pull free.

'Where are the documents?' she shouted. Blood poured down her arm and she ground her boot against my arm. My bones were ready to snap, my skin bubbling against the fire.

'In my bag!'

She released me and turned her back on me for the briefest moment. It was enough. I grabbed her leg, tripped her. She tried to catch herself but her other foot went in the fire, sending burning coals skittering across the floor.

Julia fell; her head cracked against a table. Her body hit the floor with a dull thud and she lay motionless.

I breathed through the pain in my head, my arm. My hand wouldn't move. The skin on my palm was black and vivid red.

Then I saw the flames. A coal had found the carpet, another a stack of papers. The fire grew fast, spreading to a pile of books, then to a chair. In moments, it was out of control and had covered the far side of the room.

I scrambled to my knees, my eyes blurred and head spinning.

I crawled to Julia. She moaned, her head rocked side to side. Blood pooled on the carpet.

'Wake up!' I shook her and her eyes fluttered open, found me.

Her hands shot to my throat.

'Give me the documents!' she shrieked and squeezed. Madness gripped her. She would kill us both.

The fire spread up the bookshelves, across to the drapes.

I wrenched at her hands, scratched at her skin, at the cut on her arm, but she would not let go. She screamed at me, her eyes wild.

I couldn't breathe. Smoke filled the room. The flames reached the desk. The papers caught in a blaze; sparks shot out. One landed on my arm. It seared into my skin and I cried through gritted teeth. Another landed in her hair, two more on her scalp.

She screamed then, and let me go, her fingers raking her hair. I backed away, knife pointed at her. She barely saw me. Her hair was alight, she patted it, flailed about, knocked into a stack of burning books and fell into the flames.

'Julia!'

The room was filled with fire and smoke. I couldn't see her but her mad endless screams echoed through the heat and flame. The fire curled across the other wall, eating the books in great bites. It would be at the door in moments.

'Julia!' I coughed, held my sleeve across my mouth and nose, squinting to see her.

Her screams were lost in the roar of the fire and in seconds, I would be too. I could not stay. Could not save her.

I found the door, wrenched it open and fell into the hall,

coughing. I crawled away as the fire spread out of the library as if chasing me, wanting to pull me into Hell with it.

I struggled to my feet, falling twice as I ran for the front door, feet slipping on dust. I finally made it outside into fresh, clean air and sucked in the cold. My chest hurt, my mouth felt terribly dry and all I could taste was ash and burnt hair.

A crash of breaking glass as the fire flared out of the library window, licking up the outside of the house.

I lay on the long grass, wet from the rain, pain searing up my hand as it met the cold air. Fire lit the windows on the lower floor, spreading so fast I could not imagine Julia would survive it. I needed to leave, yet all I could do was stare. I shook, from cold and heat, from fear and the release of it.

The pages were gone. Julia Chatton was gone.

But I was not. I breathed. I hurt. I still held the knife.

Was it over? Was I free? Not yet, for if I was found here, all would be lost.

'Get up,' I told myself. 'Get up now.'

I was on my feet, dizzy and aching all over. Another window smashed and fire lit up the night. I was sure I heard a bell. A crowd gathered on the street. I could not risk being seen. I stumbled around the garden to a back gate, stole through it and, shielding my face, I ran.

46.

My journey back to Oxford was a blur of pain and constant worry I would be found and arrested. My appearance drew looks of concern and disgust in equal measure but no one stopped me and no one helped me. I stumbled through London to Paddington station. Around every corner I saw Julia's burned face jump out at me. Her charred fingers clawing for my throat, her screams echoing inside my head. I knew I would hear that sound for the rest of my life and I resigned myself to it.

I do not recall if the train was busy or empty, but no one sat by me; perhaps the stink of fire and the blood on my face kept them away. None but the conductor bothered me and even he did not linger past punching the ticket I dropped on the seat. I did not know the time, nor the day, as I staggered across Oxford, my scarf wrapped around my blistered hand. It had swelled so much to be unrecognisable. The tight, burned skin stretching, threatening with every movement to rip apart. I'd never known a feeling like it. Tears pricked my eyes and I didn't dare think what might become of my hand.

Every step was torture. The Botley Road stretched ahead of me so impossibly far I thought I would never make it. But my legs carried me where my mind could not and I found myself outside a familiar door. I knocked with my good hand and as the door opened and I saw the kindly face of Harry's mother, I collapsed.

*

I woke in a hospital bed. The features of the room slowly came into focus. The wood-panelled walls, the high windows, tall green plants in the corners, nurses moving about, efficient in their whites. The Radcliffe Infirmary.

I lifted my hand. It still hurt but not as severely. It was wrapped in a clean bandage, my fingers peeking out the top.

'Hello, sweetheart,' said the woman beside me. Harry's mother. She put her knitting in her lap and smiled.

I tried to smile back but all that had happened to me these last few months came rushing at me. Tears came, for my father, my home, for Harry and what I had done to him now and years before, for all who had suffered because of me, for Julia Chatton and her terrible fate, and for myself. All because of a book. Harry's mother held me and let me cry until I fell back to sleep, exhausted.

When I woke again, the sun was down and the nurses were closing the curtains while others brought dinner. Harry snoozed beside me and I choked back my tears at the sight of him. Safe. Unhurt.

A newspaper lay on the bedside table. A headline on the right side of the first page read, *Fire Blazes in Belgravia Mansion, One Dead*. I dared not read it, for what if it mentioned me? But I knew I had to. I pulled the paper to me – even such a small effort hurt – and ran my tired eyes over the article.

They did not know who the body was but it was suspected to be Julia Chatton, the owner of the house that had belonged to her late father. She was known to spend days there, to keep it tidy. The fire gutted the lower floor of the house and the rest of the structure was deemed unsafe and must be torn down. The article closed with a mention of her husband and son. My heart broke for kind Mr Chand and for the child and what I had cost them both. I could not keep the tears from my eyes.

Harry's hand was suddenly on mine. He had woken, seen me upset, and was beside me in an instant. I leaned into him and he held me until the guilt eased, though I knew it would never leave me entirely.

'You're here,' I said to him and my voice was broken, stripped raw by the fire.

'Of course.'

I looked up at him. 'Did the man, Devlin, did he . . . ?'

'He tried. But the boys from the press gave him a seeing-to, chasing him halfway up the Banbury Road. I don't think he'll be back.'

A weight lifted from my chest and I felt I could breathe again. Without his employer, would Devlin risk coming after us any further? He was a hired man and I couldn't see his loyalty lasting beyond his final payment.

Harry moved from the uncomfortable edge of the bed back to his chair and pulled it closer. His smile faded as he looked at me. What a state I must be. My hair singed, the bruise and cut on my cheek swollen and black, and my hand.

'The doctor says you should be well enough to go home tomorrow. The burns are healing well and your hand isn't broken, just bruised.'

I closed my eyes. 'I'm sorry, Harry. I'm so sorry.'

He shook his head, then kissed my hand. 'You have nothing to be sorry for. Do you want to talk about it?'

Yes. No. But I knew I must. I coughed and my chest burned.

He handed me a glass of water. I took a long drink and told him all that had happened. He deserved the truth, especially now I had come so close to losing him. There would be no secrets between us, I promised myself that, and should he still wish to be with me, knowing the full me, then I would give him my heart. Harry listened, patiently. When I spoke of Charlie and our night together, he paled and sat back.

'I won't keep anything from you anymore,' I said. 'I swear it.'

What had happened when we were young lay unspoken between us. I knew he felt it too, my lies and secrets hurting him once again. But it was a pattern I was determined to break.

'I need some time,' he said quietly. I saw in him his heart broken afresh by my actions.

He stood and tears filled my eyes. 'Harry, please.'

He put out his hand to stop me. 'Just . . . some time, Lily. That's all.'

I bit my lip and watched him leave as I had done so many years before. This time was different, for back then I had been so angry and afraid of loving him, losing myself to him, that I watched him go without caring if he came back. Now I cared. Now I wanted him to turn and come to me and forgive me. I was gripped with a new kind of fear that he may never. That I would truly lose him.

I rolled onto my side, aches blazing across my body. I cradled my ruined hand and closed my eyes to hold in the tears.

*

I was discharged the following morning with instructions on how to change the dressing on my hand, and a bottle of lime-water liniment and linseed oil to apply daily. I made my slow way home, by myself, and I had never felt more alone.

I stood before the bookshop and barely recognised it. The sign, gold lettering on green-painted wood, seemed drab and small, the windows covered in a thin layer of grime obscuring what lay within. I unlocked the door and pushed it open. It had only been a few days but several letters lay on the floor. I saw from the return address in the corner that two were from the bank. I didn't have the energy to face whatever they said so I left them there, went to my room and lay down. I felt I could sleep for a week, that this fatigue would never leave me but, slowly, as the day went on, life returned to me.

I had half expected Devlin to be standing there when I went downstairs, twirling his blade, that predatory look in his eye. But the bookshop was empty, still. Too empty, without my father. Despite growing up here, it was my father's space and without him, I didn't know how to live in it. If, indeed, I even could.

I went to the front door and picked up the letters, took them to the office. I sat in my father's chair, heard that all too familiar creak of the wood and settled, for a moment, before I let more bad news in.

Three letters. One to my father and one to me, both from the bank, which I found curious. The third looked like a circular. I opened my father's letter first, my big, bandaged hand making it an awkward endeavour but, eventually, I managed it.

Dated the day after his funeral, it was another demand for payment. It listed the books I'd given the bailiffs, what felt like a lifetime ago, and what they fetched at auction. It was a paltry sum and the outstanding debt was still crippling. It irked me that they'd received so little for the books but I knew they hadn't been valuable enough to clear the balance. It was time to pay the piper, it seemed, and all I had to give was the roof over my head.

I opened the other letter from the bank, the one addressed to me, and could not believe what I was reading. It was dated just two days ago.

Thank you for your final payment to clear the balance of the debt owing. We at London & Country Bank appreciate your business and should you need a loan in future, we will be pleased to offer favourable rates.

The balance, cleared? In one payment. I read it three times before I believed it. Who would do such a thing? Who had nearly two thousand pounds spare to give to me?

Ambrose? I barely knew the man and, as kind as he was, I could not see it. But there was one person who might, who could.

I grabbed my jacket and threw it around my shoulders, for my hand would not fit inside the sleeve. I took the letter with me and went out into the late November air.

I went to the bindery but the doors were locked and it was only after knocking twice to no avail that I realised it was Sunday. The days had blurred into nameless chunks of time, spent in different beds, in different corners of the country. I'd lived on trains, running from a man with a knife, and now I was here, and the Sunday church bells of St Giles began to ring.

I went to Mr Caxton's home, just a few streets away in the cosy confines of Wellington Square. His house was a fine old Oxford pile, a three-storey stack of pale stone, and large windows, sitting opposite a tree-filled public garden. Even in winter, the green space was verdant and well maintained.

I'd been here a few times, though always for work, and I felt nervous as I lifted the knocker. A man I did not know opened the door. He was around the same age as Mr Caxton and a little taller but his smile was as wide and welcoming.

He took in the sight of me, of my hand. 'You must be Lilian.'

I blinked, nodded. 'I'm sorry, I don't believe we've met.'

The man put his hand to his forehead. 'Where are my manners! I've heard so much about you it's as if I know you. I'm Robert.'

From inside, Mr Caxton called, 'Bobby, who is it?'

'Your overworked and undervalued apprentice,' Robert called back.

He shook his head to me in a conspiratorial way.

'Get her inside, will you?'

Robert ushered me in and I was immediately struck by the warmth of the house, and of my hosts. Robert hung my jacket and led me through to a parlour where Mr Caxton sat on one side of a well-worn Chesterfield sofa. He set down his newspaper and looked up at me.

'I'm sorry to intrude,' I said.

'Don't be silly.' Robert threw up his hands. 'Let me put some coffee on. Leave you two to chat.'

Mr Caxton patted the empty seat next to him as Robert disappeared through a far door, followed by the sound of running water and clinking china.

'What an adventure you've had, Miss Delaney,' Mr Caxton said, eyes flicking to my hand and back. 'Are you in one piece?'

'I have all my fingers, but I'm not sure I'm whole.'

'Your hand, how is it?' He looked suddenly worried.

'Burned, painful, but unbroken. The doctor doesn't believe there will be lasting damage,' I said and his shoulders seemed to relax. His easy smile returned. 'I don't know where to begin.'

'You don't need to explain anything to me.'

'I do. And I will. But perhaps not today. It is all very raw still and I have another matter that brings me here.'

I handed him the letter from the bank and he did not need to read it for a knowing look to come over his face.

'Was this you?' I asked.

'You think I have money to waste on banks and book-shops? Dear me, Miss Delaney, what do you take me for?' he quipped, his mouth drawn in a wry smile. But I saw through it, as he knew I would. 'It was not entirely philanthropic, you understand.'

'What do you mean?'

'I had hoped to speak to you when you were recovered but I suppose, you were never one to wait.' He sighed and gave me back the letter. 'It was not a gift or charity. It is an investment. When you resigned your post, I realised how much I liked having you around, even if it was only to get me a pastry in the morning.'

I let out a small laugh that ended in a cough and aching lungs. 'How have you survived without a morning Danish?'

'Barely. That's how. It was selfish of you to leave an old man to his own devices. So I have ensnared you by paying off the debt in your father's bookshop.' He sighed again, as if forcing himself away from the jokes to the truth of the matter. 'You are an exceptional talent, Miss Delaney, and I kept you apprentice too long. I was afraid you would leave, you see, and you did anyway so more fool me.'

'He was a huge fool!' came Robert's teasing voice from the kitchen.

'Shut up, traitorous wretch!' Mr Caxton shouted back and Robert laughed.

I saw immediately their relationship and remembered all those times Mr Caxton had talked of never marrying, never having children. He did not need a wife, for he had a husband. Knowing my mentor – my friend – had someone who clearly loved him warmed my heart.

'Mr Caxton, what are you saying?' I asked.

'I wish to expand the bindery to incorporate Delaney's Bookshop,' he said and I could not hide my surprise. 'And not only that, I wish to take you on as a partner, not an apprentice. We would be Caxton and Delaney Bookbinders and Sellers of Rare and Valuable Tomes. We'll work on the name but you understand the idea.'

I did. And I could not believe it. I opened my mouth to speak but no words came, for the size and shape of the offering seemed far too big for me.

Robert appeared with a tray and sat in a chair opposite. He looked, excitedly, from me to Mr Caxton and back.

'You told her, then,' he said, grinning. 'Look at the poor girl, she's horrified.'

Mr Caxton tutted at him and turned to me. 'Lilian? If you're not keen, I don't expect you to return the money of course. Consider it back pay if you'll not accept it as a gift. I understand if you wish to set up on your own. A young person must spread their wings.'

He rambled on, giving me all these scenarios for my future, talking about the money, the presumption, apologising for it. He blinked more and wrung his hands. I confess, I enjoyed his discomfort and held on to it a moment or two longer than was necessary.

Then I let myself smile and I put my good hand on his. 'I'd be honoured.'

The air went out of him in one gust and he eyed me. 'You did that on purpose, didn't you?'

'I can't think what you mean.' I picked up a biscuit from the tray and ate it in one bite.

Robert clapped his hands. 'I like her!'

Mr Caxton grew red-faced. 'You wait till you know her better.'

'Truly, Mr Caxton, I can think of nothing I want more. Thank you.' I squeezed his hand. 'Thank you.' His small eyes creased in a smile. 'Though we will have to look at that name. Delaney and Caxton has a nicer ring to it.'

'My good humour only goes so far, Miss Delaney.'

We laughed together and Robert called for a celebration. We clinked teacups and I spent the most wonderful afternoon in their company. We talked of this new venture, the ideas for the bookshop as well as the bindery. We even spoke of taking on an apprentice. I almost wept for the joy of it after living under a sword for so long.

I returned to the bookshop exhausted but smiling. My head and hand throbbed. The cut on my cheek had scabbed tight and the bruise was turning a ghastly shade of purple. I didn't dare take the bandage off my hand yet, too afraid of what I would see and the pain it would bring.

Inevitably, in the solitude of my home, as I attempted to tidy my father's office, my thoughts turned to Isabel and William. All this began with a burned book and ended with a burned hand. According to the elder Dr Ashburn's journals, William was clutching the book, pulled from the fire, before he died. His last word, Isabel, or maybe just bell. I wondered about Isabel, if she was still alive, if she knew what became of her son. Sadness weighed on me at his distant loss and that of the pages. The confession that had consumed my life for so long was gone. But their story was not. I remembered it, how they had fallen in love, her father's anger, the confinement, and secret communications. The puzzles . . .

The puzzles. My breath quickened.

I looked around the desk, found a scrap of paper and pencil. In the final part of her confession, Isabel spoke of a puzzle she'd made just for William. She rang the bells, she said, so he would know the source of the puzzle. The bells. Or, the Bells.

I pulled up the chair and held the paper with my bandaged hand, thankfully my left so I could still hold the pencil and wrote down the titles of all the books as I remembered them.

A Song for a Knave
He Sings His Devotion

Orpheus in the Tower
Love's Last Aria
When Love Lies Unsung
The Lyre's Broken String

Anagrams again? It could be instructions, a name, a time and date, a place. I set about deconstructing the *Knave* title. I tried a dozen words, but nothing seemed right. Surely it could not be so complex, so painstaking. She would have wanted William to solve it fast to meet her. There would have been no room for mistakes or misinterpretations. It had to be simple for him but unknown to most.

My head ached but I racked my memory for clues. But nothing came. I knew there was a puzzle they had made together, solved together, but my memory was foggy.

Perhaps it wasn't an anagram. Perhaps something more overt. Obvious. I looked at the list of titles and realised a mistake.

They were in the wrong order. I had written them in the order I found them, not the order of the books as Isabel intended. I wrote them out again.

A Song for a Knave
The Lyre's Broken String
He Sings His Devotion
Love's Last Aria
Orpheus in the Tower
When Love Lies Unsung

I stared at them for what felt like an age, my eyes began to blur. It had to be here somewhere. The answer was right in front of me. What had Grieves said about the name Fahig Peal? I had everything I needed to solve it and so I did again, but this time I lacked a German-speaking woman in a café. I closed my eyes and pulled myself through their story. Isabel's unhappy home life, their meeting at the theatre and the sparks that flew between them and then Henley. Where she had spotted William working out a puzzle. Paris. The Seine.

A double acrostic, he'd called it. The first letters read top to bottom and the last read bottom to top made the solution.

My breath caught. I read the first and last letters of the titles and wrote them out with a trembling hand.

ATHLOW GRANGE

I dropped my pencil and pressed my hand to my mouth. I was right. The puzzle was real. The place real. She had gone there, fifty years before, to wait for him. A country house, by the sound of it. I needed to find it. Perhaps one of the staff or someone in the local village would know what happened to her. It was the last thread of this story and I could not leave it untied.

47.

I had written to Ambrose who, of all my acquaintances, would be the most likely to know Athlow Grange or at least be able to find it. It did not take him long. Two days later I received a letter from him and a promise of a visit soon to hear all about my brush with fiery death, as he put it and to hear the ending of the story he was so invested in.

Athlow Grange was a country estate in Gloucestershire, near Fairford, only an hour or so by train from Oxford. At the same time, I wrote to Dr Ashburn and asked him to send along the birth and marriage certificates. I would have them with me, should I find any news of Isabel.

I packed a new satchel, for my other had been lost in the fire, and made my way to the station. My bandaged hand was no longer fat and swollen and I was able to wear a much smaller dressing, though my wrist was still too stiff and sore to move.

Harry had not been to see me and though I had tried to call on him once, his mother gave me only a sympathetic look and pat on the arm.

'He just needs some time, you understand?'

I did. I could not blame him, though I left his house deflated and afraid. My lies and mistakes had caught up with me and now I was paying for them. I would give Harry the time he needed. I only hoped he could forgive me. Again.

I wiped a tear from my eye as I climbed the steps to the train station. There was a branch line train to Fairford and from there I would find a carriage. I had criss-crossed this country by rail and where I had once been nervous of the great machines and the indecipherable timetables, now I could read one as well as I could read my own name. The smell of the steam was invigorating and even rushing the platform at Swanage to escape Devlin could not dull my appreciation.

As I rode the train west, I wondered what became of him, though, given he had not bothered me or my family – for that is what I considered Mr Caxton and Harry, especially now I had no true family left – for a week now. That wonder did not last. The man was gone and I was no longer afraid of him.

I also thought of the Bells, Agnes and Deidre, and resolved, once my trip was done and my affairs in order, to visit them and tell them the ending of this most dramatic tale.

I was on the morning train and the heavy winter mists still clung to the fields. It was December now, and the chill had deepened. Where the wind curled the fog, it revealed frost-covered meadows and bare, silvered trees. I had always loved winter, how one can look out over a landscape so changed while still remaining warm and safe within. It was a season of firelight and reading, of stories by candle, of darkness held back by the light. Although we were entering the shortest days, I felt like I was emerging into spring. After months of Hell, just as Dante had done, I had come forth once more to behold the stars.

*

Athlow Grange was a Tudor manor nestled on the side of a gentle hill, surrounded by trees. At some point in the morning it had begun to snow and the bare trees were covered in a thin, diamond-like sheen. The sculpted hedges were outlined in white, and the house itself was topped with an ivory blanket. I stood at the end of the long pathway where the gates were closed but not locked.

The building was beautiful, made of yellow Cotswold stone. It shone golden against the white. It was a hidden place, not grand or imposing. It fitted into its landscape and all but disappeared within it. I was nervous as I approached the door and thought more than once about turning around and not bothering whoever was inside. There was little chance Isabel was here after fifty years. It could be anyone opening that door. But I had to try.

I knocked and it took some time but eventually the door was opened by an older lady in a maid's uniform.

She frowned at me. 'Help you?'

'I hope so,' I said and my breath turned to smoke before me. I dug my hands into my pockets to keep them warm. 'I am looking for someone who may have once lived here. A lady named Isabel Chatton.'

The maid's frown deepened and her eyes turned dark. She went to close the door. 'No one here by that name.'

I put my hand against the wood to stop her. 'How about Mrs William Heathfield?'

The maid paused, looked me up and down. From inside, I heard a faint voice.

'Let her in, Daisy.'

'Daisy . . .' I stared, open-mouthed at the maid. The older

woman looked uncomfortable at my awed expression and led me inside. She took my coat then bid me follow her to a mercifully warm parlour.

Seated in an armchair by the fire was an elegant, thin lady in her sixties or seventies. She wore a grey dress and her long white hair hung over her shoulder in a neat plait. She was pale, her skin almost translucent, as if she wasn't there at all.

'Are you . . .' I began but could not finish, for it seemed impossible.

'Am I?' she prodded. She wasn't smiling and did not seem very happy to be bothered on a weekday morning. But I could not stop staring at her.

Finally, my voice and manners returned. 'I apologise, I am somewhat overcome . . . It's just, you're Isabel. Aren't you?'

She looked past me to Daisy. Daisy! Her long-time maid who had helped her and William. The maid, no doubt more a friend and companion now than employee, nodded and stepped from the room.

'And who are you?' Isabel asked, then she frowned. 'Dear Lord, sit down. You're making me twitch bouncing foot to foot like that.'

I forced myself to smile, for I was dumbfounded. Seeing her was seeing a ghost, or a character from a novel come to life. I took a chair opposite her.

'Why are you here, miss . . . ?' she said, clasping her hands in her lap.

I tried to calm myself. 'My name is Lilian Delaney and I'm a bookbinder.' Her eyebrow arched. 'I found . . . your story. Yours and William's. I found the books you made for him.'

At that, her whole demeanour changed and her strong voice became breathless. 'You did?'

'I know what became of him and I know the fate of your son, Isaac.'

She pressed her hand to her mouth and at once, tears came to her eyes. 'Isaac . . .' She shook her head as if to shake away the rising tide but she could not. 'Start at the beginning please and leave nothing out.'

'It began with a burned book, *A Song for a Knave*, and the letter it contained within the binding. It was given to me by Dr Ashburn, junior,' I added as her eyes widened. 'Quite by coincidence, for he is an avid book collector and had no idea what the book was. From there, your story consumed me.'

I went on to tell her all that had happened, how I found the books, how I found her confession piece by piece, and was pursued by those who would have it for themselves. I told her of Julia and the poor woman's fate and that of the pages, of Devlin and his blade and my father, all I had lost along the way. I spoke of the authors, Deidre and Agnes, and finally of my trip to Dr Ashburn.

Isabel listened to every word, her expression ranging from sorrow to disbelief to anger and back. She mourned her life; that was apparent. She grieved even now after fifty years for the family and future she had lost and my heart broke for her.

'His father kept a journal and it spoke of the days after Isaac's birth and William's . . . his death. I solved the puzzle you left him. The double acrostic. That is why I'm here and why, to be frank, I was so surprised to find you still here.'

'I told him I would wait.'

She was lost in her memories, her hand clutched to her chest as if trying to hold her heart together.

I reached into my satchel and took out the documents, the

proof of her life and love and what that love produced. I held them as if the paper might shatter, then handed them to her. 'These belong to you.'

She took them with a trembling hand, stared at them as if she could not believe she was seeing them again. She looked so fragile in that moment, her pale skin turned even more ghostlike.

I felt a great stab of guilt. To come to a woman like this, so clearly living in grief, was cruel. I was being selfish looking for my answers while opening up old, barely closed wounds.

'I'm sorry. I will go,' I said and rose.

She blinked, as if suddenly noticing I was there. 'Stay. Please. So few know of my William, even less my son. It is painful, yes, but not all pain is bad. Stay.' She looked back down to the documents, her eye lingering on the birth certificate. 'What became of Isaac?' she asked, her voice timid as if afraid of the answer.

I lowered myself back to the chair. I smiled, for at least this tale had a happier end. 'The elder Dr Ashburn and his wife raised him. From what the younger doctor said, Isaac had a joyful life, wanted for nothing, and he is now a doctor himself.'

The tears came again and she held her hand to her mouth, nodding. 'That is good. Is he . . . Have you seen him?'

I shook my head. 'He lives in America, in New York. I have the name of his hospital. I thought you may want to write to him. Give him these so he may claim the fortune.'

'The fortune . . . That money has brought nothing but pain to all who would claim it. Silas, Julia, they went mad for want of it.'

'Julia had a son. A male heir to that line has a strong claim. He could take it from you.'

She sighed and looked down at the proof in her hands. 'You may be right. I suppose that is Isaac's choice to make.'

We sat in silence for a while, the only sounds the pop and hiss of the fire and the gentle ticking of the grandfather clock in the corner. I didn't know what to feel. I could only stare at this woman. She was not quite as I had imagined her from my reading. She looked smaller, not the large presence she had become in my life, but she was beautiful. Her features delicate and sharply honed. I could imagine those features flush with youth and the blush of love. I could see her staring from her upper window at her lover below, sneaking out to meet him.

'Your story,' I began, breaking the silence. 'It changed my life. Saved it, really. Before I found that letter, my life was on a narrow path, confined between a father who tried his best but did not know how to love, who saw for me only one way to live, and another man who until recently, did not see my value. They both kept me small though it was not with any malice on their part. But your story, it cracked open my world and my heart and showed me its true size. I had given up on love for myself but you and William . . . you never gave up on each other, even now you wait for him and I wish for that. For someone to be waiting for me, though Lord knows I don't deserve it.'

Isabel reached for my hand. 'Thank you. Although you did not know William, that someone out there knows our story means we live still. He lives. Not just in my memory any longer but in yours too. You have given me a gift today and I am grateful.'

Tears came to my eyes and for a moment we held each other's hands.

'May I ask . . .' I said and wasn't sure I should continue but my curiosity could not allow it to go unasked. 'There is a part of your story you left out of the confession.'

She nodded. 'The duel.'

'Did William really kill Julian?'

'He did. William became so enraged by Julian's mockery of me and our sham engagement that he challenged him. It was a cold morning, the mists heavy, and Daisy and I snuck out of my father's house before dawn. I was terrified of every noise, that my father would hear and know and it would be somehow worse for me than total confinement.

'Daisy found a carriage in a nearby street and we rode west to Osterley Park. With every bump of the wheels, my baby wriggled, as if he knew he was going to see his father.' She paused, smiling. 'I can still feel that, when I close my eyes, that heavy, strange feeling of life inside me. It was so brief and I miss it, even now. The sky was turning grey, dawn was coming and we were running out of time. I was worried, for Osterley was expansive and there could be any number of places for an illegal duel. But we found them on the edge of a small lake. Pre-dawn mist clung to the grass, and the dew, in the new light, had turned silver. Within the mist, were five outlines of men. William, Julian, their seconds and an overseer, though I could not tell who was who, for everyone was turned pale and blurred.

'Those who I supposed were William and Julian came together, turned, and began to pace away. I ran. As fast as my condition would allow but they were too far. I tried to call out but I could not breathe, and any movement was slow and laboured. Daisy was beside me, arm around my waist.

'I shouted but at the same moment, the pistols shot. Birds fled their trees and for that moment, the world ceased its turn. They both hung there as if held by God's thread. Then time seemed to catch up and one of them stumbled, then the other, and they both fell.

'I ran down the hill, fearing every second I would fall, my feet slipping on the grass. The other men looked upon me with horror. The overseer fled at once. Julian lay writhing on one side, growling like a caught bear. His second, a man I recognised as one of Julian's cohort, rushed towards him. William's second, a young man I've never seen, was at his side but looked more frightened than I. William was on his back, breathing heavily, eyes staring at the sky. The second, babbling something about William paying him to be here, was more trouble than he was help. I snapped at him to run and he was away like a jackrabbit. William had been hit in the arm, little more than a graze. But Julian . . . he had been hit in the stomach, a terrible wound. Julian's man was kneeling beside him, pressing his hands onto Julian's gut. My cousin snarled and snapped at him, and in between his anger came sharp sobs. He was afraid.

'William put his hand to my stomach. I recall his touch as if he were here now. He felt our child. He kissed me without a care for anyone else and said we would be a family. I told him he must escape arrest first. His expression turned grave and I believe the magnitude of his act came down upon him at once.

'Julian's movements had calmed, his anger faded. He looked

at me, saw me, and his bloody hand reached for me. But I did not reach back. An awful gurgling sound came from his mouth and he fell forever still. The second sat back, breathing hard, covered in blood. Then the man looked at me, at William, and ran. I found the two pistols and hurled them into the lake.

'We did not linger further. I led William to the carriage but it was them supporting me far more, for the flight and panic had taken its toll and my legs threatened to give way. Daisy held me on one side and William on the other. I told William to take our carriage and go, find a safe place and write to me under a name only I would know. Another of our puzzles. He agreed, kissed me, and put his hands upon my stomach. He told our baby how much he loved him, that he would be there for him always. Then he was away. Daisy and I took the other carriage, returned to my home before the house woke.'

Isabel looked to the door, where Daisy now stood. I hadn't heard her come in but she looked at her mistress with undisguised affection.

'Daisy and I never spoke of it again, until now.' Isabel looked back to me. 'There you have it. Our whole story. William was not perfect. He was impetuous, had a temper. He made his mistakes but I forgave him. I would forgive him again. That's what real love is, seeing the heart behind the mistake and loving it still.'

I could only think of Harry. Of the man I loved. I prayed he would see through my mistakes, for they were many.

'How about some lunch?' Daisy asked and Isabel agreed.

I did not stay, for I needed to see Harry. It was not a simple wanting any longer but a fierce need. I must get to him, hear from his own lips if he could ever forgive me. I could not wait as Isabel had. She and William had missed their chance and my heart ached for her, but I would not do the same. I loved Harry. As much as I tried to force the feeling away over the years, I could no longer.

I hugged Isabel as I left. She cupped my face in her hand and smiled. 'Thank you for coming. You have brought him to life again, and my son . . . I believe I will write to him. Isaac deserves to know who his father was and that for the brief time their lives coincided, he was loved.'

'He also deserves to know who his mother is,' I said gently and Isabel's eyes shone with tears.

Daisy gave me a sandwich for the journey, ever the caregiver even to those she did not know. I left Athlow Grange feeling light for the first time in months. The story complete, the questions answered and gaps filled. My shoulders loosened and my step quickened. I glanced back once at the snow-brushed house, where warm light glowed from every window and could not help but smile. I hoped these women had found some happiness in the decades since William's death. I hoped they would be happy once again.

48.

I returned to Oxford, to the bookshop, and set about putting it right. The floors and shelves were dusty and the smell of old books had become overwhelming, being shut up for so long. I aired the rooms, washed the floors and, over the next day, catalogued the remaining books of true value. There weren't many and most were stalwart, uninspiring volumes, a mainstay of every collector. I resolved to modernise while keeping close to my father's methods. The traditions had their place, as they do in every endeavour, but without change, fresh light and air, one cannot grow. Mr Caxton knew this now, though it had taken him a while to see it and, when I arrived at the bindery, it was with a new, odd feeling in my chest: that of equals working together, not of master and apprentice.

The bindery was warm, the fires lit early and the sun bright through the front windows. Mr Caxton smiled at me as I entered.

'You're late, Miss Delaney.'

'Now I'm a partner, I may arrive as I like.'

He weighed my words and huffed. 'Only if you bring—' I produced a paper bag and set it on his desk. He laughed. 'Fine, fine. You are on time, for once.'

We talked through our new arrangement and the way it would work. It was exciting, a new chapter, but still, a dark cloud hung over me and would not be shifted. Harry had not been to see me. He had asked for time and I was giving it, but at what point would this time turn into forever?

As I left the bindery at the end of the day, the joys of my work faded and worry over my heart began. I walked the short path to my home, coat tight to my chin to keep out the chill. I turned into Victor Street, eyes to the pavement, and did not see the figure outside the bookshop until I was almost upon him.

I looked up as I approached and jumped, for in the darkness I could have sworn it was Devlin, his bowler obscuring his face, the silver glint of a knife in his hand.

But it was Harry who stepped out of the shadows.

Harry who saw my fear and moved to comfort me.

It was Harry.

'Sorry, Lily. Didn't mean to scare you.'

I couldn't believe he was here, after so long thinking he had forsaken me. 'It's . . . I'm fine. You're here.'

He stepped to me, took my hand. 'I'm here.'

I rushed into his arms and he wrapped his around me, held me tight, then tighter, and that was answer enough. He was mine. Our love was stronger than my mistakes and he felt it too.

'I'm sorry, I'm sorry,' I kept saying until he hushed me with a kiss.

The dark cloud over me was whipped away and I saw only sun and stars and the path they lit for us.

We went inside and it was then I noticed Harry carrying

a bag. He didn't, usually, but what did that matter? I was too happy to wonder, to ask, to care.

'I found Isabel, the woman who wrote the confession,' I said, for I didn't want any other secrets between us. He deserved the ending to the story as much as I did. 'She waited for him for fifty years, knowing he'd never come. I waited for you, too.'

He squeezed my hand. 'I'm sorry it took me so long. But it was a lot to hear, you know, the books, then this man you saw.'

My shame coloured my cheeks. 'I'm so sorry, Harry.'

'You don't owe me an apology, Lily. I owe you one. I didn't listen to you when we were younger. You said you didn't want the family, the mother's life, but I tried to force it on you and then I hated you for taking control of yourself, even if you did it in a way I . . .' his voice cracked and I could tell the grief of our past was still present in him '. . . in a way I didn't agree with. But it's done now and you and me can start again.'

I pressed my hand to my mouth and could barely speak, could only nod, for the ache in my chest threatened to over-whelm. I wrapped my arms around him and held him for what felt like forever.

Eventually, we parted and he wiped my tears with his thumb and said, 'The story of this woman, the books, it's over, isn't it?'

I nodded and felt sad for the loss. 'No more obsessive searches across the country.'

'Are you sure?' Harry said, and he had a gleam in his eye I had rarely seen. An excitement, a conspirator's eye.

'What do you mean?'

'I found something.' He reached into his bag and handed

me a package wrapped in brown leather. 'It was beneath a floorboard at the press. I'd heard rumours about a hidden book from the old printers. When I found it, I knew I had to show you.'

I unwrapped it and revealed the most curious book I had ever seen. The cover was made of hammered silver, thin and light as paper, tarnished with age. My curiosity outmatched any lingering worries from the last few months, for surely no book could be as much trouble again.

My fingers instinctively ran over the endpapers, the plain silver cover, the shaped banding on the spine.

I smiled up at Harry. 'Tell me.'

ONE PLACE. MANY STORIES

Bold, innovative and
empowering publishing.

FOLLOW US ON:

@HQStories